Trained as an actress, Barbara Nadel is now a full time writer. She has worked as a public relations officer for the National Schizophrenia Fellowship's Good Companion Service, and prior to that was a mental health advocate in a psychiatric hospital. She also worked with sexually abused teenagers and taught psychology in both schools and colleges. Born in the East End of London, she now lives in Lancashire.

Praise for Barbara Nadel:

D1022887

A Passion for Killing

Barbara Nadel

headline

First published in 2007 by
HEADLINE PUBLISHING GROUP

First published in paperback in 2007 by
HEADLINE PUBLISHING GROUP

4

Cataloguing in Publication Data is available from the British Library

978 0 7553 2134 6 (B Format)
978 0 7553 3752 1 (A Format)

Typeset in Times by Palimpsest Book Production Limited,
Grangemouth, Stirlingshire

Printed and bound in Great Britain by
Clays Ltd, St Ives plc

Headline's policy is to use papers that are natural, renewable
and recyclable products and made from wood grown in sustainable forests.
The logging and manufacturing processes are expected to conform to
the environmental regulations of the country of origin.

HEADLINE PUBLISHING GROUP
A division of Hachette Livre UK Ltd
338 Euston Road
London NW1 3BH

www.headline.co.uk
www.hodderheadline.com

To my favourite carpet dealers.

Acknowledgements

This book was written with enormous assistance from Tribal Collections carpet dealership in Göreme, Turkey. Without the expert guidance and help provided by Ruth, Faruk and Hüseyin I would have been totally lost. The world of carpets is fascinating and fun but also intricate and complicated. So a big thank you to all those involved, which includes the many carpet buyers and aficionados that I talked to as well. Any errors that may be found within this book are nothing to do with any of my tutors – they are totally and utterly all my own!

Glossary

Bakkal – grocery shop

Balık Pazar – fish market

Belediye – local council

Bey – as in 'Çetin Bey', an Ottoman title denoting respect, still in use today following a man's first name

Çay ocağı – a small space in a public building, often under the stairs, from which tea is dispensed from a samovar by a usually very old functionary

Efendi – an honorific Ottoman title denoting a person of high status. Always used when addressing a prince or princess

Gulet – a wooden yacht

Han – tradesman's hall, inn. Sometimes called a caravanserai

Jandarma – while the Turkish National Police Force are responsible for law and order in the urban districts, the Jandarma cover the rural areas. They are a paramilitary force under joint control of the military and the Interior Ministry

Kapalı Çarşı – Grand Bazaar

Kapıcı – Doorkeeper. Blocks of flats have kapıcılar, men who act as security, porters etc., for the apartment community

Kilim – flat woven rug

Mısır Çarşı – the Spice Bazaar

MIT – Turkish Secret Service

'Mehmet' – affectionate generic name for the 'average' Turkish solider. Like the British 'Tommy'

Namaz – Muslim prayer, performed five times a day

Nargile – a water or 'hubble bubble' pipe used for smoking tobacco

Pide Salonu – a restaurant specialising in the slightly leavened style of bread known as pide. This may be eaten with a variety of toppings including eggs, vegetables, meat and cheese

Rakı – aniseed-flavoured alcoholic spirit

Sigara Börek – savoury pastry shaped like a cigarette

Vizier – minister. The Grand Vizier was the Ottoman equivalent of a Prime Minister

Zabıta – dedicated market police. The Zabıta check that weights and measures are correct

Cast of Characters

Çetin İkmen – middle-aged İstanbul police inspector

Mehmet Süleyman – İstanbul police inspector, İkmen's protégé

Commissioner Ardiç – İkmen and Süleyman's boss

Sergeant Ayşe Farsakoğlu – İkmen's deputy

Sergeant İzzet Melik – Süleyman's deputy

Metin İskender – young İstanbul police inspector

Dr Arto Sarkissian – İstanbul police pathologist

Abdullah Ergin – an İstanbul Tourism Police officer

Fatma İkmen – Çetin İkmen's wife

Zelfa Süleyman – Mehmet Süleyman's wife

Muhammed Süleyman – Mehmet Süleyman's father

Raşit Bey – an elderly carpet dealer, a friend of Muhammed Süleyman

Mürsel Bey – a spy

Haydar – Mürsel's sidekick

Peter Melly – an official at the British Consulate and a carpet collector

Matilda Melly – his wife

Wilhelmus (Wim) Klaassen – an official at the Dutch Consulate

Doris Klaassen – his wife

Kim Monroe – wife of a Canadian consular official

Nikolai Stoev – Bulgarian Mafia 'Godfather'

Emine Soylu – wife of murder victim Cabbar Soylu

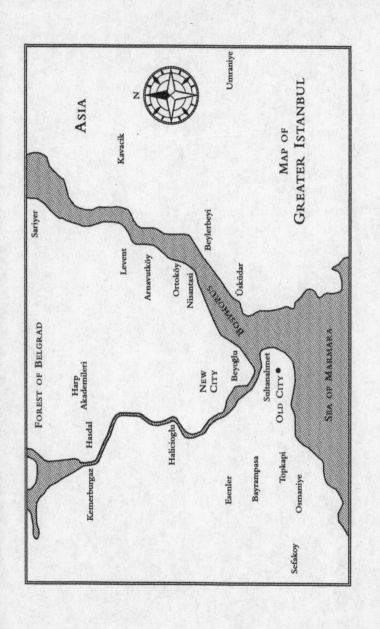

Prelude

By modern standards the carpet was immense. It must, the elderly carpet dealer reckoned as he passed his expert eye across the piece, measure at least three metres by nine metres.

'They rarely make them like this any more, Muhammed Efendi,' he said to his tall and equally elderly companion.

'No,' the other replied – a little sadly, the carpet dealer felt. 'No, Raşit Bey, this carpet is from another time and place entirely.'

And then both the carpet dealer, Raşit Bey, and his friend Muhammed Efendi looked back at the small, rather shabby wooden house that was the latter's current abode.

'Come, let us sit and take tea under the apple trees,' Muhammed Efendi said as he guided his friend over to a table and chairs set underneath some trees to the left of his lawn which was now almost entirely covered by the rich, enormous carpet.

Raşit Bey breathed deeply as he walked, looking around the verdant garden with great pleasure. 'The springtime in İstanbul is hard to better, is it not, Muhammed Efendi?'

'Impossible, in my humble opinion,' Muhammed Efendi replied.

They sat.

'My son, Murad, will bring tea presently,' Muhammed

Efendi said as he offered Raşit Bey a cigarette from his silver and mother-of-pearl case.

'Thank you, Muhammed Efendi,' Raşit Bey said as he took what was a very cheap cigarette from what he knew was a very valuable box. But then that was so typical of a certain section of the old aristocracy. People like Muhammed Süleyman Efendi, or 'prince' Muhammed, lived gracious poverty-stricken existences in Bosphorus villages like this one – Arnavutköy – if they were lucky. If they were not, they lived up in the high rise, scrappy suburbs out near Atatürk Airport. Muhammed Süleyman, although never personally having done a day's work in his life, was very fortunate in having two sons who worked very hard. The eldest, a hotel manager, as Raşit Bey understood, now approached the elderly men with a tray bearing tea glasses and an ashtray.

'Ah, Murad,' Muhammed Efendi said as he watched his son serve himself and his friend. 'Thank you.'

Murad, who was a pleasant-looking man in his forties, first bowed and then lit the cigarettes of both men before returning to the small house he shared with his parents and his own young daughter.

Once his son was out of sight, Muhammed Efendi turned to his friend and said, 'You know it isn't right that Murad should still be alone at his age.'

'Ah, but Muhammed Efendi, your poor son's wife died in such terrible circumstances. Maybe he feels that looking after his daughter and being, as I know he is, such a good son to you and your wife is enough for him now.'

Muhammed Efendi shook his head sadly. Murad's wife had died in the great earthquake of 1999, leaving her husband to mourn bitterly and to bring up their daughter Edibe alone.

2

He'd returned to his parents' house in Arnavutköy almost immediately where, his father imagined, he would remain for ever unless things changed quite dramatically. But Murad was not the reason why Raşit Bey was in his garden now and so he turned his attention back to his friend and the business he wished to conduct with him.

'So now, this carpet, Raşit Bey . . .'

'Is a wonderful Ottoman Court Carpet, as I know you know, Muhammed Efendi.' He leaned forward, stiffly, and took a corner of the great carpet between his fingers. The pile was thick, luscious and contained, as he knew that it would be, a high proportion of silk in the weave. 'What, if I may be so bold, is its provenance?'

'It belonged to one of my aunts,' Muhammed Efendi said. 'Do you remember the Princess Gözde? She lost her fiancé in the Great War when she was sixteen and spent the rest of her life in mourning. She was a recluse and so, even though she was my father's sister, I saw her only infrequently.'

'Did she live in one of those large wooden palaces up in Nişantaşı?'

'Yes.' Muhammed Efendi smiled. 'By the end of the fifties most people had forgotten her existence. The house was in a state of disrepair, and she could afford neither gas nor electricity. When one night, just prior to her death in 1959, a thief broke in and saw her, he assumed she had to be a ghost and ran screaming from the building. Upon her demise, the house and all her effects were bequeathed to my father, her brother. This carpet graced the floor of the enormous entrance hall to that palace. I believe it was made at the end of the eighteenth century.'

It was beautiful in that rich, ornate fashion that had so

3

appealed to the wealthy Ottoman mind. Probably, Raşit Bey calculated, produced in Usak in the 1790s, it was a mass of thick tulips, roses, hyacinths and carnations. He was certain it was the product of the expert weavers from the Anatolian city of Usak. They had produced carpets for the Ottoman court from the 15th right up to the 20th century.

'Fortunately,' Muhammed Efendi continued, 'my father had the good sense to empty out the Princess Gözde's house immediately after her death. Like all of those old Nişantaşı mansions, it is no more.' He sighed. 'It burned to the ground in the early sixties and was replaced by some hideous block of flats. We used this carpet in my father's old house for several years afterwards but when we came here, it was, of course, far too big for any of the rooms. Until today it was rolled up against the wall of the dining room.'

'And now you would like to obtain an opinion on the piece?' Raşit Bey knew that Muhammed Efendi was desperate to sell. Just simply observing the brand of cigarettes he was now smoking told him that. Muhammed Efendi usually had his cigarettes made for him and so if he was reduced to the dirt-cheap 'Birinci' brand, things had to be tight. But Raşit Bey knew better than to talk overtly of money, even though he recognised that the carpet was worth a considerable sum. Money talk to someone like Muhammed Efendi was most vulgar. The carpet dealer would have to proceed with caution.

'I would like an opinion, yes,' Muhammed Efendi said as he sipped his tea thoughtfully. 'But in your own time, Raşit Bey. Things like this cannot be rushed.'

'No, indeed.'

The sun was shining, the spring flowers were fully in bloom and the few birds that braved the cat-patrolled garden of the

4

Süleymans, were singing. So even the scene that surrounded him said nothing to Raşit Bey about being rushed in any way. But the carpet dealer knew. He knew the fine manners and what they concealed, he knew that Muhammed Efendi was loath to take the assistance his sons very frequently offered to him. He knew the old prince would far rather sell things than either earn money, which at his age was probably out of the question anyway, or take it from others.

'Give it some thought,' Muhammed Efendi said as he put his cigarette out and then almost immediately lit up another.

'Yes, I will.' Raşit Bey could have told him what the carpet was worth and what he could pay him for it on the spot. But such haste would be seen in a very dim light. He would, he thought, leave the old prince alone for a few days before following up the matter with a polite telephone call.

And so with the formal part of their business effectively concluded, the two men spoke of other things – Muhammed Efendi of his granddaughter who had just started primary school, and the carpet dealer of his shop and its many comings and goings. Generally trade was good and Raşit Bey was very happy about how well his grandson, Adnan, was progressing in his business.

'If only I could say the same about Yaşar,' Raşit Bey said, shaking his head sadly as he spoke.

'Yaşar?'

'The young man from the coast,' Raşit Bey replied. 'Used to work for my brother Cengiz in his carpet shop in Antalya. He's been with me for just over a year now.'

'Oh, yes.' Muhammed Efendi frowned. 'Didn't he, at one time, used to have his own factory or something?'

'No, not exactly.' Raşit Bey finished the hated Birinci cigarette and then sipped his tea. 'He just organised the sale of carpets the women in his village produced. Cengiz did business with him for several years before he offered him a job in his own shop. He did well for my brother, and he's ambitious, so he eventually came on to me here in the city. He's a bright man.'

'So what is the problem, Raşit Bey?'

He sighed. 'Well, if I could find Yaşar, then maybe I would be able to answer that question, Muhammed Efendi.'

'He's missing?'

Raşit Bey shrugged. 'If you include today, he hasn't been to work for three days now – without a word of explanation.'

'Have you visited his home?' Muhammed Efendi asked.

'Yes. But he isn't there. The kapıcı of his building hasn't seen him.'

'What about his family? In Antalya, did you say?'

'A village just outside. I have no contact details,' Raşit Bey replied. He sighed. 'To be completely candid with you, Muhammed Efendi, both myself and my brother know almost nothing about Yaşar Uzun beyond his English language and carpet-selling skills. He talks very little about his past and I, to be truthful, have little interest in it. All I know is that he is a charming and personable young man who makes me a considerable profit on what he sells. I'll have to contact my brother.'

Muhammed Efendi frowned. 'Have you informed the police?'

'No!' Raşit Bey waved a dismissive hand. 'I'm sure there's a good explanation and I don't want Yaşar to get into any trouble.' Then, without thinking, he added, 'We all know how the police can be, don't we?'

6

As soon as he'd said it, Raşit Bey realised he'd made a mistake.

'I know how my youngest son Mehmet is, Raşit Bey,' Muhammed Efendi said slowly and gravely. 'He is a very good police officer.'

'Oh, yes, but of course!' Red to the ears, Raşit Bey said, 'Muhammed Efendi, I apologise unreservedly. I had quite forgotten that Mehmet Bey works for the police department . . .'

'He is an inspector,' Muhammed Efendi said with obvious pride. 'His mother doesn't approve, of course, she thinks the job is beneath him, but . . . My Mehmet has solved murder cases, Raşit Bey. The boy has a brilliant mind and is most discreet too.'

'I am sure.'

'A missing person is nothing to him,' Muhammed Efendi said. 'If you want me to, I can ask my son to look for this Yaşar for you. He will find him.'

'You think so?'

'I am certain of it,' Muhammed Efendi replied. 'Leave it with me, Raşit Bey. I will speak to Mehmet and all will be well.'

Raşit Bey leaned forward and took one of Muhammed Efendi's hands in his. He then kissed it and raised it to his forehead as a sign of his humbleness and respect. Carpet dealers, even old ones, are rarely of this ilk. Muhammed Süleyman the prince knew that the man both needed and deserved him to deliver on his promise to speak as soon as he could to his son.

The victim was known to him. Not perverted in any way, this

man had a wife to whom he was faithful, and a child. Morally one couldn't fault him – at least not where sex was concerned. No, this man was a fine example of proper Turkish manhood – serious, masculine, respectable. In his business dealings, however, and in one serious personal regard, there was something that did not entirely conform to the image of the perfect Turkish male. This man broke the fingers of his competitors, he routinely threatened the lives of his enemies' women, and he killed people. More significantly, he had killed an entirely defenceless innocent. There was no excuse for such a thing in civilised society. This man was a gangster and so he had to go – at least that was the mindset the killer chose to adopt for this assignment. Unlike previous victims, this one was to be despatched during the hours of daylight. It was just easier and more convenient that way. One does, after all, have to consider the logistics of the thing every time a fresh kill comes into focus. No kill is, or can ever be, the same. The received wisdom on this was perfectly correct.

The killer made his way to the İstanbul Hilton in the district of Harbiye and lost himself completely in the great crowds of package tourists, harried staff members and busy conference delegates who choked the entrance lobby and reception area. He made his way up to the ninth floor where the gangster was waiting to meet a person who was, the killer understood, a provider of drugs from Afghanistan. But whether that person did indeed turn up for their meeting or not can never now be known. Drug dealers do not tend, after all, to tell people about their cancelled or abortive meetings. No, the body of the gangster was eventually discovered by a member of the hotel staff the following morning when the rather fat guest who had only booked in for one night was found dead on his hotel room floor. And so as Muhammed Süleyman Efendi and his friend Raşit Bey talked of this and that in the pretty garden in Arnavutköy, the İstanbul police put the stabbed body of the gangster into a mortuary van destined for the Forensic Institute and further investigations.

Chapter 1

Inspector Çetin İkmen liked to visit his friend and colleague Inspector Mehmet Süleyman when they were both present in the police station. İkmen, in spite of over thirty years on the force, had never managed to settle his mind to paperwork. Just the thought of it made him want to do something else – anything else. And so as soon as his sergeant, Ayşe Farsakoğlu, returned from lunch, İkmen left his chaotic desk and made his way down the long, grey corridor towards the clean and ordered office of his much younger friend. When he got there he found that the door was open and his friend was talking on the telephone. As soon as he saw İkmen, however, Inspector Süleyman ushered him in with a wave of his hand.

'Yes . . . Yes . . . I'll do my best . . . Yes . . .' He sounded weary, something that was clearly underwritten by his heavily drooping eyelids. He motioned for İkmen to sit, which the older man did with a small, arthritic grunt.

'Yes . . . Yes, I know . . . Yes . . .' He wrote something down on the back of a cigarette packet.

Mehmet Süleyman, tired and middle-aged, nevertheless had the kind of spectacularly good looks that seem to defy both age and lifestyle. As he continued to murmur platitudes into the receiver he first offered İkmen a very rough Maltepe cigarette, which İkmen took with a smile, and then lit one up for himself.

'Yes . . .' He pinched the skin at the top of his nose between his eyes with his free hand and then shook his head in what looked like exasperation. İkmen smiled. Whoever his friend Mehmet was talking to was trying his patience, which was far from limitless at the best of times. Middle-aged he might be, but Mehmet had not yet reached the rather amused acceptance of most things that İkmen's extra seventeen years had conferred upon him. But then, İkmen mused as he smoked on thoughtfully, being fifty-seven had to have some advantages.

'Yes, all right . . . Goodbye.' Mehmet Süleyman replaced the handset on to the receiver and sighed. 'Well, today is certainly shaping up to be something really quite special,' he said with a liberal smattering of irony in his voice.

'Why's that?' İkmen asked. He knew there had been a flurry of activity around his friend's office earlier in the day but he hadn't really known what it was about. He and Ayşe tended to lock themselves away, much as it irked him, when they were preparing themselves to give evidence in court. That was still five days away but they needed their records of their investigations into what had been a very brutal killing to be in order and to hand, and in İkmen's messy office that was quite a feat.

'Do you know about the body found on the ninth floor of the Hilton this morning?'

'I heard something about a body in a hotel somewhere,' İkmen replied. 'But you know how it is, Mehmet?' He shrugged. 'Court in five days' time and we need to put this acid killer away for good. What he did to his wife was, well . . . My evidence needs to be first class and, as usual, my paperwork is in a state of chaos.'

12

'You must thank Allah for sending you Ayşe,' Mehmet Süleyman said as he ground his cigarette out in his ashtray.

'She is, as you say, a marvel,' İkmen replied. 'She's almost as efficient as you were when you did the job.'

Mehmet Süleyman smiled. It was over ten years now since he had worked as İkmen's sergeant, but he still remembered those days with enormous affection.

'But this hotel murder . . .' İkmen began.

'Ah, yes. Well, he was discovered by a member of the hotel staff at 8 a.m. Stabbed, the victim is male, middle-aged and apparently he was known to the boys in vice. Unsubstantiated involvement with drugs; heroin and cocaine it is alleged.'

İkmen frowned. 'Name?'

'Cabbar Soylu, forty-five, from Edirnekapı . . .'

'I know Cabbar Soylu,' İkmen said with some distaste evident in his voice. 'Nasty fat Mafioso. Clever though. Vice are right, he's never been caught actually doing anything that could lead him to our cells. But he's known. He likes threatening the wives of those who are in opposition to him and his "soldiers" are not to be trifled with either. So why are you involved? I thought you were still working on the peeper investigation?'

'I am,' his friend replied. 'Soylu's killer is almost certainly the peeper.'

İkmen frowned. The as yet unknown criminal known as the 'peeper' had been terrorising, and more latterly murdering, young homosexual men in İstanbul since the autumn of the previous year. There was a definite sexual element to these crimes, the assailant was known to masturbate in front of or over his victims, who thus far had all been young and attractive. Cabbar Soylu had been neither. 'Hardly seems to fit what we know about the peeper so far,' İkmen said doubtfully.

Just briefly, Mehmet Süleyman averted his eyes. 'On the face of it, no,' he said. 'But it's the peeper, all right, and so that means more work for me.'

What he didn't and couldn't tell İkmen was how he knew that this murder was probably the work of the peeper. Süleyman had been assigned to the peeper investigation from the very start and, at one point, he had come very close to getting a victim to provide him with a useful description of this man. The peeper always worked from behind the protection of a mask, but on this particular occasion the victim, a young man called Abdullah Aydın, had managed to remove it and see his face. It was at this point that another agency, in the shape of a very charming but sinister man Süleyman knew only as Mürsel, had effectively taken the reins of the investigation from him. Mürsel, Süleyman's boss Commissioner Ardıç had told him, worked for an organisation that concerned itself with national security. To Süleyman this could mean only one thing: MIT, the Turkish Secret Service. But this was, if not denied, not confirmed either, and no names of any specific agencies were ever actually used by anyone involved. But whoever they were, the man known as the peeper had at one time worked as one of their agents and was now dangerously out of control. In order to allay public fear, the police would continue to investigate the peeper's crimes, but it was Mürsel and his people who pulled the strings and who would also eventually take charge of the offender's 'disposal'. It was Mürsel who had told Süleyman that Cabbar Soylu was almost certainly a peeper victim. Unhappily for Süleyman, no one apart from Ardıç and himself could know about any of this, and that included his good friend Çetin İkmen.

'And now on top of this new murder I also have my father,' Süleyman said as he attempted to ignore the doubt and slight suspicion he could see on İkmen's thin face.

'Your father?'

'On the phone just now. He wants me to look for some carpet dealer for him.'

'Why?'

Süleyman sighed. 'My father has this old friend called Raşit Bey. He runs one of the oldest carpet dealerships in the Kapalı Çarşı. Every so often my father offers him a kilim or a tapestry or a carpet, usually from my grandfather's old house. You know how it is.'

İkmen nodded. Whenever the old man couldn't pay a large utility bill or needed to repair his ridiculously extravagant car, he generally sold something. It had to be, İkmen had always felt, a depressing way to live one's life. Not for the first time, he was glad that the only thing he had ever possessed in abundance was children.

'So Raşit Bey', Süleyman continued, 'was at Father's house this morning, looking at probably the largest carpet my father still possesses and he mentioned that one of the people he employs has not turned up to work for the last three days. The kapıcı of this man's building hasn't seen him and Raşit Bey is worried.'

'Your father wants you to find this man,' İkmen said as a statement of fact.

'Yes.' He scowled. 'Isn't life grand?'

İkmen laughed.

'But he is my father, and so what can I do?' Süleyman said. 'He expects me to deal with this personally, which I cannot do, but I cannot let him know that.' He shook his head slowly.

15

'I will have to ask İzzet to go over to the man's apartment and see what he can find. But I can't really spare him.'

'Where's İzzet now?' İkmen asked.

'On his way over to Dr Sarkissian's laboratory to observe the autopsy,' Süleyman said.

It was already almost half past two, which seemed rather late for the pathologist to begin his work. 'It's only just started?'

'Yes.' He looked his friend straight in the eyes. 'You know what scenes of crime are like in public places, how difficult it can become. And the hotel is effectively a place with public access.'

Yes, İkmen did know that. What he also knew was that corpses found in public places usually meant that work at the scene of the crime was conducted under pressure from all sorts of people – the local council, public officials and in this case, he imagined, the management of the Hilton Hotel. 'Public' corpses were generally removed first and briefly to the Forensic Institute for the harvesting of samples and then on to the pathologist in haste rather than slowly. But then this was Mehmet's investigation, not his, and so there were probably all sorts of pressures surrounding the incident that he didn't know about or understand. However, he made a mental note to ask the pathologist, who was also his oldest friend, about his latest 'subject' when he could. As of that moment he couldn't, try as he might, equate the homosexual killer known as the peeper with that rough thug Cabbar Soylu.

'So why don't I look into this carpet dealer thing for you?' İkmen said finally with a smile.

'I can't ask you to do that!' his friend replied. 'You've got mountains of paperwork to go through and only five days in which to do it. No, that isn't fair on you.'

'What, taking me away from the thing I hate most about

16

this job?' İkmen laughed. 'My dear Mehmet, I would pay you to deliver me from it.'

'Yes, but . . .'

'Ayşe is so much better at paperwork than I am. She enjoys it.'

'Çetin, you're the one appearing in court, not Sergeant Farsakoğlu.'

'I know,' İkmen said. 'But I trust Ayşe. She knows what we need and what we don't. And besides, this carpet dealer thing will probably only take a few hours. You know what carpet men are like? He's probably having a passionate liaison with some woman somewhere.'

'He's not been seen at his apartment.'

'Well give me the address and I'll start there anyway,' İkmen said. 'Leave your sergeant to do his duty at the mortuary. I'll deal with this carpet man.'

Süleyman shrugged. 'As you wish, Çetin.' And then he pushed the empty cigarette packet he'd written on earlier across the desk towards his friend. 'His name is Yaşar Uzun and this is his address.'

İkmen looked down at the writing on the packet and frowned.

'Er, Sergeant Melik, would you mind coming in here for a moment please? I need to ask you something.'

İzzet Melik hoped that he would now be leaving the pathology laboratory with its sickening smells and disturbingly familiar body parts sitting in kidney bowls, but that was obviously not to be the case. Dr Sarkissian the small, almost circular Armenian pathologist, wanted to speak to him about something in his office.

17

'Doctor . . .' Melik walked into the doctor's office with heavy feet. Fortunately he didn't spend his every working day watching autopsies, it was very bad for his digestion. As he sat down opposite the pathologist's desk he stifled a rather sick-tasting belch.

'Now, sergeant, I don't want you to take this the wrong way, but I have to ask you some questions about our victim, Cabbar Soylu, before you leave.'

'Yes, sir.'

İzzet Melik had a few questions of his own about what he had been told was the latest peeper victim. But he settled himself to answer Dr Sarkissian's queries first, if he could.

The Armenian sighed, his face assuming a grave aspect before he spoke. 'Sergeant, I will be honest with you, as I will be with Inspector Süleyman, and tell you that I believe Mr Soylu's corpse has been tampered with by someone.'

This was not a situation that was totally alien to İzzet Melik. His stomach lurched and he calmed himself by stroking his very thick, black moustache before replying. 'Indeed.'

'Yes, and because it troubles me, I had a brief conversation with my colleague, Dr Mardin, who has some small experience in this area,' the doctor said. 'When I was away on vacation last autumn, you, sergeant, so Dr Mardin tells me, attempted to assist her in the investigations she was conducting on behalf of the police at that time. I understand from Dr Mardin that her fears have never been satisfactorily allayed.'

İzzet Melik felt the Armenian's myopic eyes, heavily magnified through his very strong spectacles, regard him critically. İzzet knew exactly what he was talking about and so he didn't even attempt to contradict him.

18

'You mean the corpse of that rent boy last November, don't you, doctor?'

'Nizam Tapan, yes.'

'The one that was . . .'

'The one that went missing for two hours between the crime scene and the laboratory. Yes, I do,' Dr Sarkissian replied. 'Nizam Tapan, according to Dr Mardin, was entirely "clean" when she got him. There was not a hair out of place and not a speck of dirt underneath any of his fingernails.'

'Yes,' İzzet said with a sigh, 'I remember.'

'Together with Dr Mardin you questioned Inspector Süleyman about it, didn't you?'

'Yes.' At first his boss had been as concerned as himself. He'd made all sorts of noises about taking the information up to his boss, Commissioner Ardıç, and beyond if necessary. But then the whole thing had just died down. No more questions had been asked and the peeper had not, until that morning, struck again – or so it was thought.

'Was the body of Cabbar Soylu clean, doctor?' İzzet asked.

'Yes, it was. There was not one fibre of forensic evidence on him,' the doctor said. 'The cause of his death was a single, very expertly placed stab wound to the heart. The assailant was left-handed, which is consistent with the profile of the offender we call the peeper. But beyond that . . . Mr Soylu was middle-aged, rather unattractive and, I understand, married with a child. Do you know why Inspector Süleyman is so convinced that this man is a victim of the peeper?'

'No, doctor, I don't,' İzzet replied. 'And to he honest with you . . .' He paused just briefly before continuing. He didn't, after all, want to speak behind Inspector Süleyman's back. He liked him. But he was troubled, too, and needed to speak to

19

someone. Dr Sarkissian was, he knew, a very old and trusted childhood friend of Inspector Çetin İkmen and everyone knew that İkmen was the most honest man in the police force. 'I don't know why Soylu has been designated a peeper victim. He doesn't fit the profile we're accustomed to.'

'So when did Inspector Süleyman decide that the peeper had killed him?'

İzzet sighed. 'Well, he was at the scene very early, just after the uniformed officers who'd been called in by the hotel management. When I got there he was on his mobile phone and, when he finally got off, he told me that Cabbar Soylu was in all probability a victim of the peeper.'

'Then I arrived . . .'

'You pronounced life extinct, the body was measured and photographed and then the team from the Forensic Institute moved in.'

'Or so it would seem,' Dr Sarkissian said.

İzzet Melik looked up into the doctor's eyes with fear building in his chest.

'The Forensic Institute tell me that the body was entirely clean when it arrived at their laboratories. What was it that happened last time, sergeant? With the rent boy?'

İzzet considered his answer carefully. None of the weird things that had happened with Nizam Tapan's body, apart from his 'cleanliness', could, after all, actually be proved.

'It would seem that the body went somewhere else before it arrived at the Institute,' he said. 'Persons unknown having gathered the evidence from the corpse then passed that information on to the Forensic Institute – or not. Nothing can really be proven in all of this, of course.'

'No.' Dr Sarkissian twirled a ballpoint pen between his

20

fingers. Behind him on the wall, a stern portrait of Atatürk looked down impassively. 'And this time, of course, I know that the body did indeed go straight to the Institute because you accompanied it, didn't you, sergeant?'

'Yes, doctor. But I didn't go inside.'

'The body was at the Institute for an unusually long time,' the doctor said as he leaned down on his desk, his large brow furrowed in thought.

'Yes.'

'But unlike Nizam Tapan's, Cabbar Soylu's corpse didn't go on any sort of excursion before it arrived at the Institute.'

'No, doctor.'

'And yet it, too, was clean!' He stood up and rubbed his bald pate angrily with his hands. 'Which is utterly impossible. Everybody picks up dirt and fibres on their clothes, even in expensive hotel suites. The Institute scientists only ever take samples, they never clean bodies of all evidence! Bodies have to go through my hands first before they can be cleaned.' He sat down again and looked İzzet Melik square in the eyes. 'I don't know why, sergeant, but I think that either the Institute did not for some reason examine Soylu or someone at the Institute is lying. And,' he sighed wearily, 'even though it pains me to say so, I have a bad feeling that Inspector Süleyman knows this is happening and why.'

İzzet Melik said nothing. But that didn't mean that he didn't agree with the doctor.

An owner of a successful carpet shop could conceivably afford an apartment in the up-market northern suburb of Nişantaşı, but not a mere salesman. Otherwise known as Teşvikiye, the district was characterised by designer shops, beauty parlours and luxury

21

car showrooms. Apartments were at a premium and generally inhabited by wealthy business people, lawyers and doctors. Looking up at the clean, smart apartment building on Atiye Sokak which runs across the junction of the super cool Teşvikiye Caddesi with Maçka Caddesi, Çetin İkmen couldn't help wondering how the salesman Yaşar Uzun managed to exist in such a place. Fiscal matters aside, quite how the young man from, apparently, some dirt village just outside Antalya, managed to cut it amongst the educated and ostentatiously monied folk of Nişantaşı, İkmen couldn't imagine. Even the beggars were fatter and better clad in this part of town.

He entered Yaşar Uzun's building via an efficiently silent revolving door. A man who could, from the looks of him, have been something relatively impressive in middle management came out of a small office to his left and asked İkmen what he wanted. Amazingly, this smart young man – probably only in his forties – was the kapıcı of the building, a post generally occupied by poor village men or rather crusty elderly gents with bowed and aching backs. But then this was Nişantaşı . . .

The kapıcı, though unimpressed by İkmen's police credentials, was nevertheless as helpful as the more traditional incarnation of his profession was wont to be.

'Oh, I don't know anything, actually, about Mr Uzun,' he said. 'It's not my place to interfere in the affairs of my ladies and gentlemen.'

İkmen rolled his eyes. Any kapıcı worth his wages knew everything about everyone in his building – their occupations, their children, their habits, lovers, plastic surgery status and pets. Nothing was sacred. One just didn't display one's knowledge openly, particularly not to a common person, such as a man who worked for the police.

22

'I'm here Mr, er . . .'

'Ahmet Osman.'

'Mr Osman, at the request of Mr Uzun's employer. Mr Uzun has not reported for work for the last three days. His employer is understandably concerned.'

'Yes, I know,' Osman replied. 'A Raşit Bey, from the Kapalı Çarşı. He came here yesterday.' He sniffed with some distaste at the memory of a person from such a vulgar part of town. 'I think he wanted me to open up Yaşar Bey's apartment so that he could look for him, but of course I refused. What my ladies and gentlemen do is their business . . .'

'Yes, well, you'll have to open up Yaşar Bey's apartment to me, Mr Osman,' İkmen said. 'Mind you, if he has been lying dead in there for three days, I'm not what you'd call exactly eager to find out.'

The kapıcı shrugged. 'Oh, I don't think that's probable,' he said. 'If something has happened to him, then it hasn't happened here.'

'Why not?'

'Because his car isn't in the garage,' Osman said.

İkmen frowned.

'Yaşar Bey went out to work on Monday in his car as usual. It's one of those American things, quite distinctive. Yaşar Bey is devoted to it. What is it now?' He pursed his thin lips and frowned. 'Oh, yes! it's a –' he smiled – 'Jeep! Yes, it's a Jeep. Yellow. It's marvellous, everyone looks at it, quite a fashionable thing, by all accounts. Not, of course, that I told his employer that the Jeep wasn't in the garage. I mean that is Yaşar Bey's private business. I tell you because you are a police officer . . .'

'So Yaşar Bey went to work on Monday and—'

'And he never returned here,' the kapıcı said.

'As far as you know,' İkmen said.

'Well of course.'

İkmen sighed. 'Get the key to Mr Uzun's apartment, will you, Mr Osman.'

'He isn't here.'

'I need to be absolutely certain about that,' İkmen said. 'Get the key and take me up to his apartment please.'

Amid a small but obvious amount of muttering, Ahmet Osman retrieved the key to Yaşar Uzun's apartment and took İkmen up the five floors to the very stylish, if spare, dwelling. As soon as the kapıcı opened the door it was obvious to İkmen that Uzun hadn't died in his apartment. It smelled of several things including stale cigarette smoke and some sort of pungent male cologne, but there wasn't even that vague sweetness on the air that usually heralds the presence of a fresh human corpse.

'How long has Mr Uzun lived here?' İkmen asked as he moved from one featureless room to the next.

'Six months, give or take the odd day.'

İkmen wondered where Uzun had lived when he first came to İstanbul. He also wondered why, unlike most of the carpet dealers he had come across over the years, the man from Antalya didn't have any rugs or kilims of his own. After all, even in an apartment of the most severe minimalism, oriental rugs were one of the few things that were always allowed. Carpets were, as his teenage daughter Gül had told him only the previous week, one of the few things from the 'old days' that were 'funky'. And Gül read every style and fashion magazine in the Turkish language.

'Did Mr Uzun go to his usual place of business on Monday?'

24

İkmen asked as he picked up a small black box containing what looked like a man's silver bracelet.

'As far as I know,' the kapıcı replied. 'He left at the same time he always does.'

'Mmm.'

Yaşar Uzun was probably with a girlfriend, or even off with a new and more exciting employer – people did sometimes just quit their jobs without explanation. But İkmen was not easy just leaving things like this and so he took his mobile from his pocket and called the station.

Mürsel was so casual about everything. Turned away into the corner of his office, his head down over his mobile phone, Mehmet Süleyman spoke to the man he called 'the spy' in a tone just above a whisper.

'It may be easy for you to lie about everything but it is not natural to me!' he hissed. 'I'm having to deceive people I know as friends! And I don't even know why I'm doing it!'

'I told you, Mehmet,' the voice at the other end of the line said evenly, 'there is a very dangerous man out there some-where whom we need to apprehend.'

'Yes, I know, but in the normal way . . .'

'This man, my dear Mehmet, cannot be captured in the normal way as you well know,' Mürsel replied. 'He is a patriot, a . . .'

'A spy like you!'

'A patriot,' the smooth voice corrected, 'gone astray. Now . . .'

'I cannot do it!' Süleyman shakily took a drag from his cigarette and then let out the smoke on a jerky sigh.

'Yes you can.' Mürsel's voice was calm but menacing. Just

as it had been that first time he had revealed his true nature and profession to the policeman – the time when he had told him that not to cooperate with himself and the other 'spies' would result in his untimely demise. 'You have no choice. You have to pretend to continue because people must believe that the police, and they alone, are involved in the peeper investigation. Don't worry, as I've told you before, you won't have to actually apprehend our man. You won't be able to. We'll do that.'

'But people can't understand why Cabbar Soylu is a peeper victim. I don't understand it myself!'

'Take it from me . . .'

'The peeper kills young homosexual men, as far as I and everyone else is concerned,' Süleyman said. 'Cabbar Soylu is a straight, thuggish . . .'

'Our man has moved on,' Mürsel said with what Süleyman felt was annoying simplicity. 'Now he targets other groups. Soylu is a peeper victim, trust me.'

Süleyman shook his head at this.

'Look, we could meet, you and I, it would be lovely. Or talk to Ardıç, he knows what's going on,' Mürsel continued. 'He's been most cooperative.'

Süleyman's boss the commissioner was the only other police officer with knowledge about the true nature of the peeper affair, and the sole person the inspector could talk to. Not that that was easy; Ardıç was an explosive and difficult individual at the best of times and this peeper thing had done nothing to improve his mood.

'I don't like the fact that people like Çetin İkmen and even my own sergeant, Melik, think that my judgement on the Soylu case is eccentric to say the least!' Süleyman said forcefully.

26

'Well, I can't help that,' Mürsel responded smoothly. 'My job is to find and apprehend our friend. Yours is simply to pretend to do so whilst remaining very poised and attractive. I know which one I would prefer to be doing.'

Süleyman wanted to say something about how Mürsel should perhaps stop drooling over him at every opportunity, but just at that moment his office telephone rang. Without even so much as a 'goodbye' he cut off the call to Mürsel and answered his landline.

Chapter 2

The Forest of Belgrad lies to the north-east of the city of İstanbul and is a great source of oxygen for the carbon monoxide-choked metropolis. So named because of the Serbs, from Belgrade, who were once entrusted to guard it by Sultan Süleyman the Magnificent, the Forest of Belgrad is now a favourite haunt of cyclists, runners and walkers. One of the latter, a middle-aged official at the Canadian Consulate called John Mclennen, was fond of taking his Irish wolfhound, Dara, with him on his various jaunts. On this occasion, because he had stayed the previous night with a friend in the village of Peri, which is just north of the forest's most familiar areas, Mclennen and the dog set out into uncharted territory along the road that leads from the village towards, eventually, the Bosphorus village of Sarıyer.

The area was characterised by deep, green gorges to each side of the road and, particularly in the very early morning, an all-pervading cool, misty calm. Peri was a 'diplomatic' village where numerous consular and NATO employees had their residences and so security was good. Crime or even general unpleasantness was rare and so John Mclennen had no fear as he walked out of the village at five o'clock on that gentle spring morning. He and Dara walked along the road at a steady pace, enjoying the lack of traffic and the sweet, early air. Because the dog was on his lead, John could look around, confident that Dara wouldn't run off while he was distracted. And so John looked. Up into the lightening blue spring sky, at the trees that lined the road beside him and into the dark and mysterious gorges that plunged so far down to the edge of the road.

Nothing beyond a vague and natural curiosity made him decide to dive off into one of the gorges to his right. He could, he later told police, just as easily have decided to go to the left. But he went right into the darkness of many thickly growing fir trees and, by his own admission, enjoyed the slightly dangerous feel of sliding down an almost vertical slope. By this time Dara was off his lead and was into the trees a good minute before his master. Once in the gorge, John first called the dog and then looked around. A couple of the trees seemed to have sustained some minor damage to their trunks, but he didn't think anything of it at the time. The forest was officially a protected area, but people sometimes tried to cut trees down illegally for firewood. In this case, it appeared that they had been interrupted before the trees were irreparably damaged. But John did not dwell upon the trees for very long. As seconds passed into minutes and Dara did not respond to his call, he became increasingly impatient with the dog and went still deeper into the trees in order to try and find him.

Now as he scanned about him for signs of his dog, John noticed that the ground at his feet was marked by a set of tyre tracks. He hadn't seen them at the top of the gorge, but they were very obvious lower down. It was all a bit of a mystery until he finally found Dara and the overturned vehicle that the dog appeared to be guarding for some reason. Whining and pacing up and down in front of what John recognised to be a

Jeep, the dog wanted his master to see something that was behind the vehicle. And so John, knowing dogs and their behaviour as he did, went knowing that Dara was probably leading him towards the erstwhile occupant of the vehicle. He wasn't wrong, although sadly the poor guy was very obviously no longer alive. John took his mobile out of his pocket and called 155.

'Yaşar is much better at doing those carpet shows than I am,' Raşit Bey said as he sucked on the mouthpiece of the nargile his grandson had just brought him. 'He has charm, he's attractive and he's so good with the foreigners who are, after all, the bulk of our customers these days. Yaşar speaks English very well, German and French well enough. His knowledge of carpets is very good, especially about Nomadic trappings – camel and salt bags, baby slings. Those are all becoming rare, I can tell you. Not that we exactly specialise in such items. We're much more "Ottoman" in what we stock.'

'You didn't attend this carpet show yourself, Raşit Bey?' İkmen asked.

Raşit Ulusan's shop was not the biggest or brightest in the Kapalı Çarşı, in fact its window display looked decidedly dusty. But then that, İkmen soon came to appreciate, was part of both the shop's charm and Raşit Bey's retail strategy. Situated in the Zincirli Han, which is at the north-eastern corner of the great bazaar, Ulusan Carpets faced stiff competition from the far more prominent Sisko Osman shop, which was well known for its immensely prestigious international clientele. Realising, many years before, that there was never any way that he could compete with a shop that sold to US and other presidents, Raşit made a conscious decision to appeal to a rather different

31

type of market. Specialising in buying largely from the old Turkish and sometimes also Arabian elites, Raşit's customers tended to be those who favoured faded glory; nouveaux riches Turks wishing to impress their friends and rather romantic foreigners, many of whom lived in Turkey as part of the expatriate community. Dusty 'Ottoman'-style windows appealed to such people very much, in Raşit's experience. To some the dust was almost an adventure in itself.

'No,' Raşit Bey tipped his head back to signal his denial. 'It's a long way out of town and my English, though not bad, is not as good as Yaşar's. Back in the old days of course, we rarely went to the home of a buyer – unless that person was extremely prominent. But now so many people want everything done for them on their doorsteps. I dislike it. And besides, I'm getting old now. Some of those shows can go on for hours. I need my bed.' He leaned forward towards İkmen. 'Are you sure you wouldn't like a nargile, Çetin Bey? I can get Adnan to bring you one, it really isn't any trouble.'

İkmen put one hand over his heart and said, 'You are very kind, Raşit Bey, but thank you, no. I will stick with my cigarettes if that is OK with you.'

'But of course.' The old man sighed.

It was just gone nine-thirty in the morning, but because it was officially İkmen's day off, he had only been up for half an hour. Four cigarettes one after the other was one thing, but a nargile so soon after rising was beyond even him. He was only in this shop because he had been unable to get to speak to Raşit Bey the previous evening. Though failing to pinpoint precisely why – he was, after all, a grown man – İkmen was concerned about Yaşar Uzun.

İkmen took a moment to take a sip from the tulip glass of

dark, sweet tea his host had given him when he arrived. Then clearing his throat he said, 'So tell me about these carpet shows, Raşit Bey. Does whoever is doing them take the carpets to the venue in a truck or . . . what happens?'

'The boys, that is, Adnan my grandson, Hüseyin, who has worked for our family for years, and Yaşar, load up the truck we use for all our carpet transport and Hüseyin usually drives it to wherever they need to be. For a show that we know will attract a lot of enthusiastic collectors we can take upwards of fifty pieces.'

'Pieces?'

'Carpets, kilims – and, recently, some antique embroidery – that can be very popular. The boys will unload the truck when they get to the venue and then Yaşar will give his presentation about the history and different types and grades of carpet and then hopefully sell some to the people at the show.' Raşit Bey leaned in towards İkmen once again and added, 'We see ourselves very much as educators in this field, Çetin Bey. Not like most of the other scoundrels who purport to sell good carpets these days.'

İkmen smiled. Programmed almost from birth, like most Turks, to treat everything a carpet man or woman said with extreme caution, this profession of honesty and expertise by Raşit Bey rather made his skin crawl.

'But then, of course,' the old man continued, 'one can only do so much, however well-intentioned one might be. Ultimately, Çetin Bey, the carpet chooses the person, not the other way around.'

Still smiling, İkmen said, 'Magic carpets.'

'If you wish,' Raşit Bey said. 'Not that I have to explain magic to someone like you, Çetin Bey.'

33

At this allusion to his late mother, Ayşe the Albanian witch of Üsküdar, İkmen put his head down a little in a small bow of recognition. He had loved his mother very much, but her old profession was not something he often wanted to discuss with people.

İkmen changed the subject. 'Do the boys all go with the carpets in the truck when they go out to one of these shows?'

'Yes.' Raşit Bey's grandson Adnan came in at that point and sat down beside the front door of the shop. 'Hüseyin drives as I said before, and Yaşar sits next to him. Adnan, you usually lie on the carpets at the back, don't you?'

The boy turned to look at his grandfather with a serious expression on his face which, İkmen saw, was sadly damaged. The poor lad had quite a pronounced hare-lip that made him appear as if he were continually sneering at everyone.

'Usually, yes,' he said. 'It's dusty and makes me cough. But I am the smallest and so I have to do it. Although I didn't do it last time.'

The old man frowned. 'No?'

'No, I sat up with Hüseyin last time, on Monday. Yaşar followed in his car.'

'Why was that?'

The boy shrugged. 'I don't know, showing it off, I expect. You know how he is with it, Grandfather, it's like his son or something.'

The famous Jeep that İkmen knew was not in the garage of Uzun's apartment building.

'I assume then that Yaşar also left the show in his own car at the end of the evening?' İkmen asked.

'Yes,' Adnan replied. 'He stayed on a bit to talk to the people at the show while Hüseyin and I packed up the carpets

34

and made our way home. It was already one o'clock in the morning.'

'Now tell me, where was this show held?' İkmen said.

But before either the grandfather or the grandson could answer, the policeman's mobile phone began to ring insistently in his jacket pocket. With a muttered apology he turned aside in order to answer it. It was Mehmet Süleyman and he was calling from the station. He took up all of İkmen's time and attention for the next ten minutes. When finally he did finish the call, İkmen turned back to look at the old carpet dealer with a grim expression on his face.

'Raşit Bey,' he said, 'did the carpet show on Monday take place in the vicinity of the village of Peri out in the Belgrad Forest?'

'It took place in Peri,' the old man said, 'at the house of a very enthusiastic collector, a Dutchman. Why?'

İkmen lit a cigarette before replying. He hated this part of the job, and always had. 'Raşit Bey,' he said, 'I'm sorry to have to tell you that Yaşar Uzun's Jeep and a dead body, which would appear to be that of your assistant, have been found in a deep gorge by the side of the road out of Peri.'

The old carpet dealer put one hand up to his chest. 'Allah!'

His grandson, equally shocked by this news, said, 'Did he have an accident or . . .'

'It would seem so, yes,' İkmen replied. 'I can't tell you very much yet except that the Jeep and the body were discovered in the early hours of this morning by a man walking his dog.'

'So you mean that poor Yaşar has lain there undiscovered since Monday night?' Raşit Bey said as the full horror of what had just happened began to sink into his mind.

'Unless he went back to Peri after the show for some reason, yes,' İkmen said. 'I am very, very sorry, Raşit Bey.'

The old man took the mouthpiece of the nargile between his teeth once again and then shook his head as he smoked heavily upon it.

Although the traffic officer who had responded to the Canadian's call for assistance when he'd found the Jeep suggested that the driver of the vehicle had just simply had an accident, police officers were dispatched to investigate. Inspector Metin İskender, one of İkmen and Süleyman's colleagues, had already left for the forest. Mehmet Süleyman, now that he had informed İkmen about Yaşar Uzun, was also out and about his professional business. Today he was out in the fashionable Bosphorus village of Yeniköy to interview Cabbar Soylu's widow, Emine. On his way back he planned to briefly stop off at his parents' house in order to tell his father the news about Raşit Bey's unfortunate assistant. But before that could happen he had to talk to Emine Soylu. After all, whatever Mürsel might believe about Soylu's murder and his contention that it was definitely the work of the peeper, it was incumbent upon the police, in the shape of Mehmet Süleyman, to explore all and any other possibilities that might exist.

The woman who greeted him at the door of what was a small nineteenth-century palace was of indeterminate age. It was rumoured that Emine was considerably older than her husband, by as much as ten years, some said. But, unlike Süleyman's own wife who was twelve years his senior, one couldn't even guess as to the age of Emine Soylu. Nothing on her face had been left untouched by the knife of a plastic

36

surgeon – not mouth, nose, eyes, cheeks or chin. That aside, however, it was obvious that she had been crying and plastic surgery or no plastic surgery, her face was pale with tiredness and shock.

'I loved my husband more than life itself,' she said without preamble as she led Mehmet Süleyman into a large room that contained a lot of very ornate lamps and several overstuffed red sofas. Pointing to one of these she said, 'Please do take a seat, Inspector.'

He sat down, took his notebook out, and apologised for intruding upon her grief.

Emine Soylu smoothed her short dark dress down towards her knees and said, 'We are burying Cabbar this afternoon. But you have your job to do, Inspector, I know that.'

According to the pathologist, Dr Sarkissian, there hadn't been any significant forensic evidence on the body. In fact, there hadn't been anything at all. Soylu had died from a single stab wound to the heart, but that was all the doctor could tell from his investigation. As he had told Süleyman in a very frank exchange between the two men the previous evening, he wasn't at all happy about releasing Soylu's body for burial. It was Muslim custom for the deceased to be buried within twenty-four hours of death – Turks in particular believe that the soul of the departed suffers terrible torment until burial is effected. Victims of crime, however, could not always be given an early burial for legal reasons and this was one of those occasions. Or rather it would have been had not the hand of Commissioner Ardiç on instruction no doubt from Mürsel, intervened. Dr Sarkissian had told Süleyman, in no uncertain terms, that he opposed releasing Soylu's body. He had also intimated that he felt something was distinctly awry with this

37

case and that Süleyman himself knew or suspected what that might be. How right the pathologist was! And yet Süleyman couldn't say anything to him or anyone else about Mürsel, the peeper and the involvement of organisations beyond either his understanding or control. In a few hours' time Cabbar Soylu was going to be buried and that would be that.

Süleyman cleared his throat before speaking. 'Mrs Soylu,' he said, 'if we are to have any success in tracking down your husband's killer, we need to know something about his life and his contacts.'

She sighed. Cabbar Soylu had been a well-known and very prosperous villain and both Emine and Süleyman knew it. 'I know you know exactly what Cabbar was,' she said as she looked up into the policeman's face with a small smile on her lips. 'And I know you want to know who his enemies were.'

'Yes.'

'Yes.' She sighed again before offering Süleyman a cigarette from her packet and then taking one for herself. 'But I can't help you with that,' she said. 'Cabbar, I know, was not always a nice man to those outside his immediate circle. He was after all a businessman and I accept that they can be ruthless. But with Rahmi and me, he was perfect.' Her eyes began to fill with tears once again. 'He kept us away from all that. He took care of us, always.'

Süleyman had met gangsters' wives and women in the past and, although Emine Soylu did look very similar to many of them, her character so far appeared to be radically at odds with those hardbitten females. There was, in fact, something of the simple rural Anatolian woman about her. It made him pursue a different, if not less relevant, line of inquiry.

'So tell me about yourself and your husband,' he said. 'Rahmi is, I take it, your son?'

'No.' She lowered her head slightly, hunching over her burning cigarette. 'Rahmi is Cabbar's son by his first wife. She died when Rahmi was born.' She looked up sharply. 'Where we come from, Inspector, women die in childbirth.'

'Where's that?' He knew it would be somewhere out in the east, somewhere hot in the summer, cold in the winter, miserable all year round. And he wasn't wrong.

'Hakkari,' she replied naming a troubled far eastern town close to the Iraqi border. Ringed by the impressive Cilo Mountains, Hakkari would be an outdoor sports enthusiast's paradise were it not for the still raw memories of the battles waged by the Turkish army against the Kurdish separatist movement, the PKK, in the 1980s and 1990s. Even in the twenty-first century Hakkari was, Süleyman knew, still dirt-poor. What it must have been like when Cabbar and Emine lived there he couldn't imagine.

'So you married Mr Soylu . . .'

'We met just over a year after his first wife died. We'd seen each other before of course, but . . . I, too, had a son at that time . . .'

'You were married before?'

'No.' She looked him straight in the eye with an honesty that was so straightforward it was intoxicating. After all, even in the twenty-first century sophisticated city women rarely admitted to a pregnancy outside of wedlock. For a woman from a place like Hakkari to do so, it was quite something. 'The father of my son, Deniz, deserted me as soon as he had got what he wanted. When Cabbar rescued me I was a destitute woman with a sick child. He brought me to İstanbul twenty

39

years ago. We married here and I brought Rahmi up as my own.'

Süleyman put his cigarette out in one of the many ashtrays scattered around that luxurious room. 'And Deniz?'

'My son is dead, Inspector. He was a very sick young man.'

'I'm sorry.'

She shook her head and smiled weakly. 'As I said, my son was sick. He died in hospital, back home.'

'Mum . . .' It was eerie, in view of what she had just said, to hear a young male voice call out to her like that.

Emine Soylu looked towards the door and said, 'Rahmi.'

Unlike his late father, Rahmi Soylu was a slim, attractive young man, in what Süleyman presumed had to be his early twenties. The only intimation that he was anything like his father was a slight steely glint to his slanted, green eyes. He walked into the room while his stepmother spoke. 'Rahmi, this is Inspector Süleyman from the police. He is trying to find out who killed your father.'

The young man looked at Süleyman with ill-disguised disdain. 'Why?'

Süleyman rose in order to shake Rahmi Soylu's hand, but the latter kept his wrists clasped firmly behind his back in what was a very ill-mannered snub.

'It's my job,' Süleyman replied. 'The State pays me to do so.'

Rahmi shrugged his narrow shoulders. 'But this is the Soylu family you are talking to,' he said. 'It is a family I now head. We take care of our own affairs.'

His stepmother, obviously appalled at Rahmi's lack of manners, reddened and then turned away.

'It is your affair, yes,' Süleyman said, 'but a murder has

40

been committed which also means that it is a police matter.'

'My father and the police were not exactly close,' Rahmi Soylu snapped back bitterly, leading Süleyman to the conclusion that perhaps Emine Soylu had been lying when she told him that her husband kept herself and her stepson away from his business. Rahmi Soylu, after all, seemed very keen to assume the mantle of a big, police-taunting man of power.

'I know what your father did and what he was, Rahmi,' Süleyman said as he leaned down just a little bit in order to speak to the younger, shorter man. 'This does not debar him or your family from access to justice.'

The young man snorted unpleasantly.

Emine Soylu went over to her stepson and said, 'Rahmi, Inspector Süleyman wants to help.'

'We can handle our own affairs.'

'Rahmi,' she put one of her hands on his shoulder. 'Some people your father may have been involved with . . .'

'Don't talk to me about things you don't understand!' He shook her hand off roughly and began to walk back towards the door. 'You're not my mother. You're nothing! All you could ever give birth to was a demon!'

And then without another word he left. Once he was out of earshot the tear-stained Emine Soylu said to Süleyman, 'You mustn't mind Rahmi, he doesn't mean what he says. It's his grief talking, that's all.'

But Süleyman wasn't so sure. There was both a hardness and an inappropriately childish petulance about Rahmi Soylu he really didn't like. Grief or no grief, to be so cruel to his stepmother was inexcusable. And what was that about Emine having given birth to a demon?

*   *   *

41

'What are you doing here?' İkmen said as he walked over to and then embraced his friend the pathologist, Arto Sarkissian.

There were five vehicles parked somewhat precariously by the side of the road, perched, as it were, on the lip of the steep gorge below. There was Inspector Metin İskender's Audi, a standard police squad car, an ambulance, İkmen's beaten up old Mercedes and a much newer and sleeker model of the same make that belonged to the Armenian.

Arto leaned in towards İkmen and said, 'Both Inspector İskender and the attending medic reckon that the victim was shot at some point during his recent "adventures". I'm here to cast my eye over the body. Although, looking down there . . .' He pointed into the deep darkness of the gorge and was not, in tandem with İkmen, comforted by the sight of İskender, his sergeant, and a white-coated medic coming up through the trees towards them.

'It's a long way down, isn't it?' İkmen said as he lit up a Maltepe cigarette. 'I wonder if it's slippery down there, or . . .'

'If I fall over, at my weight, I will break something,' the Armenian said with some passion in his voice. 'Either the rest of you will have to hold me as I walk down or we will have to get a crane in from somewhere!'

İkmen rolled his eyes up towards the bright blue spring sky. 'Arto, I don't think that industrial machinery will be required,' he said. 'I think that's just a little over-dramatic.'

'Do you! Do you!' His large face was white with fear, his small dark eyes staring out wildly from behind the thick lenses of his spectacles.

'Yes, I do.'

Fifteen minutes later, however, having struggled alongside his colleagues to get the terrified Arto Sarkissian down into the gorge unharmed, İkmen was no longer as sure as he had been about the amount of dramatic potential inherent in a crane. In retrospect it seemed to be almost a missed necessity. Sweating heavily after his long slide down the gorge, İkmen, along with Metin İskender, surveyed the overturned Jeep while the doctor got to work with the body on the forest floor.

'What makes you think that Yaşar Uzun has been shot?' İkmen asked as he offered his colleague a cigarette.

İskender took the proffered Maltepe with a grunt and then said, 'The large hole between his shoulder blades was a bit of a clue.'

A dapper and attractive man in his early thirties, Metin İskender had the reputation for being a somewhat spiky individual. Not that he was as bad as he had been when he'd first joined the force. Although the majority of Turkish police officers originate from working-class families and districts, the tough Istanbul neighbourhood of Ümraniye, which was where Metin was born and brought up, had a fearful reputation for poverty and ignorance. Pulling oneself out of such a place, as he had done, was an act of great willpower and courage and did not allow one to tolerate either prejudice or criticism.

'Oh.'

'I also noticed something odd about the tyre tracks,' İskender continued.

'What was that?'

'They only appear to start halfway down the gorge. The ones near the road have been brushed over – literally – with an actual broom, by the looks of it.'

İkmen sucked on his cigarette and then said, 'So someone didn't want Mr Uzun and his lovely car to be discovered.'

43

'It would seem so,' İskender replied. 'The "mob" strikes again if I am not much mistaken, Inspector İkmen.'

The latter sighed and then said, 'Yes. Or so it would appear.'

As well as being very beautiful and healthy, the Forest of Belgrad had for some time had a more sinister reputation as graveyard for the various poor souls who had had the misfortune to cross one or other of the city's brutal Mafia bosses. Gorges like it provided excellent natural dumping grounds.

'The last whereabouts of Mr Uzun are back in the village,' İkmen said as he looked up the gorge to the road above. 'Monday night.'

'Any idea what he might have been doing?' İskender enquired.

'Selling carpets to foreigners,' İkmen replied.

'Oh. I see.' The words were spoken with a slight curl of the lip as if Metin İskender had a bad smell under his nose.

İkmen laughed softly. 'Not keen on carpet dealers, Metin?'

'It's a job.' He shrugged. 'Men must work. What more can be said?'

'Ah, but there are carpet dealers and there are carpet dealers, are there not?' İkmen said.

'Well . . .'

'And this particular carpet dealer was assistant to Raşit Ulusan, one of the oldest and most respected dealers in the Kapalı Çarşı. Raşit Bey can boast ambassadors and industrialists amongst his customers as well as the Süleyman family. Mehmet's family and the Ulusans have been trading, apparently, for many years.'

Metin İskender grunted by way of reply. He, too, knew and liked Mehmet Süleyman but he, probably rather more than most, found the issue of the man's Ottoman past difficult.

Although married to a very successful middle-class business woman, Metin's understanding of once-powerful people from pre-Republican families was limited. He also, in common with a lot of people, had little patience with such families' avowed poverty in the twenty-first century. It was Metin who changed the subject.

'Of course some of the body and about half of the face has been eaten by something,' he said as he started to make his way over to the corpse and the doctor attending to it. 'I don't know what animals live in this forest, but I expect our friends in the mob are only too educated on the matter. Luckily both his wallet and his mobile phone seem to be intact.'

'Yes.'

İkmen began to move over towards the body too, but then stopped just as the rich, meaty smell of rot began to assault his nostrils. Yaşar Uzun's death did look, on the face of it, like a classic Mafia hit – except that most mobs he knew very rarely took the time to cover their tracks or even bother to hide what they had done in any significant way. He did have a feeling about Yaşar Uzun – he'd experienced it right from the start – things here were not all that they seemed. As he took his mobile phone out of his pocket, İkmen smiled. His late mother had been exactly the same. But back then, in the forties and fifties, her abilities had been interpreted as the result of witchcraft. In Üsküdar where the İkmen family lived in those days, Ayşe İkmen had been the local witch. As he flicked his phone open, İkmen wondered whether the district still had a witch and, if so, whether she was any good. He lit yet another cigarette as he scrolled through the host of numbers he had stored in the telephone's memory and then, coming to the one that he wanted, he sighed and pressed the 'select' button. A few seconds later an elderly voice answered.

'Ah, Raşit Bey,' İkmen replied. 'I am so sorry to bother you at this difficult time, but could you please give me the name and address of the person who hosted your carpet show last Monday night?'

The old man said that he would, provided İkmen could wait for a few moments while he went into his office to retrieve the information. İkmen said that was fine and, while he waited, he looked at the deep, still slightly misty forest around him. It was gorgeous.

Chapter 3

'Yes, I remember Emine Soylu, or Koç as she was then, and Deniz, her son, too,' the phlegm-swamped voice of someone Süleyman could barely understand in the Hakkari gendarmerie said. Some of the eastern accents were difficult to decipher. But then for some of the people 'out there' Turkish was not really their first language. Often it was Kurdish and, in the case of the Suriyani Christians, it was Aramaic. Not that this man, whatever his name was, was likely to be a member of either of those groups. No, he was just a member of the local jandarma, a paramilitary force that acts in lieu of the police in some rural districts, and he had an accent you could cut with a knife.

'I believe that Cabbar Soylu married her and took on the boy, Deniz?'

Süleyman was sitting in his car outside his parents' house with his mobile phone jammed against his ear. He'd started making inquiries of Hakkari as soon as he'd left the Soylus' house. After all, if this investigation was to proceed as usual, and Mürsel was very keen for it to do so, he had to explore the background of the victim at the very least. Also it was quite propitious that this roughly spoken man had called at this time. He had not, after all, relished the prospect of telling his father about the death of Raşit Bey's assistant. Death in

47

all its forms, even of those he didn't know, saddened Muhammed Süleyman to a quite disproportionate degree these days.

'No,' the other replied shortly. 'Cabbar married Emine all right, but Deniz went to the hospital at Van.'

Rahmi Soylu had described Emine's child as a 'demon'. Süleyman wondered whether he was deformed but his colleague in Hakkari said that he wasn't.

'Deniz Koç was mad,' he said. 'Cabbar had him put into the institution outside of Van. It was for the best.'

'Why was that?'

'Oh, he was violent, biting –' had he said 'biting'? – 'touching, hitting . . . you know . . .'

Süleyman did have some experience of psychiatric institutions. Apart from the fact that his psychiatrist wife had patients in several of them, over the years his job had taken him into a few in and around İstanbul. Then of course there had been his mother's uncle Ahmet who, due to shellshock sustained during the First World War, had died in one such place. Not that anyone ever spoke about him except in whispers. If Cabbar Soylu had put his stepson into an institution it cannot have been a decision lightly taken – madness, even by association, remained a palpable stain upon one's family.

'I believe Deniz died,' Süleyman continued. 'I get the impression that was some time ago.'

The phlegmy man seemed to laugh. 'No,' he said, 'Deniz Koç died last year. September. He killed himself. They always do.'

'Oh, I . . .' He turned to see the confused face of his mother at the car window, her fingers tapping on the glass.

'Mehmet! What are you doing?'

48

He put his hand over the mouthpiece and said, 'Mother, I'm on the phone! I'll be in in a moment.'

'Mehmet?' She looked confused, her heavily powdered face frowning against the outside of his window.

'Yes,' the man on the phone continued, 'took his own life and condemned his soul to damnation.'

'Right . . .'

Süleyman pressed the button to lower his window and then said to his mother, 'I'll be in in a moment! This is business, Mother!'

'Oh, well, if you must shout at your poor mother . . .' His mother flounced off back into her small wooden house with more of the air of a teenager than that of an elderly woman. But then that was his mother all over, she had never – and would never – grow up. His father had indulged her too much for that to ever be possible.

'Inspector Süleyman?' the voice at the other end of the phone said.

'Yes . . .' Süleyman raked one nervous hand through his thick, greying hair. His mother always had an adverse effect upon him in almost every scenario he could name. But he cleared his throat and said, 'So, but, Cabbar Soylu, what did you make of him . . . ?'

'Cabbar?' the man laughed, properly, so it seemed, this time. 'A loveable rogue. He has a record, as you must know, but here he was just involved in petty crime. He stole from bakkal shops, dealt illegal cigarettes to soldiers, you know . . .'

'You wouldn't describe him as a gangster?'

There was just a moment of silence before the other man said, 'No, not here in Hakkari. I heard he later did well in

İstanbul and I wondered if it was by that criminal method, but Cabbar left no family behind when he went away from Hakkari. His mother went with him, his father and brother were dead by that time. Last I saw of Cabbar was at Deniz's funeral here last year. Word was that he and his family were off to start a new life in Europe somewhere.'

'Emine Soylu didn't mention it,' Süleyman said.

'Oh, well, maybe he changed his mind,' the other said. 'But whichever way it was, it was kismet that he die at this time. Where it happens matters little.'

'Somebody killed him,' Süleyman said slowly. The idea that kismet, the Islamic concept of a preordained fate, was the prime mover in the death of an individual was still a prevalent notion, even amongst sections of the police force and particularly in the countryside among the peasants and the jandarma. Süleyman, for whom kismet wasn't a totally serious consideration, tried to be patient with this man's point of view.

'Yes, but it was his time, Inspector,' the man continued almost cheerily. 'Life, which must conform to the Will of Allah, was always so.'

'Yes . . .' And then amid a brief further exchange of religiously inspired niceties their conversation finished.

Süleyman took a few moments to think about what he had just been told before getting out of the car and going towards his parents' house. Deniz Koç had been, apparently, 'mad', although quite what his actual diagnosis had been, he didn't know. Out in the wild and remote east maybe he didn't even have a diagnosis. After all, Cabbar and Emine Soylu must have put him in that place towards the end of the seventies or early eighties at the latest. A time when things had been very bad, very violent all over the country. Political unrest of the rightists, leftists and the Kurdish population had culminated in the imposition of martial law in 1981. Süleyman remembered it well. Cabbar Soylu's early years in İstanbul must have been tough, he'd subsequently done very well for himself. His success, however, could not, by its very nature, be applauded. Soylu had been a gangster and a thug and his life was not going to be any great loss to anyone beyond his family. If the peeper had killed Cabbar Soylu, did this mean that the peeper, as well as disliking homosexuals, hated gangsters too? Süleyman got out of his car and wondered about the types of people the peeper could conceivably dislike and how Mürsel could possibly know about that.

Mr Wilhelmus Klaassen of the consulate of the Netherlands in İstanbul was an extremely tall, dark-haired man in his late forties. Like most Dutchmen he spoke flawless English but, in addition, he spoke Turkish too, which was quite a treat for İkmen. Mr Klaassen's Turkish was the best the policeman had ever heard coming from the mouth of a foreign national.

'How long have you been in Turkey, Mr Klaassen?' İkmen asked as he followed his host into the latter's enormous modern home.

'Three years now,' Mr Klaassen replied. 'And you don't have to be formal. Call me Wim, please.'

Wim. He was so friendly and seemingly open that İkmen was almost tempted to ask him to call him 'Çetin'. But thirty years plus of maintaining a professional distance from 'the public' militated against it and so he just smiled as he sat down in a very large chair beside a very bright window.

Wilhelmus Klaassen and his wife Doris lived in one of the higher up and more prestigious parts of Peri. Their property consisted of a two-storey house with four bedrooms and two bathrooms as well as a considerable garden with a swimming pool. Every room afforded spectacular views of the Belgrad Forest, like the one İkmen was gazing at now. Stunned, he was still trying to take in the knowledge that 'Wim' had only started to learn Turkish one month before his posting to İstanbul when 'Doris' brought him a very welcome glass of tea.

'We have to learn other languages, Inspector,' she said as she handed the glass and saucer over to him with a smile. 'No one but the Dutch speaks Dutch.'

'Not many people outside Turkey speak Turkish, present company excepted,' İkmen said and then with a view to just getting the next question over with because he had to, he said, 'Do you mind if I smoke?'

Western people, especially Americans and Canadians, didn't generally like smoking and so he didn't have very high hopes. But he was to be pleasantly surprised.

Wim laughed. 'Oh, you look so worried, Inspector,' he said. 'Don't be.' He took an ashtray off one of the many coffee tables in that vast living room and gave it to İkmen. 'I am a Dutchman, I smoke cigars. It's what we do.'

The three of them passed pleasantries then about the house, the view and the various lovely things the Klaassens had in their home before they got down to what they all knew they had to talk about.

'How well did you know Yaşar Uzun?' İkmen asked as the couple both surveyed him sympathetically with their big, blue eyes.

52

'Not very well,' Wim replied pulling on a long, black cheroot as he did so. 'We know Raşit Bey. We were introduced to him and his shop by the previous Dutch consul who did a lot of business with him. It was from the previous consul that Doris and myself kind of inherited Raşit Bey's carpet shows. When he left we took over. We first met Yaşar last year when he came along with Raşit Bey to see how things were done. Then this year he came just with the boys and gave, I must say, an even better talk than Raşit Bey. His English is – was – excellent. Do you know how his car came to come off the road, Inspector?'

'No.' He hadn't told them that it was thought Yaşar Uzun had been murdered. Plenty of time for that shock later. 'So tell me about this carpet show, Mr, er, Wim, if you will.'

The Dutchman shrugged. 'Once a year the boys and either Raşit or Yaşar come to us for the evening with a selection of their carpets. Doris and myself are avid collectors of village carpets as I'm sure you can see, Inspector.'

There were various brightly coloured rugs hanging on the snow-white walls and spread out across the floorboards, but İkmen didn't have a clue about what precisely these carpets were.

'Our friends likewise,' Wim continued. 'And because Raşit Bey and his boys are so knowledgeable, we like to buy from him.' He looked at İkmen with a sudden serious cast in his eye. 'Do not take this the wrong way, Inspector, but there are a lot of useless, cheating dealers out there . . .'

'Oh, you don't have to tell me about cheating carpet dealers, Mr – Wim, I can assure you,' İkmen replied.

'Raşit Bey's prices are very good,' Doris put in. 'And the Nomadic Trappings he gets hold of are amazing. A couple

53

we knew from the Swedish consulate, they love those. Turkoman camel bags, baby slings, salt bags, even sometimes old dowry trappings. Raşit Bey has so many wonderful pieces.'

Including, İkmen remembered, some of the Süleymans' carpets from their many and various defunct palaces.

'So anyway,' Wim returned to the subject at hand, 'the show. On Monday Yaşar and the boys arrived at about four in the afternoon with the carpets. Unloading from the van took them just over an hour, they bring so much. Then Doris made us all some drinks and sandwiches and we sat talking in here until our guests started to arrive at about seven.'

'What happened then?'

'Well, it took a while for everyone to arrive, people come from both here in the village and from İstanbul too.'

'All consular people?' İkmen asked.

'Some. We have friends in the NATO coterie too,' Wim said. 'On Monday night we had people from the Netherlands, Sweden, Israel, Canada, the United States, United Kingdom and one couple of Turkish friends too. Yaşar started his talk, which is about the different types and grades of Turkish carpets, at about eight fifteen. By the time all the buying and selling had finished the boys didn't get away with the remaining carpets until, I suppose, about twelve-thirty.'

'Mr Uzun, I understand, stayed on a little after the carpets had gone.'

'Yes, Doris made him coffee,' the Dutchman said. 'He was tired and asked for a coffee before he set off back to İstanbul. We talked. Amongst other things we bought a very rare Turkoman tent-door decoration. Inspector, forgive me, but was Yaşar's accident of a suspicious nature?'

But before İkmen could answer, the front doorbell rang and Wim excused himself in order to answer it. Because of the open-plan nature of the lower floor of the house both İkmen and Doris Klaassen could see who was at the door almost as soon as Wim. It was a rather flustered-looking, thin man in his fifties who spoke English with a pronounced British accent.

'Oh, Wim,' he said distractedly, 'God! You haven't heard from that bloody Yaşar Uzun, have you? I called the shop yesterday, but they say he's missing. I've rung and rung his mobile . . .'

'Ah, Peter, yes, come in,' Wim replied also in English. 'You must talk to our . . .'

'I had a deal with that bastard!' the Englishman continued. 'Months of negotiation. Now, possibly, I can complete . . .'

'Peter, this is our guest, Inspector İkmen from the İstanbul police,' Wim said as he gently ushered the much slighter man into his living room. 'I am afraid that he has some bad news about Yaşar.'

İkmen looked up into a small, grey face and began, 'You are a friend—'

'Mr Melly was at the carpet show on Monday night,' the Dutchman explained a little nervously now, İkmen felt. 'He is from the British Consulate.'

'Mr Melly.' İkmen rose and extended his hand, which the Englishman took in what could only be described as a cursory manner.

'Yes?'

He remained standing even after İkmen and the Dutch couple had seated themselves once again. İkmen looked up into a pair of craggy-browed dark grey eyes. 'I am afraid, Mr

Melly, that Yaşar Uzun is dead,' the policeman said. 'And in answer to your question, Wim, we do have some grounds to suppose that the reason Mr Uzun's car left the road was not purely accidental.'

'Fuck.' The Englishman dropped into the nearest empty chair and immediately lit a cigarette. 'Shit.'

'It's a shock, isn't it?' Wim said in the English they were obviously now all using. 'And you say it might not have been an accident, Inspector?'

'You mean someone killed Yaşar?' his wife, her brow furrowed in shock, interjected.

'It would seem so,' İkmen said as he looked at the Englishman who was visibly trembling.

'But how? He . . .'

'I can't tell you any details at the moment, Mr Melly,' İkmen interrupted. 'However, if you had business which, from what you have said so far, would appear to be unfinished, with Mr Uzun, I will have to ask you a few questions. If you don't mind, that is.' One had to, İkmen knew, be very careful around diplomats. They could, if they wanted, just disappear back to their own countries in a very short space of time. Every policeman he had ever met, both Turkish and foreign, hated dealing with them. Holding on to a diplomat was, as one British policeman had once told him, like trying to grab on to water.

'I don't expect you to believe everything about this, Inspector,' Peter Melly said as he put his coffee cup back down on the little occasional table Doris Klaassen had provided for him. 'I'm not sure that I really truly believe it myself in the cold light of day.'

56

'I'm listening,' İkmen said, his fingers steepled reflectively underneath his chin.

The Englishman sighed. 'It seems like I've been dealing with Yaşar Uzun for ever,' he said. 'But in reality I suppose it has to be at the most eight months. I adore carpets and I love history.' He stopped in order to take a deep breath after which he said, 'He, Yaşar, had a Lawrence carpet for me.'

İkmen frowned. 'A Lawrence carpet?'

The Englishman and the Dutchman exchanged a look before the former turned back to İkmen once again and said, 'I suppose I should have guessed it wouldn't mean anything to you; as a Turk, I mean, I . . .'

'Well, you are right in that regard, Mr Melly,' İkmen said. 'I've heard of kilims, just today of "village carpets", but of Lawrence carpets, I am afraid I am totally ignorant.'

Peter Melly lit a cigarette. İkmen noticed it was a very smart Black Sobranie. 'Lawrence, as in T. E. Lawrence, was a British military hero of the First World War,' the Englishman said. 'He, er, he fought with the Arabs against the Ottoman Empire in 1917 and 1918. We, um, we regard him as a hero . . .'

'Lawrence of Arabia, yes,' İkmen said with a smile. 'I have seen the movie. Peter O'Toole and Omar Sharif. Yes, he was a heroic figure for you.' He looked pointedly across at the Englishman. 'The Ottoman Empire was by then a dying and corrupt administration. Some years later, as I am sure you are aware, Mr Melly, Mustafa Kemal Atatürk changed everything.'

'Yes . . .'

'So Lawrence of the Arabs . . .'

'Ah, yes, well,' Melly continued, 'Lawrence collected oriental carpets. It is well documented and, of course, to own one of his carpets would be quite a coup. Expensive, but a

57

coup all the same.' He leaned forward, his face a taut mask of excitement. 'Yaşar Uzun had such a thing. I have seen it, held it. I was in negotiation to buy it.'

'Were you.'

'I had to have it!' Peter Melly said and then, through gritted teeth, he added, 'Had to!'

Although by no means a carpet aficionado, İkmen, like everyone else, was well aware of the trade in 'famous' carpets. The fact that some celebrity or historical icon had owned a particular carpet could increase its value considerably. A picture of a carpet supposedly once owned by the nineteenth-century English explorer Charles Doughty had appeared in the newspapers only a few months before. This fragment, which is all that it really was, had been valued in the tens of thousands of dollars. But then that carpet had been verified by experts as a genuine item.

'How do you know that this Lawrence carpet really is a Lawrence carpet?' İkmen asked.

After first looking up at Doris, who duly went off to the kitchen to get more drinks, Peter Melly said, 'It's quite a tale. Do you have some time?'

Until Arto Sarkissian had finished his autopsy on Yaşar Uzun, İkmen theoretically had all the time in the world. But then even if he hadn't he was now intrigued. Lawrence of Arabia was a troubling and indeed incomprehensible figure for him. That a man should go away from his country and become as one with another, seemingly more primitive people, was deeply strange. 'Yes,' he said, 'I have some time.'

And so after Doris Klaassen had finished replenishing everyone's drinks, the Englishman began.

58

'Lawrence's speciality was blowing up trains,' he said. 'The Turks, er, Ottomans, built the Hejaz railway through Arabia originally to transport pilgrims to the Holy Cities of Mecca and Medina. But when war broke out, of course, they used it to carry troops. I don't know exactly when Lawrence came into possession of the little Lavar Kerman prayer rug Yaşar Uzun was selling to me, but I know that he was an enthusiastic collector and that his Arab irregulars routinely looted Turkish transport trains. It's basically how our government, the British, paid these men. But anyway, the man to whom Lawrence eventually gave the Kerman was a young enlisted chap, a Brit, who was his batman in Cairo . . .'

'Batman?' İkmen frowned.

'Sort of like a servant,' Melly explained. 'Privates, non-commissioned men, can, or rather could, act as servants to officers. Cleaning their kit, pressing their uniforms, doing their housework, basically. This young man, Private Victor Roberts, was Lawrence's batman. He gave Roberts the Kerman as a way of expressing his thanks for the young lad's efforts. According to Roberts, Lawrence told him the rug had been taken from a Turkish transport train just outside a place called Ma'an which is, these days, in southern Jordan. Lawrence and his men blew the train up and then looted whatever they could find which included this rug. It's still stained with blood Lawrence claimed had belonged to a young dead man, a Turk, of what he described as "unusual beauty".'

'I think I've heard it said that Lawrence was homosexual?' Wim said.

Melly shrugged. 'It's very possible. No one really knows.

59

But anyway, Lawrence gave the rug to Roberts who carried it with him all the way to Constantinople.'

'İstanbul.'

'Constantinople as it was then, Inspector,' the Englishman said to the Turk who shrugged his assent. İstanbul indisputably had indeed been Constantinople – up until as late as 1930. 'We, the British, as I'm sure you know, occupied the city after the First World War until your man Atatürk took it back in 1923.'

'Our War of Independence.' İkmen smiled. A lot of foreigners still failed to appreciate that, at that time, Mustafa Kemal Atatürk and all the rest of the Turkish nationalists were literally fighting for the existence of their country.

'Yes, well, exactly. It must have been a very confused and confusing time for all concerned. Vis-à-vis the carpet, however, what happened next I don't know for certain, but it would seem that Roberts gave the Kerman away to someone in İstanbul.'

'Which was how Mr Uzun eventually came into possession of it, I assume,' İkmen said.

'Not exactly,' the Englishman replied. 'Yaşar is from Antalya on the Med coast. He came into possession of it there. He says he got it from some old chap in an ancient back-street antique shop in the old town. The story goes that the Kerman came into Antalya on a cruise ship sometime back in the 1980s. A member of the crew, a Turkish chap, told the tale I've just told you and sold it to the antique dealer who squirrelled it away for years. Somewhere along the line, or so Yaşar said, the Kerman had gained the reputation for bringing ill fortune. Maybe the bloodstains on it helped to build that reputation. Load of rot, of course.'

And yet İkmen knew how powerful the designation of something as 'unlucky' could be across so many levels of Turkish society. In spite of whoever had owned the carpet and whatever it might have been worth, İkmen could imagine that an elderly back-street antique dealer would be wary lest such a thing attract the attention of the Evil Eye and bring misfortune in its wake.

'And you have proof that this Kerman carpet did indeed belong to Lawrence?' İkmen asked as he lit up another of his cheap Maltepe cigarettes. 'I mean, the reports of a man on a cruise ship can hardly be regarded as reliable.'

'Yaşar found a photograph of the carpet on the Internet,' Peter Melly replied. 'It's of Lawrence and Roberts with the Kerman in Cairo. When I saw it the rug came in a wooden chest, which I think Roberts, or someone, must have put it in later. But the photograph, which I have also seen in books, was taken by the American journalist, Lowell Thomas, who followed Lawrence during the latter part of his career in the desert. I've a copy of the picture myself if you want to see it. It shows the carpet clearly and in its entirety.'

'You have nothing to prove to me in that regard, Mr Melly,' İkmen said. 'Whether this carpet is genuine or not is of no interest to me. What I do have some interest in, however, is your relationship with Mr Uzun. Had you paid for this Kerman – is that its name?'

'Yes. From the city of Kerman or rather the nearby town of Lavar – hence Lavar Kerman – in southern Iran,' Melly said as if by rote. 'Yes, I had, or rather in part.'

'What does that mean?'

'I'd paid him half and I was to get the other half. Money like that doesn't grow on trees.'

61

'How much money are we talking about?' İkmen asked as he flicked a long sausage of ash from his cigarette into his ashtray.

Peter Melly lowered his head as if ashamed of what he was to say next. He took a deep breath. 'A hundred and twenty thousand. Pounds. I raised it on the house I own back home.'

The Klaassens, who obviously hadn't known about how much their friend was willing to pay for this carpet, exchanged shocked looks.

'That was the first payment,' Melly continued.

'The first payment!' İkmen, his cigarette now shaking between his fingers, nearly fell off his chair. 'What . . .'

'We agreed, Yaşar and myself, on an overall price of a quarter of a million pounds,' Melly said quickly.

'A quarter of a . . .'

'Inspector, this is Lawrence's valuable Lavar Kerman carpet we're talking about here!' Peter Melly leaned forward in order to make his point more forcefully. 'Not only that, it's a fabulous piece! I've got carpets from all over the world but I've never seen or experienced anything like this before. The central motif is a glittering weeping Tree of Life, quite unique, almost alive . . . I had to have it!'

Or, İkmen thought, if Raşit Bey and his magic theory was to be believed, maybe the Kerman had to have Peter Melly.

'So what you are telling me then, Mr Melly, is that you do not yet have the Lawrence carpet in your possession.'

'No.' Suddenly deflated he put his head down again, on to his chest. 'No, Yaşar still has it. The deal was that I only got it once full payment had been made.'

'And that will not happen now, will it?' İkmen said.

'I've almost raised the other one hundred and thirty . . . I'll gladly pay Yaşar's family for it,' the Englishman replied.

İkmen sighed. 'Well then, I had better find the Lawrence carpet so that they can take possession of it, hadn't I, Mr Melly?'

Chapter 4

'The bullet that killed him came, so ballistics tell me, from a Beretta 92 pistol. You will, Çetin, be familiar with this weapon because . . .'

'I have one myself,' İkmen said. 'The department obliges me to carry one.'

'Even though you so very often conveniently leave yours locked inside your office drawer.' Arto Sarkissian smiled. 'Yaşar Uzun was killed by a weapon that is a standard issue police department piece.'

'Doesn't mean that he was shot by any of our officers,' İkmen said.

'Doesn't mean that he wasn't either,' the Armenian replied. 'Ballistics are going to want to check everyone's gun.' Then holding his hands aloft he said, 'Nothing to do with me.'

'I know.'

They were in the doctor's office which, mercifully and unlike his laboratory, had windows. Not that the sight of the grim, litter-strewn car park outside, now darkening under the evening sky, was anything one might actually want to look at. But just having visible access to the outside world gave İkmen some little comfort in what was otherwise a place of confinement, reeking of bodily fluids and death. How his friend managed to work and remain cheerful in such a place had always been a mystery to him.

65

'I hate guns,' İkmen said as he lit up a cigarette and then gulped down what remained of the rather nasty coffee Dr Sarkissian's assistant had made for him.

'I know.'

'I hate the way they make some people feel powerful. So often a gun is just a smokescreen used to cover an inadequacy a sick individual feels he has to make up for in some way.' And then changing the subject rapidly, he said, 'Mehmet Süleyman's peeper victim, Soylu, he was stabbed, wasn't he?'

'Yes.' The Armenian took off his spectacles, rubbed his eyes and then put his glasses back on again. 'I've actually been meaning to talk to you about that, Çetin.'

'Why?'

The doctor told him about 'clean' corpses, both Soylu's and that of the rent boy, the peeper's first actual fatality.

'This is all new to me,' İkmen said in response to this barrage of worrying information from the doctor. 'Who, if not the Forensic Institute, is cleaning these bodies up, do you think?'

'Nizam Tapan the rent boy was taken to some laboratory outside the city before he was given over to the Institute, or so Sergeant Melik asserts.'

İkmen frowned. 'Does he.'

'In Soylu's case, the body went straight to the Institute but was not, I understand, seen by the usual team until he'd already been in the building for some time. Dr Arslan, who heads up the team these days, said the corpse was clean of almost all environmental evidence by the time it got to him. It certainly was when it came to me.'

'Any idea why?' İkmen asked.

66

'Not a clue.' There was a pause before he spoke to İkmen again. This wasn't easy. 'But I fear that Mehmet Süleyman does.'

For a moment the Armenian's words just hung in the air like a bad smell. İkmen barely, or so it seemed, breathed.

'Both Sergeant Melik and my assistant Dr Mardin certainly brought the Nizam Tapan case to his attention last November,' Arto Sarkissian continued. 'He said that he would do something about it and then – nothing; the case was dropped. Now this. I don't even know why Cabbar Soylu has been designated a peeper victim anyway, no one does. Except Inspector Süleyman.'

Outside, the sunset call to prayer began its sinuous wash across the many, many mosques of İstanbul. İkmen imagined his wife as he knew she would be, praying. How nice it must be, he thought, to have such ironclad certainty in your life!

'Mehmet Süleyman is not corrupt,' İkmen said softly at length.

'No . . .'

'And yet, Arto, I assume this conversation has to involve you asking me to challenge him about the events you have described.'

'Don't you think this is serious, Çetin?' the Armenian asked.

'Yes.' İkmen looked up into his friend's face, frowning. 'And I don't doubt that what you, Dr Mardin and Melik say is true. But Mehmet Süleyman? I can't believe him capable of wrongdoing . . .'

'I don't believe that he is willingly concealing evidence either,' Arto replied. 'But what has happened is nevertheless wrong and I, at least, need some clarification. I've tried to talk to him myself, but to no avail. So, Çetin, yes, I do need

67

you to talk to him about this. You are his friend, he loves and respects you, and I don't want to have to take this up to Ardiç, I really don't.'

'No.' Quite what the explosive commissioner of police, Ardiç would do about such a situation, İkmen didn't know. Old and disillusioned as he was, Ardiç still had the reputation for being a vicious and unpredictable adversary. İkmen shook his head as if to dislodge the image of a fat, enraged Ardiç from his mind and said, 'But to get back to my body, Arto. Is there anything else I need to know?'

'Yes. Your carpet dealer was shot after he had brought his vehicle to a halt. He was in his car when he was shot. From short range and, I think, he turned away from his assailant. So the murderer was outside and shot into the car as Uzun twisted his body away.'

'So he pulled over for some reason.'

'Yes, but then once he was dead, he and the vehicle were pushed down into the forest below. Then the tracks were, as we've seen, erased.'

'Mmm.' İkmen frowned.

'Apart from that,' Arto said, 'Yaşar Uzun was in good health. He smoked cigarettes and, sometime recently, cannabis, too. But he wasn't what I'd call a user of cannabis. I think he was just a man who enjoyed the occasional – what do they call it – joint?'

'Yes. So no grim diseases or heroin abuse or anything like that?'

'No. You know, Çetin, that Inspector İskender thinks this might have been a Mafia hit.'

'Yes.' İkmen sighed. 'But then we all know that their influence stretches into most corners of society, carpet trading being

68

only one of the more obvious arenas. All I have to do is to work out which particular mob is responsible. Could it be the delightful Edip family of Edirnekapı, or maybe what remains of my local gangsters, the Müren family? But then again maybe . . .' He rubbed his tired face with his rough, leaf-dry hands. 'Arto, do you know much about the English soldier called Lawrence of Arabia?'

His friend knew as much as İkmen, basically what he had gleaned from the famous 1960s film. But he didn't know anything more and certainly the whole carpet thing was a total mystery to him – except in one regard.

'I do know that provenance is important,' the Armenian said. 'For instance a carpet that can be proven to have belonged to a significant member of the old imperial family could fetch a very high price. Even those enormous carpets that can be difficult to sell because of their size can fetch big prices if they belonged to, say, a sultan or maybe a prominent grand vizier.'

'Yes, but Arto, a quarter of a million sterling!' İkmen said as he shook his head at the vastness of the amount. 'Sterling!'

'To an Englishman it is probably worth that,' the Armenian replied. 'My brother recently paid over a hundred thousand dollars for a genuine nineteenth-century palace carpet that was proven to have belonged to the Ottoman architects, the Balian family. They built Dolmabahçe palace and so most Turks know of them, but to us they are especially significant as the most important Armenian architects in history. My brother was happy to pay what he did in order to secure what he feels is part of our heritage. This Englishman, Melly, obviously has similar feelings.'

'Yes,' İkmen sighed. 'But now I've got to go and look for

the fucking thing.' He took a folded piece of paper out of his jacket pocket and then unfolded it, spreading it out across the doctor's desk. 'Here's what it looks like. Melly gave me this printout of a photograph Uzun took off the Internet.'

The black and white printout showed two men holding a carpet up between them. The man on the left of the picture was young, tall, and wore a slightly dusty-looking military uniform. The man on the right was much smaller and older and, although his features were of an obviously western European type, he wore traditional Arab robes, even down to carrying a curved knife in the belt around his waist. İkmen pointed to this figure and said, 'That's Lawrence.'

'I gathered that,' Arto replied. 'With, I assume, this Roberts person you spoke of and the famous carpet.'

'Yes.'

'Interesting.'

'Yes,' İkmen said, 'isn't it.'

Although it wasn't possible from the photograph to see what colours had been used in the Kerman, one could deduce the approximate size of the piece, which had to be around about one and a half metres long by one metre wide. And, although it wasn't possible to make out everything in the way of detail around the borders of the carpet, the central section was very clear to see. It was also extraordinary. A tall thin weeping willow, or Tree of Life, as Melly had described it, dominated the carpet. Delicate and at the same time sinuous, in the hands of these two foreign and, in Lawrence's case, alien men, the Kerman was like a precious traveller from another time if not another world entirely. Its central design struck something deep inside İkmen. He didn't know what it was, but when he had first seen this picture tears had risen, as from a great

70

underground river, and burst across his eyes like a rain shower. The Englishman, Melly, had said he completely understood why that had happened.

Mehmet Süleyman just wanted to get home to his wife and son, but the man he knew as Mürsel was insistent.

'We can't just talk in the street!' he said as he led Süleyman down Meşrutiyet Caddesi towards, the policeman feared, his usual haunt of the dusty Londra hotel bar. Mürsel, as well as being what most people would call a spy, was also a very sexual being. By his own admission he was attracted to both women and men and the rather charming faded grandeur of the Londra bar appealed to many men who enjoyed the company of their fellows. For Süleyman however, it was sometimes a little too much. Being leered at by Mürsel alone was quite disturbing enough.

Mürsel smiled. Tall, handsome and exquisitely dressed, he was probably in his early forties – about Süleyman's own age. 'Oh, don't worry,' he said as he led the policeman past the Londra and seemingly up towards the even more chi chi Pera Palas hotel, 'this place I have in mind will not be brimming with lovely young men. It will be brimming with only you and me, I hope.'

He turned into a very grubby and unpromising-looking doorway to his left and beckoned for Süleyman to follow him. The buildings just to the south of the Londra, on the same side of the road, were also of nineteenth-century vintage. Four storeys or more in height, the grimy stucco-encrusted façades looked uniformly neglected. Open doors, like this one, frequently revealed litter-strewn halls and the usually sightless lower windows were more often than not covered in fly posters for bands and slightly fanatical political organisations. Inside there was often a rather dodgy-looking lift and this building was no exception. But Süleyman got in after Mürsel, without any questions or comments about where they might be headed. After all, if this place, wherever it was, turned out to be another venue in which Mürsel attempted to seduce him, there was nothing novel in that. Mürsel always tried, so far without success, to seduce Mehmet Süleyman. Wherever they were going in this uncomfortably small lift was unlikely to make any difference to that.

As the lift slowly ascended, Süleyman attempted to look at anything except Mürsel's sensual, mildly amused face. Knowing something about what people like him did, which involved a lot that gangsters also did, made the policeman cringe. There were, he knew, far less destructive and far more honourable ways in which one could serve one's country. But then like everything else in life, being or not being a spy was a choice and he had chosen to most definitely pass on that option.

The top floor of this particular building turned out to be the fifth. Mürsel got out first and led Süleyman along a depressingly dusty corridor towards a very nondescript door. Before he opened it, he said, 'Welcome, Mehmet, to the most magnificent view of this city you will ever see.'

The entire rooftop area was set out like a lush garden restaurant. Funky metal tables and chairs nestled in amongst great shady palms, long-leafed tobacco plants and tubs of very brightly coloured tropical-looking blooms the policeman could not even begin to identify. It was all very gorgeous although it was as nothing compared to the enormous copper bar that stretched across the entire front end of the space. And that in

72

turn was as nothing to the truly amazing view of the city that lay beyond the bar and its serried ranks of rakı, blue curaçao, vodka and gin bottles that reflected in a golden glow across the bar's deep coppery surface. With the sun setting in the west, across the Golden Horn which Süleyman was now looking down upon, everything made of either stone or metal shone with a pale yellow glitter.

Mürsel at his shoulder said, 'So down directly below us we have Şişhane district, then the Horn, then across the water to the Old City, Balat, Fener, and all those old neighbourhoods. Then' – he pointed across the Golden Horn towards the north-west – 'up there, is Eyüp.' He smiled. 'Where your Ottoman ancestors would have been girded with the Sword of Osman, my dear Mehmet. Fancy a country boy like me knowing something like that.'

To be girded with the Sword of Osman in the Holy Mosque of Eyüp was the Ottoman monarchs' equivalent of the coronations performed by western European royals. When a sultan came to power one of his first acts was to show his people he was their legitimate ruler by being girded with the Sword of Osman as soon as he could. Mehmet Süleyman could indeed count several sultans amongst his ancestors but that was not something he dwelt on at length and so he ignored Mürsel's allusion to it and sat down at the bar in order to enjoy the view.

'So how do you know this place?' he asked, aware, as promised, of the complete and utter emptiness of this wonderful place. 'It's amazing.'

'It's also not yet officially open,' Mürsel said as he sat down next to Süleyman and lit a cigarette. 'It's a little early in the season as yet. It'll be heaving come June, with the beautiful

73

people, the monied set. One of our friends is the owner.' He looked down into the street below and said, 'Oh, look, there's Haydar!'

Haydar was a sort of henchman of Mürsel as far as Süleyman could tell; a lesser spy of some sort. Süleyman looked down into the street but all that he could see were a couple of young girls carrying boutique bags, a few bored-looking taxi drivers slumped against the sides of their vehicles, and a small clutch of obviously drunk homeless men. None of them looked even remotely like the tall, powerful figure of Haydar. But then Süleyman had frequently failed to notice Haydar in the past, that was Haydar's skill.

Mürsel got up from his seat and moved behind the bar. 'Well, I don't know about you, but I am going to pour myself a rakı,' he said as he grabbed hold of one of the bottles labelled 'Altınbaş Rakı'. 'What would you like, Mehmet?'

'I don't want a drink.' Süleyman lit a cigarette and then added as if as an afterthought, 'Thank you.'

Mürsel shrugged and then poured. 'Your choice.'

'What I want is for you to tell me how I can manage to convince others that Cabbar Soylu is a peeper victim when I have no idea why that is myself,' Süleyman said, feeling anger rising in his chest. Speaking on the telephone to Mürsel hadn't managed to alert him to the seriousness of this situation, maybe face-to-face would do the trick. It was why Süleyman had requested to meet with this man now.

But Mürsel just laughed which didn't seem like a good start. 'Oh, Mehmet, what . . .'

'This is no laughing matter!' He said it through ground clenched, tense teeth. 'Beyond the fact that you have told me so, I have no reason myself to suppose that Soylu is a peeper

74

victim! And nobody except Ardiç knows about you!'

'Ardiç is very important.' Mürsel took a swig from his glass, a drag from his cigarette, looked at the amazing view, and then sighed. 'Look, Mehmet,' he said, 'I can't, as you well know, tell you much about myself or my . . . well, my department, we will call it, but the person you call the peeper . . .'

'One of your agents gone wrong or mad or . . .'

'A colleague for whom the strain of the important patriotic duty we perform became too much,' Mürsel said. 'I can tell you that his targets are not just confined to active homosexual men. Anyone not entirely in tune with the moral purity and upright standing of a good citizen can also attract his eye, shall we say.'

Süleyman frowned. 'So is this a religious crusade?'

'Oh, no, no, no! Quite the reverse! No, our man is, shall we say, desirous of removing the morally suspect, superstitious, unthinking or brutal elements from society.'

'By killing them,' Süleyman said.

'Yes.'

'Mmm.' He put his head down for a moment and smoked in a concentrated fashion. 'The morally suspect, superstitious, unthinking and brutal elements represent a large proportion of any population in any country. That is a lot of killing.'

'I know.'

'And yet' – Süleyman shook his head – 'is he not morally suspect himself, this peeper of yours? If I remember correctly when he was simply terrorising young men in their own homes, he masturbated in front of them. He tried to rape that boy Abdullah Aydın, the only one so far to have actually seen his face.'

75

'Safe now, in our custody,' Mürsel said with a smile.

'What gives him the right to make these judgements about people?'

'I didn't say he was right or that the situation was one of rationality,' Mürsel said. 'We believe this individual is on a form of mission . . .'

'How does he decide who to "hit"?' Süleyman asked. 'Why Cabbar Soylu? There are plenty of other gangsters in this city, some even more vicious than he.'

'I don't know,' Mürsel replied. 'How could I? I am not insane, am I?'

'And he is?'

Mürsel shrugged.

'And yet you know him?' Süleyman asked.

Again Mürsel just shrugged. But of course he knew him! Those sorts of people, the ones whom Mürsel and the peeper worked for, wouldn't send someone who didn't know the offender out to track him. That would be both stupid and a waste of resources.

'There must be something that singled Cabbar Soylu out as the peeper's first mobster victim,' Süleyman said as much to himself as to Mürsel.

'Maybe, but it's nothing I have any knowledge about,' the other replied. 'Soylu was just a thug without whom the world is far better off.'

'You sound like you share some of the peeper's opinions,' Süleyman responded sharply.

Mürsel leaned across the bar and placed one of his hands against Süleyman's left cheek. 'I do wish you'd come to bed with me,' he said. 'You'd have to do nothing but enjoy your-self. I can be very tender and sensual . . .'

76

'No.' He pulled his face away from Mürsel's hand and stood up.

'You know you want to really,' Mürsel purred.

Süleyman, flustered, said, 'No I don't! I'm married. I love my wife. I love all women.'

'And yet I see the lust for men in you, Mehmet.' The spy sighed. 'Oh, but I am so intoxicated by boys and girls who play hard to get! It is my curse!'

'What nonsense!' Süleyman pulled his jacket down and straightened his tie. 'I'm surprised you're not afraid of ending up as one of the peeper's victims yourself,' he said.

Mürsel moved around from behind the bar and stood in front of the policeman. 'Oh, he could never catch me. He and I know too many of the same tricks. He wouldn't get you either, if you were with me.'

Big brown flashing eyes glittered at Süleyman in front of the now dramatically setting sun.

'I'll take my chances on my own,' he said and then with a small bow he began to make his way back towards the dusty corridor and the cramped little lift.

'Leaving so soon?' Mürsel said.

'I need to find some sort of plausible way to tell my colleagues that the peeper is on a moral crusade,' Süleyman said, 'and that we have absolutely no way now of predicting any future victims. Gangsters, gay boys . . . What next? Whores? Deserters from the military? Religious leaders?'

He left, to Mürsel's frustration, as he found Süleyman so very alluring. But he took his mobile phone out of his pocket and called down to Haydar, who was in taxi driver gear on this occasion, and asked him to follow Süleyman to make sure that the policeman got home safely. He then made another call, which meant that he wouldn't have to spend the rest of the evening without further masculine company.

Not too much had been said about anything in the Melly household since Peter had returned home that evening. As usual his wife Matilda had prepared their meal with great care and precision and her husband had enjoyed it so far as he could enjoy anything very much. Unknown to Matilda, Peter had given one hundred and twenty thousand pounds to a man who was now deceased. He had a receipt, of course he did, he wasn't a total fool, but it didn't say what it was in respect of. Although signed by Yaşar Uzun it could have been a receipt for anything. At the time, Yaşar had said he felt it best not to specify anything on the docket about the Lawrence carpet. The existence of the rug was to be their secret; his, Peter's and Matilda's (Yaşar never knew how much Wim Klaassen did or did not know) – not, of course, that Matilda Melly had any idea about how much her husband had been willing to pay for his beloved carpet. And now that she knew that Yaşar Uzun was dead she seemed to be rather more concerned about him than about the Lawrence Kerman.

'Poor Yaşar,' she said as she worked away at the knitting that seemed to be continually in her hands. 'How dreadful!'

'Yes . . .' Her husband sighed. God, what a predicament! How he was going to get his hands on the carpet now he couldn't imagine. Who, for a start, would he buy it from? It wasn't as if Yaşar had been selling it through Raşit Bey's business, after all. No, the Kerman had been just between the two of them, Yaşar and Peter, a private sale. Well, he could kiss goodbye to the one hundred and twenty grand he'd paid up front, that was for sure! Not that that mattered at all. The

Kerman was what mattered, the bloodstained Lawrence Kerman.

He'd seen it once, held it in his hands in all its old bloodied glory. What a piece! Its emotional impact had been instant, history raw and immediate, like a kick in the guts. Yaşar had brought it and the sandalwood box in which it had, apparently, been kept for many years over to the house about a month after Peter had first seen that picture of Lawrence, Roberts and the Kerman in Cairo. His hands had sweated and trembled as he touched it. Dappled in places with old brown bloodstains, the colours of both the features and the ground were stunning. The light blue of the background rendered it startling but the whiteness of the wool used to make the carpet was beautiful. The outer borders were decorated with a mass of gorgeous flowers, in red, blue and deep magenta. In the middle, however, inside the feature known as the 'mihrab' or prayer niche was the source of the Kerman's power for Peter Melly. A tree of life in the form of a golden weeping willow. A symbol not only of earthly beauty but of paradise beyond the grave, woven in awe at the path of the divine. He'd known right from that moment that he had to have it, whatever the cost of the piece might be. It didn't matter. And so negotiations had opened at that moment, but he still didn't know where the Kerman was kept. He assumed it had to be somewhere in Yaşar's apartment, but he didn't know where that was; Yaşar would never tell him. Of course, with hindsight, he should never have told the police about the Kerman at all. He should have gone straight away to Raşit Bey and demanded to know Yaşar's address. He was a diplomat, an important person, he could do that. Armed with that information he could have attempted to break in and get what was really, at least in part, his property. But he hadn't known that Yaşar was dead until that İkmen chap had told him. Then he'd been so shocked the whole lot had just come tumbling out of him like verbal vomit. But someone had killed Yaşar, it seemed, and that was truly terrifying because neither Peter nor the police knew why. Was it because of the Lawrence Kerman? Had someone as yet unknown killed him in order to get hold of the piece? If Peter knew of its existence he imagined that others over the years must have done so too. After all, Yaşar hadn't exactly been backwards in coming forwards about it to him. Lawrence's name had simply come up casually in conversation in Raşit Bey's shop one day and the next thing Peter knew, Yaşar was on his doorstep. He wondered again where the precious carpet was and just the thought of it made him break out into a sweat.

'I can't think why anyone would want to kill poor Yaşar, can you, darling?' Matilda wittered over the top of her knitting. She was a plump woman who looked exactly what she was which, Peter had felt for years, was very boring. Knitting, fiddling about in the kitchen making gooey cakes, going to dull little Anglo-Turkish dos with equally dull local women – that was Matilda. He tried to convince himself that he owed her little, and anyway, the house back in the UK was only in his name. He'd bought it just before they got married. He could in theory do whatever he wanted with it. Except that to do that would upset Matilda and, strange as it was, he was really averse to doing that.

'No,' he said in short reply to her wittering. They should have had children. There was so much silence and just sheer, albeit comfortable, boredom between them. If they had had children, maybe, Peter felt, he wouldn't have become quite so obsessed by oriental carpets. He idly scanned around the vast,

80

white sitting room – a space almost identical to that of the Klaassens' – with the exception of more than a few carpets. There were village rugs, kilims, early Anatolian rugs in bold primitive designs, a rare Kumkapı silk Hereke of dazzling beauty as well as Bandirma and Giordes columned prayer carpets. A wonderful collection by anyone's standards. But Peter Melly would have given them all up for just a hint as to the whereabouts of the Lawrence Kerman carpet.

Chapter 5

'I knew that Yaşar lived up in Nişantaşı these days, but I imagined he had some sort of room,' Raşit Ulusan said in answer to İkmen's question about his ex-employee's apartment. 'When he was in Sultanahmet when he first came to the city, he shared a small apartment with four other men. It was all that he could afford. I thought he'd just moved up to Nişantaşı to be posh. You know, live in something not much more than a cupboard just for the sake of the address. Status meant a lot to Yaşar.'

'Clearly,' İkmen agreed. 'But what he had, Raşit Bey, was a three-bedroom apartment on Atiye Sokak, Nişantaşı, with garaging for that very expensive Jeep. I might also add that the apartment was very well and tastefully furnished. Whatever you were paying him . . .'

'Was obviously not enough for a lifestyle like that,' the old man said. 'Oh, Allah, poor Yaşar, what had he got himself involved with?'

'You don't know?'

The old carpet dealer leaned forward to take the glass of tea his grandson had set down in front of him earlier. 'Know what?'

İkmen, who had already gulped his tea down, lit a cigarette. 'Well, Raşit Bey,' he said, 'there are two possible ways in which Yaşar could have made all this money. One we know about, the other is mere speculation. Do you know whether Yaşar had any connections with any of the local mafias?'

'The mob?' Raşit Bey shrugged. 'Which one? The Russians, the Bulgarians, Azerbaijanis, our own . . .'

'All. Any. Whatever.'

He shrugged again. 'You know as well as I, Çetin Bey, that the mob, from whichever direction it comes, is and always has been interested in the carpet trade. To a greater or lesser degree every dealer I know has had at the very least a visit from these people. I myself have been "visited" although many years ago now.' He smiled. 'Fortunately, my clientele and some of my friends are powerful enough to have removed that threat from Ulusan Carpets. I shall say no more. Why do you ask about Yaşar and the mob?'

İkmen, smiling too, now, had suspected that Raşit Bey's business had some very powerful friends. But maybe that had not extended to Yaşar Uzun. 'The manner of his death was, or could be, typical of a mob-style hit,' he replied. 'We've as yet found no other connections, however. What we do know is that around about the time he acquired the Nişantaşı apartment, he was given a hundred and twenty thousand pounds sterling by one of your customers.'

The carpet dealer's eyes widened. 'A hundred and twenty thousand *pounds*!'

'Yes, from a Mr Peter Melly at the British Consulate.' İkmen then went on to report what the Englishman, backed by the Dutch couple, had told him about the Lawrence carpet. He showed Raşit Bey the photocopied picture of Lawrence, Roberts and the Kerman carpet that Melly had given him.

Shaking his head, the carpet dealer said, 'I've never seen

this photograph or the carpet in it in my life. A Lawrence carpet? Allah!'

'You've heard of such things?'

'Who has not?' the carpet dealer said. 'Carpets that once belonged to the famous are big business. Lawrence was a collector. The British and the Americans love anything to do with him. How did Yaşar come into possession of such a thing?'

'We're not sure,' İkmen replied. 'We don't even know where it is.'

'At his apartment?'

'No, we've looked.' İkmen first sighed and then said, 'I'm sorry, Raşit Bey, but I am going to have to search these premises.'

Sometimes he hated his job. Raşit Bey was a decent man and the hurt expression that clouded his face did not make İkmen feel in any way good about what he had to do.

'Inspector?'

Süleyman looked up from the papers on his desk and said, 'Yes?'

İzzet Melik was cradling his telephone receiver underneath his ear. One of his hands covered the mouthpiece. 'I've a man who won't give his name. But he's from Hakkari. He says someone here spoke to a Captain Ceylan from Hakkari about someone called Deniz Koç...'

'Yes, that was me,' Süleyman said. 'What does he want?'

'Says he has some information. Is this something to do with Cabbar Soylu?'

'Yes.' Süleyman put his hand out for the telephone. So it had been a captain he had spoken to from Hakkari. Melik gave him the receiver and watched intently as his superior took the call. 'Inspector Süleyman. I took a call from Captain Ceylan . . .'

'Ceylan knows nothing.' The voice was even harsher and less distinguishable than the Hakkari jandarma's had been.

'Who is this?' Süleyman said.

'Someone who knows Hakkari jandarma station,' came the rather ominous reply. 'Listen, Inspector, Ceylan told you that Deniz Koç killed himself. It isn't true. He was murdered.'

'Murdered?'

'Smothered. I can't tell you who did it. I don't know. But what I can say is that he was at the Perihan Hanım Institute in Van when he died. And it was his stepfather who ordered it done.'

'Cabbar Soylu?'

'Yes.'

'But why? Deniz was out of the way . . .'

'Cabbar wanted to go to Europe. Emine was nervous about being so far away from Deniz. Then the boy "died". You work it out.'

'Yes, but this is just conjecture, you—'

'Look, someone I know works at the Perihan Hanım. Deniz Koç had a pillow placed over his face. He was, as usual, drugged out of his mind, so he didn't struggle. If Cabbar Soylu is dead, then I am glad. He murdered an innocent.'

'Who—'

But the line went dead at that point, leaving Süleyman staring helplessly at the mouthpiece. When he did finally come back to himself he said, 'İzzet, see whether that call can be traced.'

'Yes, Inspector.'

He took his mobile phone out of his jacket pocket and said, 'I need to go outside for some air.'

İzzet Melik, aware that 'getting some air' was not really one of his superior's habits, said, 'Yes.'

Süleyman left and, as soon as he had managed to find a comparatively quiet corner of the station car park, he called Mürsel.

İkmen knew the Kapalı Çarşı and its shops well enough to know that checking every item of stock in Raşit Ulusan's carpet dealership was not going to take five minutes. He had three uniformed officers to help him, as well as his sergeant, Ayşe Farsakoğlu. But darkness was falling and they still hadn't got beyond the main showroom and the one small office behind it. In this, one of the oldest parts of the bazaar, successful shops like Ulusan Carpets had many, many other store rooms and sometimes workshops too. Quite often these rooms were spread out on different levels. In the case of Raşit Bey's business as well as the ground-floor rooms, there was a vast basement and three other floors that were accessed by a rickety metal staircase to the left-hand side of the main entrance. On top of that, the fact that it had been a slow day for business across the Kapalı Çarşı had meant that one of his officers, young Hikmet Yıldız, had spent most of his time shooing away other curious carpet, gold and antique dealers. Upon reflection, İkmen thought that what he should have done was call upon the services of the Zabıta, the dedicated market police, to help him keep order outside the shop. But, as usual, when he had his teeth into a case, he had been in a tearing hurry. It was well known that the more time that passed after a murder had been committed the less likely the police were to make an arrest.

'Nothing in the office, sir,' Ayşe Farsakoğlu said as she made to follow a uniformed constable to the back of the show-room. 'I'm going to start in the basement.'

'All right,' İkmen replied. 'Where's Roditi?'

Ayşe Farsakoğlu waved her copy of the photograph of the Kerman in the air. 'Oh, Allah!' she said. 'In those rooms upstairs. I don't know how many there are or where they lead . . .'

'I imagine to another dimension, sergeant,' İkmen said. 'Like you, I've never seen so many rooms, corridors or—'

'There are five rooms on three levels, two staircases and two corridors,' Raşit Bey said as he handed İkmen a glass of tea and then wearily sat down in a chair. 'Çetin Bey, can't my boys help your officers to sort through these piles of carpets?'

'No, I'm afraid not,' İkmen said. 'We have to do it, and anyway, I think your lads are fully occupied clearing up the mess we've made, don't you?'

Raşit Bey looked at his grandson Adnan and general assistant Hüseyin sweating heavily as they attempted to put the carpets and kilims the police had looked at back in good order.

'I have called my brother Cengiz in Antalya and he has located Yaşar's family and informed them of his death,' Raşit Bey said as he gestured for İkmen to sit down. 'His mother and a brother are apparently on their way.'

'They will come to you?' İkmen sat down although the sight of Constable Yıldız talking to another man in a very animated fashion outside had caught his attention.

'It is the least I can do,' Raşit Bey replied. 'I spoke to my brother a little about the Lawrence Kerman and he said there had been talk of such a thing in Antalya, but many, many years ago. I told Cengiz not to mention it to the Uzuns. I assumed you would want to do that, Inspector?'

'Yes . . .'

İkmen had been paying attention on one level, but he was also looking very intently now at Yıldız and the tall young man who was with him. The latter was, if he was not mistaken, crying.

'Excuse me, please, Raşit Bey,' İkmen said as he got up and made his way towards the shop doorway.

The first thing he heard his officer say as he opened the door was, 'I can't do that, Abdullah, he's—' and then seeing İkmen's rather troubled face, Hikmet Yıldız said, 'Sir?'

'Just wondering who you were talking to, Yıldız,' İkmen said.

'Oh, this is Sergeant Ergin,' Yıldız replied. 'He's with the um, the Tourism Police.'

'The station up on Yerebatan Caddesi?'

'Yes.'

As the name implied, the Tourism Police concerned themselves exclusively with helping foreign visitors to the city when they found themselves the victims of pickpockets, prostitution scams, etc. In İstanbul, the officers were stationed at a jolly-looking pastel-shaded Ottoman building in Sultanahmet, and spoke English and German and, usually, one or two other foreign languages. This one, whom İkmen now knew was called Abdullah Ergin, was both out of uniform and crying bitterly.

'What's the matter?' İkmen asked.

'She's gone!' the tall young man blurted out miserably.

'Abdullah! The inspector is very busy! I told you!'

'But what if she has been murdered! Only Çetin Bey can

be certain to find who has done such a thing! Oh, my Handan! Where are you?' And then he descended into full-scale weeping once again. A mercifully small group of carpet men looked on dispassionately.

Hikmet Yıldız, obviously embarrassed by what was happening, turned to İkmen and said, 'I'm sorry, sir. Abdullah is a friend. His wife went out shopping the day before yesterday and hasn't returned. He's been left with their baby, which his mother is taking care of. He fears his wife may have been murdered and he feels that you are the best person to look into that, sir, because, of course, you are the greatest solver of crimes in this city. No villain is safe when—'

'Spare me the over-blown praise, please, constable,' İkmen said. And then realising that he had violated one of the corner-stone tenets of his own people – to praise effusively where praise was due – he said, 'Sorry, Yıldız.' He then looked across at the weeping Tourism cop and said, 'You've contacted all relatives and friends?'

'Of course!'

'All right. Now listen to me, go to the station and report your wife as a missing person. Tell whoever takes the details that I have sent you. Officers will start looking for your wife based upon what you tell them, immediately.'

'Yes, I know.'

'Of course you do,' İkmen said. 'You are one of us and as such we will do our best. When I get back to the station, when-ever that may be, I will check on the progress of the search and I will make contact with you. Give me your mobile number.'

Abdullah Ergin took his mobile out of his pocket, pressed a few buttons and then read a number off from the phone's

LCD screen. İkmen, for whom mobile technology was still a bit of a problem, copied the number down on the back of a packet of Maltepe cigarettes.

'Çetin Bey, I . . .' Tears flooded down his slim, pale cheeks with probably even greater force than before.

'Go to the station, Sergeant Ergin,' İkmen said, aware that Constable Roditi had now come down the metal staircase from the upper levels of the shop and was holding what looked like an old rug. He obviously wanted to talk and so İkmen waved the miserable figure of Abdullah Ergin away and then turned towards Roditi.

'Yes?'

'Inspector, I think I'm getting some sort of carpet blindness,' Roditi said. 'I'm looking at the picture you gave us and then at this rug, and I don't know whether there's any similarity or not.'

It didn't help that the picture Peter Melly had given İkmen had been in black and white. Of course, by virtue of its age, that was to be expected, but it was scant consolation to those trying to pick the Lawrence carpet out from piles of other old carpets and rugs. Not that İkmen entirely understood what his officers were going through. The picture of the Kerman, with its amazing central tree motif had had an immediate emotional effect upon him that meant he could not possibly mistake any other piece for it. Raşit Bey had said that the motif in question was indeed a Tree of Life – just as Peter Melly had said – a very potent occult image across the Christian and Jewish worlds as well as that of Islam. He took both the rug and the picture from the hands of poor, tired old Roditi and looked at both with a sigh. There was absolutely no similarity between them. But Roditi had been looking at carpets for over eight

91

hours, he was middle-aged, he was tired, and İkmen knew that
he had a daughter currently going through a very acrimonious
divorce.

'You take over from Yıldız,' he said and then he nudged
the younger man who was still watching his distressed friend
walk towards one of the many exits from the bazaar. 'Hikmet?
Sergeant Ergin will be all right.' He pushed the picture of the
Kerman into one of Yıldız's hands and said, 'Take over from
Roditi. Up the metal staircase . . .'

'I've done the room on the right,' Roditi told him. 'I'm
about halfway through the one on the left. Then there are two
rooms above that and one in the roof.'

Hikmet Yıldız's eyes widened.

'Go on,' İkmen said as he ushered him over towards the
staircase. 'Go and look at carpets. Perhaps if you learn enough
when you've had it with policing, you can open a shop of
your own.'

The younger man trudged heavily up the metal staircase.
İkmen offered Roditi a cigarette, which he took with a grateful
nod. After a moment of silent puffing he said, 'Inspector?'

'Yes?'

'Do you really think that this Uzun hid the Kerman in his
own shop?'

'Not really, no,' İkmen said as he too took and lit up a
cigarette. 'But if we don't do this and the carpet does turn out
to be here . . . No, Roditi, if it exists it must be somewhere
and Mr Melly of the British Consulate claims to have seen it
with his own eyes.'

'Perhaps he's got it himself, sir, the Englishman.'

'That has occurred to me, Roditi, yes,' İkmen said. 'And I
will be interviewing Mr Melly as well as everyone else who

92

was at the Klaassens' home in Peri on the night of the carpet show. Have you ever been out to Peri, Roditi?'

'No, sir. Don't much like the forest. Can't stand all the insects.'

'It's an odd place,' İkmen continued as he watched several of the traders nearby shutter and then lock up their premises. It was nearly closing time at the Kapalı Çarşı. Soon all but Raşit Bey and his employees and the police would be gone. Then the great bazaar would be dark, silent and given over only to the ghosts İkmen knew had to be around in abundance on such an ancient site. 'Peri', he continued, 'is basically a diplomatic village. The British school is over there. It's a very modern and very neat village. No one parks their car in the middle of the road, there are private security guards to keep everybody safe . . . the shops are amazing. Coffee shops, pet shops, beauty parlours, a bakkal that sells truffles from France and complicated teas from England.'

'Sounds very nice, sir.'

'Yes, doesn't it? But it isn't,' İkmen said. 'There may be no dirt or bad behaviour or ghosts like there are in abundance here in the Kapalı Çarşı, but I know where I'd rather be.'

'Would you?'

'Yes.' İkmen looked up into the darkening vaulted ceiling of the venerable old Han and imagined, or maybe just caught, a whiff of a few old turbaned spectres haunting its arches. 'Peri, on the surface, is not real. Nothing can be when decay exists underneath anything. Yaşar Uzun was murdered just outside this very nice clean place and I am yet to be convinced that some nice clean person, as opposed to some unsavoury gangster, wasn't responsible for doing it.'

*　　　*　　　*

'We're being followed and so I'm going to say what I have to very quickly.'

A bemused İzzet Melik sat down opposite his superior and surveyed his opulent surroundings. Although the extravagant Art Nouveau grandeur of the Patisserie Markiz, not to mention the glamorous waiting staff, were completely in accord with what Melik felt Süleyman would find attractive, the inspector's demeanour was paranoid in the extreme. A young man with porcelain skin who came over and asked whether the gentlemen were ready to order was told by a tight-lipped Süleyman, 'Not yet. Leave us.'

Apart from two elderly ladies who sat conversing happily over by the front window, Patisserie Markiz was empty. Watching the door all the time as he spoke, Süleyman lowered his voice and said, 'İzzet, what I am about to tell you must remain secret between us and only us. I can't adequately express the seriousness of this except to say that if you break this confidence you and I are dead men. Do you swear to keep what I'm about to tell you only to yourself?'

There didn't seem to be too much choice. 'Yes . . .'

Ever since he had discovered that the call from Hakkari had in fact originated from that city's jandarma station, Süleyman had believed that someone, Melik in all probability, needed to go out there to find out what was going on. But he couldn't send him out there knowing nothing. If the man who was the peeper knew that Cabbar Soylu had killed his stepson – if indeed that were true – then it was very possible that was why Cabbar had been selected from so many gangsters for death. Mürsel had said that the peeper was on some sort of moral crusade and the murder of a defenceless and innocent mad boy was about as amoral as it got. Not that he had arrived at his decision to tell his deputy some of what he knew lightly. Right from the start, Mürsel had told Süleyman he would kill him and anyone he told if he ever divulged anything about the peeper's status to anyone apart from Commissioner Ardiç. And so far he hadn't. But now he was about to do so before whatever creature Mürsel had detailed off to pursue him this time came in to Markiz and sat down beside them.

'İzzet,' he whispered gently, with a smile on his face, as if to a lover.

'Sir.'

'The criminal we call the peeper, is not what he seems. He is an agent of the security services . . .'

'MIT?'

'No . . . yes,' he stuttered over what he really didn't fully know or understand. 'I don't know, something like that. But . . . he's gone insane or something, this person, and his own people are trying to find him. Ardiç but only Ardiç knows. We have to investigate or look as if we're investigating. They, his people, follow me. You must go out to Hakkari to look into whether Cabbar Soylu did indeed kill Deniz Koç.'

'Yes, but sir, if we're only pretending to look for this peeper . . .'

'The peeper is on some sort of moral crusade.' Süleyman put his hand over Melik's which was laid out across the table. The sergeant flinched but the waiter smiled and changed his mind about trying to get an order from the two gay gentlemen just yet. 'I think he's targeting people who are not just bad but amoral too. I mean, look at the young boys he attacked last year.'

'The queers?'

'Yes. A number of those boys used the Saray Hamam in

95

Karaköy which is a notorious haunt of very promiscuous gay men.'

'Yes, but sir,' İzzet whispered back, 'not all of those boys went there, did they?'

'No, and so I'm going to interview them again. If I'm right, there will be something else that marks them out, something wrong that—' He stopped talking as soon as a tall, elderly man came into the patisserie and sat down at a table opposite their own. 'So what would you like to drink, İzzet?' he said as he beckoned the perfect waiter over to their table.

İzzet Melik, still stunned from the onslaught of the madness Süleyman had seemingly descended into, finally looked down at the tasteful little menu in the middle of his place setting. 'Er . . .'

'I think I'll have tea myself,' Süleyman said. And then, looking up with a smile at the waiter, he added, 'And a slice of apple strudel too. İzzet?'

'Oh, er, I think I'll have an espresso and, er, yes, I will have apple strudel too, sir, er Mehmet, thank you.'

The waiter bowed. 'Gentlemen,' he said, and went on his way to the enormous glass cake cabinet at the back of the shop. Filled with sweet things that were not just tasty but fabulous to look at too, İzzet Melik under normal circumstances would be entranced. But not now. Now he was confused and worried because Süleyman was behaving very, very oddly. All the wisdom of criminology was against the idea that Cabbar Soylu could be a peeper victim and yet Süleyman had named him as just that. Süleyman wasn't stupid and so it was possible that someone else was telling him how to think and what to do. But whether that person was a spy . . . There was, however, one thing that did give İzzet Melik much pause and that was the issue of forensics. Someone had tampered with evidence into the death of that male prostitute last year. He, Dr Mardin, Dr Sarkissian and Süleyman had known about it, even if the latter had very quickly dropped the subject. Now, again with Cabbar Soylu, there was evidence of tampering with forensic material. Dr Sarkissian would almost certainly have told Ardiç about any suspicions he might have and yet there had been nothing forthcoming from that quarter so far. Even the suspicion of evidence-tampering signalled a full-scale investigation. Usually. But then those involved in the dark arts of national security were not usually involved.

İzzet Melik put one large, rough hand up to his now aching head just as his apple strudel was set down in front of him by a very elegant, perfumed hand.

Chapter 6

Mary Doyle was annoyed and she didn't care who knew it. Doris Klaassen, in her quiet, Dutch way, felt that Mary was behaving like a caricature of a ball-breaking American woman. She knew that her husband Wim, the English couple, Peter Melly and his wife, as well as the Israeli Pinhas Rabin, were all thinking just about the same thing. But trapped with her inside Wim's Toyota people carrier there really was no escape. Doris looked out of the window just as Mary started again.

'Who the hell does he think he is?' she said. 'Telling – ordering – us to come to him?'

'Mary, it is quite normal for police to ask people to come into police stations to give evidence after a crime has been committed,' Wim said gravely. 'Inspector İkmen is not doing anything out of the ordinary.'

'He could have come to our homes,' Mary Doyle continued. 'I mean, it's George who works at the consulate, not me. I don't need to come into the city. It would have been better for me if this Turkish inspector had come to my house.'

'But I'm driving you, aren't I, Mary?' Wim said. 'And so there really is no problem, is there?'

'No, but...' Mary Doyle had never had any children. At fifty-five she was bored with her overworked diplomat husband. All she could bring herself to like about poor old

George Doyle in recent years was his bank balance. If Mary had any passion in her life it was for gazing at and buying vast quantities of oriental carpets. 'I only came in to the carpet show towards the end. I missed that fabulous Van kilim that you bought, Wim. Goddammit! I'd had to go to that God-awful reception with George. I didn't get away until after ten.'

'But you saw Yaşar,' Wim Klaassen said. 'And that is the point. Everyone present at the show must give a statement to the police. Mary, you know that some people were only with us for an hour because they went to the same reception that you did. But the inspector must see all of these people too.'

'I know, but . . .' She carried on, to the amusement of most in the car, but to the annoyance of Peter Melly. Mary bloody Doyle was grating on his nerves which were already strung out like piano wires over this Yaşar Uzun affair. All the loud-mouthed American had to do was make a statement about her uninteresting life to the police. He had a priceless carpet to somehow find and get back to the UK! Matilda didn't know about the one hundred and twenty grand he'd already spent on the Lawrence carpet, but he couldn't keep information like that from her for ever – thank God the only friends who did know, Wim and Doris, were good at keeping schtum. Thank God also that Matilda hadn't been at the show the night Yaşar died, so the police didn't want to see her. She'd hitched a ride into the city to get more bloody wool or some such nonsense.

'Oh, Wim, do you have to smoke?' Mary Doyle whined as soon as the Dutchman put an unlit cigar in his mouth.

'No, Mary, of course not. I am sorry.'

The Israeli, Pinhas Rabin, who was the only other person

in the car apart from the Klaassens who could speak Dutch, said to Doris, 'Does that woman ever shut up?'

Both Wim and Doris smiled.

It was nine-thirty and at ten he was due to interview all the people who had attended Yaşar Uzun's carpet show in Peri. Being mainly westerners they were bound to be horribly punctual, but İkmen felt he had to make at least a little time for this poor distressed man sitting in front of him with his baby in his arms. Abdullah Ergin didn't really look like much of a sergeant even in the Tourism Police just at that moment. His eyes were still wet with tears but then his wife had still not been located.

'Tell me about Handan,' İkmen said and then made a funny face at Ergin's very contented baby Ali, who smiled back at him broadly.

The Tourism policeman shrugged. 'Well, she has black hair and green eyes, she's thirty . . .'

'No, no, no,' İkmen said, 'you've given us a photograph of Handan and we know how tall she is and all of that. No, I mean what does she do, what type of person is she?'

'What does she do? She looks after me and Ali and our apartment on Professor Kazim İsmail Gürkan Caddesi.'

'You live very close to the job.' Professor Kazim İsmail Gürkan Caddesi is an extension of Yerebatan Caddesi where the Tourism police station is situated.

'Yes, Allah has been kind to us,' Abdullah Ergin replied. 'Handan goes shopping in Tahtakale most days for meat and vegetables and rice. Sometimes while she's down there she'll go into the Mısır Çarşı just to look at all the expensive sweets and spices.'

İkmen nodded. His wife Fatma, like a lot of women in and around the Sultanahmet area, did much the same. Although Fatma usually went with her daughter Hulya and grandson Timür and was in no way shy about buying sweets if not spices and herbs from the Mısır Çarşı.

'On Wednesdays she'll usually go over to the Akbıyık Caddesi market. Her parents live over there in Cankurtaran and so she goes to see them at the same time. Handan is a housewife.'

'She does nothing else?' Ergin was a humble, poorly paid Tourism policeman, what else would his wife do? But İkmen had to ask. His question bore fruit. Abdullah Ergin's face darkened.

'Sergeant Ergin?'

The sergeant breathed in deeply, then out in a long, slow stream. 'Some time ago she said that she wanted to learn to speak English,' he said. 'She said that maybe if she can do that she can get a job in one of the tourist shops or restaurants. I don't know about that, but I offered to teach her a little, you know how it is.'

İkmen imagined that he probably did. He'd seen it many times before. Men teaching their wives the odd word or phrase when they felt like it. He wasn't impressed, although he tried hard not to show it.

'But then she found there is a class for English,' Ergin continued. 'It's free, it's just for women, and children can go along too. Every Tuesday morning at an office above a pide salonu on İncili Çavuş Sokak.' In Sultanahmet, just around the corner from İkmen's apartment. 'So I took her,' Ergin said. 'There were about six women there, just like Handan, and it was run by three western ladies, one I know was Canadian.'

102

Ergin looked down at the floor with furious eyes.

'Did Handan enjoy her classes?' İkmen asked.

'Oh, yes,' he looked up. 'She did well. Started talking about getting a job. These women were encouraging her to do that. But I said no, maybe later, maybe when our family is complete. It was then she told me she didn't want any more children. She talked about fulfilling herself.'

'What did you do?' İkmen asked.

Ergin looked down at his son with sad eyes. 'I forbade her to go back.'

'And what did she do?'

'She disobeyed her husband.'

'You know this for a fact?'

'Yes.'

İkmen sighed. He'd been up nearly all night looking, fruitlessly, for the Lawrence Kerman and now here he was talking to a man whose wife had left him because he didn't want her to learn English. Uncharitably, İkmen imagined him beating her. So many men still felt it was their right.

'How do you know that she disobeyed you, Sergeant Ergin? Did she go back to her class?'

'The Canadian woman, Mrs Monroe, she told me she hadn't seen Handan for months. Everyone at that class said the same thing. But I don't believe them. I think that she carried on going to classes, that they put ideas in her head, and that now she's gone off to "fulfil" herself!'

İkmen thought about lighting up a cigarette but then, remembering that there was a baby in the room, he decided against it. Even his own daughter could be funny about smoking around children now. When his lot were babies everyone had smoked and nobody had ever said anything.

103

'This Canadian woman,' İkmen said, 'is she a teacher or . . .'

'Her husband works for the Canadian Consulate,' Ergin said. 'I see.'

İkmen glanced down at the list of diplomatic officials he was shortly about to interview and quickly spotted the name 'Mark Monroe – Canada'.

'Would you like me to speak to these ladies?' İkmen asked. 'Yes.'

'Very well. Now is there anything else you can think of that may give a clue as to where your wife might be?'

He shrugged. 'No, I . . . Listen, Çetin Bey, you know how it is to be a hard-working man. Handan, well, Handan and I, we don't talk, you know. I come home from work, I eat, maybe watch a little television, and then I go to bed. Life is hard.'

'Mmm.' İkmen knew what he was talking about. He'd been working hard, and harder, for twice as many years as this man. The difference being that he and his wife did, in spite of everything, still talk. They often rowed, but not talking with Fatma had never been an option. But then Fatma had never been afraid of her husband. She'd never had any cause to be. Handan Ergin was not so fortunate, İkmen felt.

'We are actively looking for your wife now and I will arrange to speak to the ladies at her class, sergeant,' İkmen said. 'I am working on another case at the moment, but I will do whatever I can for you and I will delegate what I cannot to my inferiors.'

Abdullah Ergin nodded his approval and then gently kissed his gurgling baby on the head.

After gaining the reluctant approval of his boss, Commissioner Ardiç, to allow İzzet Melik to travel to Hakkari, Mehmet

Süleyman set off in the direction of the district of Sirkeci. This is a largely commercial area of the old city down by the waterfront, dominated by Sirkeci Railway Station, which was once the terminus for the Orient Express. Süleyman, who needed to visit an apartment above a car showroom on Muradiye Caddesi, bade farewell to his sergeant at this point and then watched for a moment as İzzet Melik drove off in the direction of the Golden Horn. He lived in Zeyrek with, Süleyman had recently discovered, his younger brother who was also divorced. On the surface, a bluff and at times misogynistic individual, İzzet was nevertheless a diligent officer and had proved himself a person his superior could trust. Süleyman hoped he would be all right out in the dry-baked wilds of Hakkari. The spy, Mürsel, had considered the entire enterprise utterly without merit. But Süleyman wasn't so sure. However, as soon as İzzet had gone, he turned to the job in hand which involved re-interviewing a boy called Esad Benmayor.

Esad, who was the youngest child of a middle-class secular Jewish family, had been one of the peeper's earliest victims. Like a lot of those early victims Esad was young and attractive and had woken in the middle of the night to see the masked man masturbating at the end of his bed. Esad, who was not a timid boy by any means, had screamed long and loud and the peeper had responded by escaping through the same window by which he had entered. Like the majority of old city flats, the Benmayors' place looked out over and was overlooked by countless higgledy-piggledy rooftops of all different vintages. İstanbul has always been a city of rooftops. But as pressure mounted, particularly upon hotels and pansiyons, to obtain even the merest glimpse of one of the city's three great waterways, building upwards had been on the increase. The peeper, above all, was known to use this labyrinthine rooftop world both as a way into and way out from the majority of his victims.

The boy, whom Süleyman had telephoned in advance of his visit, was alone when he arrived.

'Dad works in the Audi dealership downstairs,' he said as he ushered Süleyman towards a large pale settee in the middle of what was a considerably large living room.

'Yes, I remember,' Süleyman replied as he sat down. 'And your mother and sister work at Sirkeci Station, don't they?'

Esad smiled. 'You remembered.'

It had been six months since Süleyman had interviewed Esad after his night-time encounter with the peeper. He had been one of the few boys the policeman was pretty sure was not homosexual. Indeed, apart from the fact that he was 'pretty', Esad, like Cabbar Soylu, was an unusual peeper victim. An enthusiastic runner, he neither smoked nor drank and was a grade 'A' student on the language course he was taking at university.

'Yes,' Süleyman responded. 'I'm sorry that I have to bother you with this peeper thing again, Esad . . .'

'One boy died, didn't he?' Esad's face darkened. 'And another one was almost killed?'

'Yes.' The male prostitute, Nizan Tapan, had been killed the previous October, just after Abdullah Aydın had been stabbed and only just survived. Because he alone had seen the peeper's face, Aydın, who also claimed not to be homosexual, was currently under guard by Mürsel's people and therefore unavailable to Süleyman.

'That's dreadful.' Esad sat down opposite Süleyman. 'But İnşallah, this peeper will be caught soon.'

'İnşallah.'

'And I am happy to help, Inspector, if I can.'

Süleyman sighed. 'Esad, I know I have asked you before, but circumstances mean that I must ask you again. Are you homosexual? As before, no repercussions will follow from this, I will not tell your parents and—'

'Inspector, I am not homosexual!' Esad shrugged and held his hands helplessly at his sides. 'I have a girlfriend. I have the same girlfriend I had when the peeper did what he did in my room. I'm really very ordinary in every way.'

And yet there had to be something about him that had attracted the peeper's attention! 'Esad,' Süleyman continued, 'please don't be offended, but I have to ask, do you ever do anything that may be construed as, er, as immoral . . .'

'You mean like sleeping with my girlfriend or beating my mother and sister or something?' He tipped his head backwards to signal his denial. 'No. Don't misunderstand me, Inspector, I am not perfect, no man can be, but I do try to be as moral as I can.'

The sound of the Benmayors' doorbell brought their conversation to a temporary close.

'That's probably Gelin, my girlfriend,' the young man said as he sprang lightly from his seat. 'She'll tell you about me, I'm sure.'

While he was out of the room Süleyman looked around at the very ordinary flat with its clean, if slightly worn, furniture and its liberal scattering of family photographs. So far, unless he was hiding some awful crime somewhere in his short-lived background, Esad Benmayor was indeed a very ordinary boy. But then when his girlfriend Gelin entered the room everything changed.

'We sometimes try to get together for namaz – performed in separate rooms, of course – when I'm not at college,' Esad said as he ushered the little turbaned girl into his living room. 'Gelin, this is Inspector Süleyman from the police, about that horrible business I had last year.'

'Oh, yes, that was horrible.' She sat down without offering her hand to Süleyman in greeting. 'We mustn't miss namaz, Esad.'

'No, of course not. Inspector Süleyman will be gone by midday, won't you, Inspector?'

'Well, er . . .' He thought Esad Benmayor was a secular Jew. Had he possibly become confused in Süleyman's mind with someone else? 'Esad,' he said, 'I'm sorry, I didn't know that you were a religious person . . .'

'Oh, yes,' the boy replied. 'Islam is everything to me.'

'Er, since . . .'

'Inspector, I was never a practising Jew,' Esad said with a smile. 'But I converted to Islam last September, a year almost to the day after I met Gelin.'

Last September. Just a month before Esad's bedroom was invaded by the peeper. 'Oh. Good.'

The girl still neither looked up nor smiled.

'Your parents gave a big party for me, didn't they, Gelin?'

Süleyman imagined that the Benmayor family were probably less than enthusiastic. And as for the peeper? Well, Esad was indeed a very good boy in the accepted sense of the word. But for someone like the peeper, if Mürsel was right about the offender, Esad would be abhorrent. To willingly move from rational secularism to something the peeper would no doubt consider to be the depths of superstition would in all probability make him very angry. It might even make him want to kill.

'Esad,' Süleyman said, 'can you remember who came to the party Gelin's parents put on for you?'

'A lot of clerics,' Esad said with a smile. 'A *lot* of clerics.'

İkmen's knowledge of the life and career of Yaşar Uzun was not unduly increased by his contact with the various diplomatic types who had attended Yaşar's final carpet show in Peri. He still had no news about the Lawrence carpet for the Englishman, and Peter Melly had been extremely agitated during the entire course of the interview. One of the Americans, a woman who had been angling to leave as soon as she arrived, had irritated İkmen intensely, but he had got on well with the Canadian, Mark Monroe. Easygoing and polite, Mr Monroe was quite happy to talk some more to the Turkish detective once all the other foreigners had left. İkmen asked him straight out whether his wife did any English teaching in the old city.

'On İncili Çavuş Sokak, yes,' Mark Monroe said with a smile. 'Kim and some other diplomatic wives teach English to a group of local women.'

'Do you know who the other ladies are?' İkmen asked.

'Yes, there's another Canadian wife, Dawn Shaw, and Peter Melly's wife Matilda from the UK Consulate. They're the main ones. Why?'

Before he could answer Monroe's question, İkmen's mobile began to ring. He apologised and turned aside to take the call. When he had finished he said, 'I am required to be at the Forensic Institute now so I am afraid that I must leave you, Mr Monroe.' He picked up his car keys from his desk. 'But in answer to your question, one of the students of the English class your wife works at has recently gone missing. The lady's husband claims to have spoken to your wife on the subject.'

'Kim didn't mention it to me.'

'Your wife told the husband that his wife had left the class some time before. Mr Monroe, would it be possible for your wife to contact me herself? I think I need to clarify this situation with her.'

Monroe shrugged. 'Sure.'

'Thank you.'

İkmen led Mark Monroe out of the building and then drove himself over to the Forensic Institute. Yaşar Uzun's personal effects were now ready for İkmen to collect on behalf of the dead man's family. They were also going to let him have a look at what had been salvaged from the carpet dealer's Jeep.

'It's a ridiculously inefficient vehicle to have in a city,' İkmen said to the technician charged with guiding him around the mangled car. 'Must cost a fortune to fill up the tank. Did you find much in it?'

'A couple of packets of cigarettes and a copy of *Time Out İstanbul*.'

'That's all?'

'That's all.'

'Çetin!'

He turned to find himself looking into the small, red face of Dr Adem Arslan, the leader of the forensic team working on the Yaşar Uzun case.

'Dr Arslan.' İkmen shook his outstretched hand.

'If you want to have a look around the vehicle, feel free,' the doctor said. 'We've finished with it now.'

'You've got everything you can from it?'

'I hope so.' Arslan dug into his lab coat pocket and removed a packet of cigarettes and a lighter. 'You know I'm still amazed that whoever killed the carpet dealer bothered to brush over the tyre tracks leading down into the gorge from the road. The mob don't usually bother to try and cover anything up.'

'No. But then maybe we've got a new hit-man in town.'

'A Beretta-wielding person with a broom. What a strange thought. By the way, have you turned your gun in to ballistics yet, Çetin?'

İkmen, walking around the large, twisted Jeep said, 'No. But I will do.'

'I know you didn't kill the carpet dealer, but the weapon used was a Beretta which you lot do use. It is just possible that the victim did stop for some reason. Why not a police officer – the broom notwithstanding . . .' He lit a cigarette while İkmen looked into the open hatch at the back of the vehicle. 'This Jeep is called a Wrangler, by the way. A lot of money for not a great deal beyond style in my opinion.'

'Four seats, but no boot space,' İkmen said as he peered inside.

'There's a small gap behind the back seats which I suspect is supposed to be used for luggage,' Arslan replied.

Talk of guns had made İkmen remember that he had promised Arto Sarkissian he would have a word with Mehmet Süleyman about the Armenian's concerns about evidence. He was just mouthing this to himself so that he wouldn't forget when he noticed something inside the car. He looked up at Adem Arslan and said, 'This, behind the back seats here . . .'

'Oh, that old rug? We took whatever samples we could get off it and then put it back. There's a rotten old sandalwood box with it, too. Broke to bits in the crash, I imagine. Terrible stained old rug, that is. I can't think why the carpet dealer would have wanted it.'

111

But İkmen knew or felt that he did. The central motif on what was indeed a very, very dirty rug was tree-like, unusual and familiar. He took his copy of the Lawrence carpet photograph out of his pocket and held it up against the poor, stained thing in the back of the Jeep. He knew he wasn't mistaken, because he could hardly breathe. He felt his heart literally jump up and down in his chest.

'Adem,' he said once he had managed to calm himself down, 'I'm going to have to take this off you.'

Chapter 7

Mehmet Süleyman stood in front of his boss's considerable desk and said, 'Sir, I believe this peeper is far more dangerous than even we first thought. His criteria for preying upon people are wider than I for one, first imagined.'

Commissioner Ardiç, Süleyman's corpulent and perpetually tired superior, said, 'Mürsel has told us that the peeper is on some sort of moral crusade. We know he doesn't like gangsters or queers – although he does seem to have tendencies himself. What can you do? Sit down, will you, Süleyman? I can't keep on looking up at you like this.'

Süleyman sat. 'Esad Benmayor, a secular Jewish boy, was an early victim,' he said. 'The peeper didn't hurt him but the boy had a nasty shock. I assumed that Esad was gay, if in denial, but he isn't. He has a very pious Muslim girlfriend and last September, just before the attack, Esad converted to Islam.'

'And you think that the boy's interest in religion was what prompted the attack?'

'I think that this man sees himself as some sort of rational cleansing system, if you like, rooting out the morally reprehensible and what he sees as the superstitious and the irrational. It's a kind of Nietzschian superman sort of . . .'

113

'The man is off his head,' Ardiç said. 'What his politics might be is of no concern to us.'

'Sir, he's targeting people at a very basic level,' Süleyman continued. 'Nizam Tapan was a rent boy and morally reprehensible. Most of the other boys actively cruised for men. Esad has gone from being a secular person to a committed follower of Islam. Cabbar Soylu may have ordered the murder of a defenceless hospital patient . . .'

'Or not,' Ardiç responded darkly. 'As I've told you, Süleyman, I'm not happy about Melik being out among the jandarma in Hakkari. They know nothing about a murder at a mental hospital in Van.'

'Well somebody does, as I told you, sir,' Süleyman said. 'Someone from the Hakkari station called here . . .'

'Yes, yes.' Ardiç reached across his desk and took a large black cigar out of a wooden box. 'But you know as well as I do that we cannot actually arrest this peeper.'

'No, sir.'

'So what we do or do not know about him . . .'

'Sir, I think that a wider section of the public may be at risk . . .'

'Murderers and religious converts.' Ardiç cleared his throat before lighting up his big cigar. 'Forgive me if I don't begin to weep.'

'If the peeper is, in his eyes, cleaning up society, where will he stop, eh? Who will be his next victim? A female prostitute? A military draft dodger? A minister of religion?'

Ardiç's face darkened.

'Sir, I just work, where I can, with Mürsel. I don't have access, as you do, to those who control him. This peeper is one of their people. They need to do something! I've spoken to Mürsel but he's so casual . . .'

114

'Maybe he gives that impression,' Ardiç said. 'But, look, when one of these sorts of people loses their mind or control or whatever you call it, it isn't as simple as just picking up some gangster. This man has been trained to kill in ways we can't even imagine. He is fitter than you and I have ever been, he knows more about breaking and entering, about making himself invisible . . .' He wiped his now sweating brow with a handkerchief. 'On top of that he is technically brilliant, I am told.'

'And so if he decides to really let himself loose on members of the public he doesn't like . . .'

'We don't know what we're dealing with. We have to let Mürsel's people take the lead on this.'

'So when the peeper completely loses control, we look as if we just don't care!'

'Süleyman, there is nothing I can do!' Ardiç thundered.

'But sir, we don't know who he's going to take against next.' Süleyman shook his head and continued, 'It could be anyone. Sir, my wife is a psychiatrist, some people see them as little short of magicians, products of drug-crazed Freudian dreams . . .'

'Now you're letting your imagination run away with you!' Ardiç said. 'There is no reason to believe that your wife or mine or anyone we know is at risk. This man targets the morally reprehensible.'

'Esad Benmayor isn't morally reprehensible,' Süleyman responded darkly. 'He's a very nice, personable boy.'

Ardiç sighed, looked up at the ceiling, and then said, 'I am doing what I can. You must continue to do what you can.' He then looked back at the younger man. 'Have you handed your Beretta in to ballistics yet?'

115

'For this carpet dealer business?'

'Yes.'

'No, not yet.' Deflated now, Süleyman stood. 'Sir, if that will . . .'

'Süleyman, just remember that whenever one deals with Mürsel and his ilk, things are never what they may seem.' He gave him what Süleyman felt was a significant look.

'Sir?'

But then the look disappeared to be replaced by his usual stern and disapproving expression. 'Hand your gun in to ballistics today,' he said. 'I want to clear all of our people as soon as I can.'

He then waved a dismissive hand towards Süleyman who left immediately. Outside in the corridor, he stood for a moment while he considered what had just been said. Obviously Ardiç knew more about the peeper and the investigation into his activities than he was prepared to admit to. The implication, however, could, Süleyman felt, mean that perhaps Mürsel's people were further along in their inquiries than he had thought. He hoped that was the case. He hoped that what Ardiç had meant didn't mean that he was just simply totally and utterly in the dark.

'Do you recognise this?' İkmen said as he spread the discoloured and stained rug carefully out on the floor. Filthy though it was, that delicate weeping tree, gently held inside the mihrab prayer niche, glowed incandescently up into the room. He looked away from it quickly, afraid he might be tempted to stare.

The young man pulled a face. 'No. Why?'

İkmen looked at the elderly woman sitting next to him, her

face turned towards the wall, and said, 'Because, Mr Uzun, this carpet belonged to your brother Yaşar.'

'Yaşar had a lot of carpets, Inspector,' the young man responded harshly. 'He was a carpet dealer, you know.'

'Yes . . .'

Yaşar Uzun's younger brother Ara and his mother Bülbül had arrived from Antalya early that afternoon. They had gone straight to Raşit Ulusan's shop, which was where İkmen was talking to them now. In the little office at the back of the shop, he was displaying what he was certain – for he knew it down to the soles of his feet – was the Lawrence Kerman to the tired and visibly distressed pair.

'Mrs Uzun? Could you look at the carpet please?'

She didn't. Instead, seemingly ignoring İkmen, she said to her son, 'Ara, Raşit Bey has kindly made some arrangements for your brother's funeral. Will you please . . .'

'Mrs Uzun,' İkmen said, 'we cannot yet release your son's body . . .'

She stared at him pointedly whilst still speaking to her son, 'Ara, go to Raşit Bey, there's a good boy.'

'Mother . . .'

'Go!'

İkmen found himself looking into eyes that did not tolerate disobedience. They were not unlike his wife's eyes when she was angry. Ara Uzun left without another word.

It wasn't every day that İkmen found himself being stared down by an elderly woman in a headscarf. Bülbül Uzun had to be at least sixty-five and yet her eyes were as clear and as threatening as those of any spirited woman half her age. After a pause, during which İkmen knew she was listening to make sure that her son had gone, she said, 'So you found the Kerman, Inspector. How did you know about it?'

İkmen told her about the Englishman Peter Melly and what her son had required him to pay for the rug so far.

'It's my job to first make sure that Mr Melly did give your son the money that he claims to have given him,' İkmen said. 'Second, I have to find out whether the Kerman is indeed worth what Yaşar claimed it was, and third, I have to establish who in fact owns the rug now that your son has sadly died. I need your help, Mrs Uzun.'

She sat impassively, studiously ignoring the carpet at her feet before she finally looked down and said, 'It's a long story.'

'I have time,' İkmen said as he lit up a cigarette and then leaned back into Raşit Ulusan's big leather chair.

'My husband's brother came into possession of the carpet in the early 1980s,' Bülbül Uzun began. 'He worked on a gulet, the Blue Cruise, you know?'

'Yes.' İkmen knew, but he'd never been. The idea of the Blue Cruise was started by the writer and painter Cevat Şakir Kabaağaç who sailed around the Aegean and Western Mediterranean in a traditional wooden yacht, called a gulet, back in the 1930s. In more recent years the Blue Cruise had become the preserve of mainly the wealthy and the foreign.

'My brother-in-law was a deck hand,' Bülbül Uzun continued. 'In other words, a servant for the foreigners on the cruise. On this occasion the foreigners were English. I don't know how many there were but there was an old man and his son. They had been in İstanbul before coming down to Fethiye for the cruise, and they came on board with many things including the Kerman rug.'

'Do you know where they got it from?' İkmen asked.

'I'm coming to that!' Bülbül Uzun said tetchily. 'Allah! You are an impatient man! Kemal, my brother-in-law, he spoke very good English.'

'He is deceased?'

'Along with my husband, his brother, yes,' she said. 'Kemal carried the luggage on board for the old man and his son. One of the things that he noticed was a very ornate sandalwood box. He asked what it was and the younger man began to tell him something about it being an heirloom, when the older man told him to be quiet. Kemal was, of course, as you would be, very intrigued.' She cleared her throat. 'Well, one night when nearly all of the guests were up on deck, Kemal heard the younger man in conversation with another Englishman. They were both drunk and the one told the other that he had a box with a carpet inside that once belonged to the Englishman Lawrence of Arabia. He said that many years before, his father had been given the carpet by Lawrence's own hands. But he, the father, had then given it to someone else. By chance it turned up in İstanbul where the old man first recognised the box and then bought both that and the rug inside from a dealer who, he said, had no idea what it really was. He boasted, this son, about what the carpet might be worth. He said that it was stained with the blood of young Turks that Lawrence had killed in the desert. He blew up our troop trains, this Lawrence, and he stole this carpet from one that he destroyed outside a place called Ma'an. It is, I think, in Arabia. Kemal wrote that name down on a piece of paper.'

İkmen stubbed out one cigarette and then lit another. 'The sandalwood box you spoke of was destroyed when your son's car crashed into the trees of the Belgrad forest,' he said. 'So . . .'

'It is not my place to speak ill of the dead,' Bülbül Uzun continued, 'but my brother-in-law Kemal was not an honest man. When the gulet stopped at Kaş the following day, when all the passengers got off, he stole the sandalwood box from the cabin of the old man. He hid it in the house of a loose woman he had been seeing in Kaş for a few months so that when the police came, which he knew they would, they would find no box or carpet in his possession. When the cruise was over he came home to Antalya with the box and the carpet and he told my husband, Orhan, all about it.'

'What did your husband say, Mrs Uzun?'

'He said he thought that his brother should get rid of it quickly. There are men, you know, who . . .'

'Men who buy stolen goods.' İkmen smiled. 'Yes, I know of them.'

'But then Kemal died.'

'Died?'

'He was in an accident in a car,' she said. 'So, because he was unmarried, my husband inherited his goods, including the carpet. He put it and everything else of Kemal's away for many years. It was a very upsetting time.'

İkmen wondered what the real owners of the Kerman, whom he imagined were probably Roberts and his son, were going through at this time, but there was no way of knowing.

Seemingly lost in a dream of the past, Bülbül Uzun stared into space.

'And then?' İkmen prompted.

She sighed. 'And then one day, Orhan took the Kerman out. It was filthy and stained and Yaşar, who was with his

120

father at the time, tried to take it and its box to throw them away. It was then that Orhan told him what his uncle Kemal had thought it to be. Later that week, Orhan went into Antalya – we live just outside – got into a fight and was killed. I told Yaşar to get rid of the Kerman then. I said it was bewitched. But he wouldn't. He was just getting involved in the carpet trade himself then and he was fascinated by it. In recent years, or so he said, he has grown to hate carpets. Maybe the Kerman and the greed and fear that it provokes turned him against them. Who knows? But during that time he read every book he could find on Lawrence of Arabia, and he watched the film – looking, always looking, for the Kerman in a picture or a description. But he found nothing. He went to work for Cengiz Bey, Raşit Bey's brother, and then he came to İstanbul, bringing the Kerman with him. It was then that things changed.'

'How?'

'He found a picture of Lawrence with the Kerman on the Internet,' she said. 'He sent me a copy in the post and it was certainly the carpet Kemal had taken all those years ago. I could see that. Yaşar told me that now he had the proof the Kerman was what it was supposed to be, he was going to sell it and make us all rich. He said that Raşit Bey had many wealthy customers, passionate collectors of carpets who would not be averse to being taken aside and shown the Kerman in confidence. Yaşar said that it was going to make him his fortune. I begged and begged him not to sell it. It is cursed. It belonged to an enemy of our people who stained it with the blood of martyrs. Kemal stole it, only making the bad fortune worse. He died, Orhan died. I told Yaşar to throw it away. But . . .'

'Your son decided to make some money out of it instead.'

'And it has killed him, as you see,' Bülbül Uzun said as she looked down at the floor and then burst into tears. 'First it murdered his true love of carpets and then it murdered him!'

İkmen took his mobile phone out of his pocket and dialled a number. When the person at the other end answered he said, 'Ah, Ayşe. Can you send an e-mail to Inspector Lloyd at Scotland Yard in London for me please? His address is in my desk diary for last year which is in my top drawer.'

Bülbül Uzun, through her tears, looked up at him questioningly.

'I want you to e-mail Inspector Lloyd a copy of that photograph of the Kerman rug with Lawrence of Arabia and the soldier Victor Roberts. We need to trace Roberts, or his descendants, I should say, I expect he is dead by this time. You will need to attach the photograph to an e-mail asking Lloyd, in English, to look for this family Roberts. He will probably be able to use the uniform of Roberts in the photograph as a starting point.' He then looked straight at Bülbül Uzun as he said, 'It would seem that we have something that belongs to the Roberts family here in İstanbul. Something that was stolen from them in the 1980s.'

He clicked his mobile shut and returned it to his pocket. He sighed. 'Bülbül Hanım,' he said, 'I am very sorry for your loss, but as you have admitted yourself, this carpet is not yours.'

She looked down at it with ill-disguised loathing. 'You think I want this?' she said. 'After what it has done to my family?'

'We have to keep it until someone can definitely prove

122

ownership anyway,' İkmen said as he began to roll the Kerman up.

'Burn it if you want. I don't care.'

If, as Raşit Bey was fond of saying, carpets chose people as opposed to the other way around, then the Lawrence Kerman seemed to have had a somewhat mischievous, not to say malignant, nature with regard to the Uzun family. İkmen found himself handling the carpet with some trepidation.

A ripple of voices outside in the shop made them both look towards the only partly curtained-off entrance to the office. Ara was nowhere to be seen, but Raşit Bey was bending down to kiss the hand of an elderly man well known to Çetin İkmen.

'Who is that?' Bülbül Uzun said as she regarded this obviously favoured customer with a frown.

'That's a man whose family used to rule this country,' İkmen said as he smiled and bowed very slightly towards the stately form of Muhammed Süleyman Efendi.

Like most of his fellows, Abdullah Ergin hadn't wanted to hand his Beretta in to the ballistics laboratory. But he'd done it anyway and now, off duty, he was wandering aimlessly along İstiklal Caddesi when he came upon Handan's erstwhile teacher, the Canadian woman, coming out of the Markiz patisserie. She wasn't alone. There was another woman with her whom he vaguely remembered from either one of his very short visits to Handan's class – one to get her started, the other to stop her going.

'Er, madam . . .' He touched the Canadian woman on the elbow to attract her attention.

Smiling, she turned and then, seeing who it was, her expression changed to one of studied neutrality. 'Mr Ergin,' she said, 'what can I do for you?'

'It is Handan, she . . .'

'Mr Ergin, I have told you that I haven't seen your wife for at least two months,' Kim Monroe said firmly. 'I will be telling the police who, I understand, you've put on to me, the same thing.'

'But Mrs, er, Handan was still going out at class time. My neighbour saw her.'

'Well she wasn't coming to my classes, Mr Ergin,' the Canadian said again very firmly.

He turned to the other woman with her and said, 'You, Mrs, er, you took classes with Handan too . . .'

'Mrs Melly stopped teaching way before you made Handan leave,' Kim Monroe said with an edge to her voice. 'She wasn't there to witness the scene you made.'

Abdullah Ergin put his head down just a little. 'I am sorry.'

'No, you're not,' the Canadian responded calmly. And then before she and Matilda Melly went about their business she added, 'But I am truly sorry that Handan has gone missing, Mr Ergin. Goodbye.'

Arm in arm the two of them made their way up İstiklal Caddesi towards the Vakko department store. Kim looked around once and saw the beleaguered figure of Abdullah Ergin still standing outside Markiz, but then she dismissed him from her mind and said, 'So Matilda, how's Peter about that rug he wanted to buy from that carpet dealer guy?'

'As far as I know the police still haven't found it,' the English woman replied.

'Yes, neither of us were at poor old Yaşar's last show, were

124

we?' Kim said. 'How did Peter get on with the police this morning? Has he called you?'

'He's OK.' She smiled. 'What about Mark?'

'Oh Mark left Doris's such a long time before Yaşar it was hardly worth them having him in. Anyway, all they seemed to want to do was to talk about that poor Handan Ergin.'

'Mark doesn't know anything about her, does he?' Matilda said as she glanced at the window of an antique bookshop.

'No, the inspector guy wants to talk to me, apparently,' Kim replied. 'I don't know what to tell him! Handan would sometimes turn up to class with bruises . . .'

'Did she?'

'Yeah, don't you remember? Oh, well, whatever. And then Ergin made her leave. Said we were corrupting her mind.'

'Turkish men,' Matilda Melly said by way of explanation.

'Some Turkish men, yes,' Kim replied.

Matilda looked at her friend coldly before she pointed to a shop front just up ahead and said, 'Look! Lace!'

When darkness came to the golden city on the Bosphorus that night neither Çetin İkmen or Mehmet Süleyman had managed to reach their respective homes. Someone else was out and about still too, someone neither of the police officers had any knowledge of.

'Have you ever seen a film called *Nosferatu*, Haydar?' Mürsel asked as he and his henchman watched what looked like a black cloak or part of a coat slither across the surface of the alleyway.

'No, Mürsel Bey,' Haydar whispered in return. 'That thing,' he tipped his head towards the alley, 'is that him?'

'I believe so,' Mürsel whispered back. 'I feel we're too late. He's already killed. But if we can get him now . . .'

'Mürsel . . .'

'Get behind him. Block his exit back on to Sabahattin Evren Caddesi.'

'He will see me!' Haydar hissed.

They were both squatting down in the doorway of the small information centre and bookshop to be found just before the Jewish Museum at the end of Permçemli Sokak. Like a lot of the streets in the district of Karaköy, Permçemli Sokak was, in reality, little more than an alleyway. It was dark even in daylight, and sometimes it was hard to believe that it was almost opposite the northern end of the wildly busy Galata Bridge. Now at night with the museum, the ex-Zulfaris Synagogue, and the hardware shop on the left-hand side, closed, only those who lived in one of the flats in the old darkened buildings came deliberately into this alleyway. And they were few. He, Mürsel and Haydar's frightening prey, had slithered out of the synagogue-museum several minutes earlier. As yet neither of the men could say whether or not there had been anyone else in there with him. But if there had been, the chances were that he or she was now dead.

Haydar reluctantly did as he was told and began to creep along past the shuttered hardware store in order to cut off the escape of the person still, apparently, motionless on the ground. Although he had seen a lot in his ten years with the service, Haydar had to admit that the one the police called the peeper was very good. If you didn't know where to look, he could make himself completely invisible. It was a good thing that Mürsel Bey did know where to look. What was not so fortunate for Haydar was that the peeper could move very much faster than most people and that included his boss, Mürsel Bey. Haydar's death was so quick and so efficient, he didn't even have time for a last thought.

Chapter 8

İkmen put the telephone receiver down with a heavy hand and then looked out of his office window at the very black night sky outside. His conversation with Peter Melly had not been easy. But then he never imagined that it would be. Even for a well-paid diplomat, one hundred and twenty thousand pounds sterling was a lot of money, particularly if one had nothing to show for it. As sympathetically as he could, he had had to explain to Mr Melly that although the Kerman had now been found, Yaşar Uzun had never been the rightful owner of it. The carpet dealer's story about having bought it from an antique dealer in Antalya had been a total fabrication. Whether a member of the existing supposed true owners, the Roberts family, could prove that he or she had a proper claim on the carpet was another matter. But Yaşar Uzun did not and never had. What was more, his mother wanted nothing to do with the carpet. If Melly could prove, as he asserted, that he had in fact given Uzun the one hundred and twenty thousand pounds, some of that money could possibly be recouped from the dead man's estate. But that would take time and as Melly himself had freely admitted, time was not on his side. He'd raised the cash, he said, on a house he owned in England, but he hadn't shared this knowledge with his wife – she was not apparently co-owner with him.

However, in spite of that, İkmen's advice to him had been that perhaps now was the time to tell Mrs Melly and get the inevitable out in the open. After all, if she was married to him, she had an interest in his property because it was also, apparently, their home. But Melly had just shouted and raved and in the end İkmen had put the phone down on him. Not that he was incapable of understanding what Peter Melly was feeling.

İkmen knew about wives, at least about his own dear Fatma. He adored her. But he'd only been home for one hour in the last forty-eight and she had called him five times since then to ask about estimated times of arrival, food preferences, his state of health, etc. Each time she called her voice was a little bit more elevated. But he had promised Arto Sarkissian that he would speak to Mehmet Süleyman soon and so he dialled his home number and waited for him to answer. But Mehmet, just like Çetin, was not at home.

'He called about ten minutes ago to say he was on his way,' Mehmet's wife Zelfa said in that lovely Eire-accented English of hers. Although her father was Turkish, Zelfa's mother had been Irish and she had spent most of her formative years in Dublin.

'Oh, I'll try him tomorrow,' İkmen said wearily. 'It's not urgent. We just don't seem to get the time we once did to talk these days. There is always so much to do! I miss him.'

'And he misses you, I know,' Zelfa replied. 'Brave new world of international crime and implementing EU standards, eh, İkmen?'

He smiled. Zelfa was a bright woman who understood her husband's world very well. 'Yes,' he said. 'You know, Zelfa, I remember when the worst young boys ever got up to was stealing chocolate from their local bakkal. When did they start sniffing gas lighters and stealing cars?'

'Probably about the same time as boys in Ireland decided that breaking into the priest's house and smashing him over the head with a cosh was a lot more fun than laughing at him behind your hand on the street,' Zelfa said. 'But we mustn't carry on like this, İkmen, it makes us sound old.'

'I am old.'

She laughed and then said, 'I'll tell Mehmet that you called.'

He'd just put the receiver down when there was a knock at his door followed by the appearance of a thin young man in front of his desk. He carried a small paper bag, which he placed, rather ceremoniously, on top of İkmen's ink blotter.

İkmen looked at the bag, which appeared to be gently steaming and said, 'I take it this is my final warning?'

'Yes,' the young man said. 'Sigara börek. Mum just made it. Eat it first, then please come home, Dad. She's driving everyone mad.'

İkmen sighed, indicated that his son should sit down opposite him, and then opened up the bag. A great waft of steam came floating out at him. He looked up at his son and said, 'You know, Bülent, that if I plunge my fingers in there I'll be scarred for life. You must have run like the wind to get here with these!'

'Mum is very angry with you,' Bülent replied. 'So the oven was hot and my escape route was very short and rapid. What have you been working on, Dad?'

'Oh . . .'

His office telephone began to ring.

Bülent said, 'Oh please don't answer that, Dad!'

The phone continued to ring.

131

'I have to,' İkmen said as he went to pick up the receiver. 'If I'm in the building I have to answer my phone.'

'Dad!'

İkmen spoke into the receiver. 'Hello?'

'Çetin, it's Mehmet,' the familiar voice of his friend Mehmet Süleyman said. 'I need to speak to you. I must!'

He sounded both breathless and rattled. İkmen said, 'When and where?'

'I don't know when. Oh, Allah, Allah!'

'Ssh! Ssh!' Poor Mehmet sounded as if he was in the midst of a crisis. His voice was full of tears. 'Come on, Mehmet, I will meet you. Just tell me where. I will wait. I promise.'

'Oh, er, at, at . . . Meet me at Uç Horan, you know, the Armenian church in the Balık Pazar. Dr Sarkissian's friend is custodian there . . .'

'Garbis Bey, yes, I know him,' İkmen said. And then, shrugging helplessly at his son, he added, 'I'll go there right away.'

Bülent waved his hands in the air and mouthed the word 'no' most emphatically.

'I don't know how long I'm going to be, Çetin,' Süleyman continued. 'Something has happened that I have to deal with first, I . . .'

'I will be with Garbis Bey in under an hour,' İkmen said.

When he put the phone down, İkmen lit a cigarette before he looked up into his son's face.

Bülent, shaking his head sadly from side to side said, 'Dad, you are dead.'

'Yes,' İkmen responded gloomily. 'I know.'

Permçemli Sokak was cordoned off by the time Süleyman arrived. Uniform had been very quick and efficient. Mürsel, who was leaning over a body that appeared to be in the middle of the little street, had called straight through to Ardiç. As Süleyman approached, Mürsel straightened up and smiled.

'Haydar,' he said as he tipped his head, seemingly dispassionately, in the direction of the ground. 'I shall miss him.'

Süleyman, shocked, took him to one side, away from the uniformed officers. 'How did it happen?'

Mürsel lowered his voice. 'I ordered Haydar to get in behind our man, but he was too quick for us. He cut Haydar's throat. He's very good.'

'But still, apparently, without a name,' Süleyman said exhibiting impatience with the apparently endless subterfuge.

'You have no need of a name, Inspector,' Mürsel said as he moved towards Süleyman with his smile still fixed upon his face. 'You will never catch him.'

'Which will put me on an almost equal footing with you,' Süleyman responded sharply. 'Those who assist me are still alive. What were you doing here, anyway?'

'There's a girl,' Mürsel said as he gestured towards the synagogue. 'Some functionary at the museum. He killed her.'

'What?'

'The peeper, he killed a girl in the synagogue,' Mürsel elaborated. 'What . . .'

'How did you know?' Süleyman asked. 'What made you come here in the first place?'

At the end of the small street the heavy traffic on Yüzbaşi Sabahattin Evren Caddesi thundered past in glorious oblivion. Out on the Bosphorus, night-time ferries sounded their horns to announce their arrival at Eminönü, Kabataş and Üsküdar.

Mürsel Bey's eyes glittered. 'Intelligence,' he said.

'What intelligence?'

He smiled again. 'If you remember, Mehmet Bey,' he said, 'when this business began and my agency and yours started to co-operate, it was understood that intelligence would only proceed in one direction. I don't have to tell you anything.'

Some of the uniformed officers around the scene began to look at the two men with some curiosity. Feeling rather vulnerable without İzzet Melik, Süleyman went through the archway to the courtyard in front of the synagogue without another word.

The Zulfaris Synagogue, now the İstanbul Jewish Museum, was a nineteenth-century building and one of the very many, particularly Sephardic, synagogues that were built in the Karaköy area of the city. The main body of the synagogue, with the women's gallery looking down from above, was exactly as it would have been when the place was built. Now, however, display cases and large bodies of text have replaced worshippers and down beneath the main hall there is a small ethnographic display. It was to the lower level that Mehmet Süleyman was directed by the uniformed officers stationed at the main entrance. Dr Sarkissian and another man Süleyman didn't know were with the body.

As Süleyman approached, the Armenian turned towards him and said, 'Her name is Leyla Saban. She was twenty-nine and a member of the local Sephardi community.'

Süleyman wondered whether his old friend the Sephardi Balthazar Cohen had known her. Or, given Leyla's age, whether his son Berekiah had. Not pretty like Berekiah's wife, İkmen's daughter Hulya, Leyla Saban was nevertheless a handsome-looking woman. And if it hadn't been for the huge bloodstain across her chest she might have looked as if she were just sleeping. Her features were at rest and seemingly untroubled.

The other man, whom Süleyman did not know, spoke next. His eyes full of tears, he said, 'She was a great scholar of her people's history. Leyla helped to run this place. She was a good girl!'

Süleyman looked at Arto Sarkissian who said, 'This gentleman lives across the road.'

'I am a Muslim scholar, Leyla was a Jewish scholar,' the man, who had to be at least eighty, continued. 'We were friends. We spoke of and enjoyed the differences between us. It is the Turkish way.'

'Yes . . .'

'My grandfather, he was an Armenian,' the old man said. Though still tearful, he was nevertheless in his stride. 'I don't care who knows it! Leyla knew it. You know what she was doing in here so late into the night on her own? She was going through archives taking notes for a book she wanted to write – a book about all the Turks who saved Jews from the concentration camps in the Second World War. If this is the work of people who call themselves religious . . .'

'This is not the work of fundamentalists of any kind, sir,' Süleyman said. 'Of that you can be certain.'

Arto Sarkissian looked up at Süleyman again and frowned. 'You sound very sure, Inspector.'

'I am.'

'Well, she was stabbed,' the Armenian said. 'One thrust to the heart. Left-handed assailant.'

Just like the peeper.

'Doctor, who actually found the body? Was it . . .'

'No, it wasn't this gentleman,' Arto Sarkissian said as he smiled gently at the distressed old man. 'He just came over when he heard the commotion.'

'I knew that Leyla was in here on her own,' the man said. 'I have given the name of her father to your officers. He lives out in Şişli. There are many Jews in those districts to the north these days.'

'So who actually found the body?' Süleyman asked.

'Oh, it was that officer from out of town,' the doctor said as he turned his attention back to the corpse. 'You must have seen him on your way in. A Mürsel Bey.'

'Was it.' Süleyman felt cold. Mürsel. How had he known that the peeper, if indeed it was him, had struck inside the museum? Intelligence? What did that mean, exactly? And what, he wondered, could the peeper have had against poor Leyla Saban? How had she transgressed his seemingly ever-more stringent and deranged moral standards?

'Yes, his sergeant was killed trying to apprehend Miss Saban's killer, so it would seem,' the Armenian said. 'I will attend to him in due course. By the way, Inspector Süleyman, where is your sergeant tonight?'

'Hakkari.' İzzet Melik and Süleyman did not always see eye to eye but he missed his sergeant's blunt, but honest loyalty now.

'What is he doing there?' the doctor asked. 'God, but that's the end of the earth almost!'

'It's a long story,' Süleyman said and then he turned to the elderly erstwhile friend of the murdered woman. 'Sir, if you wouldn't mind coming outside and telling me exactly what happened from your point of view . . .'

'You will find him, won't you? Leyla's killer . . .'

At that moment Mürsel came into the room and just before he turned aside to look at a display cabinet given over to nine-teenth-century wedding dresses, he smiled at Süleyman who

136

fixed him with his eyes and said, 'Oh, yes, sir, we will find Leyla's killer, you have my word on that account.'

His English friend was very drunk, but then if Wim Klaassen had just lost the equivalent of approximately two hundred thousand euros, he would probably be drinking heavily too.

'How could he do it?' Peter Melly said as Doris poured him yet another large gin and tonic. 'What a shit!'

Doris gave her husband a meaningful look and then made off into the kitchen to make some coffee. It was very late and she, for one, wanted to go to bed.

'It was his uncle who stole the carpet, not Yaşar,' Wim said. 'And to be fair, Peter, I don't think that it was in Yaşar's plan to die before he completed his deal with you.'

But Peter Melly was in no mood to listen to facts. 'Yaşar lied! And now the fucking police are actively looking for the family of bloody Lawrence's batman, Roberts. Fucking Yaşar's uncle stole the carpet from them, so they think, and so legally it belongs to them. And where does that leave me?' He drained his glass and leaned in shakily towards his host. 'Fucked is where it leaves me! What am I going to tell Matilda?'

'Just what Inspector İkmen told you to tell her,' Wim replied calmly. 'The truth.'

'The truth? The truth! The truth is, Wim, old mate, that my wife and I were mortgage-free, I'd paid the fucker off until Yaşar came into my life. The house I bought in good old Henley-on-Thames just before I got married for a hundred and fifty grand has now doubled in value. That's three hundred grand to go home to – except that it isn't. Now it's one hundred and eighty. It's less if I go ahead with the loan I'd arranged with the bank to pay Yaşar the rest of his money. That leaves

137

me with about fifty grand. Do you know what kind of hovel you can expect to get in Oxfordshire for that sort of money these days? For our three hundred thousand we were going to buy a flat on the river when we went home. Matilda has her heart set on it. That the house was never hers is immaterial. She's been married to me for ever so she expects things. What will I be able to give her now? A fucking bedsit in Reading! Men get divorced, taken to the cleaners, for less! I haven't lived alone since I was at Oxford, for God's sake!' He began to cry.

Wim passed him a box of tissues and then excused himself to go into the kitchen. As he entered, Doris was pouring water into the coffee percolator, shaking her head.

'I want Peter to go home,' she said forcefully to Wim. 'There's nothing we can do for him!'

'I know.'

'You'll have to drive him home yourself if necessary, Wim,' she continued.

'He won't be easy to shift. He doesn't want to go home and have to face Matilda.'

'Well, he'll have to sometime.'

'I know, but . . .'

'By turns he deceives that woman and then treats her as if she were some kind of saint,' Doris said as she angrily wiped down an already clean work surface. 'Matilda Melly has flaws just like the rest of us. More than some of us!'

Wim looked hard at his wife and frowned. 'Matilda is very quiet, very meek. But of course she'll be angry when she finds out about their house . . .'

'Oh, you men are so slow! Sometimes, Wim, appearances can be deceptive,' Doris said. She regretted it instantly.

138

'Doris?' Wim moved in close to her and said, 'Do you know something about Matilda that I don't?'

She looked him straight in the eye and said, 'No.'

'Doris?' He knew that she was concealing something. Women could be very hard to read, in his experience, but Doris was in general easier than most.

She turned away from him. 'Wim, I don't know anything about Matilda. I just find it difficult to believe that she is really so perfect.' She looked back at him again. 'Maybe I'm just a bitch.'

He smiled. Doris was about as far from being a bitch as a woman could get. But he let whatever it was that was buzzing about in her head go and said, 'I must go back to Peter. Perhaps some coffee . . .'

'Absolutely. Any minute.' She watched him go with a smile on her face. But then her features dropped as she turned back to the percolator and her own thoughts. Yes, Matilda did annoy her with her good works and her knitting and her soft, soft voice. But what really annoyed Doris was the fact that the domesticity and devotion were only part of the picture that was Matilda Melly. If Peter had financial secrets from Matilda, she had a few secrets from him that were of an entirely different nature. But that was not, Doris reminded herself firmly, any of her business. Unlike her husband, Matilda had never come to either herself or Wim in order to pour out her heart. No, what Doris knew about her had been stumbled upon on a flying shopping trip one afternoon late on in the previous year. Matilda had not even known that Doris was there.

It was half past two in the morning by the time Mehmet Süleyman reached the old door, which was slightly ajar, leading to the Armenian church of Uç Horan. The figure that sat, red-eyed, in the little wooden hut just in front of the church grounds said, 'You know that when my son Sınan was little he used to call this place "The Church in the Cupboard". We all came to Arto's cousin Sylvie's wedding here. Sınan must have been about four and from then on it was "The Church in the Cupboard". He still calls it that.' İkmen smiled softly at this, his own fond memory, and repeated, 'The Church in the Cupboard.'

It was easy to see why. The main entrance to Uç Horan and the courtyard around it is accessed via a small, ancient door in the right-hand wall of the Balik Pazar. Back in the fishy crowdedness of the Balik Pazar, it is difficult to imagine that anything larger than a wardrobe can possibly be behind such a door, much less a church built for, at one time, a very large Christian minority. Now, however, in the depths of the night, all was quiet, almost reverential.

'Where is Garbis Bey?' Süleyman asked as he watched İkmen lock the outer door behind them with a very rusty-looking key.

'I had Bülent take him home,' İkmen said. 'He's too old to stay up all night.'

Süleyman looked around rather nervously. 'Is Bülent here?'

'No. I told him to take Garbis Bey home and then go back to Sultanahmet. He wasn't exactly overjoyed, but then who would be at the prospect of an interrogation about me and my movements from my wife?'

Süleyman frowned.

'I haven't been home for more than an hour in almost three days. My life is full of dead carpet dealers, filthy, mythical rugs and news that our case against the acid killer has been

140

postponed. Poor Ayşe, after all that preparation . . . Now I've promised to be here until eight when I'll let Garbis in to do his job.' He shrugged. 'Fatma is not happy and who can blame her?'

The two men embraced.

As he pulled gently away from his friend, Süleyman said, 'The peeper has struck again. A young Jewish woman in Karaköy.'

İkmen shook his head sadly. 'Do you have any . . .'

'Çetin, can we go into the church?' Süleyman asked, looking around at the empty courtyard with a considerable amount of nervousness.

'You told me that you wanted to talk,' İkmen replied. 'So we will. I'm quite happy to go into the church if that is what you want. I'll just go and put the lights on.'

'No!' Süleyman nervously placed a hand on İkmen's arm. 'Can't we light a few candles or something. I don't want too much light – it might attract attention.' İkmen shrugged. His friend was obviously very nervous. 'OK,' he said, 'if that's what you want, Mehmet.'

A box of candles was by the front door and as Süleyman followed İkmen into the church they lit two apiece and both watched the enormous, incense-scented space flicker in the pale yellow candle-light Süleyman whispered, 'Çetin, I want to tell you something, but I've been told that if I do, you and I will be killed.'

İkmen looked up at his much taller friend and then, holding his candles aloft, at the enormous crystal chandeliers that hung from the vaulted ceiling of the church, he asked, 'Who said that, Mehmet?'

From outside there came a noise that might have been a

footfall. Süleyman paled and ran quickly outside the church to find out what it was. But there was nothing to see out there and so he returned, sweating, re-lighting the candles that had snuffed out when he ran.

'I don't know,' Süleyman said as he made an effort to calm down. 'Ardiç says it would be foolish to use names like MIT . . .'

'Oh, spies!' İkmen smiled. 'Ardiç is involved?'

'Not with the threats of death, but yes, he knows about these people. Like me he is obliged to work with them. It's to do with the peeper . . .'

'And no doubt the fact that the bodies of his victims frequently go to places Dr Sarkissian thinks they shouldn't.' İkmen took his friend's elbow and led him to a pew at the back of the church. They both placed the candles in the sand box positioned in the niche in the church wall. 'Arto asked me to talk to you about this, Mehmet,' he said.

'But Çetin . . .'

'And if MIT or whoever want to threaten me personally, they can come and see me themselves,' İkmen said as he sat down. 'So come on, what's this all about?'

Although his voice quavered as he spoke, Süleyman told İkmen everything about Mürsel and Haydar, about who the peeper might be and what his motives were perceived to consist of. He was scared but he was also relieved, in a way that he hadn't been when he had told İzzet Melik only part of the truth in the patisserie. When İkmen asked him why he had chosen this moment to break his silence, and had chosen to talk to him and not to Ardiç, he said, 'As I told you, Mürsel's bosses speak to Ardiç. Mürsel and his superiors have the bodies of the peeper's victims examined and keep the results to them-

142

selves. Dr Sarkissian is quite correct to be concerned. But it seems that Ardiç trusts these people and, by extension, Mürsel. But I don't. The bosses I don't know about, but I'm rapidly coming to the conclusion that Mürsel Bey is not all that he seems. Even if he doesn't appear at a murder scene he seems to know where the peeper has just been and what he has just done for a lot of the time. Earlier tonight the peeper apparently killed Mürsel's sidekick, Haydar. Mürsel says that the man we know as the peeper is a highly trained agent who is expert at avoiding detection and capture. The police have no hope of apprehending him. But so far Mürsel, himself one of these "people", is not having any more success than ourselves. The body count of peeper victims is mounting. He must be stopped!'

'Mmm.' İkmen frowned. 'What do you think this Mürsel character might be up to?'

Süleyman pushed his fingers up into his hair. 'I don't know. But I don't feel that he is, for whatever reason . . .' And then he shook his head and said, 'No, that's not true. If I am honest, as I always am with you, I fear that Mürsel is actually assisting this peeper.'

'But surely his spymasters or whatever one calls such people would be aware of that?' İkmen said. 'These are people who, if I'm not mistaken, are psychologically evaluated on an almost permanent basis, are they not?'

'So we're led to believe, yes. Look, Çetin, I know this is all completely crazy and I don't have any evidence for it, but I have this terrible feeling . . .' His normally handsome face was almost ghostly in the thin, eerie light from the candles.

'I, as you know, always trust such intuitions myself,' İkmen said. He let his eyes wander across the just discernible pictures of saints and angels that adorned every wall of the church and then he said, 'What are you going to do? If this Mürsel is trained in the art of espionage, it's unlikely you will catch him out.'

'I know.' He sighed. 'There is one way, by getting closer to him, that might work.'

'What do you mean?'

In spite of the overtly religious nature of his surroundings, Süleyman saw in his mind a replay of the occasion upon which Mürsel had attempted to paw him. The look of the spy's greedy, drooling mouth had made him shudder. But he didn't share Mürsel's passion for him with İkmen. He knew that the older man would consider the course of action he was contemplating to be far too dangerous. It was. But it was something else too, something that made the ends of Suleyman's fingers fizz with what could be excitement. He said, 'I don't really know, it's just an idea. I need to think about it.'

'You know that you should go to Ardiç.' İkmen held up a hand in order to silence his friend's protest. 'Yes, he is involved, but from what you have told me he doesn't know what you suspect about this Mürsel.'

'But can I trust him?' Süleyman asked and then qualified what he had said, 'Sometimes I do think that maybe he shares some of my suspicions about Mürsel, but then again that could just be a bluff of some sort. Not meaning that Ardiç is corrupt, you understand. Just that this higher agency takes precedence over him and even his superiors. National security, you know?'

'Mmm. Yes, it would take some confidence to approach such a subject. Well, it certainly puts my case of the dead carpet dealer in the shade,' İkmen said with a small, weary smile.

'Yaşar Uzun.'

'Yes.' İkmen rubbed his almost scarlet eyes with his fingers and said, 'His, it would seem, is a long story. Oh, by the way, I saw your father at Raşit Bey's shop this morning.'

'Yes,' Süleyman shook his head and sighed. 'Poor Father. He called me. He gave Raşit Bey an absolutely enormous court carpet to value the day you started looking for Yaşar Uzun. Father is in the same financial situation he is always in, but he had great hopes about this piece, which is very beautiful. Sadly for Father, Raşit Bey says that the carpet will not realise as much as could be hoped because of its size. It's lovely, but far too big for a modern house or even an ordinary old one. It came from a palace. But Father is unhappy and thinks that Raşit Bey is being overly pessimistic about its value. I am inclined to think that Raşit Bey is probably in reality overvaluing the carpet to save my father's feelings. But what can one do?'

And then in spite of the fact that Süleyman had opened their discussion with such dangerous and frightening ideas and information, the two men now turned to rather more trivial matters. A lot of it was about carpets and most specifically about the Lawrence carpet itself. İkmen had developed quite a fascination with this item. Süleyman didn't know a great deal about T. E. Lawrence, but he had seen *Lawrence of Arabia* on several occasions. It was not, he admitted, easy viewing for him.

'Those Ottomans who fought in the desert were my ancestors,' he said.

'And mine,' İkmen added. 'At least two of my grandfather's brothers fought in the Great War.'

'Yes, but with respect, Çetin,' Süleyman said, 'I expect your ancestors were of the peasants with no boots variety.'

145

İkmen smiled. 'They were poor *Mehmet*s* who fought for their sultan, yes.'

'Whereas mine sat about in places like Damascus drinking champagne and listening to Offenbach.' Süleyman shook his head yet again. 'You know they used to actually talk in terms of the men being replaceable entities? Thousands would die and they'd just send back to Anatolia for more! The Arabs, and that Lawrence person, humiliated us!'

'It was a long time ago.'

'The film wasn't.'

They looked at each other but neither of them said anything. There was a scene in the film where T. E. Lawrence, played by Peter O'Toole, is sexually propositioned by the Turkish governor of the Arab town of Deraa. It was not easy viewing for anyone, but especially not for patriotic Turks. It also, for Süleyman, brought to mind the image of the very sexual Mürsel yet again.

Süleyman finally left İkmen at just before six in the morning. He needed to go home and wash and prepare for a day of autopsy reports, press releases and, hopefully, some information from İzzet Melik in Hakkari. He wondered whether he had yet discovered who had made that mysterious phone call to his office from the Hakkari jandarma station.

İkmen opened up the main door out into the Balık Pazar and then embraced his friend before he walked through it.

'Be careful, Mehmet,' he said. 'Those people, the ones we spoke of earlier, they are not like us. They have no restraints . . .'

Süleyman stepped out into the fish market which was now coming alive in a whirl of red snappers, mussels, lobsters,

* 'Mehmet' is an affectionate generic name for the 'average' Turkish soldier. Like the British 'Tommy'.

146

squid tubes, shouting men in flat caps and hordes of very loud, hungry cats.

İkmen closed the 'Church in the Cupboard' off from the rest of the world again, took his mobile phone out of his pocket and, with a very grave expression on his face, he made a very important call.

Chapter 9

That a lot of police work so often involves nothing more than the relentless pursuit of paperwork trails has become something of a cliché. It doesn't, however, make it any less true.

After first organising tea and some spare packets of cigarettes for her superior, Ayşe Farsakoğlu settled down to tell İkmen what she had discovered.

'First,' she said as she took a light from İkmen's shakily proffered lighter, 'I had a call from England just before you arrived, sir. Scotland Yard say that they have identified a Roberts in the north district of London whose grandfather, he says, was the servant of T. E. Lawrence. They will send someone round to interview this man.'

'That's good.' İkmen rubbed what he knew was a ghastly visage with a nicotine-reeking hand. If only he'd accepted Garbis Bey's offer of breakfast . . .

'Now with regard to Mr Yaşar Uzun . . .'

İkmen's phone began to ring. He visibly froze. Ayşe flicked her long black hair behind her ears and bent over his desk in order to pick it up. But before she did so, she said, 'Fatma Hanım has called several times already to speak to you, sir.'

İkmen puffed on his cigarette and then said, 'Call me a coward if you must, Ayşe, but I cannot speak to my wife just at the moment.'

149

Ayşe took the call which was from Fatma İkmen. She told her that her husband was indeed at work but out at the present moment. She lied well and without apparent embarrassment which, İkmen felt, could be seen as either an advantage or a disadvantage in one's inferior.

'All right,' Ayşe said as she retrieved a sheaf of papers from her desk and then sat down in front of İkmen again. 'Mr Uzun had only one bank account as far as I can tell. It's with the Yapı Kredi in Beyoğlu and on 1 October last year he deposited sixty thousand pounds sterling in cash into that account. That is on exactly the same day that Mr Melly from the British Consulate claims he gave one hundred and twenty thousand pounds sterling to Uzun as a deposit on the Lawrence carpet.'

'Has Mr Melly given us the receipt Yaşar Uzun gave to him yet?'

'We have a faxed copy of a receipt for one hundred and twenty thousand pounds signed by Uzun, but it doesn't say what the money is in respect of. Although apparently his UK bank, HSBC, as requested, took down the serial numbers of the sterling notes issued. He must have been nervous about the transaction.' She pushed a piece of paper with the Yapı Kredi Bank logo at its head over the desk towards him. 'But as you can see there is a shortfall of exactly a half.'

'Yes. Maybe Mr Uzun, buoyed up by his immense good fortune, decided to go on a spending spree.'

'There is some truth in that, sir,' she said. 'For instance, he moved into his Nişantaşı apartment within days of that deposit and he may well have paid for his beloved Jeep with cash. I have yet to follow that up. Mr Uzun also possessed some nice clothes, a few of them Italian, and some reasonable furniture. But nothing spectacular. However, so his landlord has told me, in spite of all that money, his rent was three months in arrears.'

'Which means that much of the missing sixty thousand pounds is still unaccounted for,' İkmen said. 'I wonder why that is? Gambling, maybe? He smoked a bit of cannabis. But we know he didn't have a cocaine habit or . . .'

'Well, sir, there is this,' Ayşe said as she reached back to her own desk to retrieve a leather-bound book. 'This is an appointment diary which belonged to Mr Uzun.' She placed it on İkmen's desk and opened it up at 3 March. 'Here in his handwriting you will see a name, Nikolai, an İstanbul telephone number, and a time – three o'clock.'

İkmen peered down at the diary through the film of water that covered his raw, exhausted eyes.

'That number belongs to Nikolai Stoev,' she said.

İkmen looked up and then let out a long and impressive breath. 'So our carpet man had dealings with the Bulgarian Mafia.'

'On some basis it would seem so, yes, sir,' Ayşe said.

'Which means, I suppose,' İkmen said, 'that I will have to go over to Laleli and see Mr Stoev and, no doubt, several of his retarded, broken-nosed henchmen too. I wonder how many uniforms I can get to take with me?'

'Oh, that reminds me, sir,' Ayşe said, 'your Beretta is ready for collection at the ballistics lab.'

'Oh, so I'm innocent of Mr Uzun's murder, am I?' İkmen said wearily. 'How wonderful. You know, Ayşe, I know that we have to go through this exercise in order to rule out officers with this weapon, but when half the bad men have Berettas too . . .'

His telephone rang again.

151

'If that is my wife, I am still out,' İkmen said.

Ayşe picked up the receiver, stated her name and then for what seemed like a very long time stared fixedly down at İkmen's desk. At the end of the conversation she put the handset down on to its cradle and said, 'Change of plan, I think, sir, with regard to Nikolai Stoev.' She took her jacket from the back of her chair and put it on. 'Constables Yıldız and Roditi and Inspector İskender are waiting for us downstairs.'

Then in answer to her superior's blank expression she added, 'I'll explain as we go, sir.'

Metin İskender was wearing the expression of slightly mocking disbelief that he usually employed when interviewing a suspect. İkmen had thought that with one of their 'own' Metin might exhibit a little more warmth. But that was not to be so. The interview room at the ornate little Tourism police station on Yerebatan Caddesi was almost homely compared to what they had back at headquarters, but Metin was obviously not letting that affect his interrogation of Sergeant Abdullah Ergin. He was going for the jugular.

'Your Beretta 92 was used to kill the carpet dealer Yaşar Uzun,' he said baldly. 'Ballistics have confirmed this beyond question. I want you to tell me about it.'

Abdullah Ergin, who only ten minutes previously had been helping a group of Japanese tourists locate the underground cistern, was still in shock. His face was white and, as he raised his cigarette up to his lips, his fingers visibly shook.

'Where were you and what were you doing on the evening of Monday, 5 April?'

'I was, er, I finished my shift at six . . .'

'And then what?'

152

İkmen didn't really like the intensive interrogation style that Metin employed. He felt that, as well as sometimes getting to the truth, it could also on occasion lead suspects to say things they had not meant to say out of panic. He tried to catch Metin's eye in order to indicate that he should tone it down a bit, but to no avail.

'Sergeant Ergin, I am asking you a question,' Metin İskender said menacingly. 'Answer me!'

'Well, I, um, I went home to my apartment on Professor Kazim İsmail Gürkan Caddesi and I had my dinner, my wife . . .'

'What did your wife cook for your dinner, sergeant?'

Ergin looked up with a shocked expression on his face. 'I don't know!' he said. 'How can I remember that?'

'I know you only work with tourists, sergeant, but even you must know that details like the constituents of a meal are used by us to test a suspect's alibi.' It was said with such arrogance that, had İkmen not known that he was using a tried and trusted interrogation technique, he would have been inclined to pull Metin up on it.

'Look,' Ergin said, 'Handan cooked me a meal of some sort and then I went out.'

'Where?'

'To my brother's apartment in Kumkapı.'

'What for?'

Now Abdullah Ergin lost his temper. 'Because I love my brother! Because we like to visit one another from time to time!'

Unaffected by this outburst, İskender said, 'How long were you at your brother's apartment?'

There was a pause during which İkmen found himself

153

looking quizzically into Ergin's eyes. 'Sergeant?'

'I stayed all night,' Ergin said and then put his head down on to his chest.

'Why? You have a wife and child. Kumkapı is not far from where you live . . .'

'Handan and I, we had an argument,' Ergin said. 'She provoked me!' He looked at İkmen. 'About that wanting to learn English business again that I told you about, Çetin Bey. All the time I was trying to eat she went on and on and on about it. I went to my brother's to get some peace! It is not the first time I have stayed all night at his apartment. Handan tests me sometimes . . .'

İkmen leaned across to İskender and said, 'Sergeant Ergin's wife is the missing Handan Ergin . . .'

'Yes, I know,' his colleague said dismissively. Ayşe Farsakoğlu, who was also in the room, raised an eyebrow at her boss. Metin İskender was way, way too abrasive for her taste.

'So, to recap,' İskender continued. 'You went home when your shift finished at six, you ate your dinner – whilst rowing with your wife – and then you went to your brother's apartment where you stayed all night.'

'Yes.'

'Did you change your clothes when you got home from work?'

'Of course! Nobody should wear his uniform when he is off duty.'

'Did you take your gun home?'

'Yes.'

'Did you take it with you to your brother's apartment?'

'No!' Ergin shook his head. 'Why would I do such a thing?

154

I left it in the top drawer of the bureau in my bedroom where I always leave it.'

'Was the weapon locked inside the drawer?' İkmen asked.

'Yes. I've a family, of course I lock such a thing away!'

'Presumably you were on duty the next morning?' İskender said.

'Yes.'

'So you went home, changed into your uniform, and took your gun out of the drawer?'

'Where it had been all night undisturbed,' Ergin said.

'Except that it hadn't and could not have been,' İskender replied. 'Your Beretta 92 was fired on the night of 5 April and it killed the carpet dealer Yaşar Uzun. It has only your own fingerprints on it. Your wife is missing and so far as I can tell we only have the word of your own brother that you were in Kumkapı on that occasion.'

'Well, my neighbours may have seen me leave . . .'

'Yes, we will speak to them,' İskender interrupted. 'Although that will prove little beyond the fact that you left your apartment building. You could have had your gun with you for all your neighbours would know.' He then looked across at İkmen and said, 'Do we have any lead at all on the wife?'

'No,' İkmen responded. 'Not as yet.'

İskender turned to Ergin and said, 'The next step, sergeant, is for our officers to search your locker here at the station and your apartment.'

'But I didn't do it!' Ergin said, a look of real confusion on his face.

'Didn't do what?' İskender said as he rose smartly from his seat. 'Kill the carpet dealer? Kill your wife? Or both?'

'I don't know anyone called Yaşar Uzun!' Abdullah Ergin

155

cried. 'You say he worked in the Kapalı Çarşı, but I don't know every carpet dealer in there. I'm a Tourism officer, not a pimp for the carpet men or the leather men or—'

'All right! All right!' İkmen held up his hand to silence him and then turned to Metin İskender. 'Can I speak to you for a moment outside?'

They called Roditi in to sit with Ayşe Farsakoğlu and Abdullah Ergin while they went outside into the corridor and lit up cigarettes immediately.

'Allah, but it's so clean in this place, I feel almost shamed into not smoking,' İkmen said as he looked around at the really very tastefully painted corridor. 'Ashtray?'

Metin İskender eventually found one on a windowsill. 'What's on your mind, Inspector?' he said as he held the ceramic bowl underneath his own and İkmen's cigarettes.

'Sergeant Ergin's lack of motive,' İkmen said.

'His gun, with his prints on it, killed Uzun. There can't be any question about that,' İskender replied.

'Yes, I know and I accept that. But whether he actually fired it is another matter. There are such things as gloves.'

'True. But we know that Uzun was shot after he had brought his car to a halt. An officer, even one like Ergin, could so easily pull a car over, as we know.'

'Yes, but when his wife went missing he came to us. I know that the guilty do do such things, but . . . I don't think that he killed Uzun. I really don't.'

'But then if he didn't kill him . . .'

'First of all, Sergeant Farsakoğlu has recently discovered a possible link between Uzun and Nikolai Stoev.'

'The current Bulgarian Godfather?'

'The same.' İkmen coughed. 'Also, if Ergin didn't shoot

156

Uzun, then maybe his conveniently missing wife did. He said he left his Beretta at home when he went to visit his brother. She had to know he kept his gun in that bureau. She probably had a key herself or knew where her husband kept his. I'd like to see whether there's any connection between Mrs Ergin and Uzun.'

İskender sighed. 'You think she might have been having an affair?'

'I don't know. Uzun was young and attractive but without, so far, any sign of a lady friend. However, you know as well as I do how these carpet dealers are, don't you, Metin? Other people's wives are often very attractive to them.'

'Yes.' İskender ground his cigarette out in the ashtray and said, 'So do I take it you will check up on Nikolai Stoev?'

'I know him, it makes sense that I do.'

'All right then, I will search Ergin's apartment,' İskender replied. 'Guilty or not, he has to remain in custody for the moment. His 92 silently damns him.'

The two men shared a brief, grim smile.

If he knew one thing about Mürsel it was that there was no way he was going to believe a complete change of heart on Süleyman's part. If the policeman was indeed going to try and seduce information out of the spy, the impetus had to come from Mürsel. But now that the autopsy, if not the toxicology, on the body of Leyla Saban was complete, Mürsel had done what he usually did just after a peeper killing and was making himself scarce. Whatever his feelings on the matter, which were mixed to say the least, Süleyman had to be patient. And there was some comfort to be had in not being subject to Mürsel's leering caresses. But only some. There was curiosity

157

too. If he were honest with himself, there always had been. Even as a boy he had wondered – about men – and Mürsel, well, he was a very attractive man . . . He had just finished shuddering, more at his own thoughts than anything else, when his office phone began to ring.

'Süleyman.'

'Hello, Inspector,' a familiar voice replied.

'İzzet! How are you? What's going on?'

'Oh, the boys at the jandarma station here are looking after me,' İzzet Melik said. 'In fact, I had a meal with several of them at a little lokanta yesterday evening. I threw up all night . . .'

'Eastern food,' Süleyman said by way of explanation.

'Eastern food, a western stomach unaccustomed to eastern food and bacteria, and no alcohol,' İzzet replied and then said stoically, 'But it was written, kismet, what can you do? Inspector, no one seems to know, or won't admit to knowing, who telephoned our office from the station here in Hakkari.'

Süleyman groaned.

'I've had to deal with some very weird accents and, to be honest, I was beginning to lose hope until just after that meal last night, before I threw up . . .'

'What happened?'

'We were talking, the jandarma and me, about how they work, how I work. I told them how when old Ali died, the Commissioner made us get rid of the çay ocaği so now we have to get tea brought in. The jandarma were horrified. One of the men told me that their cleaner, a local woman, makes tea for them. Then another of the lads remembered something; this cleaner's husband works at the mental hospital in Van where Deniz Koç died.'

'Good. Are you going to interview this woman?'

'No, but one of the patrols is taking me over to Van this afternoon and I'm going to try to speak directly to the husband.'

'Well, proceed carefully, İzzet,' Süleyman said. 'If Cabbar Soylu did indeed order his stepson's death then those who perpetrated the act will not have any love for you. But get as much as you can and then perhaps I can talk to the authorities out there about exhuming the body – if our suspicions become strong enough.'

'Yes, Inspector.'

'Don't lose sight of our peeper in all of this either, İzzet. If we are right, then he somehow found out that Soylu had ordered the death of Deniz and I can't see how he would have discovered that in İstanbul. They may not know it, but someone in that hospital, or connected to it, possibly knows who the peeper is. Be careful.'

'I will. What's happening there, Inspector?'

Süleyman told him about Leyla Saban, but not about Haydar. There was no need for İzzet to know about the death of the spy's best friend. But İzzet did want to know what Süleyman intended doing next and so the senior man was forced to tell him. It was all quite above board – questioning residents local to the Zulfaris synagogue, reviewing the evidence provided by the Forensic Institute and Dr Sarkissian . . . . He didn't tell him what he had in mind with regard to Mürsel. He wouldn't tell anyone about that.

Matilda Melly's reaction to her husband's confession was both muted and violent at the same time. When he told her that he had given Yaşar Uzun a deposit on the Lawrence carpet without her consent, closely followed by the amount involved, she hadn't reacted at all. When he told her how he had raised the capital, she had choked on her tea, but she hadn't actually said anything. It was only when Peter launched into the details about what was to happen next, specifically the likelihood of their never seeing any of the one hundred and twenty thousand pounds again, that she spoke.

'You've been very stupid, haven't you?' she said as she shielded her eyes with her hand from the bright springtime sun that had just begun to invade the terrace at the side of their pool.

'You think I don't know that?' her husband responded angrily. He was pale and, she knew, hung over from a drinking session he'd had somewhere the night before.

'You were duped.'

'Yes!'

'Conned.'

'Yes!'

'Stitched up . . .'

'How many ways do you want to tell me I've been fucked, eh, Matilda?'

She shrugged, looked briefly across and beyond the rooftop of the Rabins' house opposite and then stared down at the knitting in her lap.

'So, basically, we have a mortgage for the foreseeable future,' her husband said. 'It means that when we go back to the UK, we'll either have to stay put in the Clarence Road house or we'll have to settle for something elsewhere if we want to be mortgage-free.'

'I want to live by the waterfront . . .'

'Well, you can't.' He ran his fingers through his greying, sandy hair.

160

'But I want to,' she responded calmly.

'Matilda,' her husband said, 'you are a fifty-two-year-old woman, not a petulant child. Just because you want something, doesn't mean that you'll get it. For once in your life, face reality!'

Still calm, Matilda put her knitting down on the plastic patio chair beside her and said, 'Peter, I faced the reality of not having children many years ago. Travelling the world was a reality I quite liked living with, but not what went along with it; first your string of affairs with foreign women and then this collecting madness . . .'

'We dealt with my affairs!' Peter leaned in to point a long, thin finger in her face. 'We weren't talking about those again!'

'And now, effectively, you throw away our future and I'm expected to deal with that too?' She stood up and said, 'No.'

He looked up at her, squinting as the sun behind her head and body blinded his eyes. 'What?'

'I'm going,' she said calmly and then began to walk towards the patio doors and into the house.

In spite of his hangover, Peter sprang to his feet. 'Going? What do you mean, going? Where?'

She turned to face him and for the first time in probably over twenty years he noticed that in spite of her pudginess and apparent compliance, she was really quite an attractive woman. 'Leaving you,' she said quietly.

He flushed hotly. 'You can't leave me!'

'Yes, I can.'

'Where will you go? Where . . .'

'To a place by the water,' she said.

'But you haven't got any money!'

'Then I'll have to get some, won't I?' she said. She walked

161

towards the stairs that led to the upper storey of the house.

'What are you doing?' her almost hysterical husband said.

Matilda carried on walking. 'I thought I might pack a bag for the moment,' she said.

'If you think that you're going to find some fucking place by the water now . . .'

'No,' she turned. 'I thought I might stay with a friend for a few days while I sort myself out. If anyone will have me. If not, I'll stay in a hotel. Then I'll go and be by the water.'

'But why, Mat –' He ran his fingers through his hair yet again and then began to cry. 'I . . .'

'You . . .' – Her eyes blazed as she turned for the first time – 'you thought more of that carpet than you did of me!'

And then she ran up the stairs and he heard her slam what had been her bedroom door behind her.

'But what am I going to do now?' Peter Melly wailed up into the vast height of his fashionable living room. 'I've lost absolutely everything! What about me!'

Five minutes later, when she came down the stairs with her suitcase, she still retained her calmness. In fact, rather than just rush out of the building as he thought she might do, Matilda Melly put her bag down and then sat on one of the sofas. 'Peter,' she said, rather imperiously, he felt, '*I* have something to tell *you*.'

Chapter 10

The noise from the ceaseless thundering traffic along Ordu Caddesi was all too apparent in the echoing bleakness of the Sofia Travel Agency. Apart from a few rather tatty posters of somewhere called 'Sunny Beach' – which had a definite air of menace about it – and some people, apparently rose pickers, in colourful peasant costumes, there was little beyond scary-looking men in the place.

'Can I shut this door so that I can hear myself think?' İkmen said as he walked towards a desk and the truly thuggish-looking individual sitting behind it.

'It's warm now, we need the air,' the man, who had an almost chewably thick eastern European accent, replied.

İkmen leaned down on to the desk. Two black-clad youths with necks like bulls moved forward. Ayşe Farsakoğlu, who was standing behind İkmen, looked up at the youths and said, 'Get back. Give the inspector some space!'

They smirked, but they backed off anyway.

'I've come to talk about a man called Yaşar Uzun,' İkmen said to the man at the desk. 'You and he met on 3 March this year, Nikolai. Now he's dead.'

Nikolai Stoev wrinkled his very wide forehead. 'And you think that I . . .'

'Shut the door for me, will you, Sergeant Farsakoğlu?' İkmen

163

said as he sat himself down in the rickety metal chair in front of the Bulgarian's desk. 'I'm not so sure that Mr Stoev will be quite so keen on fresh air now, in view of what we're about to discuss.'

Ayşe Farsakoğlu went and did as he had asked her and then stood behind him, staring at the craggy face of Nikolai Stoev.

'So, Nikolai,' İkmen said, 'how many denials will I have to endure before you admit that you knew Yaşar Uzun?'

The Bulgarian smiled, revealing as he did so several golden teeth. 'None,' he said. 'I remember Yaşar Uzun, a very pleasant man, a carpet dealer. He came to me because he wanted to buy some property in Bulgaria.'

İkmen, somewhat taken aback by this, coming as it did from the usually most elusive Stoev, said, 'And did you manage to get him to buy anything? At Sunny Beach, perhaps?'

Nikolai Stoev laughed. 'No, he wasn't interested in old communist resorts like Sunny Beach. For us Bulgarians sometimes that big communist-style architecture can be quite nostalgic, but not for you people.'

'Then why do you have a picture of Sunny Beach on your wall here?' İkmen asked.

Stoev shrugged. 'It reminds me of home. It pleases my poor old Slavic heart.'

'So what, if anything, did interest Yaşar Uzun?' İkmen lit up a cigarette without offering one to his host. Like most gangsters, Nikolai Stoev could easily afford his own cigarettes. With people like him traditional Turkish manners were, İkmen had always felt, purely optional.

'He bought a very nice house in Balchik,' the Bulgarian replied. 'He bought it just from a photograph I showed him on that day in this office. I am a brilliant salesman.'

İkmen, frowning, wondered why and how anyone would buy a property without ever actually seeing it. 'What is Balchik and how much did he pay?'

'Balchik is a very lovely Black Sea resort. It has pretty, whitewashed houses and wonderful botanical gardens.' Nikolai Stoev turned to one of his men, said something in Bulgarian, and watched with İkmen as the man made his way to a staircase at the back of the shop. 'He's going to get the account book to see what Mr Uzun paid,' he said to İkmen. 'I think he paid in cash . . .'

'So how did you persuade Mr Uzun to buy this Balchik place?' İkmen asked as he offered Ayşe Farsakoğlu a cigarette and then flicked his own ash on to the floor.

'I didn't,' the Bulgarian said. 'Mr Uzun came here knowing all about Balchik. He asked for it specifically. He wanted a house near the waterfront and Queen Marie of Romania's old palace. The Romanians ruled that part of my country for a while in the 1920s and 1930s.'

'Do you know why he wanted this particular place?' İkmen asked. A very short, thick-set individual gave him and Ayşe a chipped ashtray to share.

'Balchik?' He smiled. 'Well, it is very romantic, Inspector İkmen! Especially for Turks. You know that Queen Marie built that palace in Balchik as a love nest for herself and her Turkish lover? She was sixty, he was twenty. The place looks like a cross between a wedding cake and Aya Sofya. Mr Uzun, I know, wanted to take a very specific lady there.'

'Do you know who?'

Nikolai Stoev took the large ledger book from the man who had retrieved it earlier and was now holding it out to him. 'Inspector, I am not Mr Uzun's mother! How should I know who this woman was?' He opened the book and then peered down at the figures written inside. 'Ah, here. Yes. Yaşar Uzun paid forty thousand euros for a three-bedroom house in Balchik. Yes. Oh, and yes, then there was the apartment too.'

'The apartment?'

'Yes, in Sofia, our capital. In a nice, nice area.' Nikolai Stoev looked up and said, 'He bought that just from the description I gave him. An excellent customer, decisive. For two bedrooms he paid just under twenty thousand euros. It's a lot of money.'

İkmen, who knew a little bit about property prices in İstanbul, raised an eyebrow.

'For us,' Stoev explained. 'Bulgaria. We are a little, new country. We are a land of great opportunity for investors, anything is possible. But for Turks . . . It's cheap. Mr Uzun did pay, as I thought, in cash with euros.'

They knew that Yaşar Uzun had the money from Peter Melly by this time, only half of which had entered his bank account. These really rather odd Bulgarian purchases had to make up for either withdrawals from Uzun's own bank account or the spending of the other sixty thousand pounds which he must have converted from sterling into euros at some point. But this was the first that İkmen had heard about any 'lady' in the carpet dealer's life.

'So, Mr Uzun, now his surviving relatives own these properties outright?'

'Yes.'

'Did he or his lady friend move in to the place in Balchik, do you know?'

Nikolai Stoev said, 'No. The house and the apartment were his, he could do as he pleased with them.' He smiled and

166

leaned across the desk conspiratorially. 'One thing I do remember was that he wanted all of the papers for the house and the apartment to be separate. He didn't want the lady to know that he had the apartment. I think that maybe he had plans to see other "ladies" when he was in Sofia . . .'

'Did you ever see him again?' İkmen asked.

'Only to give him the keys and his paperwork the following week. It was very quick and he was an excellent customer. I have friends in the legal profession back home.'

'Most people who traffic heroin and prostitutes have some sort of connection to the judiciary,' İkmen said with a smile.

'Inspector!'

'Oh, don't worry about me, Nikolai, I'm not going to take your organisation down today.' İkmen took his notebook out of his pocket and placed it in front of Stoev. 'I need the addresses of the two properties you sold Uzun.'

Nikolai Stoev gave this job to one of his minions.

'I hope he can write,' İkmen said acidly as he watched the distinctly simian man slowly copy what was in the ledger into İkmen's notebook.

'He can.' Nikolai Stoev smiled. 'You know, Inspector, you should consider buying somewhere in Bulgaria. A lot of people are moving to my country. It's very cheap for Turks.'

'For some Turks,' İkmen corrected. 'Not me.'

'Oh, that's a shame.' He leaned across his desk again and then tilted his head towards Ayşe Farsakoğlu. 'If you had a little place, you could offer your lady policeman a little "holiday". Just the two of you, a little career development . . .'

İkmen's hand flew across the table and caught Stoev's neck in a sharp-fingered grasp. 'Don't push it, Nikolai!' he said as he watched the gang of shady men move in around him. 'Remember who you are and know that it is only because it suits *me* that today is not the day when I come for you and your monkeys. It will not always be so. Tomorrow may very well be different. Now, Mr Stoev, where were you on the night of the fifth of April?'

Apart from the fact that she regularly attended the Neve Şalom Synagogue, which implied at least some sort of religious faith, there was nothing that Süleyman could discover about Leyla Saban that would make her an obvious peeper victim. She wasn't promiscuous in any way, she was certainly not a gangster, and had not, as far as he could tell, ever killed anyone. But then some of these, particularly the latter victims, were not obvious. Maybe the peeper had now really lost his mind. Maybe now anyone in the least bit 'imperfect' would do. It occurred to Süleyman that perhaps Leyla had just been an opportunistic victim. But if that were so, he wondered what the peeper could have been doing hanging around the Jewish Museum after it had closed.

'Here is my Leyla,' the old man said as he laid the heavy photograph album in Süleyman's lap. 'That's her with her little brother, my son, İzak. He will be devastated . . .'

Süleyman looked down at the photograph of a teenage Leyla Saban with a boy of about seven or eight and said, 'Mr Saban, your son . . .'

'İzak moved to Israel last year,' Fortune Saban said sadly. 'I didn't want him to go. He said he wanted to fight for Israel. I begged him to stay here and do his military service for his real country, this country.'

Maybe that was the flaw, Süleyman thought, maybe Leyla's

brother's apparent disloyalty to the state was why she was killed.

'My wife Zeynep passed away and so the children have been my world ever since.' Fortune Saban began to cry. 'Now İzak has gone and my Leyla is dead . . .'

'I am so very sorry, Mr Saban,' Süleyman said. 'I'm sorry that I have to disturb you now, but I have to try and find out as much as I can about Leyla in order to have any chance of catching her killer.'

'I know. I know.' He dried his eyes on the sleeve of his pullover and then said, 'Inspector, I apologise, you sitting there without even the offer of a glass of tea! How ill-mannered of me! Zeynep would have been disgusted.'

'Oh, please, Mr Saban, don't trouble yourself,' Süleyman said. 'It really is of no importance. However, if you don't object, if I could have an ashtray . . .'

'Oh, yes, yes, of course! I think I have one in the kitchen,' Mr Saban said as he rose slowly from his chair and began to walk out towards the hall. 'I don't smoke myself. İzak does, Zeynep did, but not me or Leyla. No.'

The Saban place was a small apartment in a nice block in smart up-market Şişli. A lot of Jews lived in the district, but not many, Süleyman imagined, lived in such shabby turmoil. There were books everywhere. Laid open on rickety sideboards with less than the normal complement of drawers, their broken spines pointing up towards the ceiling. Old clothes hung haphazardly from the backs of broken chairs – a clear sign of brains and efforts concentrated on much higher things than cleaning. He went back to looking at the photograph album. Leyla Saban had been, from her photographs, a lively young woman. What looked to be the most recent picture of

169

Leyla showed her again with her brother, he now towering over her and smiling. İzak looked very much like his father, but Leyla didn't.

Fortune Saban gave Süleyman a very old Efes Pilsen ashtray and then looked with him at the picture of his children.

'If you have to know everything then that is what I must tell you,' the old man said as he sat back down in his chair once again.

'Mr Saban?'

'Leyla was not my biological child, Inspector,' Fortune Saban said. His deep, dark eyes screwed up against what he had just said, all but disappeared. 'I brought her up as my own. Leyla never knew. İzak will never know.' He opened his tear-filled eyes and smiled. 'Thirty years ago I was teaching at a school in Hakkari. Unmarried. I was old then! I employed a cleaner. The first was an elderly lady who eventually became too infirm to carry on, then another woman and then, out of nowhere, came Zeynep.'

'Your wife was your cleaner?'

'She just arrived,' the old man said. 'Little more than a child. No papers I ever believed were her own. My Zeynep was not the Zeynep Habib whose identity card she carried. My Zeynep was not a Jew. I had to teach her many things about our life before we came back to İstanbul.'

'But your son . . .'

'My beautiful Israeli son knows nothing of this. What would he do if he knew I thought his mother was a gypsy?'

'Do you?'

Fortune Saban shrugged. 'I don't really know. But there she was, Zeynep, in Hakkari, young and beautiful and preg-nant. She didn't ask me to marry her, I offered. I loved her

170

from the very first moment I saw her until the second that she died. I have never known who Leyla's father was. I have never wanted to.'

Süleyman put the photo album down beside his chair and then lit a cigarette. The town of Hakkari was turning up again in this peeper 'drama'. He wondered whether it was relevant, part of a pattern . . . . 'That is quite a story, Mr Saban.'

'To be only between ourselves, Inspector,' the old man said.

'Yes.'

Then Fortune Saban pointed to a large photograph of an extremely beautiful and striking woman which stood upright on the lid of an old piano in the corner of the room. 'That is Zeynep,' he said. 'See how lovely she was!' Again he cried. 'To lose that which you love the most is the hardest test God makes us take.'

Süleyman let him cry. There was nothing he could say that would ease the old man's pain. Years of experience working with the relatives of murder victims had served only to underline his complete lack of utility.

When Fortune Saban had finished crying he said, 'Mr Saban, didn't you ever ask Zeynep about her background? Where she came from?'

'Not really,' Fortune Saban said. 'She didn't like it. If I did ever quiz her, all she would ever say was that she came from poverty and brutality a nice man like me couldn't even imagine. I have always believed, Inspector Süleyman, that Leyla was the result of my poor Zeynep being raped. Out east families throw girls so dishonoured out, don't they?'

Süleyman left the Saban apartment as much saddened as intrigued by what he had discovered there. Unwittingly, Leyla Saban had lived a lie. She wasn't Jewish, even her 'Israeli'

171

brother wasn't really Jewish. Was the lie she led what had caused offence to the peeper, or was it her brother's seeming desertion of the armed forces of the Republic of Turkey? Family secrets. Süleyman knew a thing or two about them. The way the casually cruel, frequently intoxicated princes that were his forebears were still revered as great and courageous Ottomans. The way his mother would insist upon telling people that his wife Zelfa was not only a full-blooded Turk, but she was also the same age as he as if Zelfa being older than he was was dishonourable or indecent in some way. He considered gloomily whether being economical with the truth about one's background was just a middle- and upper-class 'thing' . . .

'Inspector Süleyman!'

Mürsel, extremely stylish in a slim-cut black suit, was standing in the little park that was opposite the apartment block Süleyman had just left.

'What a beautiful spring day!' he said with a smile as Süleyman approached. 'You know I'm really beginning to feel as if we are at last leaving the winter behind us.'

'Yes.'

'So where have you just been, Inspector?' the spy said as he lit a long, green cocktail cigarette.

'You know exactly where I have been, Mürsel Bey,' Süleyman responded, now smiling himself. 'You know everything that I do and when I do it.'

Mürsel's smile faded. 'I'm glad that you recognise and accept that now,' he said.

'What choice do I have? I get the impression I can only find out what you want me to. Hakkari . . .'

'Where you've sent the unfortunate İzzet Melik . . .'

'Is . . .'

172

'From my point of view, wholly irrelevant.'

'Mr Saban lived there.'

'So he might have done. But now you're pushing, which I don't like,' Mürsel said with a smile.

Had Süleyman been planning to try and seduce what he felt Mürsel knew about the peeper out of the spy at that moment, then he knew that he hadn't made a good start. But then it soon became apparent that he really didn't need to try too hard.

Mürsel laid a long, slim hand on his shoulder and said, 'You know that we are closing in, don't you, Mehmet? I'm appalled that Haydar died, he'd been with me for years, but . . .'

'When is his funeral?'

Mürsel put his head on one side as if struggling to think and then he said, 'It was this morning, I believe. I . . .'

'But forensic . . .'

'Yes, it was this morning. I remember now.' He smiled again.

'Did you not go?' Süleyman was almost frightened to know what the answer might be.

'No.'

'Ah.'

Mürsel moved his arm along Süleyman's shoulders and then snaked his other hand around his waist. 'You're shocked?'

Süleyman shrugged. If Haydar had already been buried the chances were that those who should have performed forensic tests on his body had probably not done so.

'Grief affects people in many different ways,' Mürsel said as his lips came within just centimetres of Süleyman's face. 'Personally, I prefer to celebrate a person's life rather than waste time in useless misery. Would you like to help me celebrate Haydar's life later on this evening, Mehmet?'

173

This was a very good opportunity and it was coming not from him, but from Mürsel. But Süleyman was suddenly afraid, and for several seconds his mouth just flatly refused to utter.

'Don't be too eager, will you?' the spy said acidly into the silence.

'Oh, er, yes, yes, I would like to mark, er, his passing . . .'

'Good. Meet me in the bar at the Pera Palas at eight.'

And then he walked off back through the little park and disappeared. Süleyman, shaking now, realised for the first time that he was sweating.

'So what do you think about the notion that Sergeant Ergin's wife Handan was having an affair with Yaşar Uzun?' İkmen said as he spooned another heap of pilaf into his mouth.

Ayşe Farsakoğlu first swallowed her mouthful before she said, 'But sir, there's no connection between them.'

'Her husband's gun shot Uzun,' İkmen elaborated. 'Ergin has no real alibi for the night of the killing and Handan Ergin has seemingly disappeared off the face of the earth leaving her baby son behind her!'

'That's terrible.'

They both turned to look at the headscarfed woman at the top of the table who continued with, 'The things that go on these days . . .'

'Fatma, it happens,' her husband said. 'People have affairs. It's life.'

'Well it shouldn't be,' his wife replied.

Ayşe Farsakoğlu, herself a veteran of several affairs of the heart, one long ago with Mehmet Süleyman, looked down and paid close attention to her food. Although aware of the fact

174

that whilst information was still building in the case of the dead carpet dealer he had to keep on working, İkmen nevertheless knew he had to make some sort of concession to his wife. So after leaving Nikolai Stoev's shop they made a detour to the İkmen apartment in Sultanahmet and a rather late lunch that Fatma İkmen insisted they both eat.

İkmen turned back to look at Ayşe again. 'Metin İskender's search of Ergin's apartment hasn't turned up anything of note.' And then he immediately changed tack and said, 'I wonder if Handan Ergin is at Uzun's place in Bulgaria!'

'Sir, Mrs Ergin disappeared after Mr Uzun had been killed.'

'But before we found his body.'

'True.'

'So maybe she shot him. Maybe it was some sort of lovers' argument that they had . . .'

'On the road out of Peri in the middle of the night?' Ayşe said. 'Mrs Ergin doesn't drive and she had a baby to look after that night. Also, how would an ordinary lady like Mrs Ergin have the presence of mind to cover up tyre tracks in the forest?'

'Mmm. Point taken,' İkmen said. 'Ayşe, that sixty thousand pounds sterling that Uzun deposited in his Yapı Kredi account – do we know whether he withdrew all or any of that?'

'No, sir, but I'll check it out.'

'Do so.'

'You're not eating!' Fatma İkmen stood up and went around the table towards Ayşe Farsakoğlu with a saucepan.

'Fatma Hanım . . .'

'How you can ever expect to get a decent husband if you don't eat, is beyond me!' Fatma said as she spooned great dollops of rice on to Ayşe's plate.

'Fatma!'

175

She looked over at her husband with a challenging expression on her face and said, 'Yes?'

Not wanting to get involved in any sort of argument about how one should and should not speak to younger guests, İkmen held his hands up in submission and said, 'Nothing!'

'But to get back to Mrs Ergin, sir,' Ayşe continued, 'Handan had a passport which was still at her home. Constable Yıldız told me that she was born in Germany you know – although she came back to Turkey as an infant. But anyway, she's either still in this country or . . .' She looked first at Fatma İkmen and then at her husband.

'Ergin or someone else, as yet unknown, has killed her,' İkmen said, finishing off the statement Ayşe had not felt able to. 'You don't know how thoroughly Inspector İskender was intending to search the Ergin apartment, I suppose, Ayşe?'

'No.'

'I'd like to know whether or not he's lifted the floorboards, or dug around in the garden.'

İkmen's mobile phone began to ring. He took it off the table and answered it, his face soon cracking into a smile. 'Ah, Metin,' he said, 'yes, we were just talking about you. I gather Handan Ergin's passport was in the apartment.'

'Yes, but in spite of almost ripping the paint from the walls, my boys have found no sign of the woman herself,' Metin İskender replied. 'However . . .'

'Yes?'

Fatma İkmen smiled at Ayşe Farsakoğlu and then took a plate of sweet pastries out of a cupboard and pushed them towards her.

'One of the Ergins' neighbours, a woman whom I get the impression spends much of her time spying on those around

176

her, said she saw a woman go into the Ergin apartment on the night of Uzun's murder,' İskender said. 'Apparently she went in just after Abdullah Ergin went out to his brother's and then she left about half an hour after that. The informant told me that the woman was a foreigner, a European of some sort. Wasn't Mrs Ergin supposed to be involved with a group of European women?'

'Yes,' İkmen said. 'The main one being a Mrs Monroe, a Canadian. Oh, and also the wife of the man Uzun was in the process of selling the Lawrence carpet to, a Mrs Melly.'

'Mmm,' İskender said. 'That's interesting.'

'Yes.' And then İkmen went on to tell him what he and Ayşe had discovered from the Bulgarian Nikolai Stoev.

'So how are you going to proceed?' İskender asked at the end of İkmen's exposition.

'I think that perhaps Ayşe should go and pay a visit to the Bulgarian Consulate to follow up Uzun's properties and I, I suppose, had better take another trip out to Peri.'

'To see these consular women?'

'Yes. They knew Handan Ergin and, I get the feeling, they might have at one time supported her linguistic ambitions in the face of Abdullah's disapproval, but whether that actually has any bearing on this case is another matter. İnşallah, all will become clear.'

'İnşallah.'

And so their telephone conversation ended and shortly afterwards Ayşe Farsakoğlu and her boss left the İkmen apartment and went their separate ways. As she put her shoes back on at the front door, Ayşe was presented with a large box of sweets by Fatma İkmen. 'For your journey,' she said as she pushed them into the younger woman's hands. Çetin, whose journey was at least five times the distance of his sergeant's, shook his head in both despair and amusement as he walked down the stairs ahead of a now smiling Ayşe.

It was only four o'clock when Mehmet Süleyman arrived home. But then he'd hardly spent more than an hour at his pretty little house for the past week. Situated in the Bosphorus village of Ortaköy, Mehmet Süleyman and his wife and son shared their charming wooden cottage with Zelfa's aging father, Dr Babur Bey. But when Mehmet arrived there was no one in and so he went straight up to his bedroom and took a shower. Then, after choosing what he was going to wear for his meeting with Mürsel, he lay down on his bed to think – or rather to worry.

What if his bad feelings about Mürsel were misplaced? What if what he said about the peeper was all absolutely true? He had, after all, believed every word Mürsel had said on the subject when he had first come into contact with the spy. He wasn't alone, either; Ardiç had underwritten everything that he had been told. But then that was before the peeper apparently went off-script. At the beginning he had been a serial offender whose hatred of homosexuals had eventually escalated to murder. Apart from the fact that he was, unlike most killers, highly trained to do just that, his actions did not diverge from what was generally accepted knowledge about offenders of his type. But then there was Cabbar Soylu, the Jewish girl and, significantly, Mürsel's sidekick, Haydar. According to Mürsel, Haydar had died because the peeper had been just too quick for him. But people like Haydar did not die easily and besides, by Mürsel's own admission, there had been two of them and only one of him. There was something wrong. He

178

didn't know what, but he felt it in every bone and organ of his body. This 'instinct' was something that didn't make itself apparent to him every day. Çetin İkmen at times lived his life by such gut feelings, but not him, not Mehmet Süleyman the rational Ottoman gentleman. Not for him cases involving semi-mystical carpets that had once belonged to a probably deranged enemy of the old empire. Leave all that to İkmen and good luck! But then what İkmen didn't have to deal with was the possibility of either inflaming or infuriating the spy Mürsel. Because as a strategy, the promise of sex in exchange for truth about what was actually happening was fraught with danger. For a start, he had – or, rather, he told himself he had – absolutely no intention of satisfying Mürsel sexually. If of course, once the seduction began, the agent gave him the choice of not going ahead. Although no bigger than Süleyman, Mürsel was almost certainly more highly trained in the arts of both attack and defence. What if he overpowered him? What if, worse still, Süleyman found himself giving into Mürsel in an act of sensual curiosity? What if he liked what happened then? In the past, he had always managed to successfully suppress those occasional sexual feelings he had for other men. What if suddenly he could not? And then there was also the fear that what he was proposing to do would be for nothing anyway. What was he going to do if Mürsel just denied everything? What was Mürsel, once in possession of the fact that Süleyman suspected him of something, going to do with him? Would he have him flung into some ghastly secret service jail? Would he kill him?

If he were honest, Süleyman didn't even really have a coherent theory about his suspicions. That Mürsel always seemed to know where the peeper had been and why he had done whatever he had done was consistent with his role as a member of the secret services. But then if he was that close, why was he consistently failing to catch the peeper? People were continuing to die because of Mürsel's incompetence, or worse. If only he could speak to someone about these things! But İkmen had his phone switched off and İzzet in faraway Hakkari was dealing with his own problems. Thus far, to his knowledge, the investigation at the Perihan Hanım institute in Van had come to nothing.

Süleyman thought about these and other things until his father-in-law returned at six. After sharing tea with him, he went back upstairs and began to dress. When his wife eventually arrived with their son at just before seven she was surprised to see her husband standing in front of his wardrobe mirror staring at his own image with still, blank eyes. He looked very smart and, as ever, very handsome.

'You look', she said to him with half a laugh in her voice, 'as if you're going on a date.'

180

Chapter 11

Çetin İkmen was not amused. Having started his investigation into the consular women of Peri at the house of Peter Melly, he was dismayed when, having moved on to the Monroes' place, he discovered that the Englishman had lied to him.

'Matilda is staying with Mark and myself,' Kim Monroe said when İkmen mentioned that he had already visited her neighbours but had been unsuccessful in tracking Mrs Melly down. 'She's left Peter.'

'Mr Melly told me his wife was out shopping,' İkmen said as he replaced the tea glass the Canadian had given him on to its saucer.

'For a new husband, maybe,' Kim said. 'That business with the Lawrence carpet and the money was just the last straw.'

'What do you mean?' İkmen asked.

Kim Monroe sat down opposite İkmen and, unusually in his experience for a Canadian, lit a cigarette. They were outside on one of those big Peri patios overlooking the Monroes' pool and the forest beyond the village. A manicured, rather disturbing idyll to İkmen's way of thinking, and one which this woman was about to expound upon.

'You're an intelligent man, Inspector,' she said. 'I don't have to ask whether or not you can see through all this.' She swept a hand across the view in front of them. 'Apart from the trees nothing here is real. Everybody has heaps of money, some of which they spend in the village store, which carries goods from Harrods in London and Macys in New York. Everyone lives in a fabulous house with servants, they have fabulous holidays, and anyone who is anyone collects either carpets, villas, jewellery or all three. I'm not knocking it, but it does encourage a kind of atmosphere of invincibility. Anything is possible, money is no object. Some people inevitably end up getting into trouble.'

'Like Mr Melly?'

'I'm sure you've noticed that Peter's house is stuffed with carpets. It's his thing.'

'But not Mrs Melly's?'

'No.' Kim Monroe looked down at the floor.

'So what was her "thing", as you put it, Mrs Monroe?' İkmen asked.

She put her cigarette out before looking up into his eyes and saying, 'This is only hearsay, you understand . . .'

'But?'

She sighed. 'But it's said that Matilda took lovers. Local men.'

'I see.' İkmen cleared his throat. 'And your evidence for this contention is?'

'I saw her once, about a year ago in Bebek.'

'With a Turkish man?'

'In a restaurant, yes,' Kim said. 'They were cosy . . .'

'Kissing or . . . ?'

'Just cosy.' She smiled. 'On its own it would have been nothing, but then more recently, late last year, Doris Klaassen saw her, she thinks, coming out of an apartment up in Teşvikiye.'

182

İkmen shrugged. 'So?'

'So at that time she was supposed to be helping out at a British Consulate kids' party,' Kim replied. 'As well as the British women, Doris and I had volunteered to help out too. At the last minute Matilda cancelled. She said that her maid, who lives over in Sarıyer, was sick and she wanted to go and see if there was anything she could do. So I went off to the consulate and I met Doris there. Doris had driven via Teşvikiye because she wanted to drop in to Marks and Spencer first. She was just going back to her car after visiting the store when she saw Matilda, a little flushed, she said, but unusually for her dressed to kill. Doris had to look twice to know it was her.'

'But Mrs Klaassen didn't actually see a man with Mrs Melly?'

'No.'

Women, both local and foreign, were inclined to dress up when they went shopping up in Teşvikiye/Nişantaşı. It was that sort of area. It was also the place, on Atiye Sokak, where until very recently Yaşar Uzun the carpet dealer had lived. Yaşar Uzun's stylish place, way beyond his means as a carpet dealer, not five minutes away from Marks and Spencer's . . . Was it possible that Matilda Melly had had her own and quite separate 'arrangement' with the man who had been doing rather dubious business with her husband? After all, if Nikolai Stoev was to be believed, someone had to have been the woman for whom Uzun had bought the house on the Bulgarian coast. However, with hearsay, one had to be careful, but İkmen felt that a visit to both Doris Klaassen and the kapıcı of Uzun's building would not be a waste of his time. But then his mobile phone began to ring and so he was forced to turn his thoughts to other things.

*   *   *

183

They didn't stay for long in the bar of the Pera Palas Hotel. For although its somewhat faded early twentieth-century glamour certainly appealed, and always had done, to Süleyman, Mürsel was clearly uncomfortable.

'I think that maybe Haydar's death is having a more profound effect upon me than I had imagined,' the spy said after he had paid the silent waiter for their drinks and then retrieved his jacket from the back of his chair. 'There's far too much chatter here. Too much music.' He looked with some distaste through to a salon that gave off from the bar where a lone pianist played 'Somewhere over the Rainbow' on a really quite battered baby grand. 'Do you fancy going on some-where else? Somewhere quieter?'

'If you like.' Süleyman smiled. And in truth, despite his misgivings about going anywhere with Mürsel on his own, quite how he was going to have broached the subject of the peeper with the spy in the Pera Palas bar had given him pause for thought.

Once outside the famous pale green hotel, Mürsel turned to Süleyman and said, 'You know I have the keys to the Saray Hamam?'

Süleyman frowned. It had been outside the well-known gay haunt called the Saray Hamam in the old red light district of Karaköy that he had first encountered Mürsel Bey. He'd been following up on leads given to him by some of the earliest peeper victims. They had all at some time or another used the Saray, in order to meet or just look at other men. It had been Süleyman's contention at that time that the peeper was possibly following his victims home from the hamam.

'Why do you have keys?' he asked. 'Surely the hamam is open for business now? It isn't late.'

'No, but it's closed at the moment,' Mürsel said. 'The owner, a charming man from Adana, a friend, is currently on vacation. Ibiza, I believe.'

'He's given you the keys?'

'Yes.' The spy smiled. 'How does a nice quiet bath sound to you, Mehmet?'

He heard his heart begin to pound, but he said, 'Great.' And so after first walking up on to İstiklal Caddesi the two men strolled down into the tiny dark streets of old Karaköy.

Two things had happened. First, Ayşe Farsakoğlu told him about the results of her inquiries about Yaşar Uzun's purchases in Bulgaria. 'The Bulgarian Consulate officials were completely in accord with what Nikolai Stoev told us about Yaşar Uzun's property in that country. So, in light of the Ergin lover theory we talked about, I asked them to check and see whether anyone called Handan Ergin had somehow managed to get out of this country to Bulgaria. She hadn't, of course, although what you might be interested in, sir, is the fact that a fifty-two-year-old English woman called Matilda Melly flew to Sofia on Wednesday, 7 April. There is no record of her re-entering Turkey.'

İkmen, who was now inside the Monroes' house and well away from Kim, said, 'But that's impossible. Matilda Melly is still here in the city.'

'All I can do is repeat what the Bulgarians told me,' Ayşe said. 'A British woman called Matilda Melly flew to Sofia on Wednesday, 7 April. Where she went after that isn't known. But it would appear that she is still in the country. Would you like me to ask the Bulgarian authorities to look for her, sir?'

'Well, yes,' İkmen said. 'Accepting the possibility that there could have indeed been two middle-aged English women in this city with the same name, this maybe raises the spectre of impersonation or identity theft too. In the past, Bulgaria had something of a reputation for this sort of thing. We must alert the British Consulate too. You're at the station?'

'Yes, sir, I . . .'

'I'll get back as soon as I can,' İkmen said. 'Mrs Melly has been proving interesting from this end of things too. But I'll speak to you about that later.'

'Sir, there's something else, too,' Ayşe said.

'Yes?'

'A telephone call from London. The man who claimed he was the grandson of Lawrence of Arabia's servant is apparently genuine. He's called Lee Roberts and seems very anxious to come out here and see the carpet as soon as he can get a flight.'

'Is he.'

'Officers at Scotland Yard are e-mailing copies of his documents to you and I've told them to give Mr Roberts our contact details.'

İkmen sighed.

'Did I do the right thing, sir?'

İkmen rubbed the side of his head with his hand. 'Yes, yes, of course you did, Ayşe,' he said. 'I'm just tired and although I want to clear this carpet thing up as soon as I can, the thought of another person to look after and talk to does not fill me with joy. I'm sure that Mr Roberts will be charming, but he is a foreigner, he almost certainly won't speak Turkish, and—'

'And I'll look after him for you,' Ayşe said. 'I need to practise my English. And anyway, sir, if he is who he says he is, he won't be with us for very long, will he?'

186

'No.'

İkmen heard a noise behind him which proved to be the front door of the Monroes' house opening. He turned to look in that direction and saw a short, lumpish middle-aged western woman. For a moment they both just stared at each other, until İkmen murmured into his phone, 'I'll call you later, Ayşe.'

'Who are you?' the woman said in what İkmen recognised as British-accented English.

'My name is Inspector İkmen, of the İstanbul police. And you are?'

'Matilda Melly,' the woman said now with a sudden and surprisingly beautiful smile. 'You interviewed my husband . . .'

'In connection with the murder of Yaşar Uzun, yes,' İkmen said. This was the first time he'd met Melly's wife and it was proving interesting. Her clothes and general demeanour were indeed dull and plain and, on the surface, she appeared so homely as to seem almost invisible. But as Kim Monroe had suggested, there was something else underneath that was entirely at odds with her plain exterior. It came to the fore in her smile, which made her something different, something beyond beautiful. Although whether that meant that Matilda Melly was or had been having affairs with anyone was quite another matter.

'Mrs Melly, I've just been to your house where your husband told me you were out shopping.'

'Did he?' She moved further into the living room and then said, 'Well, he was lying.'

'I gather from Mrs Monroe—'

'I've left Peter,' she interrupted baldly. 'I'm going to stay with Kim and Mark until the consulate get my passport organised. That's where I've just been, to the consulate.'

187

Frowning, İkmen said, 'What do you mean, "get your passport organised"?'

In light of what Ayşe had told him about a Matilda Melly travelling to Bulgaria on the seventh of the month this was, İkmen felt, about to prove interesting.

'I've lost my passport,' Matilda Melly said.

'When?'

She shrugged. 'I don't know. Peter and I had a row early this morning. I won't bore you with the details, but suffice it to say that I decided I'd had enough. I went upstairs to pack my things and it was then that I discovered I couldn't find my passport. As soon as I got here I phoned the consulate, who asked me to come in immediately. I've been there all day.'

'So when did you last see your passport, Mrs Melly?'

She looked behind him to where Kim Monroe was now standing in the patio doorway. 'What?'

'When did you last see your passport?' İkmen reiterated.

Matilda Melly pulled her chin backwards and suddenly looked very, very plain once again. 'Why? I've told my consulate. What is it to you?'

'There is a very lively trade in stolen European Union passports through this city, Mrs Melly. As a police officer I am bound to investigate any such passport that appears to be missing.'

'It hasn't been stolen,' Matilda Melly said now with one of her smiles again.

'Hasn't it?'

'No. I've misplaced it. I hadn't seen it for weeks. I'm careless, it—'

'Mrs Melly, a person as yet unknown entered Sofia in Bulgaria on a British passport in the name of Matilda Melly

188

on the seventh of this month. The age given on the passport was the same as your own and this person has, since arriving in Bulgaria, apparently disappeared.'

'What?' She sat down on one of the Monroes' sofas where she was quickly joined by her friend Kim.

'Mrs Melly,' İkmen said, 'I have a lot of questions I must ask you. I think it might be better if you accompany me to the station.'

Instantly, and in a high-pitched girlish way, she began to cry.

Mehmet Süleyman tucked the top of the really very small peştamal around the edge of his underpants and then looked at himself in the full-length mirror at the far end of the men's changing room. Apart from the colourful checked cloth around his hips he looked very white. He was also, he noticed now for the first time, going just slightly grey across his chest. But this was not the time for either vanity or self-doubt. Mürsel was waiting for him in the hararet where, he had told him earlier, he would give the tired policeman one of his very efficient, as he had put it, massages. What this actually meant, Süleyman tried not to speculate upon. It was, in common with the mystery of who exactly was operating the boiler that provided the steam for the reportedly closed hamam, something that was as yet concealed from him. After slipping a pair of enormous takunya clogs on his feet he made his way unsteadily towards first the soğukluk, the cooling down room and then into the hot and steamy hararet.

A hamam or Turkish bath generally had four main areas: the camekan or reception area where tired bathers could lie down, drink tea and smoke cigarettes, the changing rooms,

189

the soğukluk or cool room, and, at the centre of the building, the red-hot hararet. The hararet was nearly always covered with marble and was frequently a domed area with light filtering down through the thick steam from small star-shaped windows. At the centre of the hararet was a great marble slab known as the göbektaşı or navel stone. It was here that massages were given by trained masseurs to tired and aching customers. Not that a trained masseur was in the Saray Hamam on this particular evening. It was just Mürsel, dressed in the same short peştamal as Mehmet Süleyman, sitting on the slab, staring into the thickening steam around his ankles.

'Ah, my customer,' he said as he watched the policeman clack his way shakily towards him. Takunya clogs were one of those inventions that defy logic in that they were completely insufficient to their purpose. One false move on a pair of takunya in a wet and slippery hamam and one could only too easily fall over and break an arm or crack one's head.

The göbektaşı was hot and so Süleyman sat down with care. The boiler must have been started hours before.

'I used to give Haydar a massage from time to time,' Mürsel said with a sad smile on his face. 'Sometimes we were far from what you would call civilisation.'

'Did you and Haydar . . . Have you worked abroad?' Süleyman watched Mürsel watch a large drip of sweat run down the entire length of his face.

Neither the smile nor the look of hungry sexuality moved. 'That isn't your business,' he said. And then with a rapidity that was truly breathtaking he darted forward and crushed his lips against Süleyman's mouth. It became a long, and terrifying open-mouthed kiss. If he were honest, Süleyman's terror was not about the fact that Mürsel was a man; Süleyman

190

knew, if with considerable guilt, that he experienced sexual feelings for other men from time to time. No, it was the all-encompassing viper-like nature of his 'lover', the way that Mürsel almost seemed to eat him while pinning his hands with enormous force down on to the hot stone below. When he had finished the spy said, 'I assume I am not being presumptuous, am I, Mehmet? I mean, why come here if you didn't want . . .' He left the issue of what Süleyman might or might not want open to the hot, steamy air.

After first shaking his head and then taking a deep breath, Süleyman changed the subject. 'Now that Haydar is dead, will someone else assist you in your hunt for the peeper? He, the peeper, seems to be gaining in confidence.'

'In your opinion.' Mürsel leaned forward again but this time he only very lightly ran his fingers across Süleyman's chest. 'Remember, sweet boy, that you really don't know anything. I, on the other hand . . .' He moved his fingers up to his mouth and licked each one very slowly. 'I know about you.'

'Do you?' Even the soaking wet hairs at the back of his head stood up.

'I know you prefer it when your wife goes on top during sex. She's a very dominant woman – usually.'

In spite of the heat, Süleyman felt his face drain of blood. 'What do you mean?'

'Giving head isn't a particularly dominant act, is it?' Mürsel replied. 'But it brings you so much pleasure, I'm sure that Zelfa doesn't mind. I know I wouldn't mind personally. In fact, I would love—'

'Have you been watching me?' His heart was hammering, his breathing laboured.

'If one has the skills, sweet boy, then one can and does.

191

The only pleasant thing about this whole ghastly affair has been you. I've always said I'll have you. And let's face it, if you were wholly heterosexual, you wouldn't have come here with me, would you?'

He was right, of course, but even so, this situation had peaked rather sooner than Süleyman had imagined. The spy was slavering for sex and Süleyman was still no nearer to finding out what was going on in Mürsel's mind with regard to the peeper and his possible relationship to the offender. Now it was Mürsel who wanted an answer. Süleyman looked into his eyes and said nothing. It was the spy's idea to go to the massage.

'Ah, well, what happens, happens,' Mürsel said cheerily. 'Let's get some of the knots out of your back, shall we? Then maybe other things will follow on naturally.'

Slowly, Süleyman lay back down on to the hot, slick stone. For just a moment he didn't turn over. But then, as Mürsel pointed out, if he didn't, a back massage would be entirely out of the question. And so the policeman complied. His back was a mass of tension knots. It was something his masseur pointed out as soon as he insinuated his long fingers into Süleyman's muscles.

'Allah, but you are tense!' the spy said as he fought to work his hands through what felt like vulcanised rubber. 'Poor Mehmet, this has to hurt.'

'Yes . . .' It did. A lot. 'Mürsel, the peeper, what is happening?'

'What?' The hands continued to knead without missing a beat.

'I'm worried. So many people are dying and we don't seem to be any nearer . . .'

'We? What is this "we" you speak of, Mehmet?'

'Well, yourself and myself and—'

'As I'm growing rather tired of telling you, Mehmet, it is my agency who will apprehend this offender. You are only where you are for show. Because of the public nature of the peeper's offences, you the police have to be in evidence.' The massage grew stronger, the fingers digging that little bit deeper. 'You mustn't catch him, he'll hurt you and I wouldn't want that, would I?'

'No . . .'

'No. I wouldn't like you to die in the way that Haydar died, would I? I'd have much more fun with you if you were alive.' Süleyman felt Mürsel's hands move down towards his buttocks.

'Mürsel . . .'

'Oh, that's a very nervous voice. What's that nervous voice about, Mehmet? Have you something to confess to me?'

Suddenly everything was beginning to sound like a threat. Suddenly not everything sounded sexual . . .

'Well, I can confess to you', Mürsel said, 'that on occasion I love to play the woman with the men in my life. If you're worried about losing your manhood to me, then don't be. I love men to give me pleasure, but I also know how "masculine" you proper Turks can be.'

But then perhaps he was wrong about the threat, perhaps it was only sexual? If it were, and Mürsel was as besotted as he imagined, then perhaps he could press ahead with his line of inquiry?

'Mürsel, I don't understand what is happening in this investigation,' he blurted. 'You're always where he, the peeper, is and—'

He felt the spy's lips plant a kiss in the middle of his back.

He also felt a rush of hot air as the man moved his leg in order to straddle him. Although he knew that he could turn over quickly and easily if he wanted to, he was vulnerable now. He was also, just very slightly, aroused.

'Mehmet . . .' The breath was hot on the back of his neck.

'Mürsel . . .'

'You know I can see the way that your face contorts with both pleasure and pain when you're very close to coming. I can see that in my mind. Of course I fade out the picture of your wife in that scenario.'

'Mürsel, I'm confused!'

'Sexual angst is not uncommon even in adults,' the spy replied. 'If, of course, this were about sex, which it isn't.'

Süleyman felt a slight pressure from one of Mürsel's hands on his right wrist. The hot breath on his neck became hotter as the spy lowered his body down close to Süleyman's. 'This is about the peeper, about how you told Çetin İkmen all about me and my investigation into his activities and your fears about that, isn't it?'

Süleyman could feel his arousal collapse, his breathing fracture and disintegrate with terror in his lungs. How had he found out about his conversation with İkmen? How?

'It isn't about sex,' Mürsel continued softly. 'I have sex with men a lot younger and prettier than you, Mehmet. I wouldn't say no, if you offered it, of course. But if you thought you might seduce whatever information you think I have out of me, then you are very wrong.'

The policeman's right wrist was suddenly pushed so far up his back it was touching the crown of his head. The pain was unspeakable, but the hand that held the wrist in place was, he could feel, barely even tense.

'Not gorgeous enough any more, Mehmet!' He slapped him hard around the side of the head. 'Treacherous too. I heard you at the church with İkmen. Bad.'

'You . . . with the peeper . . . you . . .'

There was a sound from over by the door into the hararet, but Süleyman couldn't lift his head in order to see what it might be.

'I told you if you told anyone but Ardiç about me, I would kill you, didn't I, Mehmet?'

'I . . .'

'So now I suppose I'm going to have to make good on that promise, aren't I?' He pulled Süleyman's right shoulder out of its socket and, above the screams of pain, said, 'Shame.'

Chapter 12

'I don't know why you keep on bringing up the subject of Handan Ergin,' Matilda Melly said exasperatedly. 'I haven't seen her for months! I stopped teaching. But poor Kim and the others were quite terrified by that ghastly husband of hers.'

'Yes, I know,' İkmen said as he puffed on yet another Maltepe cigarette. 'But, Mrs Melly, you have to understand that you have connections to both Mrs Ergin and Yaşar Uzun, two people involved in—'

'That neighbour of Handan's you took me to see, she didn't know me from bloody Adam!' the Englishwoman cried. 'I wasn't at Handan's apartment on the night Yaşar died! I was at home, in bed!'

It was certainly what her husband was saying. Matilda Melly had been at home while he went to the carpet show and Handan Ergin's nosy neighbour had not identified Matilda as the woman who came to see the young wife on the night that Yaşar Uzun was shot. Admittedly, the neighbour said that all westerners looked the same to her, however . . .

'Mrs Melly, just today you have separated from your husband. Could you please tell me—'

'Just today I found out what he paid, so far, for that bloody carpet!' Matilda Melly cried. 'It was the last straw!'

'You have been having problems in your marriage?'

'You could say that, yes.' The Englishwoman sniffed as if she had an unpleasant smell underneath her nose. But then that wasn't surprising. İkmen's office, even to Ayşe Farsakoğlu's well-accustomed nostrils, was not the pleasantest place in the world. The mixture of dust, stale smoke and sour tea was not suitable for all tastes.

'And these problems,' İkmen continued, 'do they involve other people?'

Matilda Melly looked up sharply. 'Even if they do, what has that got to do with you? I've done nothing wrong!'

Ayşe Farsakoğlu for one had to agree. Mrs Melly had, as far as they knew, done nothing wrong. As she watched their superior, Commissioner Ardiç, get into his brand new BMW with his driver, she wondered about just what İkmen hoped to achieve by this line of inquiry even if his English was absolutely stunning.

'Mrs Melly, no one is saying you have done anything wrong,' İkmen said. 'All I am doing is trying to establish connections between people if they exist. We have a number of people across both the Handan Ergin and the Yaşar Uzun investigations who know each other and have relationships of various sorts.' He flashed one of his totally charming smiles. 'I am just a poor policeman, Mrs Melly, I cannot always keep all of this information in my head.'

She visibly softened. But then, as Ayşe Farsakoğlu knew only too well, the İkmen charm offensive, in full flight, rarely failed especially with women.

'I'm sorry, Inspector,' Mrs Melly said with a very lovely smile of her own now. 'My husband . . . Some years ago, Peter was unfaithful to me. We got over that, somehow, but . . .'

'The quarter-of-a-million-pound-carpet was too much for you,' İkmen said.

'Yes! And when I realised he wanted to mortgage the house again to pay off the second payment, well . . . I didn't want to lose my house, and my future too, for the sake of a carpet, Inspector!'

'I can understand that.'

'Well, that is more than Peter could!'

'I'm sorry.'

She shook her head girlishly. 'That's all right.' She was, Ayşe Farsakoğlu felt, really quite flirty and pretty in certain lights too. She was just very slightly coming on to old İkmen.

'So you were at home in bed at the time of Mr Uzun's unfortunate death . . .'

'Yes. I didn't hear Peter come in. I was sleeping by then – we sleep at the front of the house – and he hadn't taken the car with him so the place was as silent as the grave, but I saw him in the morning.'

'Do you drive?'

'God no! No, I'm afraid I taxi across the city. Expensive, I know, but . . .'

'And you haven't seen Handan Ergin?'

'For months, no! As I said, her husband made his position quite clear to Kim Monroe. I liked Handan when I taught her. But I haven't seen her since I stopped teaching.'

'No.' İkmen shifted in his chair before, smiling yet again, he said, 'So did you ever meet the carpet dealer, Yaşar Uzun, Mrs Melly?'

She looked up at the ceiling as if attempting to find inspiration to her recall up there. 'Yes, yes, I met him once last year, I think.' She looked down again now and into İkmen's eyes, 'At Raşit Bey's shop in the Grand Bazaar.'

'And what did you make of Mr Uzun from your short acquaintance?' İkmen asked.

She shrugged, looked up to the ceiling again, and then said, 'Not a great deal.' She smiled. 'Carpets are really Peter's interest, not mine, as I imagine you know!'

İkmen laughed. 'Quite so. Quite so. Well, Mrs Melly, I'm very sorry to have inconvenienced you like this, but you know how it is. One of my officers will drive you home.'

'I can go?' She looked surprised.

'Yes.'

'Ah.' Matilda Melly stood up. She then took a deep breath before she bent down in order to retrieve her handbag from the floor.

'Sergeant Farsakoğlu will accompany you downstairs,' İkmen said and then, turning to Ayşe, he continued in Turkish, 'Get Roditi to take her home.'

'Yes, sir.' She turned to the Englishwoman and made a gesture towards the door. 'Mrs Melly?'

'Oh, thank you.' She leaned across İkmen's desk and shook his hand before walking towards the door after the younger, much slimmer woman. However, just as she was going through the doorway, a deep, dark voice called her back.

'Oh, Mrs Melly!'

She turned and saw him smiling at her from behind his desk, lighting yet another cigarette. 'Yes, Inspector?'

'Do you sometimes like shopping in Nişantaşı?'

'What?'

'Nişantaşı, do you like shopping there? In Marks and Spencer, Armani . . .'

'Not generally, no.' And then she frowned. 'Why?'

Still smiling he shrugged, 'No friends in that area or . . .'

'No. Why should I have friends in that area?'

'There is no reason, it . . .'

'Then why are you asking me about it?' Her voice was tetchy, even if her face was entirely impassive.

'As I said to you before, Mrs Melly,' İkmen said, 'it's all about connections, relationships between people.'

'But I have no connection to Nişantaşı. Why would I? If I wanted to go to Marks and Spencer I would wait until I went home to go there. Their stuff is much cheaper in the UK.'

'I see.' He looked across at Ayşe who was frowning. 'Well, that is very good then, isn't it, Mrs Melly? Thank you.'

She watched him smile again and then look down at the papers that littered his desk, before she said, 'Inspector.'

And then slowly she made her way out of his office and into the corridor beyond. As soon as she was out of earshot, İkmen called Matilda Melly's husband.

Mürsel was far more physically fastidious than the man who had recently entered the hararet to join him.

'Shooting shouldn't be done in an enclosed space, I want to live,' he said as he held Süleyman down on the göbektaşı so hard that the policeman could feel his right cheek beginning to burn.

The other man, whose words was more a collection of growls than proper speech, said, 'Lift the head, I'll cut the throat.'

'And splash about in his blood for the next hour? I think not,' Mürsel replied.

'Because you desire him . . .'

'Oh, don't start with that!' Mürsel exploded. 'I have nothing

201

on you. You who have pleasured yourself all over your victims!'

'I did what you wanted!'

'You did what you wanted, too!' Mürsel replied. 'You did that well before I came on the scene. Mad bastard.'

Süleyman, still gagging with pain, tried to look up at who Mürsel was talking to, but found that even the slightest movement of his head was far too painful to allow him to continue. Strangely, even to himself, the policeman couldn't get over what Mürsel had said to him earlier. Although terrified, part of his mind was still smarting from the way the spy had so spitefully disparaged his appearance. Over the years people had said many negative things about his wit, his intelligence and his morals, but never, ever his looks. That he was so disturbed about something so trivial made him vain and despicable in his own eyes. A sexually irresponsible, vain and stupid man.

'I'm going to snap his neck,' Mürsel said very matter-of-factly. 'Clean, quick . . .'

'You don't want to do anything with him first?'

'No. I'm not you. I . . .' There was a pause then, a long one, during which, it seemed, no one moved. Mürsel's grip was still tight upon his hand and now dislocated shoulder, but there was something in the character of that hold that had changed. He didn't know what . . . 'On your chest,' he heard Mürsel whisper. 'Look down, look down! On . . .'

'Oh . . .'

'Keep . . .'

'You've an identical red dot on your back I think you'll find,' a very cultured and entirely different voice boomed across the marble and the steam. Now, just very slightly, Mürsel's hold on Süleyman's wrist began to slacken. 'You're lined up in my sights. Let the police officer go.'

'What?' Mürsel was suddenly speaking at increased volume now. 'So you can shoot me?'

'I can shoot you anyway. We can shoot both of you. It's over.'

'What is?' Silence again. Then Mürsel reiterated, 'What is? What's fucking over? Nothing's fucking over until I say it is! You do what I say! I'm in charge! I don't need you! Who authorised you? I didn't ask the department for help! I don't need any help!'

His voice had suddenly gone into something Süleyman hadn't heard before. Rough, guttural eastern tones. 'Well? Well?' Süleyman felt the force of these words as they poured out of what felt like his weakening captor.

The sound of feet running and scuffling against the hot slick floor was followed by a slight whirring sound and then a dull, damp thud somewhere across the other side of the space. Mürsel gasped.

'He . . .'

'He', the unknown voice said, 'was a dog we and you knew had to be put down some time. He tried to run. We've done it now. Stand down. Move away from the police officer. Stand down. That's an order.'

Mürsel yanked Süleyman's hand back up to the top of his head again. 'And if I don't?' he said. 'What if I don't?'

'You are a patriot. You will obey the orders of your superiors. I am your superior, Mürsel. Obey me. To do anything else would be the action of a traitor.'

A long time passed, or rather it seemed like a long time to Süleyman. The voice of the man who had come to reason with

Mürsel was not familiar to him. It had to be the voice of one of Mürsel's people. Some other twisted, shadow-person. The water around the base of the göbektaşı was now streaked with fine threads of deep red.

'Do you want to die as a traitor?' the unfamiliar voice said. 'After all you've done in the past? After where you've come up from?'

Mürsel didn't answer for a while, nor did his hold on Süleyman slacken.

'Come along,' the voice said. 'There's nothing we don't know. It's finished.'

'Nothing?'

'Nothing.'

'I thought I was better than that.' It was a statement made with great sadness in the voice. But then Mürsel cleared his throat and addressing Süleyman said, 'You probably don't realise it, sweet boy, but you were only two centimetres from death. I only had to move my fingers and . . .' He let go of Süleyman's hand and what sounded like a regiment of heavily armed soldiers ran across the hararet towards the spy and the still motionless policeman.

'Don't move.' A face almost totally obscured by first a helmet and then an elaborate mouthpiece and microphone crashed into Süleyman's line of vision. Somewhere behind him, he could hear the metallic snap of handcuffs being secured around wrists. The 'helmet' and his fellows had to have been sent by Mürsel's employers, MIT – or whoever – finally as convinced of their agent's corruption as Süleyman himself.

'There was another man, I think,' Süleyman said to the helmet, which he now saw had very deep-set, black eyes.

204

'He's dead,' the helmet responded. 'Someone's going to have a look at your shoulder.'

'I think it's dislocated . . .'

'I'm sure it is,' the helmet said.

Süleyman felt a pair of confident hands move around his shoulder and a short way down his arm. The helmet looked up and widened his eyes. He then nodded before saying to Süleyman, 'Inspector, my colleague can put that back in for you now. It'll hurt . . .'

'I'm not afraid of pain.' He was a man and a Turk, of course he wasn't!

The helmet nodded to his colleague and Süleyman first felt as if his shoulder was being ripped off before the pain settled down into just an excruciating burning sensation. They turned him over and sat him up immediately. Staring, white-faced, into the now subsiding steam, Süleyman was confronted by a scene that resembled something from a futuristic horror film. Tall, slim creatures, dressed in what looked like heavy black leather, stalked the hamam, their heads covered by great black helmets, their faces obscured by mirrored visors.

'Allah!'

Of course they were men, or women, who certainly worked for a very powerful security agency. But they were not police, they were not, thankfully, people whom Süleyman had knowingly come into contact with before. He looked for Mürsel amongst their ranks but he didn't see him. As if in anticipation of questions about the spy, the man who had spoken to Süleyman earlier said, 'He's gone. You're safe. Can you walk?'

He said he'd give it a try. Of course he was shaky, but he didn't want any of them to have to carry him. Whatever these people had seen of his 'performance' with Mürsel, he still felt the need to hang on to some shred of dignity.

'How did you know . . .'

'Let's get you out of here, sir.' The man attempted to take his one good arm, but Süleyman shrank away from him. In the process he found himself looking down at the floor and the body of a very tall, thin man who was dressed in something that looked like a wet or ski suit. His face was entirely nondescript and in death seemed completely at peace. His fingers, curled lightly at his sides, looked so delicate, like the feet of some large, rather vulnerable bird.

Süleyman didn't have any need to ask the identity of the body. After collecting his clothes, he just let himself be guided out of that terrible place and into Commissioner Ardiç's brand new BMW, which was waiting for him outside in the courtyard at the back of the building.

'So if Mr Melly says that his wife was at home when he returned from the carpet show, and you believe him, then she cannot be our culprit,' Ayşe Farsakoğlu said as she sat down opposite her boss and then lit up a cigarette.

'If you believe him, true,' İkmen replied.

'Mrs Melly told us she doesn't drive and her husband has just confirmed that to you,' Ayşe continued. 'So it would seem . . .'

'Yes, it would seem that Mrs Melly lives an entirely blameless life. The Ergins' neighbour didn't know her and yet . . .' İkmen leaned back in his chair and lifted his feet up on to the top of his bulging waste-paper bin.

'And yet what?'

'Nişantaşı,' İkmen said. 'We know she was seen in Nişantaşı.'

'Yes, but she didn't say she'd never been to Nişantaşı, did she, sir? What she said was that she didn't generally go there. She was only, it is alleged, seen in Nişantaşı once. The notion of her having affairs could just be so much gossip.'

'Yes, it could,' İkmen replied. 'I have no doubt that in closed communities like the diplomatic corps, all sorts of jealousies and accusations occur. But, Ayşe, there was also Mrs Melly's body language.'

'Her body language?'

'When she was talking about Yaşar Uzun, she looked up at the ceiling. Specifically when she was talking about having met Yaşar only once and having not noticed that much about him on that occasion, she was looking away. She looked towards me and smiled when she talked about how she had met Yaşar at Raşit Bey's shop and when she detailed her husband's interest in carpets.'

Ayşe frowned.

'Basic psychology,' İkmen said. 'She looks into my eyes when she is telling me the truth, she looks away when she is lying. She didn't meet Yaşar Uzun only once and she did take more than just a passing interest in him. Mrs Melly's lying technique was very bad, almost infantile. I've seen far better than that in the course of my career.'

'So you think that she's guilty?'

'Of something, yes.'

'What do you mean, sir?'

İkmen smiled. 'Her husband spends all of his time with his carpets, she's probably a rather bored diplomatic wife – she may well have taken Yaşar Uzun to her bed. But whether she killed him . . . How, in fact, she did that while in her own bed and without recourse to transport . . .'

207

'Sir, to my mind, that just isn't possible. The crime scene is a good two kilometres from the Mellys' house. And anyway, why would Mrs Melly kill Uzun whether she was having an affair with him or not?'

'Anger, maybe? Yaşar Uzun took a lot of money from her husband. Mind you if, as she claims, she has only just discovered that fact, we come to an effective dead end there.'

'The Tourism cop killed him,' Ayşe said simply.

'You didn't think that initially. You felt there was no connection between the two. Why have you changed your mind?'

'Because logically it makes sense. Ergin's gun killed Uzun. If, indeed, his wife, whom he could have also done away with too in my opinion, was sleeping with Yaşar Uzun. It explains why Ergin killed Uzun and why Mrs Ergin is still missing.'

'But how did Mrs Ergin, a conventional, if slightly rebellious, housewife, meet and have a relationship with a smart operator like Yaşar Uzun? With his quarter of a million pounds sterling and his love nests in Bulgaria, this was a very ambitious carpet dealer. What would he want with an ordinary housewife like Handan Ergin, not to mention the baggage represented by her baby and her police officer husband?'

Ayşe, her brow now furrowed with thought, said, 'Maybe Mrs Ergin met Yaşar Uzun when she was having English lessons with the diplomatic women. Mrs Melly and the others all knew him and the place where the lessons were held is only a short walk from the Kapalı Çarşı.'

'Yes, but again, why would he?' İkmen said. 'Why have an affair with such a poor prospect when, surely, a lot of far more attractive single women were available to him?'

'But, sir, if you remember what Nikolai Stoev implied about Uzun's property deals . . .'

'One house for the girlfriend, the apartment for "other ladies", yes. But Handan Ergin had nothing to offer Yaşar Uzun! Why bother to set her up somewhere?'

'Perhaps he loved her?'

İkmen looked up at his deputy and slowly smiled. Silly old fool, he'd forgotten about that – love. Totally irrational and frequently irritating beyond belief, it could, if not bring them any closer to a solution, explain some of what was becoming a veritable tangle of a case. After all, if his Fatma, a clean-living, sincerely religious woman could love him with all his scepticism and vice, anything was possible.

'Maybe he did,' İkmen said with a sigh. 'Maybe when Ergin suspected his wife of continuing with her English classes, what she was actually doing was going to visit the carpet dealer. I'm going to ask the Bulgarian authorities to observe Uzun's properties for a while. It cannot be just coincidence that someone carrying Matilda Melly's passport chose to fly to Sofia.'

'Maybe not, although you said yourself, sir, that Bulgaria has in the past been somewhere that is easy for those whose documents are not all that they should be. I've heard myself that passports are copied there.'

'Passports are copied everywhere in the world,' İkmen said gloomily. 'And before you ask, hot passports have never, in the past, been of interest to Nikolai Stoev. Having said that, if one were to come his way . . .'

İkmen's mobile phone began to ring and so he turned aside in order to answer it.

Ayşe enjoyed these work conversations. İkmen called them

'case conferences' and he'd been sorting out his own and whoever was his sergeant's thoughts like this since the days, long ago, when Mehmet Süleyman had been his inferior. The constant questioning wasn't for everyone and Ayşe knew that some of the detectives, like İskender, preferred to go through theories and evidence in the privacy of their own heads. This allowed the detective involved to take all of the credit should he or she solve a case in this way. Inspector İskender, although very attached to his sergeant, was rarely in any great hurry to give him any credit for anything. İkmen, on the other hand, was always very happy to sing Ayşe's praises. 'We need', he was always telling her, 'more women higher up in the police. You, Ayşe, are my personal mission in this regard.' Although she secretly doubted that she would ever become a detective. She still hoped, at thirty-three, to be someone's wife and mother some day.

'Yes, sir, thank you, sir,' İkmen said into his mobile phone before ending the call and then putting the instrument back in his pocket.

Ayşe looked at him questioningly.

'That was Commissioner Ardiç,' İkmen said with a smile on his face.

Because the name 'Ardiç' rarely elicited a smile from anyone, much less İkmen, Ayşe said, 'Sir?'

'It would seem, Ayşe, that Inspector Süleyman has finally solved the problem of the man known to us all as the peeper.'

'He's caught him?'

İkmen took his jacket off the back of his chair and slipped it over his shoulders. 'Sort of,' he said. 'He's on his way back to the station now and would apparently really like to speak to me. Ayşe, during the course of our case conference, it occurred to me that I haven't been back to re-interview the

210

kapıcı of Yaşar Uzun's building in Nişantaşı. If anyone could identify this mystery girlfriend it would be him. Now I know it's already really late and . . .'

'I'll bring up the details on the system,' Ayşe said as she logged into her computer with a smile.

İkmen lit a cigarette, checked his pockets for keys, and then said, 'Get taxis to and from Nişantaşı, the department will pay. I don't want you driving around on your own in the middle of the night.'

'Sir, my car is in the car park, it . . .'

'Do as you're told. You can get a cab into work tomorrow too,' İkmen said as he raised one warning finger up to her. 'Parts of this city are not safe even for a police officer on her own.' He then made his way towards his office door and, just before he let himself out, he said, 'Thank you.'

The commissioner didn't stay long. He had a function to attend along with his wife. As if to underline this point he let his hands wander to the tight bow tie around his neck several times. As soon as İkmen had entered the room he had seen that Mehmet Süleyman had been both injured, for his right arm was in a makeshift sling, and thoroughly bawled out by a still-lowering Ardiç.

'Tell him it was you who effectively saved his life,' the commissioner said to İkmen just before he pushed his way out of Süleyman's office. 'For what it's worth.'

He then slammed out into the corridor leaving İkmen alone with a very white and crestfallen Süleyman. The older man sat in what was usually İzzet Melik's chair and waited for his friend to speak first. It took a while and when he did it sounded petulant. 'You told Ardiç about Mürsel.'

211

'Yes,' İkmen said, 'I did. I broke your confidence in order to hopefully save your life.'

'Which I thank you for.' He looked up with darkened, wounded eyes. 'If the commissioner hadn't spoken to Mürsel's superiors, hadn't got those operatives to follow us, I would now be in Paradise – or somewhere. But why didn't you just tell *me* to go to Ardiç myself? I know I said that I feared—'

'Mehmet, you were living in the paranoid world of that spy! I've seen people deal with "those" people before, it makes you crazy!' He leaned forward and looked into Süleyman's eyes. 'I knew you would never go to Ardiç. You'd gone into that place in your head where everyone is under suspicion. Reasoning with you was, I knew, impossible and so I did what you couldn't. I called Ardiç and I told him. He in turn told me nothing. But I was afraid, of what you might do . . .'

'How did Ardiç find me? I suppose "they" must have told him to come and take me away.'

İkmen shrugged. 'I don't know anything about what has happened this evening. I'm here because I want you to tell me.'

And so, inasmuch as he could, Süleyman told İkmen what had happened, what he had done, if not what he had felt, and what had been done to him.

'I know that what I had in mind was desperate and stupid,' he said, 'but so many people were dying. And there appeared to be an acceleration.'

'Which nearly cost you your life and brought with it much pain and, from what I can gather, humiliation for you.'

Süleyman turned his head away. Now the memory of Mürsel's fleetingly erotic caresses made him shudder. 'The peeper is dead. Those "futuristic" MIT people shot him.'

212

'Ardiç was working with them. I wonder when he first knew about Mürsel? When I told him what you'd told me, on . . .' İkmen paused. 'You've a very badly made sling around your arm,' he said. 'I'll take you home, get your wife to put it right for you.'

'Provided she still wants me,' Süleyman said gloomily.

'What, the woman who worships the plates you eat from? Oh, Mehmet!' He was about to laugh when suddenly the look on his friend's face struck him as something more than just post-traumatic gloom. İkmen sat forward and said, 'Mehmet, did that Mürsel . . . You say he suddenly went from trying to seduce you to . . .'

'He said some negative things about me.' It was almost as if the words were threatening to choke him. 'It's nothing.' He looked up then and forced a smile. 'İzzet called. My phone was off.'

'Did he leave a message?'

'Yes, but I haven't listened to it yet. My arm . . . I can't . . .'

İkmen stood up and walked across to the stand where Süleyman had hung up his jacket. 'Do you want me to listen to it?' he asked as he slipped a hand inside the jacket and took out Süleyman's phone.

'Yes.'

After a little fumbling with what was an unfamiliar phone to him, İkmen managed to call up the ansaphone and listen to İzzet Melik's tired, seemingly eastern dust-soaked voice. He didn't understand it, but he relayed the basics of it to Süleyman. He said, 'Apparently since he managed to assure him that Cabbar Soylu was indeed no more, the cleaner's husband is prepared to talk about Deniz. That must mean something to you . . .'

213

For the first time in what seemed like for ever, Süleyman smiled. At last İzzet had managed to make contact with the right person and, apparently, get him to talk. 'Oh, yes it does,' he said. 'I think it could mean justice for a poor innocent who didn't deserve to die. We've had a lot of those lately.'

'Too many,' İkmen agreed. And then he put the mobile phone back into Süleyman's jacket and held a hand out towards him. 'Come on, I'll drive you home.'

Unlike in the case of the masked man in the hamam, Süleyman was happy to take İkmen's hand. He rose with diffi-culty. 'Allah!'

'So do we know why Mürsel and the peeper were in league?' İkmen said as he just very lightly steadied his friend with one strong hand.

'Not for certain.'

'Will we ever know, do you think?'

Just once before, İkmen had been forced to have dealings with those engaged in 'security', in his case both foreign and domestic. Süleyman knew this had happened, he also knew that the older man had hated the whole process. It had, he had said later, made him feel dirty. 'I have no idea,' Süleyman answered. 'There is no way of knowing with these people.'

'I see,' İkmen said with what his friend knew was under-standing.

They walked slowly towards the office door.

'I must answer İzzet's call,' Süleyman said as he took his mobile out of his jacket pocket with his left hand.

'Once we're in the car, I'll dial and you can speak,' İkmen said. 'Oh, and by the way, Mehmet, I don't know exactly what nasty poison that spy spat into your ear earlier this evening, but I'd just like to point out that all of my daughters have

214

been in love with you at one time or another. At the moment it is Gül, whom you may or may not have noticed staring up at this office window on her way to and from school.'

'Çetin, you don't know . . .'

'I know a man whose basic beliefs about himself have been shaken,' İkmen said. 'In your case your honour and your looks. And seeing as a creature like Mürsel is entirely without honour . . . As I have said, Mehmet, people, mainly women although by no means exclusively, find you irresistible.'

Süleyman, in spite of the pain from his shoulder, smiled. 'Çetin, how do you know all these things about people? I mean, I know that your mother was a witch . . .'

'Well then, there is your answer, isn't it?' İkmen replied as he led his colleague out into the dimly lit corridor beyond the office.

Of course witchery, magic, or whatever one chose to call the supernatural was, he believed, involved in much of what İkmen did on an everyday basis. His 'feelings' and 'hunches' fell into this category, as did his sometimes frighteningly uncanny ability of knowing where his children were, especially when they didn't want him to. But sometimes, as in this case with Süleyman, it was just knowledge of the person coupled with basic psychology. Süleyman only indulged in self-deprecation when he was really low and, as İkmen had told him, because he could in no way imagine how Mürsel could have impugned his honour, it had to be his looks that were attacked. Although he had personally never seen him, İkmen imagined that Mürsel was probably jealous. That or just so horribly frustrated that thwarted desire had spun viciously into spite. After all, according to Süleyman, he had very shortly after the start of the supposed massage

215

turned very calmly to the subject of Süleyman's death. But then 'such people' were ever thus – good or bad, it was their job.

Chapter 13

'Kim, I am begging you,' the Englishman said through a welter of stale alcohol fumes. 'Don't take her, let me. It could be my last chance to talk to her, for God's sake!'

Kim Monroe was used to her friend and neighbour Peter Melly getting drunk on occasion, but this first thing in the morning phenomenon was a new one on her. Of course it had only come into being since all the Lawrence carpet business Matilda had told her about, not to mention the latter's desertion.

'Peter,' Kim said as she bodily blocked his way into her house, 'Matilda is going back to Britain tomorrow morning and I have agreed to take her to the airport.'

'I don't understand why she's going home!' Melly said as he ran his fingers through his mop of untidy, greying hair. 'I told her it was all right. If she stayed, we could work things out!'

'She doesn't think so.'

'And besides, the police here, they might still want to ask her questions . . .'

'But they've interviewed her already, Peter,' Kim replied. In spite of knowing that Peter Melly was an irresponsible shit, she was sorry for him at that moment. 'They've done.'

'Yes, but there's still the issue of her passport!'

'Which, if you'd been in to work, you'd know is resolved,'

Kim said. 'Your immigration guys are working with the Bulgarians to track it down. Matilda's got a temporary.'

'Well, why didn't I . . .'

'Know? Because you've been drunk for days, Peter,' Kim said. 'You know, if I were you I'd get sobered up and off to work. You're having a rough time, but you don't want to lose your job too, do you?'

He turned away into the Monroes' lush front garden and made his way back towards the clean and quiet road beyond. Kim shut the door and then went back into her kitchen where Matilda Melly was waiting for her with a cup of black coffee in her hands. As Kim entered she handed it over and said, 'What did he say?'

'He wants to drive you to the airport tomorrow.' Kim took a big swig from the cup and then sighed. 'For what it's worth, I think he really knows he's screwed up. I think he's genuinely sorry and he is lost without you.'

'Yes, but does he love me? Really love me?' Matilda replied. And then she answered her own question with, 'No.'

'How can you be so sure?'

'I just know,' the Englishwoman said with a smile.

'How?' Kim was, she knew, intrigued. If Matilda 'knew' that Peter didn't love her, how had she come to that conclusion and what, if anything, was she measuring his lack of love against? Sure, he had in the past been inattentive and unfaithful. But now, he seemed to be desperate to keep his wife. A case of not knowing what one had until that thing was under threat . . .

Matilda Melly smiled. 'Because real love isn't selfish. Real love takes risks that are about the couple as opposed to the individual. Real love fills your soul.'

218

'And so is that how you once felt about Peter?' Kim asked. But the Englishwoman just shrugged.

'Was there someone else at some time? Is there . . .'

'No.' She looked up sharply. 'Why?'

Kim sighed. She had been meaning to tell her, but Matilda had got back so late from the police station the previous evening that she had not had a chance. 'Matilda, I saw you once, in Bebek, in a restaurant with a young man. Doris saw you once in Teşvikiye . . .'

'I wasn't with anyone in Teşvikiye!' the Englishwoman said. 'Did you tell the police I was in Teşvikiye?'

'Yes, I had to. Inspector İkmen asked me outright. It was the time you were supposed to be helping with the consulate kids' party. I couldn't lie!'

'Oh, couldn't you?' Matilda Melly suddenly snapped. 'Oh, so that's why İkmen kept on to me about Teşvikiye and Nişantaşı and what I was and was not doing there! God! I was shopping, Kim. You've all got kids, you don't know what it's like to be like me! Suddenly I just couldn't do it, couldn't be with other people's kids, and so I went up to Nişantaşı for some retail therapy to make myself feel better.'

'But you didn't tell anyone!'

'No, because it was my business,' she said. 'Just like the boy in Bebek is my business.'

'Was he, the young man . . .'

'The young man in Bebek was an afternoon of really good sex,' Matilda said. 'Peter thinks I'm just some sort of sexless knitting machine, but I have needs. If you say anything to Peter, by the way, I will deny it! If you say anything to anyone, I will deny it!'

'Matilda . . .'

'If my husband still has any money to give, I'll want my share,' she said. 'Twenty-five years of loveless . . .'

'Peter does love you, in his way, and anyway, what will you do? You can't take afternoons with boys . . .'

'I'm going home,' Matilda said. 'I won't be having afternoons with Turkish boys back there. I won't need to. People love me at home.' She looked very sad.

'Yes, but . . .'

'I'd better go and make a start with my packing,' she said. And then as she began to make her way out of the kitchen, she added, 'Oh, and you don't have to take me to the airport tomorrow, Kim. I'll just pack my things now and then take a taxi to a hotel in town. I'll spend my last night in İstanbul on my own. It'll be better that way.'

'Matilda . . .'

'That way I'll know that no one will be judging me.'

Kim Monroe watched her leave with a mixture of relief and sadness. Matilda Melly was, and probably always had been, a very lonely and unhappy woman. The last thing she had ever needed was to be married to a man who was so obviously a dickhead.

'On the day that Handan Ergin went missing, exactly half the money she and her husband had saved in their account disappeared.'

'And Sergeant Ergin didn't notice that until today?' İkmen said as he looked across at Metin İskender with an expression of incredulity on his face.

'Odd as it sounds, amongst people of their type, the woman was apparently in charge of the finances. He's been too busy looking for her to be bothered about money.'

220

Inwardly İkmen smiled. When Metin İskender spoke about 'people of their type' he meant working-class folk rather like, if not as poor as, his own parents. Until he made a conscious and very brave decision not to indulge in crime or drugs or any of the other ills that afflicted his home district of Ümraniye and to get himself out, he was at a far lower social level than the Ergins.

'We actually found this out ourselves,' Metin continued. 'The Ergins are with the Garanti Bank and I made a routine request for information. That was what I found.'

'So maybe Mrs Ergin, far from having gone missing, is actually out in the big wide world somewhere on her own, out of choice?' İkmen said.

'Maybe. Not that this changes anything with regard to her husband's involvement in Yaşar Uzun's death,' Metin İskender said. 'One's own brother, as I think you will agree, Çetin, is far from a suitable alibi.'

'Indeed, although we must still establish motive.'

'Which is why every officer in this city should be looking for Mrs Handan Ergin. Find the wife and, I believe, we may well have found the motive. After all, if Handan was having an affair with the carpet dealer and she knew that her husband, a police officer, had killed him, she could be a very frightened woman. I for one can see only too well why she might have run.'

'If you put it like that, I must concur,' İkmen said.

İskender leaned forward frowning. 'Although I sense you still have doubts?'

'Oh, I always have doubts about everything, Metin,' İkmen said with a smile. 'It is my blessing and my curse. You know that Uzun deposited sixty thousand pounds from Peter Melly

221

into his account last October? Ayşe discovered from his bank that he took it all out in bits and pieces over the following four months.'

'So?'

'So did he pay for his Bulgarian property with that money, converted into euros? And if he did, where is the sixty thousand sterling from Melly that is still missing?'

Metin İskender shrugged.

İkmen looked up at the ceiling and said, 'Allah!' And because he didn't effectively have any answers he then changed the subject. 'Did you hear that Mehmet Süleyman finally got the peeper?' he said.

'Shot him, yes. Rather a shame, that,' the younger man replied. 'Although from the little the commissioner told me, it would seem that this person was the most archetypal friendless loner I, at least, had been expecting. I mean, who in his right mind breaks into people's bedrooms and performs acts of masturbation? Whether they murder or not, that type is always basically the same.'

İkmen, who knew more about it than he wished to expound upon to his colleague, and who also didn't share İskender's rigid view of personality, kept his counsel. However, before either of the men could speak further, Ayşe Farsakoğlu entered her superior's office bearing glasses of tea for both İkmen and İskender.

'Thank you for that, Ayşe,' İkmen said as she placed the tea down in front of him.

'It's nothing.'

Ignoring her completely, İskender stirred a cube of sugar into his tea and then said, 'So it was Stoev who reckoned that Uzun had a lover . . . But do we have any other evidence for this contention?'

222

'We may do,' İkmen said as he turned to his sergeant with a smile. 'How did you get on with the kapıcı of Mr Uzun's building last night, Ayşe?'

She made a point of looking into the beautifully arrogant face of Metin İskender. She didn't like him. 'Mr Osman, the kapıcı, was most elusive on the subject, sir,' she said.

'Oh, that's a shame,' İkmen said.

'However, when I realised that it was the fact that I was female that was holding Mr Osman back – his embarrassment you understand – I asked to speak to his wife,' Ayşe said.

İkmen smiled again, with obvious pride. His protégée had a very resourceful head on her attractive shoulders.

'Belkis Hanım, Mrs Osman, was very illuminating,' Ayşe continued, still looking at Inspector İskender. 'She told me that many women came and went from Mr Uzun's apartment. Some were, he told her, clients, a few others apparently, his sisters. Now knowing as we do that Mr Uzun only had brothers . . .'

'So some of these women were Turkish and some were foreigners?' İkmen asked.

'The clients tended to be foreign, yes, sir,' Ayşe said. 'When I asked Belkis Hanım whether or not she might be able to identify any of them, she said that it would be difficult. Apparently amid such thronging hordes picking one from the other would be well nigh impossible.'

'Yaşar Uzun was a busy man.'

'Odd, don't you think, that his employer was apparently ignorant of his philandering?' İskender said as he looked with just slightly more regard at the face of Ayşe Farsakoğlu.

İkmen shrugged. 'Raşit Bey is old, I don't think that he's always actually in his shop these days.'

223

'There's his grandson and the assistant.'

'Well, we could go back and talk to them again,' İkmen said. 'But I don't know how much good it would do. I mean, Metin, you must have seen a few carpet men at work over the years? There's so much flirting that goes on with the female customers, how can anyone know what is real and what isn't? The boys may well have thought he was just messing around. After all, in the absence of Raşit Bey, Yaşar was in charge, and the lads were unlikely to question him. And besides, some of these women he took back to his apartment may well have met elsewhere.'

'But some of them were Turkish,' İskender said, 'so one of them could have been Handan Ergin.'

'Maybe.' And then turning to Ayşe, İkmen said, 'Good work, sergeant.'

'Oh, there's more,' Ayşe said.

'More? How very wonderful, sergeant,' İkmen said with one eye on the perpetually unimpressed İskender.

'Something that Mr Osman was happy to talk to me about was a visit he had from a man called Mr Kordovi,' Ayşe said. 'He came early yesterday afternoon asking to see Mr Uzun. Mr Kordovi, Mr Osman told me, works for a car showroom up in Şişli and had come to collect the three unpaid instalments on the carpet dealer's Jeep. Mr Kordovi was understandably upset to hear of Mr Uzun's death but, according to Mr Osman, he was incandescent with fury about his ruined vehicle.'

'Oh, dear.' İkmen leaned back in his chair and looked up at the ceiling. 'So this means – what?'

'It means, sir,' Ayşe said, 'that Mr Uzun spent sixty thousand euros on property in Bulgaria, and he must have paid

224

some sort of deposit on his apartment and on the car. But I can't see that, given current exchange rates, he can have spent much more than sixty thousand pounds sterling.'

'Which, given what we know about his bank account, leaves another sixty thousand . . .'

'Numbered notes,' Ayşe put in.

İkmen smiled. 'Numbered notes still unaccounted for.'

Metin İskender, who had been listening to what passed between his colleagues with interest, said, 'Mr Melly definitely gave Yaşar Uzun one hundred and twenty thousand pounds?'

'He says he did,' İkmen replied. 'He certainly took that amount, raised on his property in the UK, out of his account. He has a receipt signed by Uzun for it. But half of it is missing . . .'

'You don't think that Melly still has it do you?' İskender asked.

'I can't think why he would,' İkmen replied.

'Some sort of scam or . . .'

'I don't think so,' İkmen said. 'He really wants that carpet. I believe he did pay for it.'

'But then who has the rest of the money? A load of sterling cash floating around . . .'

'Mr Uzun had no investments,' Ayşe said. 'And his family don't seem to have come into money or assets.'

İkmen shook his head. 'Well, I suppose as a matter of course, we will have to search Mr Melly's property. But I will be very surprised if the cash is there. What we need to do, I think, is try to identify some of the women Uzun went with. One or more of them, maybe this special woman Nikolai Stoev talked about, could have come into some nice wads of sterling. Not that that would necessarily bring us any closer to Uzun's killer.'

'Sergeant Ergin is not inclined to confess,' İskender said.

'Well, if he didn't do it, why would he?'

'If he didn't do it, why are his prints on the murder weapon?' the younger man countered.

İkmen heaved a very large sigh and said, 'I don't know. I really don't.'

And, uncharacteristically for İkmen, he looked totally and utterly at a loss.

Süleyman had just got off the phone to İzzet in faraway Hakkari when the car the commissioner had sent for him arrived. Zelfa, who had assisted him with the phone during the course of his conversation with his sergeant, said, 'My God, darling, a chauffeur too!'

'I can't drive,' Süleyman said as he pushed the sling she had provided him with at her face. 'And anyway, that young man isn't a chauffeur, he's just a constable.'

'Yes, I know,' Zelfa said as patiently as she could. 'I was being funny.'

'Oh.'

'It's Irish humour, you wouldn't understand,' she said as she guided him to the front door and then opened it for him.

Ardiç had sent the car not just because he wanted to make sure that Süleyman got to work, but also because the two of them had something they had to do together.

'You and I are extremely fortunate in being able to do this,' the commissioner said as he led Süleyman down into the bowels of police headquarters.

226

'Do what, sir?' Süleyman asked as he followed the large man down brooding, dusty, unfamiliar corridors.

'What we are about to do,' the commissioner replied.

'Sir?'

A little while later, underneath what Süleyman imagined from the tangle of pipe-work and the rattle of water in the ceiling above their heads was probably the boiler room, Ardıç stopped and said in little more than a whisper, 'Down here there used to be more cells than we have now.'

'Down where? Where are we?' Süleyman, tired from his recent ordeal at the Saray Hamam as well as not feeling entirely healthy on the painkillers he had been given, was feeling the strain.

'In the bad old days, back in the seventies,' Ardıç said, 'we had to have more cells than we have today.'

'Why was that?'

'Oh, come on, Süleyman, I know you weren't very old back then, but you were alive!' Ardıç blustered. 'The 1970s? Political unrest? You must remember how the leftist and rightist factions used to shoot it out in the streets around here? Even with these cells down here we could barely contain them! Before the coup in 1980, there were thousands of suspects for all sorts of really stomach-churning crimes. You must remember!'

'Sir, I wasn't even ten when the seventies began,' Süleyman said and then added a little sheepishly, 'and we lived in Arnavutköy.'

'Oh, yes,' Ardıç said a trifle acidly, 'I forgot you come from a Bosphorus village.'

'Yes . . .'

'And you went to a lycée too, didn't you?' the commissioner said, referring to the French style of private school favoured by the wealthy and upper classes.

With anyone else Süleyman would have spoken up proudly for his school, but with the commissioner he just mumbled, 'Yes, sir.'

'Well, welcome to what was my world,' the commissioner said as he continued along the corridor with his arms flung out at his sides. 'Some communist, I think he was, broke my nose down here. İkmen had his nose broken too at about the same time, if I remember correctly. But that was on the street, I think. He never would properly protect himself even then . . .'

'But, sir, what are we doing here now?'

Ardiç stopped in front of a door which he looked hard at for a few moments before he said, 'We are here, Inspector, to have a once and once only chance to speak to someone we both know rather better than we would like.'

Ardiç pushed the door open and, as Süleyman looked over the commissioner's shoulder, he saw what was unmistakably the figure of Mürsel sitting on a chair between two figures dressed in exactly the same black leather suits and helmets as the people who had saved his life at the Saray Hamam. Mürsel, his head low down on his chest, was handcuffed, shackled at his ankles and bleeding from cuts to his head and his mouth.

Ardiç led the way without a word, striding into that dark, windowless, musty-smelling room and sitting himself down at one of the two chairs directly in front of the spy. After just a brief hesitation, Süleyman sat down on the other chair and then waited with his head bowed to see what might happen next. There was an atmosphere of violence – recent and long since past – in what Süleyman felt was a vile and poisoned place.

228

Ardiç cleared his throat. 'Mürsel's superiors have agreed to our posing some questions to him, prior to his being taken –' he looked at the black-clad men for some sort of answer, but when none was forthcoming continued – 'somewhere. We're not to take any of this information out of this room. This exercise is purely to satisfy our curiosity. It's a gesture of goodwill from, er, MI . . .'

'We don't use names, do we, commissioner?' The voice coming from the spy was much less rounded and sophisticated than it had once been. It was almost as Süleyman had heard it when Mürsel was shouting at the men in black back in the hamam. Rough and eastern. It was also a little muffled this time too. It seemed that Mürsel had lost a couple of his teeth.

'I call you Mürsel, because I don't know what else to call you,' Ardiç responded. 'You can call me whatever you like. Your people tell me that the peeper was called Nuri Koç.'

Süleyman looked at Ardiç and said, 'Cabbar Soylu's wife was a Koç before she married him.'

'Mehmet!' Mürsel said sounding drunk as he did so. 'So good to see you!'

'Mürsel,' Süleyman cut in quickly, 'Koç? The name . . .'

'I went to school with Nuri Koç, out in the countryside. A dirty place you wouldn't go to, Mehmet. We did our military service together. We were both chosen, from our batch of recruits, to serve our country as a career. But when that all got far too much for Nuri, as it can for any one of us, I looked after him.'

'When you say it all got far too much for Nuri, do you mean when he started looking at young men in their bedrooms?' Commissioner Ardiç asked.

'Nuri had died.' Mürsel sucked some red-tinged drool back into his mouth. 'In his head. People in our line of business sometimes do. We see and do things that . . . well . . . it's sometimes difficult to retain respect for one's superiors. Especially when such people commit acts that in "ordinary" life would land a person in prison. Nuri lost control, he did what he wanted without reference to his employers. I began to hear that he was dangerous. He was, I recognised, living inside what I knew had in the past only been his fantasies. He was both sexually attracted to and morally repelled by those not entirely in tune with accepted society. Because I was his friend, I was given the task of bringing him in.'

'So why did you then collude with him?' Ardiç said. 'You say you were a friend but . . .'

'Nuri and I were never anything more than friends, commissioner,' Mürsel replied. 'But I colluded, as you put it, for my own purposes. From the moment I was told that Nuri had gone mad, disappeared into his own head, whatever you may call it, I had an agenda. I never for a moment thought that I wouldn't kill Nuri in the end.'

'But he was your friend!' Süleyman said.

'Yes.' He attempted a very small smile but then gave up when the pain became too intense. 'But my job was to eliminate the risk from Nuri in whatever way I could. I am excellent at my job. Nuri was dangerous to the public.'

'And yet, I say again, you colluded with him!'

'I allowed him to do whatever he wanted provided he did some things for me.'

'That was very dangerous, wasn't it?' Ardiç said. 'What with your own people and later on ourselves, the police?'

'I had the absolute trust of my own organisation . . .'

'Except that you didn't,' the commissioner said. And then turning to Süleyman he continued, 'Apart from the public nature of Koç's crimes, we were brought in to watch Mürsel, or rather I was. Something was suspected, I wasn't told what, and I was ordered not to even breathe such a thing to you. But then when Nuri's brother-in-law became his victim, things began to change.'

'I take it you're referring to Cabbar Soylu?' Süleyman said.

'Nuri's brother-in-law. Yes. You know he killed Nuri's sister's boy?'

'My sergeant has been investigating that possibility,' Süleyman replied. 'So it's Hakkari that you, a country boy, as you once said to me, come from? You, Nuri, the Soylus . . .'

'Kumru, the woman I know her husband told you was called Zeynep Saban. She came to Hakkari, our city. She was a nomad from somewhere. Very pretty. She'd do anything for a handful of food and some cigarettes. I had a lot of fun with her just before Nuri and myself went to do our military service. I am Leyla Saban's father. I met Kumru, poor soul, quite by accident shortly before her death. She recognised me immediately and told me everything. Sort of a death-bed confession I suppose. Imagine.' It was said with tight, outraged lips.

'Leyla Saban was a very accomplished young woman . . .'

'Leyla Saban was a Jew,' Mürsel replied. 'Not that I minded her religion. No, what I minded was her existence. I've served my country for thirty-one years without a slip. I come, I go, I leave nothing of myself behind. Sex with Mürsel Bey is always safe sex, Mehmet Bey. I am nothing and no one and I take considerable pride in that. After all, when one doesn't exist one is truly free and in my profession it is then and only then that one can become absolutely and without a doubt the

231

best. I couldn't have a daughter! What if someone found out and used my own blood against me? What if they attempted to blackmail me by threatening her? What would I do? As time passed anxieties about Leyla and what she might mean for me grew.'

'And so you allowed your friend Nuri . . .'

'Have you ever seen that old Alfred Hitchcock movie called *Strangers on a Train*?' He didn't wait for an answer but continued, 'It's about the swapping of murders. One man does a murder for the other and vice versa. Motive, opportunity and all the usual markers you people use to track murderers are therefore removed. In the movie it is only one of the men, the mad one, who wants to do this, the other, the sane man, is distinctly reluctant to comply. In the case of Nuri and myself, however, compliance and, some would say, madness existed on both sides. I killed Cabbar Soylu for him because Nuri's sister, poor Emine, didn't deserve to be childless. Deniz, Nuri's nephew, was an innocent boy, but Cabbar had him put down like an inconvenient family pet. Of course even after all these years Cabbar would have recognised Nuri and so I killed him. He'd known me only slightly.'

'And Nuri killed your daughter.'

'Yes.' His calmness was bald and terrifying. 'Quickly and painlessly. I had told him I didn't want her to suffer. Who she was wasn't her fault. After her death I did think that Haydar and myself could take Nuri down, but as you know he killed Haydar and then I had to engage with him one more time, partly in order to kill you, Inspector Süleyman, but also so that I could finally end it all for Nuri. Haydar, by the way, never knew about any of this. As far as he was concerned we were just out to bring my friend in and that was that.'

232

'Why did you want to kill me?' Süleyman said as he watched the spy roll what looked like a very swollen tongue around a visibly dry mouth.

Mürsel coughed. 'You were to be the peeper's last kill. You had started to make some worrying connections with my old home town and Deniz Koç, etc. But I knew that I could counter whatever you managed to dig up. No, you were just simply a body that was convenient. The peeper had progressed through frightening young men to the murder of young men to full-scale insane assassination of anyone he felt like killing – that was the idea.'

'Nuri started like that.'

'Nuri did indeed begin on his own from that standpoint. He was mad and alone and when I found him I knew that I could, if I was careful, use him for my own purposes. All I had to do was look after him, which I did, and then gradually persuade him to kill Leyla Saban. Her death could hopefully get lost in his long list of carnage. But as luck would have it, rumours about Cabbar Soylu and the possible unnaturalness of Deniz Koç's death had begun to circulate. Several of our operatives in the east were talking about it. It wasn't difficult to pass on what was family information to Nuri. He went berserk – at first. He calmed down when I told him I had a plan. He was so full of hatred for Cabbar he hardly even noticed when he killed poor Leyla.'

Süleyman shook his head. 'But to kill your own child . . .'

'So unnatural,' Mürsel sighed. 'For you it must be. But for me it is different. Policing is a job. What I do, however, ah . . .' He smiled. 'That is something else. That is life and death to my country, that is an honour for anyone who is deemed fit to do it!'

'Yes, I agree,' Commissioner Ardiç said, 'what you people do is vital. But when you use what you do to kill innocents for your own ends ...'

'I didn't have Leyla Saban killed for my own ends!' Mürsel cried. 'I had her killed so that her existence couldn't compromise my loyalty or bring my reputation into disrepute!'

'No one would ever have known!' Süleyman said. 'Fortune Saban was, as far as Leyla knew, her father. He loved her and she loved him and even if she had known about you, she would never have called you Father! And besides, to allow that Nuri to do what he did to those young men ... Mürsel Bey, you have a very twisted and evil sense of what is honourable!'

'So you think that Cabbar Soylu, the killer of a poor mad boy, deserved to live?'

'Yes! To stand trial and account for his crime. Absolutely.'

'The state doesn't execute anybody any more, Mürsel Bey,' Ardiç said gravely. 'Like it or not, that is what the State has decided and you as a servant of the State and, by your own admission, a proud one at that, must abide by its rules.'

'It's different in ... in our line of work,' Mürsel replied.

Süleyman looked into the face of one of the black-clad guards – it was completely impassive. 'Well, if it is, then it shouldn't be,' he said forcefully. 'Our country is not some third-rate dictatorship, we are not some arrogant superpower! We are, Mürsel Bey, the inheritors of a fantastic civilisation and a truly great republic.'

'Your patriotism is impressive, Mehmet Bey ...'

'Yes, because unlike yours it is genuine! I do not use my country as some sort of cover for ...'

'No, no, but of course you don't.' Ardiç put a steadying

hand on to Süleyman's arm. 'That is not at issue, Inspector. No one could doubt your loyalty to your calling. But time is short and I am aware that our friends here are . . . needful, shall we say, of being elsewhere. Is there anything else you wish to ask Mürsel Bey before we go?'

Süleyman thought for a few moments about all the things one might want to ask a man who had ordered the death of his own child, but then he decided that whatever those things were he neither wanted nor needed to know about them. The only thing that remained in his mind now concerned not Mürsel but Nuri Koç.

'Mürsel,' he said, 'did Emine Koç know that her brother was in the same service as yourself?'

'She knew he was successful,' Mürsel replied. 'They would see each other occasionally, until the last five years.'

'When Nuri changed, became out of control?'

Mürsel shrugged. 'Yes. She was told he was missing.'

It wasn't going to be easy telling Emine that her brother, who was now dead himself, had killed her husband. And quite where he was going to start on the subject of Deniz, Süleyman really didn't know.

'Nice girl, Emine,' Mürsel smiled. 'Very accommodating. Unlike Kumru she didn't require payment.'

Süleyman felt his face go white. He did not, after all, know too much about Deniz Koç's birth – apart, of course, from his illegitimacy.

'You're not saying that you . . .'

'I'm not saying anything, Mehmet Bey,' Mürsel said with absolutely no side or irony in his voice at all.

'But . . .'

'Inspector?' Ardiç was standing now, his huge body

shuffling uncomfortably about on top of his small, almost dainty feet.

'Sir?'

'We should go,' he said. 'I feel our time is up.'

Süleyman looked across at Mürsel as he sat, slumped and bloodied between his captors.

'What will happen to him?' he said as he looked again into the totally impassive faces of the men who guarded the spy.

'I don't know,' Ardiç replied simply.

Süleyman stood.

'But whatever it is, it was written,' said Ardiç who was at heart a religious man. 'Allah is merciful.'

And then without any further conversation, the two policemen left that small hidden room underneath their familiar offices and squad rooms. As the door closed behind them, Süleyman took one last look at Mürsel and saw for the first time ever that his eyes were filled with fear.

Ardiç, shuddering with either cold or fright or both, took hold of Süleyman's one good arm and pulled him roughly along the corridor.

'I hope never to see this place again in my lifetime,' he said as he puffed his way back towards the stairs. 'I pray to Allah that you never do so either, Inspector. And, by the way, Emine Soylu is never ever on any account to know that her brother was the peeper or that he arranged for the murder of her husband.'

'No, sir.'

'Abdullah Aydın, the only person who ever actually saw the peeper's face, doesn't know who he was and will be released by Mürsel's people soon,' the commissioner said. 'They will make up some name for the offender in due course and young Aydın will just tell what he saw, which was very little. Soon the whole affair will have just melted into the dust.' But then he looked up at Süleyman's doubtful face and added, 'Or maybe not.'

Chapter 14

Peter Melly's office on the first floor of the British Consulate in Beyoğlu was, though not state-of-the-art, extremely large. If one ignored the scarred and battered desk, the threadbare carpet and the rather tired decoration, Melly's office was very grand. It had to be, İkmen felt, at least four times the size of his own humble place of business. Not that the policeman looked about at his surroundings for long. As he sat down in front of the obviously hungover Englishman, he came straight to the point.

'Mr Melly,' he said, 'I'm afraid I have to tell you that we have only as yet managed to account for half of the money that you gave Yaşar Uzun for the Lawrence carpet.'

'Half? What? Sixty grand?' Peter Melly sat back heavily in his chair and then said, 'It is safe, isn't it, the Kerman?'

'I have it locked inside my office,' İkmen replied and then thought briefly about the dingy old filing cabinet the carpet was currently locked in. Hardly where a fanatic like Melly would have put it. But then, unlike Melly, İkmen didn't want to look at the Kerman any more than he had to. There was, he felt now, something both mesmeric and wrong about the piece. Looking at it would take up far too much of his time if he allowed it to do so. The Kerman perhaps had chosen him in that negative way it had chosen Yaşar Uzun. İkmen inwardly shuddered. 'Mr Melly, the money?'

'Oh, er . . . Well, I don't know,' Peter Melly said. 'I gave Yaşar a hundred and twenty thousand pounds. How should I know what he might have done with it?'

'Can you think of anyone else who might have come into possession of the money?'

'No! Why should I? I gave that money to Yaşar in good faith. I don't have a clue . . .'

'Mr Melly, if I were to search your house . . .'

'Well, you wouldn't find sixty grand, that's for sure!' Peter Melly cried. 'Christ, I wish you would! I'm totally skint!'

'Skint?'

'Penniless. Without money,' the Englishman said. 'Search the house if you must, but . . .'

'I'm afraid that I will have to do so,' İkmen replied.

Peter Melly put his hand in his jacket pocket and took out a bunch of keys. 'Here you are,' he said as he threw them across the great scarred table at İkmen. 'Knock yourself out.'

Before he took the keys, İkmen said, 'Mr Melly, wouldn't you like to be present at the search?'

'No.'

'Well, can I get Mrs Melly to come over? I understand she is staying with Mr and Mrs Monroe.'

'That's up to her,' Peter Melly responded curtly. 'She is, she says, flying home to England tomorrow. I don't know whether she'll still be interested in our home.'

İkmen did not reply. The look of pain on Peter Melly's face was distracting. Whatever Melly and his wife may not have had in terms of a relationship was, he felt, far outweighed by the sheer habit and comfort – albeit probably unconscious – of their being together. That applied in even the worst of marriages and it hurt.

For a while İkmen tried to persuade the Englishman to return to his home for the search. But he wouldn't. He was, he freely admitted, not interested. None of his own carpets even approached the Lawrence Kerman in his eyes and now that Matilda had gone he was bereft. He had ignored her for years, but now that he was truly sorry it was obviously too late. And so İkmen left and went back to the station to gather up his search team. Ayşe Farsakoğlu was the first officer he saw.

'Sir!' she said as she watched him slowly and wearily cross the station car park.

He took his cigarette out of his mouth and walked over to her. 'Ayşe.'

'Sir, we've had a telephone call from Scotland Yard. Mr Roberts, the owner, we think, of the Lawrence carpet, is getting into Atatürk Airport tomorrow morning.'

'Are the officers in London satisfied that this Mr Roberts is who he purports to be?'

'Yes, sir, they seem to be,' Ayşe said. 'I hope you don't mind, sir, but I've offered to meet Mr Roberts at the airport.'

İkmen shrugged. 'As you wish,' he said. 'What is one more or less greedy carpet-fancier to me?'

It wasn't like him to be bitter. But she could see that he was depressed. Whatever had passed between İkmen and Mr Melly had obviously far from cheered the policeman.

'I've told Mr Melly that we're going to search his property,' İkmen said as he walked with Ayşe back towards the station. 'He's no interest in being there and so we will briefly detour to the house of the Canadian couple the Monroes to see if Mrs Melly would like to attend. I have the keys.'

'Yes, sir.'

241

And then he stopped suddenly and, looking up into the cheerful light blue sky, he said, 'You know your Mr Roberts, Ayşe? You know what depresses me about his visit?'

She frowned. 'No, sir.'

'The lack of proportion inherent in it,' İkmen said. And then seeing that she didn't really understand he continued, 'I can easily discover who owns a contentious and valuable carpet but I cannot seem to get any closer to whoever has taken Yaşar Uzun's life. I've no doubt that the carpet dealer was a lying gigolo, but he didn't deserve to die and I am as far, it seems, from his killer as I was at the beginning of this investigation.'

'I'm sorry, sir, I—'

'Oh, it's no one's fault!' İkmen cried. 'It's just . . . You know, Ayşe, when I first saw that Kerman rug all covered in filth in the back of Uzun's Jeep, I was captivated. I looked at that dully glowing Tree of Life motif and I was hooked. When I was locking it away in my office I found myself wondering how often I would go and take sly, slightly guilty peeks at it in the days to come. But do you know I haven't done that once.'

'We have been busy.'

'We're always busy! But if I want or need to find time for something, I will find it,' he said. 'But with that rug, I didn't. I put it away, I left it alone, I moved on. And do you know why?' He smiled. 'Because it isn't important.'

'A lot of people would beg to differ,' Ayşe put in darkly.

'I know,' İkmen replied. 'I know. But compared to a human life . . .'

'Oh, compared to a human life it is nothing,' Ayşe said. 'That is self-evident.'

He put his hand on her shoulder and said, 'You're my kind

of person, Ayşe. You'll probably never be rich, but . . . Oh, come on, let us get some young, energetic types together and go and search Mr Melly's house. It will yield absolutely nothing, but . . .'

She was, she said, packing to go away on a short holiday.

'It's all been so horrible and I'm so tired,' Emine Soylu said as she led Süleyman into her elaborate but strangely impersonal living room. 'Please sit down, Inspector.'

He went to where she had indicated and, being careful not to knock his injured arm or shoulder as he did so, he sat down. Now that he was here, he was nervous. Although how he might have felt had he been obliged to tell her the whole story of her husband's demise, he didn't know. Statements taken by İzzet Melik now from several members of staff at the Perihan Hanım Institute in Van left little room for doubt with regard to the fact that Cabbar Soylu had ordered Deniz Koç's death. A male nurse was actively being sought in connection with the crime. However, with regard to who had killed Cabbar Soylu the picture was complicated by the fact that Nuri Koç's name was never going to be allowed to come out into the public domain. The offender was dead and the official line was that he had been a particularly disturbed vagrant. This was the story that Süleyman dutifully told Emine Koç now.

'You shot him yourself?' she asked as she looked at his injured right arm a little doubtfully.

'Yes,' he replied. 'We fought, which is where this injury has come from, but then I managed to get hold of my gun and that was, well, that was the end . . .'

'You did a good thing,' she responded forcefully. 'Such people do not deserve to live!'

He wondered whether, had she known the truth, she would have felt the same. But then he didn't know whether she had loved her brother Nuri or not. He had, in his own way, loved her.

'This is good news,' Emine Koç said as she lit up a cigarette and then leaned back in her chair. 'Now perhaps Rahmi will stop chasing shadows.'

'Your son looks for reasons, revenge . . .'

'Cabbar's son, as he never tires of telling me these days, looks for vengeance, yes,' she replied. 'It is almost as if my marriage never existed, as if I am nothing.'

She stared straight ahead of her, the intensity making her face look both very old and very young and vulnerable at the same time.

'And yet you are financially secure?' He still baulked at moving on into the subject of her real son even though he knew he had to get to Deniz eventually.

'Yes,' she said. 'Rahmi of course has money, but this house is mine, I have other means provided by my husband too. He was a good husband.'

Süleyman smiled, but out of nervousness rather than joy. Emine Soylu had loved her husband. He had provided well for her and, Süleyman felt, in his own brutal way had cared for her too. But things were going on right at that moment in Van and Hakkari which meant that not telling Emine what her husband had done was not a viable option.

He leaned forward in his over-stuffed seat. 'Mrs Soylu,' he said gravely, 'there is no easy way to tell you this . . .'

'What?' Sitting forwards again, her eyes were awash and glowing with fear. 'What do you have to tell me? What?'

'Mrs Soylu, we have reason, strong reason, to believe that

244

your late husband Cabbar Soylu was responsible for the death of your son, Deniz Koç in 2003 . . .'

'What?'

'Mrs Soylu, your son Deniz was living at the Perihan Hanım Institute in Van . . .'

'Yes. Yes, but Deniz died. They think that he may have taken his own life. They do, people like Deniz, he . . .'

'Mrs Soylu, I am very sorry,' Süleyman said, 'but I would not be telling you this unless we had enough evidence to at least begin an investigation. My sergeant is currently in Hakkari, helping the authorities there pursue the man your husband instructed to kill Deniz for him.'

'But why would Cabbar do that?' Emine Soylu said. 'Why?'

'Mrs Soylu,' Süleyman said gently, 'your husband, I am told, wanted to move to Western Europe, set up business there in some capacity.'

'He talked of it, yes.'

'And what was your opinion about that, Mrs Soylu?'

She shrugged. 'I was, well . . . I like Paris very much, you know, Inspector. Rome is a little, well,' she forced a laugh, 'Italian for my taste, but . . . Cabbar was very keen. I . . . What can I say . . .'

'You said you wouldn't go, didn't you, Mrs Soylu?'

She just looked at him through her big, wide eyes, which had only now just started to get wet from her tears.

'You couldn't be that far away from Deniz, could you? Here in İstanbul was OK because at least you were in the same country but in France or Italy or, worse still, in Britain or Ireland . . .'

'I only saw him twice a year as it was,' she said. 'I couldn't, I wouldn't desert him! It was wrong! I told Cabbar, I . . .'

The realisation crashed across her face like a wave. She threw herself down on to the seat beside her and cried. 'I killed him!' she screamed. 'My poor son, I killed you! Allah! Allah!'

It was to Süleyman a very primitive display of grief as one might indeed see around grave sites in the east. Even her voice had coarsened. Would she soon, he wondered, start tearing at her face as the working classes were wont to do even in the city? Selfishly he hoped not. He always found that so hard to stomach. He looked around that over-stuffed room for something other than the screaming woman upon which to focus. There were hideous lamps, hideous family photographs treated to look like bad oil paintings, ghastly rugs, unpleasant coffee tables . . . Everywhere he looked there was evidence of gangster 'taste' in full and lurid flight. And then suddenly there, too, was Cabbar's son, Rahmi Soylu, his young face a mixture of irritation, 'manliness' and a little bit of concern.

'What's going on?' he said as he approached the settee upon which his stepmother was slumped. 'What have you said to her?'

'I'm afraid I've had to give your mother some bad news,' Süleyman replied. And then looking down at Emine Soylu he said, 'Mrs Soylu, do you want me to tell Rahmi? Do you . . .'

But she just wept – screamed and wept. Rahmi Soylu looked down at her with ill-disguised contempt and said, 'Someone tell me what this is about.'

Süleyman took a deep breath. 'We have discovered that your stepmother's son Deniz was murdered.'

The young man shrugged and said, 'But he killed himself, didn't he? He was mad.'

'Mr Soylu, I am afraid our suspicions have been roused to

the degree that we are now seeking to exhume the body of Mr Koç . . .'

The crying stopped abruptly and immediately. Both men turned to look at a wild and livid Emine Soylu. 'Exhumed? Dug up?'

'Yes, Mrs Soylu, I'm afraid that if we want to try and confirm what has been alleged . . .'

'Dug from the ground!' She sat or rather reared up on the settee.

'Mrs Soylu . . .'

'But his soul will be in torment! You!' She pointed one long, red-tipped finger at Rahmi. 'This evil, this outrage, is because of your father!'

'My father?' His face contorted with sudden and frightening rage. Süleyman made ready to put himself between them. 'What's my father got to do with your dead lunatic? Look at yourself, you could only carry weak, deformed things – you could never carry a child of my father's. Don't blame my father for . . .'

'Your father killed my son!' Emine Koç screamed into his face. 'He had him murdered!' And then in spite of all of Süleyman's good intentions she launched herself at Rahmi, kicking, screaming and clawing with all of her strength. It took considerable force from a weakened Süleyman as well as from the young victim himself to pull her off. When eventually a very shaken Rahmi Soylu was freed, the policeman bundled him out of the room with a promise to tell him the full story on his own after he had finished speaking to his stepmother.

When he went back into the sitting room, he saw Emine Soylu wiping her bloodied nails calmly on a tissue.

'Mrs Soylu . . .'

'Would you think me evil if I told you that part of me actually enjoyed giving that young man a beating?' she said a little breathlessly. 'He's grown so arrogant in recent years! I told Cabbar. "You give your son too much!" I said. But he wouldn't listen. He spoiled him. I did too.' She looked down at the floor. 'But it was Deniz I always wanted. He was my own flesh and blood.'

Süleyman sat down again. 'I am so sorry to have to bring you such bad news, Mrs Soylu,' he said. 'I cannot imagine what you must be feeling.'

'With not even a husband or another, real child to comfort me,' she said. But then she looked up and suddenly smiled. 'I've been here before. I know how old I look in spite of all my operations. Horror does that to you. I know that Cabbar's friends always thought that I was older than him. But I am younger – a lot younger. Inspector, do you know how old I was when my Deniz was born?'

'No.' A horrible cold feeling stretched across his back as he remembered what Mürsel had said about Nuri Koç's sister, Emine. She had, he'd told Süleyman, been 'accommodating'.

'I was twelve years old,' Emine Soylu said simply. 'Raped by boys old enough to go and do their military service. That's horror.'

Raped. Just a child. Raped, left not by one man but by a group. What she had been doing out, alone, with boys in a conservative town like Hakkari, Süleyman couldn't imagine. But she told him and then he knew.

'I was with my older brother Nuri at the time,' she said. 'The boys were his friends. There were four. He was going into the service with them. He knew what they'd done. He called me a whore at the time. Bastard! Men are like that where we come from. They take women by force and then they brand them sluts! Later on I let my brother believe that I had forgiven him. A while ago my brother Nuri was reported as a missing person. I was glad. I hope he's dead. I never have and never will forgive him.'

Kim Monroe and Matilda Melly had, apparently, argued that morning and the Englishwoman had since taken herself off to somewhere in the city prior to her flight back to the UK.

'Matilda was pissed that I told you I thought she might be having affairs,' Kim said as she followed İkmen into the Mellys' large, white sitting room.

'Start in the kitchen,' İkmen said to the two young constables who had accompanied himself, Ayşe Farsakoğlu and Kim Monroe into the property. He then turned to the Canadian and said, 'Thank you for agreeing to witness our search, Mrs Monroe. I feel a lot more comfortable about being in the home of a diplomat now. Did you explain to Mrs Melly that you were only telling me what you believed to be the truth?'

'I tried,' Kim Monroe replied. 'But she wasn't listening by then.'

'Did she say what she might do when she gets home to England?'

'She said people who really love her are there. Her mom and dad, I guess. Inspector, shouldn't Matilda be around to follow up on her stolen passport situation?'

İkmen, who was now looking over at Ayşe Farsakoğlu as she looked through various carpet-stuffed cupboards, said, 'The British have issued her with a temporary replacement and she has given them a satisfactory statement. They are

249

working with the Bulgarians and our own immigration people. As long as she provides a genuine address in England she can do as she pleases. She's done nothing wrong.'

'No.'

'Now,' he said, 'you, Mrs Monroe, have a house identical to this one, do you not?'

'Ours is a little bigger, I think,' Kim said, 'but, yeah, the layout is the same.'

'So tell me,' İkmen said, 'which of the four bedrooms upstairs is the main bedroom?'

'The one at the front, over the street door,' she said.

'I will begin there,' İkmen said. And then he turned to Ayşe. 'I'm going up . . .'

'To the Mellys' bedroom, yes, sir,' Ayşe said. 'I know my English isn't perfect, but I do understand . . .'

'I apologise.' He began to climb the stairs that were in the corner of the great white sitting room.

'Oh, Inspector,' Kim Monroe said just before he breathlessly reached the top stair.

'Yes?'

'Don't forget that Matilda's room is at the back overlooking the garden.'

There was a pause before İkmen said, 'What?'

'Matilda's bedroom,' the Canadian said, 'it's at the back opposite Peter's room. Just so you can know which is where and what . . .'

'Mrs Monroe,' İkmen butted in forcefully, 'am I right in deducing from this that Mr and Mrs Melly didn't actually sleep together?'

'No, they haven't done for years, Matilda told me. She's got her own computer system and all her stuff in the back room,' Kim said and then, noticing for the first time that Ayşe Farsakoğlu and İkmen were looking at her in a strange way, she shook her head. 'What? What have I said?'

'Sergeant Farsakoğlu,' İkmen said gravely, 'will you supervise my search of Mrs Melly's room please? If her computer is still here, I'm going to switch it on.' He then turned to Kim Monroe and said, 'I had been led to believe that the Mellys still slept together. Both their alibis for the night of Yaşar Uzun's death rest, in part, upon that notion.'

Kim Monroe bit her lips tensely.

Chapter 15

Hotels and pansiyons in Turkey are obliged by law to take passport details from foreign nationals who wish to stay at their premises. In some establishments, but not all, this is computerised. Where it was not, rather laborious records were kept on paper. Fond of computers, though he claimed not to be, Çetin İkmen was, now that he had checked the guest lists of most of the hotels and pansiyons which were computerised, flinching at the thought of his officers having to wade through the mountains of handwritten papers that were still normal in many places. In such establishments time, and sometimes, the entire concept of haste had long been forgotten.

'Mr Melly,' he said as he leaned across his desk towards the white-faced Englishman in front of him, 'are you sure you have no idea where your wife might be staying?'

'I've told you no,' Peter Melly said as he contemplated an office far smaller and shabbier than his own. 'And anyway, İkmen, I don't really see why you are so insistent upon finding Matilda.'

'As I told you, Mr Melly, it is because she lied,' İkmen said. 'When I interviewed her, Mrs Melly told me that "we" – I quote – "sleep at the front of the house". We. You and her.'

'Well, I didn't exactly . . .'

253

'You both provided alibis for each other,' İkmen said. 'And yet you have separate rooms!'

'Well, maybe that night we decided to . . .'

'Oh, come, come, Mr Melly,' İkmen said, 'do not insult my intelligence! You and your wife either sleep together or you do not! You told me that you saw your wife on the night that Mr Uzun died and yet if you do not sleep together there is no way that could have happened. So what is it to be? Did you or did you not sleep with your wife on the night that Yaşar Uzun died?'

Between his favourite bar, the Balık Pazar for a little shopping and, bafflingly, the UFO Museum on Büyükparmakkapı Sokak, Mr Peter Melly had been a difficult man to find outside the strictures of the British Consulate. On top of that, pinning him down about the state of his obviously deceased marriage was still not proving easy. But İkmen had had the bit between his teeth for hours now, ever since that casual remark that Kim Monroe had made about the Mellys' bedrooms.

'Well, Mr Melly?'

The Englishman sighed and then said, 'Well, no, I didn't. Things haven't been right since that posting to Paris five years ago. There was a Frenchwoman, as there tends to be . . .'

'So you did not see your wife until the following morning?' İkmen said.

'Well, I may have done, but . . .'

'So it is possible that she could have been out when you arrived home from Mr and Mrs Klaassen's carpet party?'

'Well . . . Yes, I suppose that physically . . .' He looked up. 'But why would my wife want to kill Yaşar Uzun?' he said. 'She hardly knew him.'

İkmen looked across at Ayşe Farsakoğlu and said, 'Sergeant,

254

can you please organise for some officers to get into the back streets of Sultanahmet. Check the records of every little hippy hostel you can find. Almost all paper in those places, I'm afraid.'

'Sir, Mrs Melly is fifty-two.'

'Ayşe, those places don't discriminate. Anybody's money is good enough for them.'

'Sir.' With a sigh she left the room.

İkmen turned back to Peter Melly and said, 'But are you sure your wife didn't know Yaşar Uzun?'

'Yes! Why would she? Matilda has no interest in carpets!'

'Maybe not, but what about carpet dealers?' İkmen said.

The Englishman's face darkened. 'If you're suggesting . . .'

'I am not suggesting anything,' İkmen replied. 'Others have suggested to me that perhaps your own infidelity might have been repaid by your wife.'

'Oh, don't be ridiculous! Matilda would never have cuck-olded me!' He crossed his arms awkwardly across his chest and then said, 'If that's that bloody Kim Monroe . . .'

'Not only Mrs Monroe, Mr Melly,' İkmen said. 'Your wife has been seen with other men. Whether any wrongdoing took place I do not know. But Yaşar Uzun was a ladies' man and some of his ladies were foreigners. In addition, we know that Mrs Melly did have a certain interest in common with Mr Uzun outside the carpet business. Maybe your wife and Mr Uzun had a, what do you call it, a lovers' tiff out on the Peri road.'

'What "interest"? What do you mean?'

'You don't believe your wife capable of an affair? Anyone is capable of an affair,' İkmen said, knowing down to the bottom of his soul that he was probably the one exception to this rule. 'But then maybe she killed Yaşar Uzun because she was so angry about the Kerman. Perhaps she was trying to get some of your money back, some of her future.'

'Matilda didn't know anything about the money until after Yaşar's death,' Peter Melly replied.

'Or so you think.'

'So I know!'

'Then why did your wife effectively use you as an alibi for the night when Yaşar was killed?'

'Oh, I don't know I . . .'

'You complied with her deception!' İkmen said. 'You would have had us believe that you slept with her that night! Why was that, Mr Melly?'

'Well, er . . .'

'Was it because you were covering for her, or was she covering for you?'

'What do you mean, that I killed Yaşar? Why would I do that? Christ, Inspector, I wanted that bloody carpet and as you must have noticed after Yaşar died, I didn't have a clue as to its whereabouts. If I had, I'll be honest, I would have taken it. I would have stolen – that I would have done!'

'But then if you did not deceive me in order to cover for your wife or yourself then you must have done so in order to cover for both of you. You both killed Yaşar Uzun . . .'

'Fucking hell, I didn't kill Uzun!' Peter Melly yelled. 'Either with or without Matilda!'

'So, then, why did you say that you saw your wife in *your* bed on the night that Uzun died?'

There was a pause during which Peter Melly first looked down at his hands and then back up at İkmen's face once again. He sighed. 'Well, it's weird, isn't it? Not sleeping with

256

one's own spouse. I mean, I know that Matilda is hardly Nicole Kidman but . . .'

'Mr Melly, are you telling me that you misled my investigation in order to save face?'

'Um, er . . .' He looked down and then up again very quickly. 'You're a Turk, you understand "honour" and . . .'

İkmen rolled his eyes. 'Mr Melly, one's nationality is entirely irrelevant here. Your wife, we now know, could have killed Yaşar Uzun. It is a possibility.'

'But why? Why . . .'

'That we have to find out,' İkmen said. 'But the fact is, Mr Melly, that your wife, who may or may not be a murderer, is somewhere so far unknown to us in this city. As one who has some responsibility for such things, I find that frightening.'

'Well, I still don't know quite why you're looking for her tonight,' Peter Melly said. 'You have her flight details. Pick her up at the airport tomorrow.'

İkmen who was now both tired and exasperated, lit yet another cigarette before he said, 'Oh, and what if your wife chooses not to take that flight? It is possible she left the Monroes' house because she was worried about the allegations of sexual impropriety which Mrs Monroe admitted to your wife she had told us about. If that is the case, she may take another booking, or even perhaps leave the country by some other means!'

'Oh, I . . .'

'Mr Melly, forgive me,' İkmen said, 'but for a diplomat, you seem to me to exhibit very little imagination. You are British, you live in a place where people make illegal entry on to your land every day. You must have to try to anticipate their various strategies. We do here in the city.'

257

Peter Melly first snorted and then shook his head. 'Not all of us are involved in immigration, Inspector,' he said. 'There are other things that diplomats do. Besides, I don't live in the UK any more and now that I'm broke I probably never will again!'

He then sank down into his seat and folded himself into a large, thin miserable heap.

It was a hideous thought, but once it was lodged inside Süleyman's mind, it wouldn't go. The four boys who had raped Emine Soylu, the four friends of her brother Nuri, had been called Emir, Berdan, Meli and Gazi. There was no mention of any Mürsel. But then, as Mehmet Süleyman knew only too well, that was not the spy's real name. That could be anything. Emir, Berdan, Meli, Gazi . . . All the same age as Nuri, they'd gone off to do their military service together – just as Mürsel had told him – with the exception of naming anyone apart from Nuri Soylu.

Had Cabbar Soylu ordered the death of Mürsel's other child, the one he may or may not have known about? Of course it was all academic now. Emine Soylu didn't know and he himself would never see Mürsel again. He doubted whether anyone outside of some almost, happily, unimaginable prison ever would.

His wife Zelfa came over and just very lightly touched his arm in order to rouse him from his reverie. He flinched just a little at her touch. To have even considered a sexual adventure, albeit with another man, outside of his marriage had been so unthinking of him. He loved her. 'Your father's here,' she said. 'I'm sorry, Mehmet.'

It was late and she knew that he was tired. But he smiled

258

anyway and said, 'It's not your fault. Do you know what he wants, by any chance?'

'I think he wants to talk about that carpet that belonged to his aunt,' Zelfa replied visibly cringing inside.

Mehmet Süleyman put a hand up to his head. 'Allah.'

'I know,' Zelfa said, this time in English, 'but he's all of a what-have-you about it and I don't know what to do.'

He didn't exactly know what being 'all of a what-have-you' meant, but he gathered that his father was agitated and he was not proved wrong.

'I thought that Raşit Bey could be relied upon to come to an honourable price,' Muhammed Süleyman complained bitterly as his son leaned forward in order to light his father's cigarette with his one good hand. 'Carpets that have belonged to prominent people are always valuable. I have heard it from Raşit Bey's own lips. My carpet belonged to my aunt, the Princess Gözde. A princess. That is almost as prominent as one can get, is it not?'

'In a sense, yes,' his son responded diplomatically. 'But Father, the Princess Gözde wasn't famous, was she? Famous, if my understanding is correct, would be someone who is brilliant or revered or mysterious. A carpet that belonged to Atatürk . . .'

'My aunt was very mysterious,' Muhammed Süleyman said gloomily. 'I remember being taken to see her as a child. All by herself in that mansion, she sat in that high-backed chair of hers like an empress. Always covered and in black, her eyes were always wet for her lost sweetheart.'

In spite of his tiredness, Mehmet had always been mildly intrigued by this admittedly very mysterious ancestor. 'How did the sweetheart die?' he asked.

259

'How did any of them die back then?' his father replied. 'In the Great War.'

'Yes, I know that, but . . .'

'I don't know who he was, of course, but he came from a very good family. The Princess Gözde always said that he was with Djemal Paşa's 4th army. Of course it was all very muddle-headed. But then the sultan, her uncle, was only a puppet by that time.' He shook his head. 'It was the time of the Young Turks, Djemal, Enver and Talaat Paşas and that mad alliance they made with the Germans. Ruined this country for years.'

'Yes, but Atatürk put it right in the end, didn't he.' It was to Mehmet a statement of fact.

His father frowned. 'Yes,' he said. 'To have retained the sultanate would have been, well . . . But it didn't happen and life proceeds. İnşallah tomorrow will bring food, light and warmth. We must give thanks for what we have and practise acceptance.'

His father had always had problems with money, all his life. Dependent upon what he did, sold, begged or borrowed, his fortunes were either up, down or just about managing. This time, however, things were bad. He'd said nothing, of course, but Mehmet knew that his parents had recently had to pay some rather large medical bills. His mother had developed diabetes and there was also the perennial problem of his father's arthritic knees. His brother, he knew, helped out in any way that he could. But Murad wasn't rich and he had a daughter to bring up, look after and school, all on his own.

'Father, if there is anything I can help you with . . .'

The old man patted his son on the knee and then said, 'No, no. It will be fine.' And then his eyes filled with tears and he said, 'But you're a good boy for asking. I am so fortunate to have such fine sons.'

He cried. Mehmet had seen his father upset many times before, but to actually see him cry was a new and alarming experience. But then, although he sometimes tried not to think about it, Mehmet had to accept that his father was old. Thin and slow-moving, his cheeks were beginning to sink into his skull and he even trembled on occasion when he was tired. And he was poor. If something didn't change soon, Mehmet could see himself and his family moving back to the house in Arnavutköy in order to contribute to his parents' expenses. Zelfa wouldn't like leaving her father's house in Ortaköy, but at least her father was solvent, fit and capable of taking care of himself. His own parents were, well, crumbling. Gently, so as not to hurt or alarm him, Mehmet put his one good arm around his father's shoulders.

It was one o'clock in the morning when Ayşe Farsakoğlu stepped back into İkmen's office. He could tell by the expression on her face that she had nothing positive to tell him.

'No Mrs Melly, I assume,' he said, waking the slumped figure of Peter Melly still sitting in front of him as he did so.

'No, sir,' Ayşe replied. 'We're down to places that look like holes in the ground and which charge junkies by the hour.'

'I don't think that Mrs Melly, however desperate, would even be able to find one of those.' İkmen then turned to the woman's husband and said in English, 'I know I asked you this about four hours ago, Mr Melly, but could your wife be with a friend somewhere in the city?'

Peter Melly yawned. 'As I told you before, Inspector, I don't know,' he said. 'As far as I'm aware she doesn't have any friends

261

in the city. Why don't you ask the gossips who told you about her "infidelities"? Maybe they know where some of these young studs Matilda is supposed to have serviced live?'

'No, sir, these were unknown men, as I think we have discussed.'

Peter Melly, an avowed adulterer himself, was filled with bitterness and spite about what his wife may or may not have done with other men. He clearly felt betrayed. It was something that was flabbergasting İkmen on a minute-to-minute basis. What, he wondered, would Melly have done had he found his wife with one of these men? He assumed he would have become very outraged and very moral. It was all, to him, extremely hypocritical. But then to İkmen infidelity was a frightening and very much closed book. He loved his wife, she loved him, and the lack of confusion that this produced was appreciated by both of them.

'So what we do now, sir?' Ayşe asked in English so that their 'guest' could understand what she was saying.

'What time in the morning does Mrs Melly's flight leave for London?'

Ayşe looked down at a piece of paper on her desk. 'Eight o'clock. And sir, I must pick Mr Roberts up from the airport at eleven.'

'Roberts?' Peter Melly sat up straight and ran his fingers quickly through his tangled hair. 'Roberts as in my Lawrence carpet Roberts?'

İkmen sighed and then said, 'Yes. Mr Roberts, who your police are sure is a relative of the servant of T. E. Lawrence.'

'So you're going to give him the carpet, are you?' His face was white with tiredness and also with a fury that was visibly gathering inside him. 'Just like that?'

İkmen turned to Ayşe and said in Turkish, 'Not a good idea to mention anything to do with that carpet with him in the room.'

'Sorry, sir.'

'What's that?' Peter Melly looked from one officer to the other with a real look of wildness in his eyes. 'What are you saying?'

'Mr Melly, I will not just give Mr Roberts the Lawrence carpet. I will need to be satisfied that he is the rightful owner and his account of the carpet's past will need to concur with that told by the Uzun family. The Uzuns, I should tell you, want nothing to do with the carpet. They don't want the thing itself or any money for it.'

'Good. But', Peter Melly said, 'that doesn't help me with my finances, does it? I'm still down by a hundred and twenty thousand pounds!'

İkmen put his head in his hands. 'Some of which, as I have told you before, Mr Melly, may be recoverable from Yaşar Uzun's estate. But first, before any of that can happen, and to go back a long way in this conversation, we have to find your wife.' He looked across at Ayşe and said, 'I'm going to call off the search tonight. We must assume that Mrs Melly is going to catch that flight in the morning. You go home and get some sleep, Ayşe.'

'But sir, what if she does not come?' Ayşe replied in English.

'The ports and border guards have already been issued with her description,' İkmen said. 'There's nothing more that I can do.'

'We don't even know that Matilda has done anything wrong anyway,' Peter Melly said. 'So do I get to go home or . . .'

'I will take you back to the consulate,' İkmen said. 'I would prefer it if you stayed there tonight.'

'Where you can keep an eye on me?' he asked challengingly.

'Yes,' İkmen responded simply. 'Exactly. I will come and collect you at five this morning and we will all go out to the airport together.'

'Five!'

'Your wife's flight is at eight,' İkmen explained. 'So she is required to be at the airport two hours beforehand, at six. She may come early and so we will be there in the event that she does.'

Peter Melly put his head down. 'I see.'

'Good.'

İkmen stood up and led Ayşe and the Englishman out into the corridor. He was completely and utterly exhausted and all he could think about was his bed. He wasn't going to be in it for long and so he had to make the most of it. How he drove Melly back to the consulate and then himself home again he would later not be able to say.

264

Chapter 16

Spring dawns in İstanbul were more soft and gently golden than their harsher, more dramatic summer cousins. Light from the east crept a little nervously across the ancient moss-covered stone of the old mosques, hamams and palaces of Sultanahmet and the Golden Horn neighbourhoods of Fener, Balat and Eyüb. It was a time for some quiet and calm reflection before the rigors and stresses of yet another day in one of the world's most populous cities. However, with Constable Yıldız at the wheel of the police car that had been sent to fetch Ayşe from her home in Gümüşsuyu and to take her to Atatürk Airport, peace was not a commodity easily had. Although young, he gossiped like an old woman. Maybe, Ayşe thought uncharitably, it was as a result of having a girlfriend who was not only much older than he was but was also a fortune-telling gypsy too. But she didn't mention the scarily formidable gypsy artist with whom, it was rumoured, the young man had occasional passionate encounters.

'I can't believe that my friend Abdullah Ergin, you know, the Tourism . . .'

'I know what Ergin does for a living, constable,' Ayşe said as she tried to carefully rub her eyes without disturbing her make-up.

'I can't believe he'd kill anyone,' Yıldız said as he raced

265

the car across the normally choked Galata Bridge. 'His parents live in the same apartment block as us. My dad and Abdullah's dad and their families all originated in Kars. You know Abdullah and me, we both have Russian women way back in our families. Kars was a Russian city for a while, there was always fighting over Kars.'

He chattered on. Ayşe hadn't a clue about whether Abdullah Ergin had killed the carpet dealer or not. The forensic evidence seemed unequivocal and he was still in custody awaiting court appearance. But there was still no motive, no actual provable connection between Ergin and Uzun. Maybe the policeman had just been clever. Although from what Ayşe had seen of him, he certainly didn't come across that way.

After crossing the Galata Bridge, Yıldız steered the car through the steep, narrow streets of Sultanahmet and then down on to the broad Kennedy Caddesi dual carriageway that would take them, ultimately, to the airport. Even in Ayşe's short lifetime this area had changed enormously. Bordering on the Sea of Marmara, districts like Kumkapı and Yedikule had once been poor places where large families with haunted eyes lived in cramped and frequently less than sanitary accommodation. In more recent years, however, this part of the city had been given a considerable face-lift and, although the poor had still not actually disappeared completely, they had moved on. Now many of them lived in high-rise blocks out by the airport like the family of Constable Yıldız and the parents of his friend Sergeant Ergin. Ayşe, although she said nothing to her driver of this, hated the area around the airport. Apparently back in the 1970s, when the airport had been called Yeşilköy after the now long-since absorbed village of that name, some of the outer suburbs near to the airport had been quite chic.

Inspector İkmen could talk at length about the beach at the district of Ataköy, which they were now passing, where back in the 1960s he and his young friends had played at emulating Sean Connery's James Bond. The great Scottish actor had just been in the city at that time making *From Russia with Love*. Now Ataköy was famous only for its shopping mall, Galleria, with its little internal skating rink. They drove on into the area where the most tower blocks were concentrated. Yıldız, pointing at one such faceless monolith, said, 'I live there.'

Ayşe, who lived in a very pleasant low-rise apartment with her divorced brother, was tempted to commiserate with him. But Yıldız seemed happy enough. He was, in fact, a very happy, uncomplicated soul from what she had observed. Hardly as deep as the sea as some men could be, in fact probably only about as deep as some of the puddles in winter, but no less admirable because of that. She sometimes thought those with few complications and probably even fewer needs were really quite fortunate. With few wants and ambitions to gnaw at them they could just simply get on with their lives, which was really what existence was about.

With his ever-cheerful expression pinned firmly to his face, Constable Yıldız drove past the military, through the police checkpoint and into the confines of Atatürk International Airport. Just before they entered the international departures area, Ayşe received a call on her mobile. It was from a very agitated Çetin İkmen. The Bulgarian consulate had news of Matilda Melly.

He saw the woman place her bag on to the conveyor belt in front of the x-ray machine and then walk though the archway of the metal scanner. She was obviously a western European of some sort and the woman they had been instructed to look for was British, but she didn't look much like the photograph he'd been shown of Mrs Matilda Melly. For a start this one was considerably more attractive.

Although the woman didn't set off the metal detector, one of his female colleagues patted her down anyway. There was no harm to it and it just made sure that the person wasn't carrying less obvious weapons like the pair of onyx knuckle-dusters one of his colleagues had found on some mild-looking Japanese man only the week before. The inventiveness of the criminally minded was a constant source of wonder to Constable Sesler and his other police colleagues who oversaw security at the airport on a daily basis. But today was slightly different, because today Inspector Çetin İkmen was in the airport looking, for some reason, for the wife of a British diplomat. She was due to get the first flight out to London, which was in just under two hours' time now. İkmen was the city's, if not the nation's, most famous police officer and so whatever this woman had done had to be serious.

The woman's luggage was still in the x-ray machine. The female officer looking at the screen had put the belt on hold and was now frowning.

'What is it?' he asked.

'There.' She pointed at two square objects that seemed to be in the middle of the suitcase. Dense and black, it was impossible to see what was in them.

'So ask her to open her bag,' Sesler said. 'Where's she going?'

The x-ray machine operator called over to the other female officer who had just finished searching the owner of the case and said, 'Where's she going?'

268

The officer asked the woman and then called back, 'Heathrow.'

'Have a look at her passport,' Sesler called across to the search officer.

What appeared to be a small altercation then ensued between the female officer and the foreign woman. The latter now appeared to be shaking with anger. She had also become, Sesler could see, now that he was closer to her, very, very pale.

'Is there a problem?' he asked the search officer who was also very obviously far from content.

'She won't let me see her passport,' she said. 'She says she'll show it at immigration.'

'What is she?'

'British, I think.'

He turned to look down gravely at the rather brassy middle-aged woman in front of him. 'We need to see your passport now,' he said. 'You must always show your passport to a policeman. It is the law.'

'Rather simplistically expressed but in essence it is the truth,' a deep, very croaky voice said from just to the left of Sesler's back. 'Mrs Melly, I must say, you do look lovely this morning. Shall we go?' İkmen said as he put his hand out towards the woman with a smile.

'Go?' she said. 'Where?'

'Back into the city. To the station,' İkmen said. 'I have news for you, Mrs Melly, about the other Mrs Melly who tried to leave Bulgaria on a bus yesterday morning. Did you know that the woman who had your passport was Turkish?'

Her eyes went blank. 'What?'

'Oh, but I think that we would be much more comfortable talking about this at the station,' İkmen said. 'There are far

269

too many people here and I think that we are holding them up.'

'I have to catch my flight.'

İkmen sighed. 'No, I don't think so, Mrs Melly,' he said. 'I need to speak to you and some suspicious articles in your suitcase have been illuminated by this x-ray machine. I would like to have a look at them. And of course your husband is over there . . .' He pointed over to where a grey-faced and yawning Peter Melly leaned up against a flashing advertising board.

There was just a very small moment when she looked as if she might try to run away, but then Matilda Melly sighed deeply, pulled the long and silky hairpiece she'd put on the night before out of her own short mop, and took İkmen's hand in hers with a tired sigh.

Ayşe Farsakoğlu accompanied İkmen, Mr and Mrs Melly and Constable Yıldız back to the station where she assisted in the search of the woman's suitcase. It was an odd mixture of things especially in terms of clothes. They ranged from the border-line pornographic basque at the top of the case right down to some blue cardigans that could have belonged to a quiet woman of over eighty. On top of this there was a huge amount of make-up and then there was something else too; something that Ayşe told İkmen about just before he and Inspector İskender went in to interview the Englishwoman. Ayşe herself had, after all, to go back to the airport in order to meet Mr Lee Roberts, grandson of the rightful owner of the Lawrence Kerman carpet. In a way she was looking forward to it as, at the very least, a chance to practise her English. But she would also have liked to have been in with İkmen too – if only to see the expression on Matilda Melly's face. İkmen, after all, had some very big news – if news it indeed was – for her. With a small wave of recognition in the direction of Ayşe, İkmen closed the door behind İskender, Mrs Melly and himself and the interview began.

'Mrs Melly,' he said as he sat down in one of the two chairs opposite the Englishwoman, 'we have it on record that you know a Turkish woman called Handan Ergin.'

'Yes. As you know, I taught her some English. A while ago.'

'So you haven't seen Mrs Ergin . . .'

'For months! No!' She laughed but it was a nervous sound that İkmen felt had little to do with any genuine mirth.

'I see.' He looked across at Metin İskender who shrugged. Until the 'other' Matilda Melly was back in Turkey nothing could be certain, mainly because the woman was refusing to tell the Bulgarians anything about herself. But they were sending her back from Sofia later on that afternoon and then they would see.

'Mrs Melly,' İkmen continued, 'my officers have found a considerable amount of money in your suitcase. I am told it is in pounds sterling. Would you care to tell me about it?'

'It's English money. I am English. It's my money.'

'How much is there? In the suitcase?'

She shrugged. 'I'm not entirely sure. Maybe about fifty-seven, fifty-eight thousand . . .'

'Not sixty thousand?'

She frowned. 'No . . .'

'Because you see,' İkmen said, 'we know your husband gave one hundred and twenty thousand pounds in cash to the carpet dealer Yaşar Uzun. Approximately half of that sum we

271

can account for due to payments made by Mr Uzun to various people. But sixty thousand pounds is still missing. My officers are counting the cash in your suitcase right now, Mrs Melly. Is there anything you would like to tell us about it?'

'No.'

'So it is your money, as opposed to that of your husband?'

'Yes.'

He sat tight against the back of his chair and then lit a cigarette. 'The money is yours, from your bank?'

'Yes, my savings.' She was beginning to look bewildered. 'What . . .'

'Because your husband, Mrs Melly, seems to think that you and he are not particularly well off.' He smiled. 'I mean, I know that he was in the process of buying the Lawrence carpet without your knowledge or permission, but with over fifty thousand pounds in the bank, surely your worries about mortgages raised on your house in England are not as serious . . .'

'Peter doesn't know about my money,' Matilda Melly put in sharply. 'It's mine. My savings.'

'Savings?' İkmen frowned. 'You mean from a job or investments . . .'

'Inheritance,' she said as she looked up and smiled full-faced into İkmen's eyes. 'From a deceased aunt.'

'About which your husband didn't know?'

Metin İskender raised one elegant and sceptical eyebrow.

'No,' she said as she looked down at the floor once again. 'No, I didn't tell him. As you can probably infer, Inspector, my husband and I do not have the easiest of marriages.'

'His infidelities?'

She first sighed and then scratched her head. 'He's a man, it's to be expected.'

272

'His spending,' İkmen continued. 'Out of control and upon things that I feel mean little to you.'

Matilda Melly looked up again. 'Carpets? Yes. Nice enough, but . . .'

'You do not have a passion for them as your husband does.' İkmen smiled. 'Not of course to say that you don't have passions, Mrs Melly.'

Her eyes, if not the rest of her face, flinched. 'What?'

'Passions,' İkmen said. 'You have passions.'

'Well we all have passions, don't we?' Again the nervous little laugh. 'Well, don't we?'

'Indeed.' İkmen looked across at Metin İskender again and said, 'Mine is my job and my family. I think that Inspector İskender is of a roughly similar mind. Although I have heard, Inspector, that you and your wife also enjoy collecting rare books.'

'Yes,' İskender replied, frowning as he did so and then starting to say in Turkish, 'What—'

'So yes, passions, interest, whatever one may call such things, are very nice,' İkmen said. And then the smile went suddenly. The effect of this was as if someone had quickly turned off all the heating in the room. 'However,' he continued, 'when such passions are for sexual congress with men who are not your husband, then the word passion can take a sinister turn. Mrs Melly, have you been having affairs with other men since you have been living in Peri?'

'That's none of your business!' Her face contorted into something that, in spite of the lovingly applied make-up, was old and bitter.

'In the normal course of events, you would be quite right, it is none of my business,' İkmen replied. 'But if one of your lovers was the carpet dealer Yaşar Uzun . . .'

273

Matilda Melly laughed. 'Yaşar? Are you kidding?'

'Kidding?' It was rare that there was an English word that İkmen didn't understand, but this was one of them.

'Joking,' she said. 'Are you joking?'

Ah.' He first smiled and then let his face drop again. 'No. No, Mrs Melly, I am not "kidding" as you say. From the evidence that I have so far it is perfectly possible to me that this situation has happened.'

'What, my having an affair with Yaşar Uzun?' She laughed. 'But that's ridiculous. I hardly knew the man. And what I did know, I didn't like. He was into carpets, for God's sake! He ripped off my husband!'

İkmen shrugged. 'Mr Uzun and your husband would, I think, disagree that the Lawrence carpet was in some way over-valued,' he said. 'But that is not relevant. Mrs Melly, if I check to see whether or not this aunt you speak of did indeed leave you money, what will I find?'

She paused for a moment before replying, 'You'll find that my Aunt Jane, Jane Harrison, left me money, some years—'

'How much?'

Matilda Melly leaned forward, a small smile now on her lips, and said, 'What, you mean how much money . . .'

'Yes.'

She didn't answer, pretending to think.

He put his cigarette out before lighting another and leaning across the table at her. 'You see,' he said, 'Mrs Melly, what you should know is that your husband Peter instructed his bank, HSBC, to make a record of all the serial numbers of the sterling notes that he gave to Yaşar Uzun.'

He looked at her face for any slight sign or change of colour, but none was forthcoming.

'And so,' he continued, 'if a significant number of the banknotes in your suitcase correspond to the numbers recorded by HSBC, then I can reach only two conclusions. Either that Mr Uzun and yourself were lovers or partners in some way and that you shared the money that was paid for the carpet by your husband. Or that you or someone you know took the money from Uzun just before or just after his death. That person may have killed him, you . . .'

'I want a lawyer,' she cut in suddenly. Now her face was pale, very pale.

'That is your right . . .'

She banged a fist down on to the table before standing up and saying, 'Now!'

İkmen looked across at İskender and then both men watched as the Englishwoman turned her body and her face to the bare wall behind the desk.

Although fully aware of the fact that he wasn't at police head-quarters because of anything he had done wrong, Lee Roberts was made uncomfortable by the look and the smell of the place. Functional and featureless, the place reeked of sweat, stale cigarettes and a sort of sweetish odour, which he later discovered was the lemon-scented cologne that a lot of people chose to sterilise their hands with both before and after eating. However, the office that the very attractive female officer ushered him into was not nearly as smelly as the rest of the building seemed to be. Tidy and clean, it was not, the young woman told him, the office of the man he had thought he had come to see.

'Inspector İkmen cannot come,' she said in her slightly husky, very sexy voice. 'Sorry. A colleague, Inspector

Süleyman, will come now. He knows all things about this problems that you have. Can I get you tea?'

Lee Roberts said that would be very nice. He was both tired and dehydrated after his flight from London. Tea would perk him up. And so the female officer yelled something unintelligible out into the corridor and then they both waited in silence for this other Inspector who, Lee hoped, really did know something about his grandfather's carpet. After all, it wasn't that Granddad's Lawrence of Arabia carpet was a simple matter. It was stolen, he knew, because of the drunken boasting of his own father. Lee had things to tell the Turkish police that he knew they didn't yet know. Things that he was aware would complicate matters, probably to his detriment. He felt for the old photograph his grandfather had taken of the Kerman many years before and then looked up and smiled. In his mid-thirties, Lee Roberts was a slim, pleasant-looking man – his smile making the Turkish policewoman blush just a little. But then it was a very open, available smile which was not surprising in view of the fact that Lee was recently divorced and openly on the lookout for a new woman in his life.

'Mr Roberts?'

He looked around for the source of the deep, male voice and found himself looking at a tall, incredibly handsome man in early middle age. The female officer who had collected him from Atatürk Airport was also looking up at the tall, handsome man with rapt attention. Lee inwardly bowed to the far superior competition and then stood up and offered the man his hand.

'Lee Roberts.' He then noticed that the man had his right arm in a sling. 'Oh . . .'

'A little accident. It is nothing,' the man said. Then he told him his name, 'Inspector Süleyman.'

'Nice to meet you, Inspector.'

Süleyman moved behind his desk and sat down. 'Please do sit down, Mr Roberts,' he said.

Lee Roberts sat.

'Now I apologise that Inspector İkmen cannot be here,' Süleyman said. 'But something very, how do you say? Something very pressing has arisen and he must go to deal with that. Scotland Yard are satisfied we understand that you are the grandson of the Private Victor Roberts who was the servant of T. E. Lawrence. You do, Mr Roberts, have the documents they told you to bring?'

'Yes.' He took the photograph of the carpet out of his pocket and then dug inside his hand luggage for his passport and birth certificate plus a sheaf of documents that had belonged to his late grandfather – birth certificate, military pay-books etc.

Süleyman passed a cursory eye over this paperwork before he said, 'We will need to make photocopies and you will need to sign a document saying that we have given the carpet back to you. I will have a copy in English for you to look at.'

'That's very kind,' Lee said.

'It's nothing.'

Lee Roberts could very easily have left it at that, taken the Kerman, gone back to Britain, and lived happily ever after. It's what his father would have done. But Lee was more like his late grandfather than his own old man. After all, it hadn't been Victor who had been so happy to find the Kerman in that antique shop in İstanbul all those years ago. He'd only allowed Stanley, Lee's father, to buy the carpet on condition that they both at some point had a stab at finding its rightful

277

owner. But after Antalya and the theft of the carpet that had been impossible. Victor, at least, had died a very sad man because of it.

'Inspector Süleyman,' Lee said after a pause. 'I have something to tell you.'

'Oh? What is that?'

'I don't own the Lawrence carpet,' Lee Roberts said. 'Victor, my grandfather, gave it away here in İstanbul, back in 1920. The person he gave it to is the only rightful owner.'

Chapter 17

İkmen looked down at his watch and then turned to Metin İskender. 'We'd better get to the airport,' he said. 'Pick up this other "Matilda Melly" from the Bulgarians.'

'What do you think they're talking about?' İskender replied as he tipped his head in the direction of Peter Melly in seemingly rapt conversation with his wife's appointed lawyer.

'I don't know,' İkmen said as he lit up a cigarette and then leaned against the corridor wall. 'But I think that, in some way, Peter Melly still loves his wife.'

'I didn't know that he didn't love her,' İskender said.

'I'm saying that he does.' İkmen smiled. 'Not that he is necessarily in love with her, you understand. Peter Melly has had affairs. But I think that Matilda is essential to him in that way that a lot of long-term wives are essential to their husbands. There is a comfort in the familiarity.'

İskender looked at him slightly questioningly. After all, İkmen himself had been married for a very long time. Not that he felt in even the slightest way that Fatma was just little more than a comfortable familiarity. Fatma İkmen was many things but a mere habit was not one of them.

While first İkmen and then İskender finished their cigarettes, they watched Peter Melly and the lawyer who had been

279

allocated to his wife talk in a huddle at a corner of the corridor. The lawyer, who İkmen recognised as one of the more fluent English speakers, was considerably overweight and frequently mopped his sweating brow with a handkerchief. Far too much rich food and probably liberal amounts of alcohol too, İkmen surmised, and then, looking down at his own bony fingers, he smiled. Not that this fat, overblown lawyer would, if he were right, do Mrs Melly very much good. If he was indeed correct, then Mrs Melly was already as good as lost.

That this Englishman, Mr Roberts, now said that he didn't own the Lawrence carpet was not what Mehmet Süleyman had been expecting. The carpet was worth a lot of money. But he was insisting it wasn't his. He was also, to Süleyman's slight irritation, beginning to expound what promised to be a long and possibly rambling story. Although not regretting taking Mr Roberts on on İkmen's behalf, he nevertheless felt that the older man was more equipped to deal with the Englishman than himself.

'When the First World War ended, this city was occupied by allied troops,' Lee Roberts said. 'Mainly, I have to confess, from the UK.'

Süleyman, who was now smoking a Gauloise, tipped his head to show that he had understood. The Allied occupation of İstanbul at the end of the Great War was not his favourite topic, but Roberts had said he had a story to tell and now he was telling it.

'So Granddad came here with the army,' the Englishman continued. 'He told me a bit about it. It wasn't pretty. There was hunger and despair and . . .'

'Our people had yet to rise again as they did in the War of

Independence, Mr Roberts,' Süleyman said. 'The Ottomans had been defeated and we do not, believe me, take defeat well.'

'No, well . . .' Süleyman looked as if he could have been a general or something in years gone by. It had not been often in his life that Lee Roberts had come across such a haughty bearing. He silently thanked God for the presence of the female sergeant who had got his tea and appeared to be a far easier character all round.

'So,' Lee Roberts said, 'Granddad was in İstanbul with the Lawrence carpet. He really treasured it, you know. Colonel Lawrence had been good to him. Granddad did some things in this city that later he was not proud of but there were some that he was proud of. The main one being when he rescued a lady from a gang of drunken sailors.'

'A Turkish lady?'

'Yes. Granddad said that her face was covered by a veil. He never in all the time that he was with her saw her whole face. But she had, he said, amazing eyes.'

'And Victor Roberts rescued her?'

'Yes. I think, reading between the lines – Granddad was quite a prude really, always found it difficult to actually give things their proper names – that the sailors were trying to rape the woman. By a combination of shouting, threatening them with his pistol and pushing them off, Granddad managed to free the lady from them.'

'He did a very good thing,' Süleyman said.

'Yes.' Lee Roberts smiled. 'He was a good sort, my granddad. I miss him.' He turned his head to one side away from the handsome man and, even more importantly, the pretty female police officer. There was no need for either of

281

them to see his tears. Victor had been dead for years, but Lee still mourned him every day. Unlike his own father, his granddad had been a decent, moral man. 'But anyway,' he continued, 'by way of a sort of reward for what Granddad had done, the lady asked him to come to her home so that she could offer him a drink and some food. He tried to decline, knowing how poor the people were at that time, but she insisted and so he escorted her back to what was, he said, a considerable house.'

'She was rich?'

'I think she had been,' Lee said. 'The way Granddad told it, she still had servants who lurked around as sort of chaperones really, but very little in the way of food. But she spoke a little English and he could speak a bit of Turkish by that time and so in a weird kind of way they got on. She was a very proud lady, Victor always said, but he knew that she and her servants were starving. For several months he took them food . . .'

Süleyman looked at this pale stranger and wondered what on earth his sad story might be leading up to. Although, unlike İkmen, he hadn't followed the whole Lawrence carpet affair through from the beginning, he was, in spite of the rambling nature of the tale, intrigued.

'He would, he said, turn up when he could which was generally a couple of times a week. As they ate, the lady slipping food underneath her veil, they talked. He told her about his life with his wife and children in North London. She spoke little about her life apart from going over what the servants were doing. But he was all right with that, understanding that the lady was a proper and reserved sort of person.'

282

'Quite so.'

Lee Roberts took in a deep breath and then said, 'Until the day that he gave her the Lawrence carpet, that is.'

Süleyman frowned. He hoped he was not going to be treated to a tale of western depravity and salaciousness. Victor Roberts had not, he trusted, taken this poor lone Turkish woman for himself and then given her a mere carpet for her troubles? But then he remembered that Roberts had never seen the lady's face.

'The lady told Granddad, out of the blue, about how she had lost her fiancé in the desert of Arabia. Apparently he hadn't even got to the, what do they call it, the theatre of war, the battle, when he died. She mourned him bitterly. The Ministry of War people here had told her that he had died on a train, one that it was said had been blown up by Colonel Lawrence. So she told my grandfather all this and when he asked her whether she knew where her fiancé had died, she said that she did. It was at Ma'an in Jordan.' He paused as if for effect.

Not being as au fait with the whole Lawrence carpet story as İkmen had been, Süleyman just shrugged.

Lee Roberts, taking the hint, said, 'The dynamited train at Ma'an was, so Lawrence told my grandfather, where he had obtained the Kerman carpet. The story went that he took it from a very beautiful dying Turkish officer. Then of course the fact that this young man's blood was all over the carpet was seen as a sort of symbolic victory over him and his people. It was honourable booty, if you like. Now, knowing what we do about T. E. Lawrence, we can put a rather more homo-erotic interpretation on this event. Not that my grandfather would have done so, but—'

283

'Are you saying', Süleyman asked, 'that the blood of this lady's fiancé is on that carpet?'

'No,' Lee Roberts replied, 'I'm not. But for my grandfather it was certainly a possibility. And I think that when he heard the lady's story he felt very sorry for her, which was why he gave her the carpet. It was, he felt, as if he were giving something of her lost love back to her. She wouldn't take it at first, but when he insisted she, apparently, held the thing up to her veiled face, kissing the wool through the gauze around her mouth. Granddad wasn't a soft man by any means, but he admitted that the sight of it brought him close to tears.'

'Indeed.'

'She put the carpet in a wooden box to preserve it from harm, which is how Granddad knew what it was when he saw it in the shop in İstanbul back in the eighties. He was shocked to see it. He had, you see, entertained some hope of trying to revisit the lady when he got to İstanbul with my dad. But he knew that if the carpet was for sale, she was in all probability dead. She would never have parted with it willingly, it meant too much to her. And when the man who sold it to him told him that the previous owner of the piece, who was indeed a lady, had died leaving no descendants, Granddad knew he really had to buy it. To him it was the only way to stop it falling into the hands of those who wouldn't appreciate its meaning.' He sighed. 'And then my stupid father went and told the world and his wife about Granddad's famous carpet . . .'

'When it was stolen?'

'Yes.'

'I see.' Süleyman nodded his head while looking at the pale

284

man in front of him. 'Mr Roberts, forgive me, but if this lady had no descendants . . . I mean, where did she come from in the city? Do you know?'

'A place I understand has completely changed character,' Lee Roberts replied. 'Nişantaşı . . .'

'Ah!' Süleyman smiled. 'Yes, there were many old mansions of the rich and aristocratic in that area.' He didn't add that several of them had been owned by his family. 'But they burned or fell down a long time ago. Now it is a very smart shopping area.'

'Yes, Granddad told me that when he did go there after he'd bought the carpet he didn't recognise anything. It made him feel very sad. The carpet dealer told him that the lady, a princess, she was, had died back in the fifties. Poor Granddad, he'd left his return journey far too long. I think that in his own way he mourned the Princess Gözde for the rest of his life. I think he may have been a little in love with her.'

For a moment, a now frowning Süleyman didn't say a word. When he did, however, Lee Roberts noticed that the policeman's face had become very pale.

'The Princess *Gözde*, you say?' Süleyman said with a slight tremble in his voice. 'Are you sure about that name, Mr Roberts?'

When İkmen and İskender eventually joined Matilda Melly and her lawyer, Mr Aksoy, in Interview Room 2 they noticed that the Englishwoman was looking far more relaxed than she had before. The last sighting they'd had of her had been of a very distressed and agitated woman. The woman had obviously spoken to her lawyer, whom the two policemen had seen

285

talking to her husband, but what had been said they didn't know.

'So, Mrs Melly, where were we?' İkmen said as he sat down, looking as he did so at a piece of paper in his hands.

It wasn't Matilda Melly who answered, but her lawyer. 'Çetin Bey,' he said in English with a smile, 'the husband of Mrs Melly would like to put right a wrong that he has done to his wife.'

İkmen looked up from the paper sharply. 'Oh?'

Shrugging his thick, meaty shoulders Aksoy said, 'When Mr Peter Melly said that he did not see his wife on the night that the carpet dealer died, he was wrong.'

Raising a very sceptical eyebrow at Metin İskender, İkmen said, 'Oh? And how was he "wrong"?'

'It was, as you say . . .' He looked towards his client for assistance.

'It was spite, Inspector,' Matilda Melly said. 'I will be completely open with you and admit that Yaşar Uzun and myself were lovers. Peter knew . . .'

'So both you and your husband lied to us.'

'Yes, we did. But then what would you do?' she said. 'Yaşar was dead, murdered. Peter and I, as lover and lover's husband, were bound to have been in the frame. We didn't want that! But then when I left, well, Peter became spiteful. He said that he hadn't seen me at home on the night that Yaşar died.'

'You sleep apart from your husband, Mrs Melly. Under the circumstances it is not strange that he should not see you when he came home from the carpet show.'

'Yes, but I always sleep with the bedroom door open. He saw me as he walked past my room. Ask him yourself.'

286

'I will,' İkmen said and then with a smile he went back to looking down at the piece of paper in his hands.

Seconds, then a minute, passed during which İkmen continued to look down at the paper and İskender just sat back in his chair with a neutral and calm expression on his face. At length Mr Aksoy leaned across the table towards İkmen and was about to speak when Metin İskender said, 'Mrs Melly, the paper Inspector İkmen is holding has on it a list of numbers. They are the numbers of the banknotes that were supplied by the HSBC to your husband to give to Yaşar Uzun. The notes found in your suitcase correspond to them. Fifty-seven thousand pounds is the total. Nothing to do with any savings at all.'

İkmen, watching Matilda Melly over the top of his list, noticed that her expression didn't change. 'Mrs Melly,' he said, 'did you know that your husband was giving Yaşar Uzun one hundred and twenty thousand pounds for the Kerman carpet?'

'Not at the time, no,' she said. 'I was furious when Yaşar told me. I think he thought I'd be pleased, knowing what I felt or rather didn't feel about Peter.'

'And yet you pretended to your husband that you didn't know of such a deal, did you not, Mrs Melly?'

'Yes.'

'And why was that, please?'

She looked at Aksoy before replying. 'Because his playing fast and loose with our money was going to give me the excuse I needed to leave', she said and then added, 'with, as you know, almost half of the money that Peter had given Yaşar. All without having to go to court.'

'Did Mr Uzun give you the money or did you take it from his dead body?'

287

A look of utter outrage settled on her face. 'I didn't kill Yaşar!' she said.

'I didn't say that you did,' İkmen replied. 'I said only that you might have taken the money from his dead body.'

'But I didn't! Yaşar gave me that money. I intended to leave Peter anyway . . .'

'For Mr Uzun?'

'God no! Not my type at all!' she laughed. Then she leaned forwards across the table. 'Yaşar gave me half the money to shut me up,' she said. 'He didn't want me protesting and spoiling his little deal with Peter and he'd still get a hundred and eighty thousand pounds at the end of it all which is no small amount. I was still unsure as to when was going to be the best time to leave Peter when, as you know, Yaşar suddenly died.'

'Mmm.'

'But the point, Çetin Bey,' Mr Aksoy the lawyer said in Turkish, 'is that Mrs Melly could not possibly have killed the carpet dealer because her husband saw her asleep in her bed on the night of the killing.'

'Provided he is telling the truth, that is so,' İkmen replied in English. 'But is he, Mr Aksoy? Or is Mr Melly saying what he is saying because he wishes to protect his wife?'

'But she has left him . . .'

'Or maybe he is protecting himself,' İkmen said. 'Maybe Mr Melly killed Yaşar Uzun.'

'Oh, I do not think that is possible,' Aksoy said in English. 'Unless you have any forensic evidence that might point towards Mr Melly as the murderer.'

'No,' İkmen replied. 'No I don't.' He looked at Matilda Melly and then said, 'In fact, I actually know that Mr Melly did not kill Yaşar Uzun.'

The Englishwoman smiled. 'How?'

'Because I know who did kill him,' İkmen said. 'It was you, Mrs Melly.'

Chapter 18

Mehmet Süleyman had left Mr Roberts with Ayşe Farsakoğlu in order to go out into the corridor to speak on his mobile to his father. Without telling the old man any details about Mr Roberts, he had quizzed Muhammed Süleyman Efendi first about relatives in general who had lived in Nişantaşı and then more pointedly about his aunt the Princess Gözde. Received wisdom in the family was that she had lost her fiancé in the Great War. Totally reclusive and permanently veiled, the Princess Gözde, whose mansion had been situated on Teşvikiye Caddesi, had died at the end of the 1950s. She seemed to fit the description that Lee Roberts had given him of Victor's 'princess' very well.

'Your grandfather inherited all of her effects,' Muhammed Süleyman told his son. 'Including that carpet Raşit Bey is being so very obtuse about.'

'So did you inherit any other effects from the Princess Gözde's house, Father?' Mehmet said in what he hoped was not too loud a voice. Mr Roberts was, after all, only just a corridor and one door's thickness away from him.

'Who can say?' the old man replied. 'When your grand-father died all of his remaining possessions were divided up equally between your Uncle Beyazıt, your Aunt Esma and myself. There wasn't that much. My father sold many things in his lifetime.'

Mehmet thought briefly about this similarity between his father and his grandfather, but then Muhammed said, 'Why do you want to know?'

Thinking as quickly as he could, he said, 'Well, I don't have a great deal to do until İzzet contacts me and we see what he has discovered in the east about one of our cases. It's a long story. But while I haven't had too much to do I have been thinking about your carpet and you know how we talked of its provenance? And also about how maybe if people knew Princess Gözde's story they might be more interested in it and . . .'

'Oh, well, then you will need to speak to your Aunt Esma about that,' Muhammed Süleyman said. 'She was the only one who ever visited the Princess Gözde on a regular basis. They got on for some reason. Go and see her. She'd be delighted to see you.'

After a few standard niceties, Mehmet ended the call. He leaned against the corridor wall and thought. Aunt Esma. He hadn't seen her for over a year – not, in fact, since the Feast of the Sacrifice. For once the entire family had been together to savour the sheep that his religious and strong-stomached Uncle Beyazıt had slaughtered in honour of the prophet İbrahim's near sacrifice of his son. The Feast of the Sacrifice was a very important Muslim festival. Not that one could have deduced this from Aunt Esma. She, as usual, had been far more interested in talking about her health than in joining in the general festivities. Tall, thin and the epitome of the unmarried and unmarriageable woman so many wealthy families used to number in their ranks, Esma lived in a tiny damp apartment down by the Golden Horn in Fener. After a few moments during which he attempted to gather his thoughts, Süleyman went back into his office.

'I apologise, Mr Roberts,' he said as he sat down behind his desk once again. 'It was necessary for me to check some facts. Now, if I am correct, I take it you would like us to try to find what remains of the family of this Princess Gözde.'

'Yes,' Lee Roberts replied. 'Whether they know it or not, the carpet will have some meaning for them. I mean, I understand that no one, not even my grandfather, could be certain that the blood on the carpet was that of the princess's fiancé. But that she believed it to be so makes it important and valid.'

Süleyman frowned. The way this man was speaking was very familiar. 'Mr Roberts,' he said, 'what do you do for a living?'

Lee Roberts laughed. 'Oh, God, was I talking psychobabble? I'm a clinical psychologist.'

'Ah.' Süleyman smiled. 'My wife is a psychiatrist.'

'So you understood the psycho—'

'Somewhat. But Mr Roberts, we must proceed. How long do you stay in İstanbul?'

'A week.'

'I see.' Süleyman offered Lee Roberts a cigarette, which he declined, and then lit one up for himself. 'Mr Roberts, I will try to find out what I can. There is a lady I have just found out about who may be able to help. If you give me your contact details here in İstanbul I will keep you informed.'

The Englishman took the printout of his hotel details out of his pocket and then wrote his own mobile telephone number on the bottom. When he'd finished he said, 'Inspector, could I please see the carpet now? I've only this old photograph of it which Victor said was taken in the garden of the mansion in Nişantaşı.' He put the photograph down on to Süleyman's desk. 'But I've never seen it in the flesh, as it were.'

293

Süleyman leaned forward the better to see the faded sepia print in front of him. It showed what looked to him very like the carpet that was currently locked up in İkmen's office. It was laid out on some dry and scrub-like grass, and behind the carpet a large, dark building of vaguely gothic design could be seen.

'Mr Roberts,' he said once he had finished studying the photograph, 'can I take a scan of this picture?'

'I don't see why not.'

'Good.' He stood up, and looking across at Ayşe Farsakoğlu, he said, 'If you would please go with the sergeant here, she will show you the carpet. Inspector İkmen has also, I believe, the remains of the box the carpet was once kept in.'

'Why would I kill Yaşar Uzun?' Matilda Melly said as she watched both İkmen and İskender light up yet more cigarettes. 'Why?'

'Because he betrayed you,' İkmen said. 'He was having affairs with . . .'

'He was always having affairs with other women!' Matilda said. 'Bloody hell, he was a carpet dealer! It's what they do, isn't it?'

'Some would say that, yes,' İkmen replied. 'But not all carpet dealers are the same and I believe few would agree to buy a property in a foreign country to share with one of his conquests. You must have been very hurt when you discovered that the romantic house he had bought in Balchik was not all that he owned in Bulgaria. He didn't tell you about the apartment in Sofia, did he, Mrs Melly?'

'I don't know what you're talking about.'

'Mr Melly has told me that you always wanted to live by

294

the sea. Yaşar Uzun and you, once you had both defrauded your husband, were going to go and live in Balchik, by the sea, where Queen Marie of Romania had once lived with her young Turkish lover. But then you discovered the existence of the Sofia apartment and you asked him about it. He denied it even existed which led you to the conclusion that he must have bought it for a purpose he didn't want you to know about. A romantic purpose . . .'

She laughed. 'This is nonsense,' she said. 'Utterly. I don't know anything about any house in Bulgaria, let alone a flat.'

'Your computer would seem to disagree with you,' İkmen said. 'There is plenty of information you have accessed about Balchik on there. I think you have a very romantic nature, Mrs Melly.'

'Also, the other Mrs Melly is of another opinion,' Metin İskender said.

'The person who stole Mrs Melly's passport?' the lawyer Mr Aksoy said.

İkmen smiled. 'Oh, no,' he said, 'she didn't steal it. Mrs Melly gave it to her.' He turned to the Englishwoman and asked, 'It's right you gave your British passport to Handan Ergin, isn't it?'

'No.' Her face was red now. Underneath all that make-up a rash was showing through. 'How do you . . .'

'Mrs Ergin told us all about it,' İkmen said. 'How you gave her the passport. How she made herself up to look old. Interesting details. She had some time to think clearly on the plane back from Sofia.'

'You mean she had time to make things up!' the Englishwoman said. 'It's rubbish!'

'Maybe, although why she should want to make such a

295

story up, I cannot imagine,' İkmen said. 'You are both in a lot of trouble irrespective of who might have done what. Mrs Ergin says that you used her husband's gun to kill Yaşar Uzun.'

A moment of stunned silence passed. Metin İskender leaned his chair back against the wall and swung his feet loosely beneath him.

'Mrs Ergin says that she gave you her husband's gun because she wanted to implicate him in a crime. As you know he stifled her, he also beat her too. She wanted to get rid of him. For your part,' İkmen said, 'I think that you had fallen out of love with the carpet dealer some time before. Your discovery of his separate apartment plans was just an excuse for what was done. So much of your recent existence would seem to me, Mrs Melly, an excuse. However . . .' He leaned on the table, took a drag from his cigarette, and then blew smoke in Matilda Melly's direction. 'Because,' he continued, 'although Yaşar Uzun had bought the little house on the Bulgarian coast for you both to share, you had not intended to live in it with him. You'd found a far better young Turkish lover than Yaşar to share that house with. You had found, Mrs Melly, the love of your life.'

Matilda Melly licked her lips before saying, 'This is what she says, is it? Handan Ergin?'

'Yes.'

'And you believe her?'

İkmen shrugged. 'I know that you killed Mr Uzun, Mrs Melly, beyond that . . .'

'I didn't kill him! She did!' She blurted. She then put a hand over her mouth and looked, terrified, at her lawyer. Mr Aksoy just simply shrugged. 'No . . . Yes . . . I . . . She wanted her husband implicated in something in order to get rid of him and I looked after the baby while she did it. But I didn't kill Yaşar! Why would I? He was an inoffensive chap deep down, he helped me get money from Peter. We shared it out sixty thousand to him, sixty thousand to me. He bought the house in which we were both going to live . . .'

'And yet you let her kill him by your own admission, Mrs Melly.'

'No I didn't! She went out that night to do something – I didn't know what! I said I'd look after the baby. She told me later about Yaşar. I was appalled.'

'I am confused,' Mr Aksoy said. 'Why would Mrs Ergin kill a carpet dealer she did not know?'

Matilda Melly looked at İkmen, shrugged her shoulders helplessly, and said, 'You think you know everything about everything. Tell him.'

'With the reservation that I do not believe Mrs Ergin killed the carpet dealer, I think that all of this happened because, Mr Aksoy, your client fell in love with Handan Ergin.'

The lawyer looked across at Matilda Melly with an expression of utter incredulity on his face.

'Now according to Mrs Ergin,' İkmen said, 'this love affair went only in one direction. You loved her, Mrs Melly, but while she was tired of her autocratic husband, she was not intending to replace him with you.'

Matilda Melly's face became a deep blood-red.

'She freely admits that she gave you the gun with which to kill Yaşar Uzun. She wanted to implicate her husband and get rid of him. But you shot Yaşar to get him out of the way, didn't you? You shot him so that once Abdullah Ergin was safely in prison, you could go and live with his wife in a lovely romantic place in Bulgaria.'

'I didn't shoot Yaşar. Peter saw me in my bed . . .'

'Oh, please!' İkmen said as he shook his head sorrowfully. 'Please! Mrs Melly, you and I both know that Mr Melly wants to change his original story in order that he may come out of this affair with something – namely you. The poor man has lost everything! Money, his carpet, and you have suddenly decided, or so it seems to me, that you are a lesbian . . .'

'Peter saw me in my bed. He is prepared to . . .'

'Mrs Melly, you have already admitted that you or Mrs Ergin killed Uzun,' İkmen said. 'Handan Ergin, like you, cannot drive. The journey from her home on Professor Kazim İsmail Gürkan Caddesi to Peri is a long one – the nosey neighbour I took you to see would have recognised her. For Mrs Ergin to go and wait for some unspecified time amongst the trees and then come back again would be ridiculous. Better that you go. You, after all, knew Mr Uzun – he did not know Mrs Ergin. He would not have stopped his car for her, not at night anyway. And yet he stopped his car for someone, who then went on to shoot him. It is my belief you had arranged to meet him on his way out of the village. You can, after all, walk to the murder site from your home. I think it quite possible that Yaşar Uzun chose to leave the Klaassens' house when he did in order to make the rendezvous with you, Mrs Melly.'

'Oh, and then I just shot him, cleared up and then went calmly back to my bed.'

'Made up, as we have seen, people find it hard to recognise you,' İkmen replied. 'But then in Peri who is going to be about at night? You went home, got into your lonely bed and your husband knew nothing about it.' He paused. 'Or rather that is what Handan Ergin has told us.'

'Mrs Ergin has told us much,' İskender interjected.

'Oh, and you believe her, do you? Because she's a Turk, I suppose!'

'Mrs Melly, Mrs Ergin has condemned herself out of her own mouth,' İkmen said. 'She wanted to get rid of her husband and she didn't care that Yaşar Uzun's death was the vehicle for that process. After going to Bulgaria she did indeed intend to meet you in London. But she was never going to stay with you, Mrs Melly.'

Matilda Melly laughed, but without much mirth. 'No, but you are wrong, you see. *She* is in love with *me*. I . . .'

'Mrs Melly, let me ask you something,' İkmen said. 'Please tell me if your relationship with Mrs Ergin was ever physical?'

Aksoy the lawyer looked shocked and even mopped his tall, outraged brow with a handkerchief. He'd heard a lot of things in his long years of practice at law, but lesbians! Turkish lesbians! His client, Mrs Melly, had said nothing to him about such 'unnatural' practices!

Seconds passed into minutes as Matilda Melly, her eyes now fixed stonily on İkmen's face, said nothing. At length the policeman said, 'As I thought. No, Mrs Melly. No, your relationship was never physical . . .'

'She wasn't ready, I didn't want to . . . Our love was pure, without men, it was . . .'

'She used you, Mrs Melly,' İkmen said. 'She knew you loved her. And then, although you had started to cool towards him by that time, when Yaşar Uzun bought that extra apartment in Sofia she used your hurt pride to propel you towards murder. That at least is my opinion. After you fell for her, carrying on teaching her was hard and so you left Mrs Monroe's little school. But you continued to see Handan in secret –

maybe to soothe the bruises that her husband gave her. Then he stopped her going to English classes and Mrs Ergin's mind became enraged.'

'I didn't do it! Handan didn't do it! Why . . .'

'You just said that she did, Mrs Melly. What are you doing? You are confused, I think . . .'

'I . . .' Matilda Melly began to cry.

'And what, exactly, did you mean, Mrs Melly, when you talked just now about "clearing up" after Yaşar Uzun's death? He was shot, his car came off the road, what was there to clear?'

'Well, nothing, it's just a figure of speech,' she said. 'I didn't do it myself and so I can only conjecture what someone might have done after the event. Clearing up is . . . well, anyone would . . . clear up . . .'

'No,' İkmen said, 'not everyone. Most people would be anxious to get away from the scene of the crime, Mrs Melly. Everything in your house will be examined by our forensics experts, especially brooms and other sweeping implements. Clearing up is important to me too.'

'I didn't do it!' Matilda Melly said through her tears. 'I didn't do it!'

'Well, then, if you didn't, you had better start telling me the truth now,' İkmen said. 'Because believe me, Mrs Melly, Mrs Ergin has told us everything on her side with only the possible exception of her shoe size. Either you or she did it! Which one of you is it to be?'

İzzet Melik returned from Hakkari later on that afternoon carrying a whole sheaf of papers and information related to the life and death of Deniz Koç. Of course until the young man's exhumed body had been properly examined, whether or not he had actually been murdered was still not certain. But the fact that a male nurse who had been largely responsible for his care, and who had disappeared shortly after İzzet Melik had arrived, was still unaccounted for was deeply suspicious. After making sure that his aunt Esma was happy to receive him later that evening, Süleyman arranged for a young constable to take him to the domestic terminal of Atatürk Airport to collect his sergeant. Süleyman was very pleased to see him. The small sigh of satisfaction that İzzet emitted when they both entered Süleyman's office seemed to suggest that he too was glad to be 'home'.

'So is there any sort of connection between this missing nurse and Cabbar Soylu?' Süleyman said as they both sat down and immediately lit cigarettes.

'Not beyond the fact that apparently Soylu always talked to this particular nurse whenever he and his wife visited, no,' İzzet replied. 'Not everyone in the east is related, you know.'

Süleyman gave him a very cynical look. 'İzzet,' he said, 'you're a man who can keep a secret, aren't you?'

'Yes.'

He half knew the tale Süleyman was about to tell him anyway, much of which had come out during the course of their odd, haunted meeting back in the Markiz patisserie. The senior man went on to tell İzzet much about Mürsel and the peeper, the unfortunate Leyla Saban and, most significantly, the role of the town of Hakkari in all of those people's lives.

'The Koç family, the Soylus, Leyla Saban's mother and the man I knew as Mürsel all had one thing in common,' he said at the end of his tale.

'Hakkari.'

'Exactly! And you say that the east is misrepresented, İzzet? Mürsel was by his own admission the father of Leyla Saban and possibly of Deniz Koç too! I tremble to think of what other relationships may have evolved within what is a very small group of people in the scheme of things.'

'True.' İzzet frowned. 'Although, Inspector, my working out in the east would not, very easily, have delivered the peeper to us, would it? I mean that was because of what you did here in the city.'

'Well, not just me,' Süleyman turned away briefly. He had not gone into the finer details surrounding the eventual arrest of Mürsel and the death of Nuri Koç. 'As I have told you, others were involved.'

'Yes, but you were there, Inspector. I was off out east and, unless this nurse when we find him eventually proves me wrong, then I wouldn't really have got any further along the trail than Cabbar Soylu. I certainly couldn't have made the connection to that Mürsel man or the peeper.'

'Maybe not.' Süleyman shrugged. 'But at least the peeper nightmare is over. It is Leyla Saban's father and Emine Soylu I feel most sorry for in all of this you know. They have lost their children. And for what? For greed, in the case of poor Deniz Koç, who died because he was inconvenient to his step-father, and in the case of Leyla Saban due to some twisted, misdirected sense of honour in the head of a father she never knew.'

'People can be vile, Inspector.'

'Yes. And don't worry, I'm not going to say anything about how much worse they are out east,' he said with a smile. 'I understand there are some very interesting places east of Kayseri.'

302

'Oh, yes,' İzzet replied. 'Lake Van is actually very beautiful and you know a lot of people are now going out to places like Mardin. There's a lot to recommend these destinations.' He paused. 'Though not necessarily the food . . .'

'Yes, I noticed that you have lost a few kilos,' Süleyman said.

'Yes . . . It was at times painful, at others just unpleasant . . .'

'Ah, but you carried on working in spite of it!'

İzzet sighed. 'Yes, Inspector, I did.'

'And although we know that the person who ordered Deniz Koç's death is himself no more, our counterparts in the east can now pursue the man who actually did the deed.' Süleyman smiled. 'Let us hope that I am tonight as adept at solving mysteries as you have been, İzzet.'

'Tonight?'

'I have to go and see an aunt of mine,' he said, 'about an aunt of hers. Great Aunt Gözde, she was called. Now she was a mystery in herself, let me tell you!'

'Before I begin,' Matilda Melly said, 'I have to know for certain that Handan did in fact say that I killed Yaşar.'

'She said just that, Mrs Melly,' İkmen replied. 'Now . . .'

'I met Handan, as you know, at Kim Monroe's English classes,' Matilda Melly said. 'We got on well. To my surprise and in spite of having a thing with Yaşar at the time, I was attracted to her. Physically. I'd never had such . . . tendencies before but . . . Well, I knew that I shouldn't do anything about it, but seeing Handan every week was torment. So I left. Fortunately or unfortunately Kim kept me abreast of what was going on in the classes, which was how I knew about the scene Handan's husband had made. It was then that I actively sought her out – I remembered where she lived from my days at the English classes. I felt so sorry for her! One day I waited on the corner of her street until she came out to do her shopping.'

'What happened then?'

'We went for coffee first of all – with the baby of course. We enjoyed each other's company . . .'

'You paid?' İkmen asked. 'For the coffee, cake . . .'

'Yes, but . . .' She pursed her lips and then said, 'It wasn't just about money. There were touches, kisses, freely given . . . Not that it wasn't innocent, you understand. We were friends. But then when she started to open up about her husband, things changed. I could see how desperate she was to get away from him. I'd already, of course, planned to leave Peter, with Yaşar. But when I discovered – I found his papers for it in his bedroom – that my carpet dealer had bought that other apartment, I felt used and cheap. He could only have another secret apartment for one reason and that was so that he could entertain other women.'

'But he entertained other women all the time,' İkmen said. 'You told me so yourself.'

'Not at my expense!' Matilda Melly responded passionately. 'The money that Yaşar had got for the carpet had been Peter's and it was meant to be for us – Yaşar and myself. Not for a horde of Bulgarian tarts!'

In the face of such obviously skewed morality, İkmen could only smile and encourage her on with her story. İskender's periodic sniffs of disgust were, İkmen felt, quite lost on Mrs Matilda Melly.

'I told Handan and she was very sympathetic. We both agreed that we'd both like to be shot, as it were, of all the men in our lives. It wasn't just her idea, it was mine too. Get rid of them all!'

'Including Mrs Ergin's child?'

'The idea was that once, well, once everything was done, we would disappear. We'd go off to England first and then decide what we were going to do from then on.'

'Except that Mrs Ergin has told us that she intended to drop you once in England,' İskender interjected.

Matilda Melly put her head down as if she were about to cry and then said, 'That may be what she *says*. If she's saying that and you're not just making it all up . . .'

'We are not making anything up,' İkmen said. 'You have my word.'

'Look, you can browbeat me as much as you like, but I will not talk about who did what and who is and is not guilty!' Matilda Melly cried.

'You said earlier that Handan had killed Yaşar Uzun and that you were innocent.'

'I was shocked, upset. I, I didn't know what I was doing! Suffice to say, Yaşar Uzun died – call it vengeance, if you will – and Abdullah Ergin ended up suspected of murder. Handan took my passport because we didn't want to be followed. She made for Bulgaria because she knew, because her husband had told her, that it was an easy place in which to buy dodgy passports. The idea was that she would ditch my passport when she got there and buy a new one in another name.'

'But it did not prove so easy, did it?' İkmen said. 'The Bulgarians have become more vigilant in recent times. And so she continued her journey on your passport and just hoped not to get caught.'

305

'Yes.'

'And you?'

'Well, as you know, I obtained a duplicate passport from . . .'

'No, Mrs Melly,' İkmen said. 'You left your friends the Monroes yesterday, came into the city and . . . Well, you disappeared. We searched the records of hundreds of hotels and pansiyons.'

'You didn't search the beds of every sex-starved gigolo in Sultanahmet though, did you?' she replied.

'No.' In spite of himself as well as the seriousness of the subject matter, İkmen smiled. 'No, we didn't do that,' he said. 'How very resourceful of you, Mrs Melly.'

She ignored him. 'And you know the rest,' she said. 'You pulled me up at the airport before I could even see the plane that would carry me back to Handan.'

'Who was nevertheless already in custody in Bulgaria,' İkmen said. 'But Mrs Melly, Mrs Ergin, as I have told you, says that you killed Yaşar Uzun. She says it was all your idea, that she was just an innocent pawn in your twisted sexual game with her . . .'

'Yes, you've told me that already,' the Englishwoman replied. 'And I have told you that I didn't do it.'

'But who are we to believe? You're saying that Mrs Ergin murdered Yaşar Uzun?'

'No.'

İkmen frowned. 'Then what are you saying, Mrs Melly?'

'Nothing.' She shrugged. 'I'm not saying I did it, I'm not saying Handan did it. I'm not saying anything.'

'Yes, but Mrs Melly,' İkmen said, 'Mrs Ergin has dropped you from a very big height. She cares nothing for you!'

'I don't care. I care for her.'

'You were quick to condemn her initially,' İkmen said.

'I was afraid. My lawyer made me do it! Advised me . . .'

'Maybe. But with or without your testimony we will convict in the end,' İkmen continued. 'By your own admission you and Mrs Ergin wanted to be free of the men in your life. Yaşar Uzun hurt you. Abdullah Ergin's wife had access to her husband's gun. No one can provide you with a believable alibi for the night of Uzun's death. Then there is forensic evidence from your home, which will be, I think, significant. I could go on . . .'

'I cannot say anything about Handan,' Matilda Melly said. 'I won't.'

'Even though she has begged us to make you out as the villain in this piece?' İkmen asked.

Matilda Melly laughed. 'Even if that were true, yes,' she said.

İkmen sighed. 'Then ultimately, Mrs Melly, I can see only a prison sentence, a long one, for you.'

'And for Handan?' Her face was taut with tension now. Maybe at last she had recognised the truly dreadful pit she had dug for herself.

'Yes,' he said as he rose stiffly from the table. It had been a very long day and there seemed to be little more to be gained from this woman at this time. 'Most certainly.'

Metin İskender rose too.

'In the same prison?' Matilda Melly asked.

And then he saw why she was so anxious and he said, 'Not if I have any control over it, no, Mrs Melly. Make no mistake, it is our job to punish you, not to help you realise your fantasies.' He moved back towards the table and said, 'You know that I pity you, Mrs Melly. Love is one thing, but what

307

Mrs Ergin offered you was only illusory and you just cannot see it.'

And then he asked the constable on duty at the door to open up and let everyone but Matilda Melly out.

Chapter 19

When he arrived at the rather funky shoe shop Inspector
Süleyman had told him to go to on Teşvikiye Caddesi, Lee
Roberts was disconcerted to see that the policeman was not
already waiting for him. Instead, there was a tall, elderly
woman with very sharp cheekbones and two old men; one
thin and very pale, the other red-cheeked and much meatier,
plus a shabby, tired-looking middle-aged man who carried a
large blue hold-all. It was he who, on seeing Roberts, smiled
and extended his hand first. 'Mr Roberts, we meet at last!' he
said as he took Lee's warm hand in his cold one. 'I am Inspector
Çetin İkmen. My colleague Inspector Süleyman was with you
yesterday.'

'Yes.' This İkmen, Lee felt, spoke even better English than
Süleyman. 'Yes, he was very kind. He phoned and told me to
come here. Where is he?'

'Ah, well,' İkmen said. 'I am afraid that for reasons that
will become obvious, Inspector Süleyman cannot be with us
today. However, we are fortunate to have with us his father,
his uncle and his aunt.'

Lee, although bemused, smiled as İkmen introduced him
to the three elderly people lined up in front of a shop window
full of lime-green trainers and zebra-skin boots.

'Mr Lee Roberts,' the policeman said, 'this is Beyazıt

Süleyman Efendi, my colleague's uncle, his aunt Esma Hanım Efendi and the Inspector's father, Muhammed Süleyman Efendi.'

As the up-market traffic of Nişantaşı thundered by, Lee shook hands with each of them in turn while İkmen explained, 'You may have noticed, Mr Roberts, that each of these people is given the designation "efendi".'

'Yes.'

'Well, to explain, this is or rather was, for it is little used today, a title given to a person of rank. Inspector Süleyman's family are related to our Ottoman sultans and so would have been, in the old days, princes and princesses,' İkmen continued. 'We think, sir, that it is possible the Princess Gözde your grandfather gave the Lawrence carpet to might have been Princess Gözde Süleyman, Inspector Mehmet Süleyman's great-aunt.'

'Is that why he isn't here?' Lee asked.

'In his position that would not be ethical,' Muhammed Süleyman said with a smile.

'Which is why I am here instead,' İkmen said. 'As an independent witness to what I am sure we all hope will be a productive meeting. Now, Mr Roberts, Beyazıt Efendi and Esma Hanım do not speak English very well and so Muhammed Efendi and myself will translate.'

Lee looked at the smiling meaty old man and the dour-looking stick-like woman with some nervousness. He wasn't used to aristocrats. In his own country such people were generally considered to be quite eccentric. 'Right.'

'So,' İkmen spread his arms wide in order to encompass the area around him, 'if you are wondering why we are here it is because this was where the entrance to the Princess

310

Gözde's mansion once stood. Above this shoe shop are several apartments that share a communal garden around the back of the block. We are now going to go there to take some tea.'

Then without another word to either the old people or the owner of the shoe shop he now led them through, İkmen made his way past the very many funky shoes and out into a large grassy space. Some chairs and a table laid with tea glasses, a samovar and sugar bowl had been set in the middle of the lawn beside what appeared to be a garden pond. However, as they moved closer to the table, it became apparent that the pond, as well as looking rather old, was also very large in size. More of a small lake than a pond.

'The wife of the owner of the shoe shop has provided tea for us,' İkmen explained as he ushered Lee to one of the metal garden seats. 'She remembers this area when the great and the good still lived here.'

'Inspector İkmen, I am confused,' Lee said as he sat.

Muhammed Süleyman, who came to sit stiffly down beside him, smiled. 'It is my sister, Esma, who really knew the Princess Gözde,' he said. 'My son, Mehmet, spoke to her for many hours last night. We have many things to show you, Mr Roberts. Much to discuss.'

'This pond you see here is all that now remains of the palace of the Princess Gözde,' İkmen said as he first poured out tea and then offered sugar to the others at the table. 'Like so many of the old palaces of Nişantaşı, it burned down in the 1960s. Now, Mr Roberts, what I am going to show you are some photographs that Esma Hanım has of the house that was once here and of her Aunt Gözde.'

He spoke briefly in Turkish to the old woman who then placed three photographs in front of the Englishman. Taking

311

his own photograph of the Lawrence carpet with the palace in the background out of his pocket, Lee looked at all four prints with a critical eye. Although he didn't really think that this strange collection of old aristocrats, not to mention İkmen who was apparently quite famous in Turkey, were out to dupe him, he knew that he had to be careful. After all, he wanted to do the right thing by his grandfather's memory and, if he could, make sure that the carpet reached the people that it should. Certainly the Gothic-style palace in his photograph and the two shots of the Princess Gözde's residence were very similar.

As Lee looked at the photographs, Muhammed Süleyman said, 'My aunt was betrothed to a young man in 1916. My sister, who knew our aunt far better than I, says that his name was İsmail Nuri Paşa and he was the grandson of one of the Sultan Reşad's ministers. Unusually for those days, the young people knew each other and they were in love. But in 1917 İsmail Nuri went to fight for his country and was sent to Arabia with Djemal Paşa's 4th army. He never came back and the Princess Gözde withered away in her house until she died in 1959.'

Lee looked down at the other two pictures the old woman had set in front of him. One was of a young woman, the bottom of whose face was covered by a gauzy veil. Small and fair, if the lightness of what could be seen of her hair was anything to go by, she sat in a chair beside a table upon which rested a large wooden box. The same ornately carved box appeared in the other photograph too. There an older version of the young woman, unveiled now, clutched the box to her chest as if her life depended upon it. Granddad Victor had always said that the Princess Gözde was a fair-skinned, light-haired lady.

'My sister says that the Princess Gözde always had that box with her,' Muhammed Süleyman said.

'Did she ever see what was inside the box?' Lee asked.

'Sadly no,' the old man replied. 'All my sister was ever told was that it was something from the Princess Gözde's lost fiancé. The Ministry of War had told her the train he had been travelling on in Arabia had been blown up. She had, she said, just this one thing left of him. How she came by it, the Princess Gözde never did say. But my sister says that it was in her hands when she died.'

'The police, they come to house,' Esma Süleyman explained. 'Auntie is dead for many days. The box is with her.'

İkmen, still standing, took something out of the blue hold-all he had been carrying. 'We think that this is what remains of the box, Mr Roberts,' he said as he handed Lee a large piece of carved wood. 'When we found the carpet in the wreck of the dealer's car, the box that had held it had been smashed. But this is one of the end pieces. Compare it.'

Although Inspector Süleyman had told him about the box, Lee hadn't actually seen what remained of it until that moment. Lee took the piece of wood from İkmen's hands and placed it on the table beside the photographs he was still studying. The carvings on it looked just like those in the photographs. He took a sip from his tea glass and saw that İkmen was laying something down on the grass beside him.

'None of these people here claim to have ever seen what was in the Princess Gözde's box. There was a lock on the lid which apparently was never unclasped,' the policeman said as he looked down at what he had just put on to the ground with a grunt. 'And so this carpet, Mr Roberts, may or may not have been inside.'

313

Lee looked down and saw, for the second time, the small, grubby-looking carpet on the grass beside him. Dull and slightly frayed around its edges, it was nevertheless quite clear at its heart where what looked like a glittering weeping willow had been woven into its design. The ground and border columns of pale blue, magenta and indigo were particularly striking and clean. Unlike the picture his grandfather had given him, the thing itself was alive with all manner of colour and, around the tree at the centre, seemingly a degree of light too. It was, however, absolutely and unequivocally the same as the black and white version that lay outside that once-fine old Gothic mansion in Nişantaşı. It looked much brighter and more impressive than it had done when he'd first seen it in the police station. 'God . . .'

'My brother and I, being men and with children of our own at that time, had little involvement when the Princess Gözde died,' Muhammed Süleyman explained. 'But our sister has told me that our father, the Princess Gözde's brother, sold most of her things.'

'Including the box?'

Muhammed Süleyman spoke quickly to his sister who replied at some length and then he said, 'She thinks so, yes. You have to understand, Mr Roberts, my father was poor at that time. He kept only a very few things from his sister's home.'

'Do you know who your father sold the box to?' Lee asked.

'Not for certain, no,' Muhammed Süleyman said. 'But I imagine it was probably to dealers in the Kapalı Çarşı. Not to carpet men, you understand. To my father it was just a box. But to antique dealers, I think.'

Beyazıt and Esma Süleyman stood up and moved around

314

the table to where İkmen had placed the Lawrence Kerman carpet. Lee Roberts looked back at the photographs on the table again. 'The carpet is supposed to be stained with blood,' he said. 'From that action against the Ottoman train. The Princess Gözde my grandfather knew believed it was the blood of her fiancé. He gave it to her because she believed that was what it was.'

İkmen sat down at the table and poured himself a glass of tea. 'Which brings us to our problem, Mr Roberts,' the policeman said.

'Which is?'

'Which is to establish whether your grandfather's Princess Gözde and Princess Gözde Süleyman are in fact one and the same.'

'The mansion in the picture my grandfather took and the one these people have from their aunt look the same,' the Englishman said. 'Then there is the box which is identical . . .'

'But the Princess Gözde Süleyman never opened the box she said had come from her fiancé in front of anyone,' İkmen said. 'So we cannot be certain that this carpet was inside. Her brother apparently sold the box to a dealer in the Kapalı Çarşı probably back in the early 1960s. Your grandfather, Mr Roberts, did not buy the box from the Kapalı Çarşı until 1981. Maybe it did just lie there for twenty years, but it is doubtful. It must have gone somewhere else before returning to the bazaar, but we cannot know. Anything could have happened in those years.'

'But it is certain this is the carpet that was taken from a Turkish military train by T. E. Lawrence?'

'Of course!' İkmen said. 'There is photographic evidence for all to see, Mr Roberts. If you wish to auction the piece

315

off, once its authenticity has been verified, you will make a lot of money. There is little doubt of that.'

Lee Roberts put his hands up to his head and said, 'Yes, but is it mine to sell or is it . . . Does it belong to these people or doesn't it?'

İkmen smiled. 'There are strong similarities that exist between your grandfather's story and that of this family, Süleyman,' he said. 'The name of the princess, her age and situation, the appearance of the sandalwood box. What is missing is a report of someone seeing the carpet. None of the efendis can say they have seen it when they have not.'

'At the moment, the carpet belongs to you, Mr Roberts,' Muhammed Süleyman interjected. 'My family cannot prove that this carpet belonged to our aunt. You may take it back to England with you. It is your choice.'

Lee Roberts looked up at İkmen.

'The police department can only provide you with details of the facts we know about the carpet,' the policeman said. 'I can't say whether this carpet rightfully belongs to these people or not. At the moment, Mr Roberts, it is yours and it is up to you what you do with it.'

Lee Roberts looked up at the three elderly people gathered around the side of his carpet and sighed.

Peter Melly looked across the table at a woman who was now a stranger to him. The young constable who was guarding the door coughed just as Peter said to Matilda, 'What the hell are you thinking?'

She visibly blanched and then replied, 'What do you mean?'

He leaned across what was an ash- and tea-stained table. God, but the interview rooms of police stations were grim! It didn't seem to matter where one was in the world, they were always dingy, grubby and depressing. 'The police are saying that you keep on changing your story,' he said.

'Just like you, then,' she responded lightly.

Peter Melly gritted his teeth. 'Not really,' he said tightly. 'I said I'd seen you in bed the night Yaşar died because I couldn't believe you capable of anything even approaching murder! Christ, Matilda, I was still trying to come to terms with what you told me when you left . . .'

'That I'd had other men.'

'Yes! That was a bloody thunderbolt. But then when on top of that I learned from the police that one of your conquests could have been Yaşar Uzun . . . Well . . .'

'You were humiliated.'

He leaned forward still further and lowered his voice. 'Of course I was! I know I've never been the most attentive husband . . .'

'Oh, you think so?' she laughed but without humour.

'But once I thought I might lose you . . .' He put his head into his hands and said, 'Look, Matilda, the Lawrence carpet has gone. The police have found who they think is the rightful owner and it sure as hell isn't me.'

'Shame.'

'But that doesn't matter.' He looked up at her again and then said, 'Look, the police have told me that you and this Handan Ergin woman are both giving them the run-around. They've taken our house apart looking for forensic evidence, but they seem pretty sure that you killed Yaşar. Now . . .' he put his head in his hands again as he attempted to deal with his heightened emotions. What he was experiencing now was difficult, sad and humiliating all at the same time. 'Matilda, they seem to think that this Ergin woman persuaded you to do it. In common with me, they can't see that you would do something like that of your own accord.'

Matilda Melly reached one hand over to her husband and took his fingers in hers. 'If I didn't love Handan so much she and I wouldn't have done whatever it is we did.'

'Killed Yaşar Uzun.'

'No one made me do anything, Peter. I did whatever I may have done completely of my own accord.'

He pulled his hand away from hers and then sat back in his chair in order to regard her from a distance. Without the make-up, hair-piece and snazzy clothes he'd seen her in when the police had apprehended her at the airport, she was the image of the old Matilda once again. His Matilda, his wife. Except that not only had she been a slut she'd also been something else too, something he had never dreamed that she was.

'You know the poor husband of your dyke lover has been released, don't you?' he said bitterly. 'Poor bastard!'

'Abdullah Ergin hit Handan, he abused her!' Matilda replied heatedly.

'Oh and so that's some sort of excuse for trying to get him banged away for life for a crime he didn't commit?' Peter Melly snapped back angrily. 'Not to mention poor old Yaşar!'

Looking down calmly at her nails now Matilda said, 'You're only bitter because of that ruddy Lawrence carpet.'

'Well, of course I am, yes,' he said. 'I had to have something in my life . . .'

'And I had to have something in mine!' his wife said as tears rose into her eyes. 'Our home, you, when you could be bothered – it wasn't enough!'

'So you took to boys and Yaşar and some woman and—'

318

'Handan is not some woman!' She shook her head whilst wiping her eyes with the back of her hand. 'Handan has never been just some woman!'

'Matilda . . .'

'I loved her from the first moment that I saw her!'

'And yet . . .' He wrestled with what he knew, mainly because it was both so alien and irrational to him. 'If you love her, why did you say that she killed Yaşar when the police first asked you? Why is she saying that you killed him if she loves you? Why have you both changed your stories over and—'

Matilda Melly laughed. 'Don't you know?'

'Know? Know what?' Peter asked.

She leaned still further forward and then she whispered, 'About confusion, silly! If we keep the police confused then they won't know whom to sentence or for how long. We'll be given the same amount of time in the same prison . . .'

'No you won't!'

'Yes, we will!'

'No, you won't!' Peter Melly insisted. 'The police will find forensic evidence to convict one of you actually of murder in the end. The other, the accomplice, will receive a lighter sentence. And besides, Matilda, when did you and this woman get together to devise this cracked strategy? You haven't seen each other since you were arrested.'

'No, but we're so close,' she said. 'We know each other's minds . . .'

'You think so?' Peter Melly first shook his head and then rose from his seat with a sigh. He'd had enough. According to İkmen the other woman, Handan Ergin, was digging his wife in deeper and deeper every time she was interviewed.

319

She had obviously never had any intention of staying with Matilda any longer than she had to. Handan Ergin had found a way out of her unsatisfactory life, or rather she thought that she had, but unlike Matilda, she had not found love.

After first asking the constable to open up the interview-room door, Peter Melly leaned down towards his wife and kissed her on the cheek. 'Co-operate with the police,' he said. 'It'll do you no good not to.'

'Afraid it might damage your career if I don't?' Matilda responded bitterly.

But Peter Melly just shrugged. 'No,' he said. 'I'm finished in İstanbul anyway. I just don't want you to spend the rest of your life in prison.'

'If I'm with Handan . . .'

'But you won't be with Handan,' he responded gently now that he was leaving. 'She's betraying you, right now, Matilda.'

'Oh, that's just a strategy, she . . .'

'No it isn't,' he said. 'Not on her part. It's the difference between a few years for conspiracy and life.'

And then her face just began to fall. A second before the constable shut the door on her again, Peter Melly saw his wife's face drop, whiten, and even line a small amount. Maybe his words had hit home on some level? He hoped so because if they had not, Matilda was going to go down for everything. That Handan woman, however much persuasion she may have used upon Matilda, was working hard to cast herself in the light of a poor, clueless innocent. What Matilda needed to do was get together enough grit to stand up for herself and fight her own corner.

But deep down inside Peter Melly knew that she wouldn't do anything like that. She didn't have it in her. Had she done so she would have burned all his carpets and punched all his mistresses years ago. Once outside the police station, Peter Melly hailed a cab to take him to the cheapest, dirtiest bar that he could think of. Maybe there he could try to forget Matilda, the female love of her life and his poor, gorgeous, lost Lawrence Kerman carpet.

Çetin İkmen had just fallen asleep in front of the television when Fatma shook him awake and said, 'You've got a visitor.'

'A visitor?' He coughed, licked his very dry lips, and said, 'Who?'

'Mehmet,' his wife replied as she cleared several teen fashion magazines from the seats next to her husband, tutting disapprovingly as she did so. 'Why do our daughters want to read such rubbish, eh? Fashion and pop stars and . . .'

'Yes, yes, yes!' her husband said as he sat up straight in his chair and then lit up a cigarette to help bring him back into consciousness once again. 'Such dreadful young children we have, Fatma! Allah, but where did I go wrong with two sons grown up to be doctors, a daughter married to the son of a friend and . . .'

'Oh, shut up, you old fool! You're half asleep!' Fatma said as she bustled out of the room clutching the girls' magazines between her fingers.

İkmen closed his eyes again and muttered, 'Allah!' His two youngest children, Gül and Kemal, were not easy kids. But they were teenagers, so what did Fatma expect? All, well, most of the older children had turned out well. And yet she moaned and moaned and . . .

'Çetin?'

İkmen opened his eyes again and saw before him the tall, smiling figure of Mehmet Süleyman.

'Mehmet!' He made as if to get out of his chair in order to embrace his friend, but Mehmet Süleyman begged him stay where he was.

'Don't get up. You must be exhausted,' he said as he sat down beside his friend and then kissed him affectionately on both cheeks. 'I've just been to see my father.'

İkmen sat up very straight and widened his eyes expectantly. 'And? Do you have good news? Did Mr Roberts decide to give your family the Lawrence Kerman?'

After first lighting up a cigarette of his own, Süleyman said, 'Well, it is good news but, for my father in some respects, it's bad news too.'

İkmen frowned. 'Roberts wants to take the Kerman back to England with him?'

'No,' Süleyman said. 'Mr Roberts has kindly given the carpet to my family. After you left him, he gave it a lot of thought and came to the conclusion that my great-aunt Gözde was in all probability the woman that his grandfather knew. So he gave the carpet to the current head of the family . . .'

'Your Uncle Beyazıt.'

'Yes, who decided that because my aunt Esma had known the Princess Gözde better than any other member of the family, she should solely own the Lawrence Kerman. As a sort of a keepsake.' He puffed heavily on his cigarette and then said, 'Father, of course, had hoped that they might all be able to jointly sell the thing. But . . .'

'Your father's financial problems continue.'

'So it would seem.' He cleared his throat. 'However, apparently Raşit Bey has found a buyer for the Princess Gözde's other carpet that my father was selling and so he won't be entirely without funds. Raşit Bey got a good price for it in spite of what Father might say. Apparently he's sold it to a footballer who has just had an enormous great modern "palace" built on the hills above Rumeli Hisar.'

İkmen pulled a face. 'Who else but gangsters and footballers can afford such luxury?'

Süleyman shrugged. 'But thank you anyway, Çetin, for helping me with what really was a dilemma. How could I, in all conscience, even have begun to approach Mr Roberts on behalf of my own family?'

'Well, I think that it was fairly obvious that your great-aunt Gözde had to be one and the same with the lady Victor Roberts gave the carpet to,' İkmen said. 'But I take your point. Was Mr Roberts happy with the way that things turned out, do you think?'

'Father said so, yes,' Süleyman replied. 'I hope so. Mr Roberts is a very decent person. He could so easily have just enriched himself . . .'

'As the carpet dealer Yaşar Uzun had intended to do,' İkmen said.

'Oh, yes, Uzun. Metin İskender told me that you've been having some trouble with the two women you arrested in connection with his death.'

'You could say that, yes,' İkmen replied. 'Changing stories, one blaming the other, the complication that comes about when one tries to get at the truth from people who are deluded or besotted or both.'

Süleyman, not really understanding what İkmen was saying, frowned.

İkmen put his cigarette out and then lit up another. 'The

323

murder of the carpet dealer had little to do with his trade,' he said. 'Yaşar Uzun had been the lover of the British diplomat Peter Melly's wife, Matilda. They met at Raşit Bey's shop, apparently, when the English husband and your father's friend were deep in carpet talk. Mr Uzun was a regular carpet Casanova by all accounts.'

Süleyman wrinkled his nose in disgust.

'Having said that,' İkmen continued, 'he didn't deserve to die for that or any other reason.'

He told Süleyman about Matilda Melly and her many affairs, including her more spiritual connection with Handan Ergin.

'Yes,' he said, lowering his voice as he did so, 'I heard that they were, er, lesbians . . .'

'Bi-sexual in the case of Mrs Melly,' İkmen corrected. 'My own opinion about Handan Ergin is that she is entirely hetero-sexual. I think that she just used the Englishwoman to help get rid of her husband.'

'Yes. Poor Sergeant Ergin!'

'Oh, don't waste your sympathy on him!' İkmen said disdainfully. 'He beat his wife and was in all ways no wounded innocent. In fact, no one in this case has been innocent, if you ask me. Peter Melly should have paid more attention to his wife, Ergin should not have been violent to his, and the women, well . . . Handan Ergin is a manipulative, psychopathic person-ality. I mean, to just give up your child as she did . . . Mrs Melly, of course, killed—'

'You're sure?' Süleyman asked. 'In spite of the changes of story and—'

'We have some forensic evidence now,' İkmen said. 'The dust on the hand broom in the Mellys' kitchen is the same as that found at the scene of Uzun's death. A pair of her shoes

324

also yielded similar particles and there was some blood on one of those too.'

'The same as Uzun's?'

'The same group, yes,' İkmen said. 'I'm just waiting for the DNA comparison now. But I know it was Matilda Melly anyway. She confronted Uzun on the road out of Peri the night that he died. We know that he was shot when his car was stationary. So he pulled up for some reason. To see his lover, the one he'd bought a house for, perhaps? No other explanation, as yet, works quite so well for me.'

'Not a Mafia hit, then?'

'No.' İkmen smiled. 'Although it was odd to have Nikolai Stoev in the middle of it all, completely and utterly innocent for once!'

'Metin said that part of the reason why you were so suspicious about the "other" Mrs Melly was because she, Handan Ergin, went to Bulgaria under that name,' Süleyman said. 'Why on earth did she do that?'

'Because I don't think that either of them believed we would ever make a connection to Bulgaria,' İkmen said. 'Also Mrs Ergin's husband was apparently of the opinion that illegal passports could still be obtained in that country. You know, Mehmet, both of these ladies were strictly amateur criminals. Their enterprise was in places very poorly thought out.'

Süleyman smiled. 'Only in places?'

'Oh, the actual execution of Uzun was really quite well done,' İkmen said. 'Framing Abdullah Ergin who they knew could, as a police officer, pull cars over and then using his own gun to do the deed on top of that, was genius. The row Handan must have orchestrated with him to get him out of their apartment that night must have been spectacular. But Mrs

Ergin should never have travelled to Bulgaria and Mrs Melly should have bent her mind to getting her sixty thousand pounds sterling back to the UK via a method other than in her suitcase. Having said that, however, even professional criminals are not perfect. If they were, we'd never catch any of them.'

'So a satisfactory end to your investigation, Çetin?'

'No more than the end to your peeper case, Mehmet,' İkmen replied.

Süleyman smiled. 'I've told you everything I am permitted to tell you about that, Çetin,' he said.

'And I would ask you for no more,' İkmen replied. 'But you, as well as I, my dear Mehmet, have the knowledge of yet more unnecessary death in your mind. Yaşar Uzun should not have died and nothing we can ever do can put that right or even begin to console his family.'

'We work with murder, Çetin. It's what we've chosen to do.'

'I know,' İkmen sighed. 'But . . .'

There was a pause during which he looked both undecided and very sad.

'Don't tell me you're thinking of pursuing another career, Çetin?' Süleyman said with what looked like real concern in his eyes.

But İkmen just laughed and said, 'No, I'm too old to change career now. Mind you,' his eyes twinkled as he carried on, 'maybe a little foray into carpet dealing . . .'

'No!' Outraged, Süleyman said, 'Çetin, really . . .'

'It's profitable, aesthetically pleasing, you get to drink a lot of tea and smoke a lot of cigarettes . . .'

'Yes, but . . .'

'Ah, I'm only joking,' İkmen said with a laugh in his voice.

'I'd never learn about all the different carpets at my age and anyway, I couldn't keep up their endless relentless patter.'

'The sales talk.'

'The dyes, the knots, all the technical stuff. Not to mention the "romance" of it all,' İkmen said.

Frowning, Süleyman said, 'The romance? What, about carpets?'

'Yes. You know. The whole carpet as a work of art angle. The "magic" carpet that chooses its owner . . .'

'That chooses its owner?' Süleyman said. 'What does that mean?'

'Oh, it's something Raşit Bey said to me right at the beginning of my investigation. Carpets, he said, choose their owners. Buyers only think that they are choosing but, in fact, it is actually the carpet that does the choosing all along. My understanding of this is that Raşit Bey at least believes that there is some sort of intelligence woven into the carpet when it is created. That is the magic.'

Süleyman snorted.

'What rubbish, you think,' İkmen said with a smile. 'And I can't blame you for that. But you have to admit, Mehmet, that if one accepts that the Lawrence Kerman did once belong to your great-aunt Gözde, it has taken a very strange, almost miraculous route back to your family.'

'You do know that what you've just said is superstitious rubbish, don't you, Çetin?' Süleyman replied.

'Yes.' İkmen shrugged. 'But if it did really belong to the old woman's fiancé, if that is really his blood smeared upon it . . . Well, maybe then it is kismet . . .'

'Maybe,' Süleyman said. 'Kismet, yes, maybe.'

'Or magic,' İkmen said.

His friend gave him a very hard and sceptical look.

İkmen, laughing, shrugged again and said, 'All right, both. Kismet and magic.' He then put a hand on his friend's shoulder and said, 'Mehmet, dear boy, I am the son of a witch, you cannot expect me to totally dismiss the supernatural and unseen. Carpet weavers and carpet dealers come and go but carpet legends and those who pursue them are as numerous as they are immortal.'

Carpets

There are various types of what are generically described as 'oriental' carpets that appear in this book. The 'star' carpet in this novel is, of course, the Lawrence Kerman carpet which, unlike the rest of the pieces described, is Persian. Intricate and embellished with complicated arabesques, the Lawrence carpet features a Tree of Life motif, which is a magical symbol common to Islamic, Christian and Judaic traditions.

Other types of carpet mentioned include:

Tribal or nomadic carpets. Very colourful carpets made by nomadic tribespeople, often whilst on the move. These are thickly knotted, high pile carpets which are very spontaneous and naive. They can be plain in terms of ornamentation but they can also be very personalised too, for instance the woman who weaves the carpet may also mix in some of her own strands of hair. Alongside the carpets, there are also nomadic trappings; woven salt bags, camel bags and baby slings. Because of the large-scale settlement of nomads in the middle east and central Asia over the past fifty years, tribal carpets and trappings are now quite rare and therefore collectable.

Turkish village carpets. Made by a village dwelling woman, possibly as part of her dowry at a set time of year. The wool and dyes used to make these carpets are pre-prepared by the same woman in advance of the weaving process. Good ones reflect the personality of the weaver and the colours used are generally indicative of the region or district in which they were produced.

Palace or court carpets. Often very large carpets made for the Ottoman court in the nineteenth century. Handmade and very ornate they were produced professionally for the court by paid weavers as opposed to village women. Frequently embellished with flowers and usually with a central medallion motif.

Kilims. A flat weave rug that was definitely the 'poor relation' in the carpet world until the nineteen seventies. Often made for prayer the design bases of these rugs nevertheless go back to Neolithic times. Geometric in design, some of the older kilims in particular can exhibit a wild eccentricity that many collectors find almost addictive. Turkey leads the world in the fineness of its kilims.

T E Lawrence

1888–1935

Thomas Edward Lawrence was the second of five illegitimate sons of an Anglo-Irish baronet called Sir Thomas Chapman. 'Ned', as he was known to his family, was a bright boy who obtained a first-class honours degree from Jesus College, Oxford after which he was employed upon archaeological digs across the Middle East. When the First World War broke out in 1914 he worked first in the geographical section of the military General Staff in London until, by virtue of his knowledge of the Arabic language and culture, he was transferred to Cairo. In October 1916 he was sent to the Hedjaz on a fact-finding mission and to meet Sherif Hussein of Mecca who had rebelled against Ottoman rule. He was subsequently given the role of British Liaison Officer in the Arab revolt serving with the forces of Hussein's son, the Emir Feisal. His achievements as part of the Arab revolt are now legendary, particularly his involvement in the capture of the sea port of Akaba. That he became in the eyes of some, and by dressing in Arab clothes and adopting some Arab manners and customs, more Arab than the Arabs was frowned upon to an extent back in Britain. But on the whole he was viewed as a heroic figure by his own people. However once the war was over, Lawrence became quickly disillusioned with regard to the treatment of the Arabs by the British, the French and their allies. In assisting these powers against Germany and the Ottoman Empire the Arabs had just, it seemed, swapped one master for another. It was with great anger and trepidation that Lawrence watched the western empires carve the Middle East up into the deeply troubled region of falsely created states we see today. Lawrence, who never married or had children, died in a motor bike accident in 1935.

The Ottoman Empire
in the First World War

By 1914 the once great and powerful Ottoman Empire was a
shadow of its former self. Almost completely absent in Europe,
the Empire was reduced to control over what is now Syria,
Iraq, Israel, Palestine, Jordan and parts of Saudi Arabia. Egypt
had long been lost to the British and places like Greece and
Albania were now independent countries in their own right.
Internally too things were changing. In 1908 the last autocratic Ottoman Sultan, Abdul Hamid II, was deposed by an
organisation called the Committee of Union and Progress
(otherwise known as the Young Turks) which was headed by
three army officers, Enver, Talaat and Djemal Pashas. The
office of sultan was held by Abdul Hamid's younger brother,
Mehmed V, who was little more than a puppet of the
Committee.

The Ottoman Empire joined Germany and its allies in opposition to Britain, Russia and their allies in the autumn of 1914.
This came about as a direct result of a secret Ottoman–German
alliance that had been signed by Enver, Talaat and Djemal
Pashas in August 1914. This alliance threatened both Russia's
Caucasian territories and the British Empire's communications
with India and the east via the Suez Canal.

The Caucasian front was commanded by Enver, who in

December 1914 threw 100,000 Ottoman troops against the Russians at Sarikamis. He lost 86% of his forces during the course of this battle. The Ottoman campaign against the British and their allies in Gallipoli in 1915 was rather more successful, largely due to the fact that it was commanded by a brilliant young officer called Mustafa Kemal, later Atatürk. In 1915–16 the Russian General Yudenich scored a string of victories over the Ottomans in the Caucuses. The war in what Lawrence called 'Arabia' (Syria, Palestine, Israel, Jordan, Saudi Arabia, Iraq) was fought against the British and the French. Baghdad fell in March 1914, Jerusalem in December 1917 and a final defeat at Megiddo in September 1918 finally put paid to the Ottoman forces and thereby the Empire once and for all.

However in spite of these reverses a modern state, the Republic of Turkey, did eventually rise from the ashes of what had been the Ottoman Empire. Under the leadership of Atatürk the country known as Turkey was born in 1923 as a secular republic committed to its own peaceful development and progress. During the course of the madness that once again engulfed Europe from 1939 to 1945, the Republic of Turkey remained neutral.

Barbara Nadel

BARBARA NADEL
Dance With Death

It is Holy Month in Turkey, but, as Inspector Çetin İkmen soon discovers, some prefer sin to virtue, no matter how deadly the consequences . . .

The body of a young woman is discovered in a cave in the remote rural region of Cappadocia, and İkmen is summoned from Istanbul to investigate. Having met a violent end, her corpse has lain undisturbed for two decades. Is she the same woman who captured İkmen's heart all those years ago? Someone in this country backwater knows who murdered her, and why.

But decades of folklore, feuding and gossip surround this community. And it is clear that some locals have no regard for the truth and are leading İkmen on a far from merry dance . . .

Praise for Barbara Nadel's novels:

'Inspector Çetin İkmen is a detective up there with Morse, Rebus and Wexford. Gripping and highly recommended' *Time Out*

'Intelligent and captivating' *The Sunday Times*

978 0 7553 3235 9

headline
review

Last Rights

Barbara Nadel

October 1940: The London borough of West Ham is suffering another night of horrific bombing and undertaker Francis Hancock is caught in the chaos. A man lurches towards him through the rubble screaming about being stabbed but there's no visible wound and Francis dismisses him as a madman . . . until the man's body turns up at his funeral parlour, two days later.

Suspecting foul play, Francis feels compelled to discover what really happened that night – but as he finds himself pitted against violent thugs, an impenetrable network of lies and his own fragile sanity, he realises that there are people who want the truth to stay dead and buried . . .

Praise for Barbara Nadel's novels:

'Unusual and very well-written' *Sunday Telegraph*

'Impeccable mystery plotting, exotic and atmospheric' *Guardian*

'Gripping and highly recommended' *Time Out*

'Intelligent and captivating' *The Sunday Times*

978 0 7553 2136 0

headline